The Day:

THE RAIN FALLS

GRACE FINLEY

Printed in the United States of America
ISBN (Kindle) 978-1-953781-06-2
ISBN (Paperback) 978-1-953781-08-6
ISBN (Hardcover) 978-1-953781-07-9

Finley Books | Phoenix, AZ
www.FinleyBooks.com

This is a work of fiction. Names, characters, businesses, events and incidents are the products of the author's imagination. Any resemblance to actual persons, living or dead, or actual events is purely coincidental.

FINLEY BOOKS

PHOENIX, ARIZONA

"Perhaps you were born

for such a time as this."

–ESTHER 4:14

1

the call

Josh West's voice had become desperate. "Canary, respond."

He waited long enough to take two forced breaths, wipe the sweat from his brow, his jaw clenched. Every inch of his skin felt coated in dirt, grime, and sweat. He fumbled with the receiver in his hand, clearing his throat. His hand smelled of gunpowder, rusty and simmering. "Canary, status."

Miles ran his fingers roughly through his sandy-colored mop of hair, walking away. He shook his head as he anticipated what the lack of response meant. "I lost focus, I wasn't covering her like I should have," he said to no one in particular. When he whirled around, his dirty face was streaked with tears. In the 14 years he'd known him, Josh had never seen Miles Kent shed a tear.

"*Canary,*" Josh persisted, his voice cracking. He hated not being able to use her name. Up until then, he had convinced himself the call sign was indicative of her love of music. She was an incredible vocalist. She had a tendency to sing whimsical melodies at random, her big unearthly silver eyes playful and dancing. He'd watched the ease in which she'd soothed a baby with a song, her voice gentle and rich. He'd seen her caught up in the message of a worship song in church, her hand raised in praise, her eyes squeezed shut. He saw her standing in the bed of the pickup truck on the open road, leaning into the back of the cab, her arms outstretched, her

1

golden-brown hair blowing wildly around her face as she sang with unbridled enthusiasm.

Songbird. Songbird would have been a better call sign, he decided silently. If her call sign was even about music, he added.

It seemed more likely, and perhaps more fitting given the circumstances, that her call sign represented her intended role in the mission; what it had been long before he'd realized. Miners used canaries to tell them when there was trouble, when the air had gone toxic. When their canary went silent, it meant their world was about to implode.

2

anomaly

16 years earlier...

If someone had put the saline solution back in its proper storage cabinet, Luther wouldn't have had any reason to open the door. If he had never opened the door, made from reinforced steel with a wheel locking mechanism, much like you might find on a submarine, he would have never heard the blood-curdling screams. If he had never heard the screams, he would have never seen the pair of feet, barely the length of his thumb, protruding from what could best be described as medical shackles around her ankles. He would have never known a child, not even three, to have needed to be restrained so thoroughly.

In addition to the shackles around her ankles, there were metal restraints over her midsection just above her diaper and another set of shackles just above her elbows.

A blindfold was reinforced over her eyes and muddy-colored hair was impossibly tangled and matted around her head. Her starfish hands were clenched tightly into fists. Her body was rigid, braced in pain.

A timer on the wall shelf indicated a duration of 17 hours, 31 minutes.

Her throat gargled and the tautness of her jaw told him she was grinding down on her small teeth.

It was apparent the diaper had not been changed in quite some time, brownish green liquid seeping through the elastic leg bands. He would believe her last change corresponded closely with the timer duration.

The vitals monitor flashed, silently alarmed that the young subject's last blood pressure reading was 170/119 and her pulse was 140, body temperature 105.4.

It was just as he considered that he should consider that she needed medical intervention that the readings began to fall. Her body settled suddenly, her legs long and loose, her palms wide and open, and her vitals eased to normal ranges over a matter of sixty seconds. The timer stopped and, in the silence, he could hear her concentrated breathing.

Suspecting at any moment someone would be returning, Luther stepped back through the reinforced steel door and sat down at his workstation. He stared at the oval orb before him and the shape within.

The thirty-two-week-old preborn child, a boy, struggled to sleep, his face tense. The use of sound generation of a heartbeat had failed to have the intended impact of simulating a natural womb for this child, as it had in others. He had all the indicators for being under severe stress. The supervising researcher had already indicated there was a high likelihood he would be disqualified from the study for which he was intended.

Until tonight, Luther had convinced himself the study was something benign. Yes, the children were born from artificial wombs, but there was a good reason for their usage. Childbirth was a high risk for both the baby and the mother. Artificial wombs would offer convenience to couples, equal reproductive rights, and allow closer monitoring and better detection of any abnormalities. Babies born from artificial wombs would be categorically healthier.

He glanced around the warehouse-sized room full of glowing orbs. He thought of the toddler strapped to a metal table just on the other side of the wall and marveled at his own naivety.

Luther recalled making the case to his mother when he first learned of the course offering. She had closed her eyes and reached for her cross

4

pendant, running it between her fingers. "Something changed for me the first time I felt you kick, Luther. I still felt like a child myself when I got pregnant, but I felt that kick--" She paused to gaze at him. "I told you: 'I don't know how, but I'm going to make a good life for us. I will always protect you.' I told you I loved you more than anything or anyone and it was the truth. We had so much quality time together those months I was pregnant."

"People adopt, momma. They love their kids, too."

"What does that do to the baby? Being grown in a lab?"

His mother's words echoed in his head as he watched PI-07-13-X3 curl his head over his torso, hands at his ears as though defending against a loud noise. Babies in the artificial wombs did not face the uneven and often unhealthy nutrition of a biological pregnancy, so they were all quite lean. This boy was no exception, his narrow arms punching at the spongy walls of the translucent womb from his tightly curled position.

Luther turned off his task light, then after checking the lab for any other technicians, he began to sing a nursery rhyme in a soft, low voice, a childhood favorite. It took persistence with the chorus, but the child relaxed, the monitors showing his heart rate slowing a bit. He found himself studying the gentle slope of his nose, how he crossed his tiny feet when he slept.

The course work was advertised in the medical school curriculum as being focused on embryonic development. For seven months, he had worked in the first-trimester lab. There he had appreciated the regimented dispensing of immune boosters, the balanced nutrition, and the more promising start it afforded babies. He hadn't considered what happened to them when they reached the next developmental stage.

It was just two days ago that he was reassigned due to a staff shortage in the advanced groups.

The hallway door flew open, bringing in a gust of humidity and nicotine. Nita was putting in her earbuds, smacking on a wad of gum as she returned from her meal break. "You alright, new guy?" She asked, raising a thickly penciled eyebrow. She had struck him as a woman of harsh extremes, given her affinity for sharp edges in her appearance. Her makeup was heavily applied, lips outlined with triangular tips and painted a dark purple. Her hair was bleached white, the roots left a midnight black. Her exposed shoulders jutted out from beneath her tank top, her shoulder blades looked downright lethal.

She narrowed her eyes, set beneath fuzzy tarantula lashes. "Did the bulb go out? How can you see over here?" She switched on the fluorescent light and the baby stirred, flipped away from the bright light. "Ugh, they get so creepy when they're older."

Luther looked from Nita to the baby, recognizing for the first time, the broad, sort of goofy smile he wore when he slept.

"What were you doing?" she asked distrustfully.

"I was following the protocol. I had taken a sample--" He motioned to the petri dish and vial filled with the baby's blood on the workstation.

"Oh, that one's just for parts now. We're not doing any more samples or including the data. You don't know the codes on the specimen sheet?"

"I guess I don't."

"Any specimen identified as an anomaly is excluded from the Proto-Immune Experiment. One lab's trash is another lab's treasure though."

"Meaning what exactly?"

"*Meaning*, a specimen with undesirable traits is useless to us, but another lab facility could use it for parts or whatever. The Franken-lab picks up every couple of weeks."

He looked closer at the baby, at his rounded features, his crossed feet. "Anomaly?"

"Did you not notice the flattened nasal bridge, the epicanthal folds, the stubby body?"

Luther took in the features as she pointed them out. "I'm sorry, I wasn't going into Obstetrics or Pediatrics. I didn't notice that anything looked off."

"Down Syndrome."

"Oh," he replied flatly.

"Yeah, probably a donation from an in vitro couple. They usually have spares after they're done having kids." She walked past him to the same door where he'd just emerged, casually climbed through, clicking her gum between her teeth as she returned. She placed the bottle next to his computer without comment. "How many more do you have to do?"

"Four more."

"That should be enough saline then. I'll have Facilities restock supplies next shift."

"Oh, is that storage back there? No one showed me."

"Not really. They're wrapping up the previous phase of the genome building experiment. There's just one specimen left."

"How many did they start with?"

She pulled out an earbud, resolving that she would be required to interact with another human for a bit longer. She attempted to mask her annoyance as she swept greasy hair from her eyes. "Uh--two dozen at least. God, that was a racket back there for a while. It's a good thing these are noise canceling."

He could hear the little girl's shrieks echo in his ears. Since her blood pressure had stabilized, she had been silent. "What are they testing on? Dogs?"

Nita glanced back toward the door then narrowed her eyes at the translucent orb in front of them, the baby within. "You're working on one. Well, not *that* one, but--" She motioned to the row of identical orbs. "We have a batch in the next lab nearly ready to start the experiment. At this point, they're just testing the limits of that one."

"Testing the limits?"

"Most subjects didn't make it past the first few tests. They're just throwing everything they have at it now to end the trial."

"By end, do you mean—?"

"If they're going to move forward with the project, *that* won't be the poster child, no pun intended." For a moment, he saw her tough facade shatter as her eyes floated over to the row of artificial wombs, the children within.

"Why?"

"Not *diverse* enough," she said distantly. Her eyes rested on one specific orb, her breathing thickening. She dropped her gaze and cleared her throat. They stood in silence for a few moments, Nita distracting herself with readings on the baby Luther had been working with, showing more interest than if she believed he was worthless. "It'd be bad PR. It's why for future batches, they're requiring the right genetic combo, so we don't waste time."

He pictured the child's pale legs and feet tinged with a sickly gray hue, how as she recovered and the blood flooded back into her toes, they turned a rosy pink.

"It's still pretty amazing what they accomplished." Her drawn-on eyebrows did not match the enthusiasm her words were attempting to convey.

The outer door opened, and a pair of young men appeared. One was scrawny with dark haphazard hair and seemed to struggle with growing a beard. He sipped a whipped cream topped coffee beverage. The other appeared a bit oversized for the doorframe and had a slower pace to him.

"'Nita, you're looking lovely," the scrawny one said.

Her face hardened in an instant. "Screw you, Marcus."

"What'd I say?"

She looked across Marcus to the other man. "I borrowed some saline. We were out."

"No problem. We have more than enough." He pointed toward the door she'd left ajar. "Noisy?"

"I just got here. It's been quiet though. New guy?"

"Luther." He corrected, but no one seemed to care. "Haven't heard anything."

"*Good*, maybe it finally died." Marcus laughed as though he had made a joke.

"Kind of not the point of the experiment, dipshit." The taller man shook his head and extended his hand. "I'm Demetri."

"The point was to build immunity or something?" Luther asked, accepting the handshake.

"Yeah," Marcus snickered. "More like making a mutant species."

"This is a big breakthrough though? What Nita has told me?" Luther offered. "Genome building or something?"

"Yeah, we can't announce the greatest advancement in genome research with *that* as our subject." Marcus glared toward the back room.

"The government building a super-race of white people? Yeah, that doesn't scream Nazi," Nita chimed in. "Although, wrong hair and eye color I guess." The simple acknowledgment that the child had eyes and hair had seemed to have given her pause, her hand suspended over the Petri dish.

"Doing all this testing on a colonizer *is* slightly satisfying."

"How is she a colonizer, Bro?" Demetri asked.

Nita sprang into action, dropping the dish into the trash.

"*It* had ancestors that enslaved my people and stole this very land we're standing on from the indigenous."

"She has only ever seen the inside of this lab. Also, you've seen that she's female. Why must you call her 'it?'"

"They're all just numbers to me."

"So, you're square then? Now that you've gotten to torture her since birth?" Nita's voice was tight and angry, but Luther doubted it was entirely related to his aggression toward the young test subject.

Marcus laughed. "No, it's screwing with me because it won't die."

She shook her head, putting a palm toward Marcus and addressing Demetri. "What was this round?" Nita asked, checking her phone.

"Pancuronium bromide and potassium chloride," Demetri said, raising his eyebrows.

"That's what they use for lethal injections," Marcus explained proudly.

"They use a sedative, too, typically," Nita added.

"To make lethal injections seem more humane. They don't do shit once the real drugs kick in."

"Let me guess, you had an ancestor who was a serial killer who got the death penalty and you're still upset?" Demetri quipped.

Marcus shrugged. "I *may* have."

"She recovered from a lethal dose of cyanide in 18 hours," Demetri said, checking his watch. "If she's recovered already? That'd be something. Especially since Lisbon has been giving her immunosuppressants."

"I thought the idea was to boost immunity?"

"It *was*," Demetri said flatly.

"I don't know where you'd go from a lethal injection," Nita remarked.

"Maybe pour acid on it. See if it melts."

Luther could not tell if Marcus was serious, but by the way Demetri turned and walked away, he believed he might be.

Nita rolled her eyes as she spit out her gum and pushed it into the bottom of the worktable. "You're like little boys burning ants under a magnifying glass."

"At first it was interesting to test how much it could take, but if nothing will kill it, we'll have to just toss it in with the others. Let nature run its course," Marcus sighed.

"By nature, he means big man-made flames," Demetri clarified, moving toward the back lab.

"Same thing."

"It's really not, Bro." There was an exaggerated groan from the door.

"Is it dead?"

"Nope and it's your turn to change her, Marcus."

"Screw that. Bring on the flames."

"Dr. Lisbon said to keep her alive. For you it won't be bad; no worse than your apartment."

"Well, I'm not doing it. I'll work on the B group today. I nominate New Guy."

"You nominate New Guy for what?" Luther asked.

"Cleaner of literal shit. Congrats."

Nita shrugged in response to meeting Luther's eye. "Better you than me."

*　　*　　*

Luther closed the heavy metal door behind himself at Nita's request, the pungency of feces finally reaching her nasal cavities. She had given him specific instructions: Unlock subject from the table, take subject to the recreation room, change diaper, lock subject in the recreation room. He doubted silently if any room here would meet even low expectations for something called a 'recreation room.'

He found his hands shaking as he unlocked the shackles, trying not to accidentally pinch her skin or apply pressure on her small body. She had flinched when his skin first made contact, so he started to speak lightly under his breath, narrating his actions, so she was aware of his location and intentions.

"I'm just going to get these restraints off you--those don't look very comfortable."

She breathed steadily. With the blindfold over her eyes, it was difficult to tell if she was awake.

"That's better. Now we're just going to get you cleaned up, little one." He decided using the word "we" might intimidate her, so he back-pedaled. "My name is Luther. I'm going to help you." He froze as he heard the words out loud. In the glimmer of time the words ran through his mind, he had thought he meant he would help her feel better in the present moment, but as he finished releasing her from the cold metal table and she turned a listening ear toward him, he realized he meant the words in a far more daunting way.

But how could he possibly help her? They said she already had a death sentence. Obviously, this work was secretive. He couldn't just walk out the door with her--and what was he to do? Raise this pale-skinned child as his own? He stared at his auburn fingers resting against her wrist. Even with her hands coated in grime, there was a stark contrast. If nothing

11

else, it would be highly suspicious that a young black man like himself, in the middle of medical school, would suddenly be the sole caregiver of a toddler who clearly did not share his DNA.

Even so, he watched his fingertips trace the imprint the steel restraints had left upon her arms. It was surprising that there weren't deep cuts where the edge of the steel had pressed. His eyes fell upon the data matrix tattoo on her forearm. He took a breath and heard himself say: "I will help you escape this place, little one."

There wasn't a detectable shift in her body, but he sensed when her attention sharpened. As he lifted her small body off the table, he felt her arm tighten around his shoulder.

The recreation room was the first door on the right. He had low expectations for its appearance and amenities, and it still managed to fall far short. The walls were lined with padding except for a large copper-tinted airplane-style window. It failed to provide much natural light. There were a few gym mats and ramps set up on the floor, and one random, deflated beach ball abandoned in center of the room.

In the far corner, there was a large muddy stain. He didn't want to venture a guess at what may have caused it.

"Okay, the bathroom's in here," he narrated. "I wonder what toiletries they've left for us, a fine establishment such as this."

To his surprise, there was store-brand baby shampoo/wash on the metal counter. The bathroom was tinted yellow by the lights and smelled strongly of cleaning products. He located the storage for what turned out to be three scratchy hand towels. He braced her over his hip, noticing that the greenish-brown ooze from her diaper was starting to slip down her leg.

"Hold on tight. I'll lay a towel down." She squeezed her arms around his shoulders, and he felt overwhelming grief as her face dug into his neck.

The thin loop towel was a pitiful barrier over the unforgiving tile floor. "I'm sorry. This isn't going to be very soft." He glanced up toward the recreation room, considering moving her to one of the pads.

"I can use potty," her small voice whispered.

He arched his neck to look at her face. She had pushed the blindfold up to rest on her forehead. Shadowed by the mask, her eyes looked to be a pale shade of hazel. The cheek facing him had a hint of a dimple.

He felt compelled to compliment her, tell her what a pretty girl she was, how well she spoke, but all of this was overshadowed by the fact that all that stood between her and death was him.

He found his chest tightening, his airway constricting, and he determined any focused attention on her angelic features would distract him from what he needed to be doing. So instead, he nodded and carried her to the toilet.

"Can you stand?"

She released a light "uh-hmm" and slid from his arms.

"I'm going to take off this diaper, but I'm going to need to clean your skin before you sit down, okay?"

"OK."

He retracted to the sink and was thankful the water turned warm quickly. He pumped out some baby wash and lathered the rough towel, making a mental note to scrub gently. "Here we go," he said, squinting his eyes as though the action somehow offered her more privacy. As he wiped the sludgy excretions from her skin, he found his eyes welling with tears. Part was certainly due to the odor, but he found his heart aching hopelessly, wondering how he would possibly be able to save her.

"Alright, little one. Go ahead and have a seat."

She did as instructed and he stepped to the other side of the heavy bathroom door.

"*New guy*," Marcus called in a sing-song voice from the hallway.

Luther stepped out of the bathroom to find Marcus hanging drunkenly by the doorframe.

"Don't bother cleaning it up."

"Why?"

"Lisbon just stopped by." Marcus made a kaboom noise followed by the fluttering of his fingers. "That's supposed to be flames," he said with a laugh. "Come on, man. I get to do the honors."

"Give me a few minutes."

"*Okay*, but there's no point. Dead colonizer walking." He peered over Luther's shoulder, pressing into the balls of his feet, looking for the girl with seditious interest.

Luther felt like the air had been vacuumed from his lungs. He turned slowly toward the bathroom, stepping in slow motion inside once he heard the toilet flush.

Her lack of muscle mass made her look even younger than she was. She wore a dirty t-shirt that hung off her like a dress and she stood in front of the sink, stretching to reach the faucet. Her hair, coated in grime and sweat, reached the bottom hem even with its impossible tangles. In the vanity light, there were glimmers of other shades beside the mousy brown. Her nose was small and rounded, her full pink lips pulled up naturally at the corners. After successfully rinsing her fingertips, she turned to face him. Her eyes met his gaze with a raw hope that seemed to cut right through him. She took a deep breath. "I going with you?"

3

construct

10 years later...

Annette Gibbons watched as the President of the United States signed the Purity Choice Bill into law. She stood over his shoulder in the Oval Office with suppressed emotion as his pen swept across the page.

It was done.

The Purity Choice Bill, as summarized for the public, sought "unwavering reproductive equity" and "right to peace." The new Congress, with its "bold freshman members" in place, passed the legislation with "overwhelming support." With a supermajority in both the House and Senate, a like-minded President at the helm, new legislation was being passed, and institutions were being restructured at a breakneck speed as part of an "ambitious agenda" to "officially disassociate the country from an antiquated structural system" and "establish itself as a leader of refreshed stances on financial institutions, social structure, cultural norms, and environmental responsibilities."

It was all very well-orchestrated and well-scripted.

Annette lifted her eyes to the sea of cameras and the faces of an adoring press, who would undoubtedly speak to the scientific breakthroughs afforded by this Bill. "A new frontier" was the selected phrase that would preside over the news cycle. Tomorrow would be: "The next phase of human evolution."

She smiled but kept her lips pressed together, remembering how public perception polls indicated she was more appealing to voters when she didn't open her mouth to smile. Her poised smile was viewed as composed and competent, but also "seductive to all genders." She made purposeful eye contact with a journalist named Christopher Loop, who had grown a full beard since she'd last seen him. He had a very popular conservative cable news show, which typically afforded him the luxury of sending staff to cover press conferences. He simply showed up in the studio to record the show, tossing about his no-nonsense approach. It was a rarity for him to cover press events. She was surprised he still possessed press credentials since his viewpoints directly conflicted with the Administration.

"They must feel like they have representation until the time is right," she had been told. "When the time is right--" The party chairman had snapped her fingers and smirked. "It'll be like none of them ever existed."

This was the same party chairman who had assured her she'd be sitting in that wingback Oval Office chair but had then pushed through Samuel-effing-Gowon and his botoxed forehead, collagen-injected mouth instead. She had known as soon as mysterious puff piece articles started making their way to publications across the nation and Samuel started finding himself repeatedly caught doing everyday things meant to endear him to the common people--jogging with a rescue dog, getting tossed about on an amusement park ride with foster kids, serving food to the homeless, jaunting into a military base to allegedly "show his appreciation for our service persons."

She couldn't say she knew Samuel well. Nobody could. He was obsessive-compulsive with anti-social tendencies--and not the entertaining kind. He was rumored to have fetishes for exotic animals and underage children. He once entertained the idea of euthanizing the homeless. He likened the military to pawns on a chess board.

The propaganda was the work of Hollywood magic with green screens, CGI, and stand-ins, since Gowon was unwilling to stand within the breathing space of blue collars. The news had the world convinced that he was a beloved leader. They chose not to report about the assassination attempts that kept him confined to the People's House grounds.

She sighed and reassessed the enthusiasm of her smile. It had slipped and Christopher Loop had noticed, one thick eyebrow perking. He kept his eyes fixed on her, shifting pointedly to the President as soon as he began taking questions from the press. The first question had come from one of the usual Administration-friendly reporters and Annette found herself losing grasp of the words being spoken, her heart thumping loudly in her ears.

"--not to mention reproductive justice. This is truly a historic day for equality and procreative--"

Annette turned abruptly. Samuel had forgotten his line and sat with a dumbfounded expression on his face as he searched for the words. He released the most unnatural of coughs, reaching for his water glass.

"Oh, excuse me. As I was saying, this is truly a historic day for procreative equity."

She caught herself mid-way through an eye roll.

Christopher Loop saw it. His hand crept up confidently.

"Oh, okay, I'll call on you, but these folks are going to think you're my favorite," Samuel said with unconvincing jest, his puckered lips pressed tightly together.

The room erupted in unearned chuckles.

Christopher Loop tapped his pen to his chin. "I'll risk it. My question is for Speaker Gibbons. Ms. Gibbons, the implications of this legislation can't be denied. This grants unprecedented control of individual rights, end-of-life decisions, among other things, to the government. Many have said that with this signing, the Constitution, the Bill of Rights, individual rights are essentially incinerated--" He took a long pause, narrowing his green eyes when she visibly tensed. "What do you have to say to those individuals?"

Annette swallowed hard, her right eye twitching at the phrasing. She found herself momentarily distracted by a piece of lint on Samuel

Gowon's shoulder. Not long ago, answers rolled off her tongue with ease. The media praised her confidence, her poise, her gumption. She remembered a time when she was receiving articles, news segments, and social media posts daily from the Party's political strategist. There was a time she was the face of the Party, a role model for girls, for women.

"This stare down from Speaker Gibbons as she drills the former surgeon general is a total mood and I. am. here. for. it.
#congressionalhearings
#reproductivehealthcareforall
#mychoiceisannette "

"#ActuallyIDo needs to trend. What a powerful statement by #SpeakerGibbons about #infantloss and the
need for #artificialwombs to give babies the best possible start."

"For the first time in my voting life, there's a candidate who I can relate to, who represents me.
#AnnetteGibbons is MY future president."

Twelve large city stations ran a feature story about her, tying into Women's History Month. The featurette included candid photographs and videos of Annette and interviews with former classmates and colleagues. Each ended with a suspenseful build-up. "Many have already speculated that Speaker Gibbons is all, but a shoo-in, for the Oval Office in the next presidential election." There were quick clips of voters and political figures vocalizing support: "She is a champion for the ages. She's exactly what this country needs."

The next publicity stunt involved a vlogger acquiring her DNA. There was a manufactured suspense leading to the results being revealed, a statement about this being an invasion of her privacy. By the time the results were released, she had gained tremendous popularity. And then the results were released, revealing her 25% indigenous ancestry and a compelling story about her great-grandmother being an activist for human rights. Additionally, she was found to be a good part South African and part Latina. There had been an entire primetime hour devoted to unpacking her ancestry. She cried about her upbringing while maintaining the message that her struggles to pave her own way have helped empower her forward.

Then came the Convention and the attention had pivoted to Samuel Gowon.

She had suppressed her anger about the situation for years now. She had still been able to answer a simple press question, even from someone like Christopher Loop. It was easy when you believed what you were selling. And she had. Hook, line, and sinker.

Until yesterday.

Until yesterday, she had believed in what she had campaigned on. She had believed in the budgets she had written that quietly bank-rolled projects that would have been trudging through FDA quicksand for decades. She had believed in the mission of the Purity Initiative and its nine hundred seventy-two pages. She had believed in the 'greater effing good' bullshit.

Until yesterday.

Her ears became aware of some muffled chattering, and she shook herself to awareness.

"Are you alright, Speaker Gibbons?" Christopher Loop's smooth voice asked, frowning. The reporters surrounding him were looking concerned. Some had blatantly cut away from the feed to cover for her, probably claiming technical difficulties.

"Oh, of course," she said, clearing her throat multiple times.

"I can take that one, Annie," Samuel said with a condescending smirk. "Chris, those allegations are simply false. Soon former procreative ways will seem archaic, as nonsensical as VHS tapes--who even remembers those? Someday you'll describe the hassle that was gone through to have children and the tremendous risks involved, and people will ask why? Someday children will learn about how our elderly and our sick suffered

19

in the past and wonder why past generations didn't do anything about it. Today we said enough. No more suffering. Today we took a tremendously long overdue step toward equity, toward embracing scientific and medical innovations that will transform our lives in a very positive way. I would tell those individuals to embrace it and be thankful to live in this time in history."

"Next question," the Communications Director announced, selecting the People's House correspondent from a more friendly network.

Christopher's forehead furrowed, seeming to ponder if he should push matters further. He jotted something down on his small notepad, then glanced briefly at Annette, who had assumed a rigid stance next to the Resolute Desk, no longer caring to appeal to public opinion polls, her jaw clenched, her lips pressed firmly together.

Mercifully, the Communications Director called an end to the press conference after the President replied to the final scripted question. Being the obedient group that they were, the press corps filed out in an orderly and efficient fashion.

"This is only the beginning, Annie," Samuel said, checking his reflection in one of the framed portraits on his desk. He ran his palm over his hair, checking for unruly strands of his black hair.

"It's an important day."

"Prior administrations have tried to pass this, but perhaps with the proper individual at the helm, we can continue to pass more priority policies. I just want to be sure you're up to the task?"

She cleared her throat. "Absolutely."

"Excellent," he said, flatly. He lifted one of the clear pens and held it out for her. "A memento of the day."

Annette took the pen and rotated it between her fingers. "Purity Act, signed into law Year 2, Day 236, Modern Time, Samuel D. Gowon, President of the United States," the pen read, Samuel's name scrawled in his rigid signature. The lotus flower symbol used for the Act was positioned above the text. "Is it made of glass?"

"Of course not. *Crystal.*"

She studied the pen and how it shimmered in the light. It was designed in such a way that the compartment housing the ink was concealed in geometric angles of the crystal. It looked like a tiny shimmering dagger.

"The agenda that has been set forth is something that needs several years to not only implement but to solidify. Longer than current term limits."

"Have you thought about starting to create a transition plan for the next Administration? I know we have time, but it's never too early."

Samuel pursed his lips in faux amusement. "No, I don't believe that's necessary. I don't plan on going anywhere."

"Have you been able to speak independently to members of the legislature about making an Amendment to change presidential term limits?" she asked, hesitantly.

"You think it's unlikely?"

"It would be a challenge. Across party lines, the vast majority support keeping presidential term limits where they are."

"Yes. These are the individuals who believe we should follow the guidance of white men who've been dead for hundreds of years." He narrowed his eyes. "I didn't suspect you were one of them."

She tried to maintain a neutral expression.

"I suppose there are always opportunities to force the issue."

"Mr. President?"

"Unexpected events have a way of removing barriers."

"Do you mean a national emergency?"

"Whatever it takes," he replied coolly. "Pandemics, civil unrest, wars—they're all so—*unpredictable*. And prevalent these past few decades—wouldn't you say?" He cocked his head to one side. "Obviously, we'd prefer a diplomatic solution, but emergency declarations are certainly handy in a pinch."

Annette narrowed her eyes.

He chuckled thickly. "I'm joking, of course. Honestly, Annie, you should see your face."

She decided to accept his claim and released her breath. "Perhaps the polls are right, that I have no sense of humor."

He waved his hand. "Forget polls. Come here."

"Pardon?"

"Listen to you: '*Pardon?*' Come here, Annie," he said, his voice uncharacteristically casual, moving his chair back from his desk.

He waited until she stepped toward him, as close as her comfort level would allow. He stood and continued to encourage her closer until her legs were touching his knees. It seemed possible that he was going to kiss her, his hot breath smelling strongly of earl gray tea, but he didn't move. The longer they stood like this, the more uncomfortable Annette became. Samuel's enjoyment, however, appeared to be increasing with each passing moment. He placed his hands on both of her arms, rotating them as a singular unit until they had made a 180-degree turn.

"Sit."

Annette looked over her shoulder at the high-back leather chair, an Oval Office fixture for many decades. She swallowed, looking up his pointy nose to his beady gray eyes. She couldn't imagine those eyes earning the hearts and votes of a record number of people.

"SIT," he repeated with such force it startled her and she reflexively reached back for the chair for support. He was smirking at her. "What do you think?"

She frowned. "It could use more cushioning."

"Right? I requested a new chair, but apparently, that takes an act of Congress," he said, crooking an eyebrow as he sat himself across in one of the boxy visitor chairs. "I jest, but I think the decorator was seriously offended at the request."

"Well, they'd have to replace the cushion at some point?" She still wasn't sure what his angle was with this interaction. He had the energy of a socially awkward kid who finally had someone over to his house and spent the whole time showing them his used gum collection.

"Every few decades you'd think. That 45 was a lard ass though." He established prolonged eye contact, smiling in a nondescript way.

Annette allowed the silence to persist, silently directing her muscles to relax into the chair back.

"I like you, Annie. You struggle with the theatrics of it all."

"Theatrics?"

"Politics. All a bunch of phonies, cut-rate actors if you ask me."

She raised an eyebrow in mild agreement.

"Right now, for example? This would be an ideal moment to seduce a career advancement out of me." He paused to issue a light smile. "But instead, there you sit."

She swallowed.

"I must admit, I wouldn't have your grit." Then, responding to her confused expression: "You were a House Representative for a single term before becoming Speaker." He narrowed his eyes. "I believe that was a record?"

Annette stiffened.

"You showed so much passion when you started. I believe you would have seized the opportunity presented by being alone in a room with the most powerful leader in the world back then. Yes?"

She lifted her eyes to the door, wishing she could be on the other side of it.

"It must be frustrating, to build so much momentum—"

"Only to have you steal my chair?" she said, raising her chin. She felt familiar levels of tenacity and entitlement rising in her chest.

His smile remained and the moment froze for a painfully long period of time, his cold eyes gazing at her with keen interest. Finally, he stood. "I feel good about this."

Annette stood, not understanding what "this" pertained to.

"We'll do tremendous things together."

She didn't quite commit to a full nod, but delicately handled their parting, like how one would handle a potentially armed bomb.

She passed through the West Wing hallways at a determined clip, her chunky heels clopping on the marble floors, all the carpets having been replaced for sanitary reasons after the third pandemic struck the country inside two decades. She kept meaning to buy quieter footwear. It would have served her well to be able to get by the press offices undetected. Mercifully, they appeared to be empty, most reporters probably recording their nightly news pieces on the People's House lawn. She tried to lighten her tread, while still maintaining a quick pace.

"Speaker Gibbons?"

Annette sighed, turning to find Christopher Loop standing in the doorway of the press office. "Good evening, Mr. Loop. How are you?"

"Fine, thanks for asking." He raised an eyebrow inquisitively. "I just wanted to make sure you were doing alright? It seemed like maybe you were preoccupied with something earlier."

"Well, it's been a lot of blood, sweat, and tears that went into this legislation." The scripted press response was supposed to continue that she was looking forward to going home, having a glass of wine, and getting right back to work tomorrow morning. This was intended to be followed by an appreciative chuckle. Ideally, this answer would be given in a presser with echoed laughs from a friendly press corps. Instead, she stood in the hallway of the most influential building in the world, third in line to hold the most powerful seat in the world and found she couldn't take a full breath. All she could see were the lifeless faces of dozens of babies and children, tossed carelessly in a pile, like some image taken from the Holocaust.

It was a hoax, the news had claimed, once they secured the airwaves again. Digitally modified, they said. A disinformation campaign. The company cited never existed. Nothing to see here.

Only she remembered the company name distinctly. The legislation and budget reports would of course be modified, but she had paperwork in her possession that included the company's name. They had a website and a Google business listing, and before it was scrubbed, the company had a Google Earth street view of their location at Glory

24

Hospital in Denver, a building featuring late 20th-century architecture and distinct, rounded, copper windows.

"Speaker Gibbons?"

She pointed toward the back exit of the building. "I need--" she wheezed, moving quickly in the direction she'd indicated.

Christopher ran to open the door for her, keeping his voice low: "Do you need a medic?"

She shook her head abruptly, her eyes quickly scanning the courtyard. She gulped for air but found she wasn't taking in an adequate amount of oxygen, her chest tightening.

"List three things you hear."

"What?" she demanded, glaring at him.

"It'll help--trust me. Close your eyes. List three things you hear."

Annette closed her eyes and tried to focus on the sounds around her. "I hear the fountains," she managed to say in one breath. "Birds. Do birds sing *at night*?" She shook off the question. "The landscaper who isn't supposed to be trimming right now," she growled, opening her eyes.

"Okay. Now, what are three things you see?"

"I see you." She said this with unintended grit, which he found somewhat comical.

"You see me trying to help you," he replied.

She rolled her eyes, clutching her chest, which was rising and falling in uneven waves. "I see the cherry blossom trees." They'd always been her favorite. She had been wanting to plan a trip to Japan during cherry blossom season for years.

"One more thing."

"I see a cracked travertine tile that hasn't been replaced in seven months."

He whirled his head around to follow her gaze. "Wow, *OK*. Now three things you smell."

Still following the rhythm of her heavy, uneven breathing, she attempted to inhale through her nose. "The grass. It was just mowed this morning." Her airway felt far less restricted. "The chlorinated fountain water."

"You should list your olfactory system as a skill on your resume."

She made eye contact with him for the first time, never having noticed the vibrancy of his green eyes.

"One more smell."

Annette frowned, closing her eyes again. "I smell cucumber, really light, mixed with freshly cut lumber." When she opened her eyes, her heart no longer raced, and she suddenly felt the weight of Christopher Loop's hand on her back.

"Are you smelling *me*, Speaker Gibbons?"

Her cheeks reddened.

"Better?"

She nodded. "I've never experienced that before."

"You're fortunate. I know a lot of people who experience them every day."

"Experience what?"

"Panic attacks."

She thought to argue that it wasn't a panic attack but feared she might tread into mental illness insensitivity. "News reporters are susceptible to them?"

His lips turned up. "*Maybe*, especially with how my network is treated. But no, I work with a veterans group."

"Oh. Did you serve?"

"Twenty years. Retired a few years back."

"I didn't know that." She swallowed hard. "Thank you. I meant for your assistance, but thank you for your service also."

He smiled kindly. "If you're not wanting to walk through the circus out the front, I've actually parked out this exit. I can give you a lift."

She knew he was right. Half the press corps would have been given orders to await her exit so they could collect the proper sound bytes. She'd hear from the committee about being a no-show. They were already planning the social media advertisements and the convention montage. "It might look--" The only word she could think of was scandalous and it sounded too seductive to say.

"I understand." His right eyelid flittered slightly.

"Thanks again."

"Have a good night," he said, tipping his brow as he started down the steps.

She watched him reach the path leading through the back gardens. He continued to grow smaller, the last orange glow from the setting sun giving way to night. When he reached the security station, she reasoned there was an adequate distance between them, and she followed his path out the less frequented gate of the People's House.

Christopher waved to her through the open driver's door of his boxy SUV as he spoke with someone on his cellphone. Annette tried to get a read on the nature of the call by the few words she had heard, deciding it was probably his producer.

"Hey, Steve? Let me call you back, okay?" He gave a friendly smile, tucking his phone in the center console. "Did you change your mind about the ride?"

"*Oh*, I was just going to walk, get some fresh air."

"Are you sure? I wouldn't walk around in this city after dark and I conceal carry."

"Handguns are banned in 30 states, including this one."

"Oh, *right*. I meant I conceal carry a unicorn bubble wand—obviously. Because the best way to deal with an armed assailant is to shower them with love and understanding—and bubbles."

"Fun fact: I have a first edition unicorn bubble wand. It has the Congressional seal and everything."

He twisted his expression. "Is that humor I detect, Speaker Gibbons?"

"Can't be. The public opinion polls say I'm incapable of it."

He smiled lightly. "Public opinion polls are used to shape public opinion, not gauge it."

"That's not a huge comfort."

27

"Whoever is running them tried to convince the public Samuel Gowon is a humanitarian *so*—take that into consideration when you're deciding about if you should take the results personally."

She bowed her chin ever so slightly, giving a curt smile. "Good night, Mr. Loop."

4
calling

The road between the Wests' farm and Wallace, Colorado stretched 210 miles. Matteo had driven the winding highway countless times, but the air in the pickup truck was different as he glanced over at his 15-year-old daughter, Esther, sitting in the passenger side, feet on the dash (he'd long stopped reminding her it was dangerous), reading a thick hardcover book. Her long golden-brown hair was loose and stretched down her arms in waves, her eyes focused on the yellowed pages before her.

"I still don't know how you can read in the car."

Her lips curled up slightly in her distracted way.

Matteo peered at the plain cover; the dust jacket removed. Dickens. Her current favorite.

His daughter had sought out literary classics since she learned to read at the age of 4, finding several in the church's rummage sale. Besides asking for a puppy once or twice, books were the only thing she ever requested. The government had been restricting new printings, citing environmental impact, so they were becoming more difficult to come by. While doing outreach work, Matteo always checked thrift shops and garage sales. Many people were naive to the implications of having only electronic versions available and started to think of printed books as a hassle to store. He'd rarely paid more than a dollar each.

While most children would never know the feel of a heavy, hardcover book in their hands, Esther's bedroom was filled with them. She had always loved the smell of books and been comforted by the presence of great adventures, deep emotional journeys, and clever storytelling. Her bedroom, with its odd shape, unusual, sloped ceiling, and impractical nooks suited her collection. Books lined plant shelves and cubbies; books filled every shelf surrounding her windows. He had created open shelving beneath the window seat to make more room. Even the right half of her wardrobe contained books instead of clothes.

"*So*—Gabriel West."

"Gabriel West," she repeated, raising an eyebrow.

"Honestly, given the choice between the West boys, I thought you would have gone for Josh."

She raised her gaze, her thick eyelashes unblinking. "I didn't *go* for anybody. *Gabe* kissed *me.*"

"About that?"

"Daddy."

"You're only fifteen."

"Oh, but I'm *very* mature," she said with a knowing smile. "Weren't you just saying that the other day?"

"Well, you certainly know how to get my goat, don't you?"

"I don't know those words."

He smiled. "If anyone knows those words, it's you," he said, eyeing the book.

"Fine, fine. 'You're only fifteen, Essie.' Go on."

"Well, you *are*—only fifteen."

"That's true," she said slowly, putting her hand to her chin. "When did *you* have your first kiss?"

He frowned. "You can't use your inside knowledge from Luke against me."

"For a boy with his eye on life in the church, you certainly got a young start–"

"I know what you're doing," he interrupted.

She furrowed her brow, as though pondering a complicated equation. "Strange that same boy would be completely oblivious to being considered the most eligible bachelor by all the lady-folk at church."

"What I'm saying is—hold on, what are you talking about, 'eligible bachelor?'"

"What did that phrase mean in the olden days? I'm sure it's roughly the same meaning now."

"And 'lady-folk'? How old do you think I am?"

"I'm sorry, how would you prefer I refer to your ladies in waiting?"

"That's worse."

She pinched her face. "Agreed. That was creepy olden kingdom times. Years before you came along."

"Centuries before, thank you."

"You're very young," she agreed, nodding repeatedly.

He shook his head, trying to find the pathway back to his originally planned conversation. "So, it *was* your first kiss-kiss?" He twisted his expression at his awkwardness.

Esther smirked. "Would you rather it wasn't?"

Matteo glared in her direction.

"I'm *sorry*, I'm being difficult. Yes. It was my first kiss-kiss. Kind of wasn't expecting it would have an audience, *but--*" She furrowed her brow, staring forward at her book, but didn't appear to be reading, her eyes no longer scanning the page.

His daughter was a logical sort, but he knew she harbored a fondness for great love stories. He'd have a difficult time believing she didn't wish such a story for herself. He remembered her cheeks turning scarlet when he walked in on her acting out a scene from a Jane Austen novel when she was eleven. The scene at the train station felt territorial and selfish, far from the long contrived great love stories of those beloved books of hers, far from what she deserved.

"It didn't seem in character for him," Matteo said, holding back from saying more.

She reached for her water bottle, taking a long sip.

"Did he say something? About being scared of going back or--?" Hearing the words out loud made him question his approach as he'd just insinuated the kiss was motivated out of fear or desperation–and not harboring feelings for her.

"He tried to seem okay about going back to Mandatory, but he wasn't."

Matteo decided against sharing some of what he had heard about the government's training antics being psychologically centered. Many enlistees weren't returning home, some writing to their families to say they'd signed on for an extended period, many more dying during "training exercises." There had been footage leaked showing seventeen-year-old recruits stepping robotically off the side of buildings. It had been discredited by the government as propaganda, misleading "disinformation" meant to undermine the government. He had been told that personal cell phones were being monitored "for public safety" as a result, though not many people could afford them anymore and the monitoring had been something people had suspected for years, a so-called "conspiracy theory." He hadn't had a cell phone in years.

"So, do you like Gabe--you know, like that?" He asked, intending to lighten the mood, or at least veer the conversation away from such *1984* matters as brainwashing and civilian surveillance.

She closed the book, taking a breath.

"Is this one of those things you don't want to talk to your dad about?"

She turned her chin toward him calmly.

"You know, this isn't biblical times. You don't have to pair up and settle down so young."

"So, we should call off the wedding?"

The truck wavered on the road.

"I'm kidding," she said reassuringly, "We can't call it off with the twins on the way."

Matteo's jaw clenched. "I know you're being a turd, but could you please tell my dad brain that? Because he's real, real tense right now."

"Do I call him 'dad brain'? Is he a different entity? Because that seems weird. Do I address your ear to speak to him directly?"

"*Essie.*"

"I'm not pregnant."

"I knew that but thank you."

"That I know of," she added with a casual shrug.

"*Esther,*" he growled, the truck bumping over the center lane lines.

"I'm not a licensed driver, but I'm more than capable if you feel like you're too distracted by all this."

"I'm fine. We're almost home, thank God," he said, resetting his hands to the ten and two positions. "When would you have learned to drive?"

She raised an eyebrow. "My closest friends both drive and they live in the middle of farmland. It's funny that it's the driving thing that troubles you most though right now."

He exhaled. "For being such a sweet girl, you really can be a turd. You know that, right?"

"I do know that, yes."

He allowed a mile of highway to pass before speaking again. "Gabe has always seemed like a good kid," he said in a grudging tone.

She smiled knowingly. "Yeah, he really *is* a good kid."

"He's good to you? He treats you the way he should?"

"He kissed me *today*. I have never gotten to know him in the context you're implying, but *as a friend*, he's very respectful." She reopened her book and resolved to move away from the conversation.

Matteo nodded, narrowing his eyes on the road ahead. Out the corner of his eye, he could see her frowning, her eyes fixed on the page. "If I could say one more thing about it?"

She raised her eyebrows. "I'm listening."

"Just because someone kisses you, it doesn't mean—"

She said nothing when he thought she might interject. Instead, she turned to listen to him, her eyes widening in their disarming way, reminiscent of her at a much younger age.

"It doesn't mean you're obligated to reciprocate if you don't share his feelings."

It would be very on brand for his daughter to add a quip to torment him; it was just the sort of relationship they had, but Esther continued to watch him in silence, waiting patiently for him to continue.

As a pastor, he had learned not to fill silences. By allowing a void in conversation, people could process things and often, they'd share more than if they hadn't been given silence. Since Esther knew him so well, she often used the tactic against him. There were very few times she'd been in trouble, but she once provided enough silence for him to doubt his approach and retract punishment for her minor infraction. This was different. The gentle blink of her eyes seemed to beg him for more guidance, more input.

"I always thought you and Josh were quite the pair—I'm just a little surprised." He added quickly: "Again, you're *only* fifteen. You don't need to worry about pairing up with *any*one."

He saw a flash of her dimpled cheek before she straightened her expression. "Why do you think that—about Josh being a better match for me?"

"You seem to have compatible personalities."

"Quirky?"

"A bit. Big personalities, both of you, but also—" he nodded toward the book. "Similar interests. Not to mention that kid has been sweet on you since he met you. Not that that should matter if—"

"'If I don't share his feelings'?" she said with a small smile.

"Yes."

"Dad, Josh *isn't* sweet on me."

"Yes, my darling girl, he is."

"We're talking about the same person, right? The guy has girls fawning over him every time we go to town. He doesn't--"

"So, what if he does?"

"He is *such* a flirt. If it is female and she has a pulse--" She finished the remark with a roll of her eyes. "His interests lie elsewhere. Believe me."

"I guess I haven't seen that side of him."

"He can be really obnoxious. It's part of the reason why Gabe and I usually split off from him when we're at the market."

When Matteo applied the behavior he saw from Gabe on this visit, he visualized him slipping a hand around Esther's shoulder and directing her away from Josh. Possessive. "You've seen him acting like that for yourself?"

She frowned, saying nothing.

"Does Josh flirt with *you*?"

"*Nooo*—" she said, smirking nervously. "He doesn't see me that way. At all. I'm not like the girls in town."

"What are they like?"

"I don't know, really sure of themselves?"

"And you're not?"

"Not in the way they're sure of themselves."

"How do you know they're so confident?"

"How they dress, how they act—'Ohh Josh, you're so *funny*.'" She play-slapped the air, her voice dramatic and high-pitched. She frowned, her cheeks reddening. "It's gross."

"Something you might discover is that the people who project the most confidence are the least confident people. That's why they need to act like--how was that again? With the hand motions and the giggle?"

She scowled at him.

"Usually, it means they're over-compensating. That's been my experience, at least."

"Well, confident or not, that's the type of girl he seems to go for."

"There's a phrase that comes to mind—'low-hanging fruit'?"

She appeared amused by this metaphor, unsuccessfully masking a smile. "That's mean."

He crooked his eyebrow.

"Accurate but mean." She twisted her face. "What's worse? Being the, as you say, 'low-hanging fruit,' or being the one—*harvesting* the 'low-hanging fruit'?"

35

Matteo winced.

"Yeah, didn't think of that, did you Mr. Matchy McMatchmakerson?" She dropped her shoulders, pinched her face. "That was embarrassing. Please delete that from your memory bank."

"Never. That shall go on my gravestone."

"Don't talk about having a gravestone."

"You're right. I'm sorry."

"Daddy, Josh is *not* sweet on me."

"Agree to disagree."

"We're friends. *Just* friends. I mean, the guy wrestles me to the ground pretending I'm a crocodile."

"That's true. He does do that."

"You're telling me that's flirting?"

He shrugged.

"Why does he narrate in that crazy accent?"

"Steve Irwin."

"Who?"

"The voice he does. It's Steve Irwin, the Crocodile Hunter. He was popular in the 90s."

"*Wow*. Are you that old?"

"Not quite. We streamed his show when I was a kid."

"What is this 'streaming?'"

"Not important."

Matteo could almost hear her belly laugh when Josh would sneak up on her, prowling around and narrating his actions in his fairly believable Australian accent. Inevitably, if put in this predicament, she'd wind up pinning him, either by using a tactic exploiting nerve endings— or if she was truly stuck, Josh would subtly open up an opportunity for her to gain an advantage.

Esther grinned to herself and shook her hair out from behind her back. "It *is* pretty funny. *Friends* funny," she clarified pointedly.

Matteo gave her a sideways look and she quickly retreated to her book again.

He decided to commit to silence. He wouldn't let her win this round. He distracted himself by thinking about when he brought her to meet his best friend, Luke, and his wife, Sara, for the first time.

The brothers had very different responses to the introduction: Gabe had been standoffish, almost cordial, but watched her with close interest and had remarked with wonder to his mom about Esther being "so pretty." Matteo remembered this distinctly because it was a recurring theme for Gabe. He'd treat her delicately, but his compliments about or toward Esther were frequently about her appearance and things Matteo considered superficial qualities. Gabe's sudden bout of assertiveness on this visit had frightened him a bit.

Josh was sweet to her, welcoming as he introduced himself. He immediately invited her, almost conspiratorially, to play. New to parenting, Matteo had felt overprotective of her as they played a bit rougher than he would have preferred, abandoning their shoes to run barefoot across the grass and dirt.

"She's not a China doll," Luke had told him, encouraging Matteo to join him and his wife in the front porch rocking chairs. Matteo had just taken a seat when Esther spotted the horses and taken off for the paddock. "Seriously, they're fine." Luke had called out to Gabe to not let her go in the paddock.

After spending a few minutes with the horses, the kids came running back to play on the swing. Before he knew it, Esther was standing on the wooden swing, ramping up speed, joyful and unafraid. It was during a backswing that the wood plank seat slipped on the rope ties, and she landed solidly in a sloshy patch of muddy grass. All three adults jumped up in alarm, but after sitting stunned for a moment, Esther started to laugh. It was pure and exuberant, and she curled over herself as the laugh rumbled through her belly. Josh ran to help, holding out his hand, and asked if she was okay. Through the giggles, she burst out with: "Yeah, but I think I broke my butt."

Matteo peered across the truck cab and found himself saying: "I was always fond of those boys, but Josh became my favorite the day he made you laugh for the first time."

She raised her eyes slowly. "What was so special about *that* laugh?"

Matteo gazed at her. "I had only adopted you a month earlier. It was the first time I had ever heard you laugh."

She smiled distantly, the dimple prominent again. She pulled her knees to her chest. "Did you try a Dad joke during that first month?"

"With a three-year-old?" He wrinkled his nose. "Fell flat."

"Yeah, my *age* was the problem."

"*Girl*," he warned.

Her cheeks beamed, her eyes twinkling.

They were both silent for a few minutes, then he noticed her becoming fidgety in her seat. "Daddy?" The skin between her eyebrows folded in its lopsided way. His stomach dropped as he anticipated what she might ask. He'd had an elevated level of anxiety when she approached him with a question ever since she was nine and read a chapter about human reproduction in a biology textbook. "At what point did I feel like your daughter?"

He exhaled deeply, pondering his response. He had learned long before she came along to take care in his words, so he never rushed when answering. When the memory came to mind that felt true in his heart, the corners of his mouth crept upward. "During our first community food pantry trip together. You came with me to get food from some farmers we partnered with. They grew fruit and vegetables in a portion of their land specifically for the pantry. They hadn't harvested it yet because they were short-handed. I was just going to have you play, maybe feed some of the animals while I worked, but you wanted to help. It was a lot of work, but you didn't complain once. By the time we were done, you were covered with dirt. You had those little jean overalls with the patches over the knees? And you borrowed my hat?" He reminisced, puffing out his bottom lip.

Esther grinned, eyeing the same distressed ball cap tucked up on the dash.

His eyes followed her gaze, his face brightening. "You fell asleep in the back seat on the drive home. When we got home, I picked you up and carried you into the house. As we reached your bedroom, you wrapped your little arms around my neck, snuggled in close, and kissed my cheek.

"You were my daughter from the day you came to live with me, but I kind of felt like an imposter up until then. At that moment, I felt like a dad."

She nodded, smiling lightly at him. For the next fifteen minutes, she seemed to struggle to focus on the words on the page, maintaining a confused expression, her mind reeling something. Meanwhile, he turned up Hank Williams to a low volume and tapped his fingers along to the music.

In the beginning, when he was new to parenthood, time admittedly stretched. It was challenging taking on a toddler alone, but it wasn't due to her being a difficult child, just the opposite. She was incredibly calm, kind, and even keeled. She showed little variance in emotion in the first few weeks, which was somewhat disconcerting. In the early weeks, he made efforts to demonstrate overt facial expressions to try to make the connection with the corresponding emotion as it all seemed foreign to her.

It didn't help that at the same time this was going on, he was taking over as lead pastor at Calvary Church. He wasn't thrilled to be starting his tenure by lying, but he understood it was a necessity. Having a child appear in his backseat at an isolated highway diner/gas station didn't exactly constitute a legal adoption process. He had told them the young girl was his niece, that his brother had been killed during his deployment and he was all she had. In all honesty, the church staff and the congregation probably would not have blinked an eye if he had told them she hatched from an egg. They were too distracted by the addition of a child to their town. They were eager to gush over her. "What a beauty!" they doted. "She looks like a little princess!" This was true--she had golden brown hair, wild and unruly waves that defied the laws of gravity, but her eyes were what took people by surprise. They were silver, shimmery with a slight iridescence.

People seemed to know better than to ask where she got her unique physical characteristics. They had likely assumed that, like Matteo, his brother (who had no children he was aware) had dark brown hair, olive skin, and brown eyes. This would deduce that she had inherited her features from her mother, but no one seemed to want to ask about her.

Almost every day someone was dropping off casseroles, boxes of decade-old hand-me-downs, toys, and books. Fewer and fewer people were having children--or rather, fewer were finding that they *could* have children. The children's ministry leader had warned that new children to the congregation were practically smothered with attention due to this. Initially, he had been concerned about her becoming overwhelmed by all the attention, but Esther enjoyed the outpouring of love immensely, the overabundance of affection seeming to fulfill something for her.

Three miles from home, the air shifted in the truck cab. Matteo silenced the stereo and Esther scrambled to sit upright. They had just taken the exit for Wallace and made the turn onto Ridge Road, the main street that ran through town. On the second block stood a Catholic church built in the 1800s. The large building was constructed of brick and featured a rooftop cross set between two steeples. It was always dressed to the nines with wreaths and twinkle lights at Christmas and featured a large Nativity on its corner lot, which provided a tremendously festive welcome to the town. Whenever they made the drive back from the West's farm after Christmas, it was a bittersweet, but spectacular sight.

The church building, the once historical site, was a smoldering heap. The only walls that remained were around the perimeter. The steeples appeared to have fallen inward into the sanctuary.

"Daddy?" There was an urgency in her voice.

Before he had a chance to shift his eyes toward her, she had thrown open her door and dropped her bare feet to the concrete. Matteo slammed on the brakes and threw the shifter into Park.

Esther was already running across the abandoned street, slowing only when her bare feet reached the splintered debris that had once been the doors to the church sanctuary. A young girl with blond ringlets, no older than six, was sitting amongst the rubble, her skin and dress coated in soot, her dirty cheeks streaked in tears. Esther was trying desperately to reach her, stepping lightly onto the pile of crumbled bricks and mortar.

5
hands

In the two months after the explosion at Saint Dominic's Church, Esther had been unable to rid her skin of the smoky residue. Her fingers wouldn't come clean, bits of ash, dirt, and dried blood persistently reappearing under her fingernails.

Matteo came home one evening after leading the men's life group to find her sitting on the edge of the tub scrubbing furiously at her hands. She wore oversized pajama bottoms he suspected belonged to one of the West boys, the waist rolled multiple times to keep her from stepping on the bottom hems. The t-shirt she wore was from the Children's Ministry vacation Bible school session themed around David & Goliath from the previous summer. She was freshly showered, her long, damp hair covering most of the logo on her back. She had a determined look about her as she scooped up the nail trimmers. They made loud, quick clipping noises as she moved along her fingertips. He stepped closer to see she had trimmed the nails down to the nubs; her skin was red and raw in places where she had been a bit too aggressive. He reached for the trimmers as she started another pass.

She gave a feeble protest, but he closed the trimmers and placed them on the countertop out of her reach. Her eyes were swollen and narrow, her cheeks blotchy as she faced him. He lowered his chin. "The offer is still good if you want to stay out at the Wests' farm."

She shook her head fiercely. "There's a lot to do here."

As usual, her logic was accurate. The community had been in disarray since the explosion. Eighty-three people had died initially, twenty died within days from their injuries. There were mass funerals daily, followed by individual services put on by families and friends of the victims. Matteo had made a point of attending every service. For the first couple of weeks, Esther had been at his side, and they attended nine separate funerals. By the third week, she approached him as he was selecting Bible verses for his Sunday sermon, still wearing his suit since there was another service to attend.

"Do you think it would be terrible if I didn't come to *all* of the memorial services?" Her eyes had glistened in the yellow light of the desk lamp. She was still wearing her black shift dress from the service they'd just attended but had pulled on cozy socks to keep from snagging her tights. She had her arms crossed over her stomach and was avoiding eye contact.

"It's part of my role as a pastor to go, Esther. You don't have that same obligation."

"I just feel like if I *don't* go—"

He leaned back in his chair.

"It feels disrespectful if I don't go. It feels selfish." A thick tear was making its way down the bridge of her nose.

"Esther," he said softly as he pushed himself out of his seat. "You don't need to be at these funerals. There are other things you can do, that you *have* been doing to help these families. You should focus on those things."

She nodded, squeezing her eyes closed. "I just don't feel like it's enough."

Matteo wrapped his arms around her. "It is, Esther. I couldn't be any prouder to call you my daughter."

Her body trembled with a wave of sobs, and she tightened her hold around his torso.

She had since stopped attending the funerals but had been trying to fill in the gaps for his absence from the church by being ever-present at the food pantry, becoming the primary vocalist for the worship band, and becoming one of the most prominent leaders of the Children's Ministry.

Now, two months later, he could see the increased involvement, the long days, were taking their toll on her.

They lived in a small two-story home attached to the back facade of Calvary Church. It was a convenient arrangement when she was young that allowed him to attend evening services and life groups. The proximity as of late had started to feel invasive. There was little opportunity to get breathing room from the endless procession of tragedy.

"You could probably use a break from all this," he said softly.

"So could you."

"That's true. But you're sixteen, I'm—" His mind trudged over the fact that in the midst of the tragedy, she had turned a year older. He felt overcome by a different sort of grief.

She pursed her lips, waiting for him to continue. He could almost hear her say "forty" in her sing-song voice, but her face fell again, and she remained silent.

"You should go to the farm, even for a little while? Get a little distance, some fresh air?"

She pondered the suggestion, her eyes softening as the prospect tempted her more and more.

"I'm sure Bree would love to have you out there to go for rides," he added softly. He intended bringing up the horse to be the final nudge to get her to agree to go, but he saw instantly that the statement had the opposite effect. It had simply reminded her that Bree wasn't being ridden very often because Josh and Gabe weren't there. While she loved Luke and Sara, the farm had far less appeal with the boys away at Mandatory. Even if she could make peace with neither of the boys being there, it probably wasn't a place where she'd find much quiet. Sara had a suffocating, motherly presence under normal circumstances.

Her face turned pale, and she swallowed hard. "I'll stay here."

Matteo leaned forward to kiss her head. "If you change your mind, it's an open offer."

"What's in your hand?" she asked, eyeing the folded piece of paper.

He'd nearly forgotten that he'd found a new message waiting in his inbox before leaving the church office. "Josh finally got your letters."

She sat up straighter, her brow furrowed. "Did you read it?" It wasn't an accusatory tone, but it gave the impression that if he had read Josh's letter first it would spoil her excitement a bit.

"He added a note at the beginning for me. I didn't read past that." He felt a twinge of guilt that communicating with the boys required an intermediary. Everything was electronic these days, but the platform required for emails contained a substantial amount of news, advertisements, and propaganda from which he was trying to protect her. The fact that she'd witnessed the aftermath of a bombing, seen severed limbs, and bodies blown to bits, witnessed raw grief in all of its forms, made his attempts to shield her from the realities of the world seem rather futile, but he didn't want to overwhelm her with anything more.

Her eyes brightened and she rose to her feet to claim the letter. She paused as she took the sheet of paper, smiling lightly when she saw the print covering both the front and back pages. "Nothing from Gabe?"

"You can read there–Josh just got access to your letters this afternoon. There's probably a delay for Gabe, too."

She frowned, her eyes scanning the top couple of lines, the part meant for Matteo. When she'd finished that portion, always a quick reader, she glanced up, taking a deep breath. "I made soup," she offered. "I was looking in one of the old cookbooks and decided to give one a try."

"Clam chowder by the smell of it," he remarked.

"Uh-huh," she murmured, her forehead creasing as she tried to resist reading the visible parts of the letter.

"That was very thoughtful of you. Thank you."

Esther gave a slight pull of her lips. "We had some bread flour that needed to be used up, too, so there's an Italian loaf that just needs slicing." She lifted her eyes cautiously. "Would you mind doing it? You remember the last time I handled a knife?" She held up her palm but had trouble locating the scar that had once stretched the width of her hand.

"Seven stitches. Yes, I remember." He nodded. "I think I can do the heavy lift on dinner tonight."

She scowled at him.

"Honestly, mia dolce ragazza, it smells amazing. Grazie. Grazie."

"I had worship band this morning, but I felt like I needed the afternoon away from things."

"I'm glad you took it, but you didn't need to spend it cooking."

"It was good for me—to focus on something else." She turned silent as she fidgeted with the fold of the paper. "Would you mind if I went and read this upstairs before dinner?"

"Of course not. I'll change and get the table set, okay?"

She nodded and jogged up the stairs to her attic bedroom, unfolding the paper as she went.

Matteo had changed into sweatpants and a t-shirt, scooped servings of the chowder into ceramic bowls, sliced the bread loaf, and put on a pot of coffee before Esther returned. He suspected this meant she had read the letter multiple times.

She had been louder on the stairs than he would have anticipated if the letter had upset her. She clattered into the kitchen in her usual way and pulled a fresh glass out of the open shelving. Her hair was now pulled into a high, messy bun on top of her head. She pinched her nose, turning toward the coffee pot.

"Aren't Italians famous for coffee?"

He snapped to attention, reflexively pulling the glass pot from the coffeemaker. The brew started dripping directly onto the hot plate with a sizzle. He shoved the half-full pot back under the drip, tapping each of the buttons to try to turn off the appliance. "I truly don't know why I'm so bad at this," he sighed as the lights on the coffeemaker turned off.

She moved toward him, shaking her head with mild amusement. "Okay, from here I can *see* coffee grounds in the pot. What did you–" She lifted the top compartment where the water looked like it was about to overflow. "I think some coffee grounds spilled out of the filter and clogged it."

"I probably shouldn't drink coffee this late anyway."

"Yeah, what were you thinking? That would have kept you up way past your normal 8:30 bedtime." She said facetiously, moving back to fill her glass with lemonade from the carafe in the refrigerator.

He smiled at her, pleased that her mood had lightened, at least for the time being. He waited for her to tuck herself into the table, her left leg folded beneath her before he briefly gave thanks.

"So, how is Josh?" he asked once they were both situated at the kitchen table. The round oak slab was surrounded by matching chairs, each with a different print cushion. His unofficial seat had green leaves that looked a little too tropical for their locale, while Esther had chosen the colorful elephant print cushion from their very first meal at the table.

Her cheeks tightened. "He's okay."

Matteo nodded. "You don't have to share anything you don't want to with me, but I do care about the kid."

"Well, should I ask 'the kid' to write longer notes to you?"

He smiled. "I wouldn't mind if he did."

She raised her spoon out of the bowl, blowing gently on the soup. "If I write him back tonight, would you mind sending it in the morning?"

"I'll scan it to him as soon as you're done if you'd like."

She nodded, her eyes drifting dreamily across the room. "Joey Farms," she said with a smirk.

"Sorry?"

"For our goat farm. Josh came up with it."

Matteo frowned.

"J-O-E-E. Our first and middle initials. Joshua O'Neil–"

He smiled appreciatively, watching her sip her soup. "The soup is really good, E.E."

She looked up at him through her lashes, dipping her spoon back in the bowl. "Hey, Daddy? You're able to do video messages, right?"

He paused. Esther had lived a fairly low-tech life, a stark contrast to his youth when everyone seemed to have a device glued to their palm. The one exception had been when a member of the congregation had recorded her singing and the video had gone 'viral.' She had been bewildered by the attention when they showed her the view count, the comment thread. "What's DC Comics?" she had asked randomly one Sunday afternoon.

"It's a comic book line–superheroes and villains."

"Do they still make them?"

"I'm not sure. They're probably all digital now. People collected the comic books for years though."

She nodded. "Huh."

He had been perplexed. "What's gotten you interested in comic books all of a sudden?"

"Oh. There was a whole conversation happening in the comments of the video of me singing. They said I look like a young Hippolyta. Based on the context, I don't think it was an insult, but I was curious who she is."

"Hippolyta is the mother of Wonder Woman."

Esther frowned. "Why does the daughter get such a cool name? Hippo sounds like–well, you know–" She puffed out her cheeks.

Matteo chuckled. "No, she's based upon Greek mythology. She's an Amazon goddess."

"Amazon means tall and like, sturdy?"

"No, *statuesque*," he said, straightening out his posture.

"Broad-shouldered?"

"Well, kind of. Athletic. A warrior."

"Do I *look* like a warrior?"

He smiled. "You're a warrior on the inside."

Her jaw dropped. "*You're* a warrior on the inside," she repeated in a mocking tone.

Matteo tried to keep a neutral expression. His daughter was striking, but she was not what he would think of as an Amazon warrior.

She was lean and fairly tall and had a decidedly feminine look to her, despite her rarely dressing the part. While she could hold her own against Josh West, for the most part, he frequently afforded her a subtle tactical advantage.

"Daddy?" Esther's voice reeled him back to the present. She looked so much older suddenly, with more pronounced cheekbones, a squared chin, and thick eyelashes that further defined her large, silver eyes. It didn't seem that long ago that she'd had softer edges, a more youthful shape to her face.

"We agreed you would not get any older."

"I made no such agreement." She frowned questioningly.

"The laptop can record video messages. I thought you liked writing though?"

"I do," she said, lowering her eyes. "I just thought—maybe it'd be nice to feel like I'm 'talking'--" Her use of air quotes and the sudden glistening in her eyes caused a sting in his chest.

"I'm sorry. Of course, you can send a video message. I didn't mean to interrogate you about it."

She smiled lightly. "I miss them."

"I know you do. We'll go down to my office after dinner and I'll get you set up."

"Thank you," she said softly.

"The soup is fantastic, by the way."

"Clams are meant to be kind of chewy?"

"They are."

"Interesting. I'm not used to eating sea creatures, but the broth part is good, right?"

"All of it is good. You're just not used to seafood. I haven't had clam chowder in twenty years. We really had canned clams hiding in the pantry?"

"Let's not think too hard about that. The can said they're still good for another year."

With their bellies full and warm, they stepped into the cool night air.

"I watered the plants this afternoon," she said, nodding to the front porch, which was covered with dozens of planters and pots filled with all different varieties of succulents, wildflowers, orchids, and roses. There were also multitudes of vines, which had threaded themselves around every wood post and now covered the entire facade of the house, stretching halfway along the wall facing the parking lot. The previous pastor had been something of a green thumb, Matteo and Esther inheriting his collection. The plants had all dried up and given the house the appearance of being haunted soon after they'd moved in, but eventually, Esther started caring for the plants, bringing the place back to life.

"I can smell the roses."

"They do recommend doing that from time to time," she said with a sideways glance. "We have gardenias now, too. They're the white ones. They're almost *too* fragrant though."

Esther had slipped into her cowboy boots with the fishhook shaped pattern sewn into the leather for the short walk outside, scuffling across the pavement loudly. Her outfit was quite something: She had tucked her blue and green plaid pajama pants into her boots, the fabric billowing out around her calves. Her decreased food intake over the past couple of months had resulted in the t-shirt looking even more oversized. She had layered on a heathered gray hoodie, which she had pulled up over her knotted hair.

Part of the concern people of his generation had with technology was the vanity aspect, the self-centered culture it had created, and the impact it had on their peers. There was too much information out there, social media had become an obsession and a curse that didn't offer enough to make up for what it took. There had been a shift, or rather, a complete course reversal for many people his age as they had children. He couldn't help but appreciate his daughter's naivety to all of it, that she had done no adjustment to her appearance before leaving the house to make a video message.

The building was locked, but they could hear voices from the classroom as they stepped inside. The noise turned out to be a bunco tournament, the round tables scattered around the room filled with a multitude of the older members of the congregation. There was a makeshift "bar" at the teacher's desk and a jazzy melody had begun to play.

"Wow. Calvary After Dark is hopping. I had no idea," Esther said, raising her eyebrows.

"Neither did I."

When they reached his office, he stepped into the darkness to turn on the desk lamp. Once seated at the desk, he navigated to his email and clicked the video icon. He considered the open emails he had minimized, the content she could access if she navigated around the computer but decided that doing too much last-minute cleanup would give her the impression he didn't trust her.

"You'll just click the red circle to record. When you're done, click the button again. The file will automatically get added to a new message, then just start typing in 'West' and he should come up. Click his name, click send, and you're done."

She nodded.

He stood and scooted around her toward the door.

"Does the green circle next to his name mean someone's available?"

Matteo turned on the spot. "Sorry?"

She pointed to something on the screen and her face brightened as a new window opened. "Oh my gosh, can he *see me*?"

"Essie?" a voice bellowed through the speakers.

"Let me turn the volume down," Matteo offered, rounding back to the opposite side of the desk. "Leave it to you to find something I didn't know about–" His eyes lifted to the video feed of a young man with a sheared head, a narrow jawline, and deep-set brown eyes. He quickly tapped the function key to lower the speaker volume a few notches.

Gabe rolled his chair closer, his eyes darting around to find the camera. "Teo," he said in a friendly voice. "It's good to see you. Well, both of you." His eyes shifted and seemed to focus on Esther's face, his smile broadening tightly. Despite the dark circles beneath his eyes, his expression was undeniably happy at the sight of her.

"I was just helping Essie get situated on the computer. I had no idea there was a video call function?"

"Yeah, it's tough though because most of us don't have the technology back home so there isn't anyone to call. I was just doing some online learning modules."

"How are you doing?"

Gabe flinched almost imperceptibly, eyes focusing back on Essie. "Better now."

Matteo noticed the continuous upturning of his daughter's smile in the inset video of their feed. He peered over at her looking fidgety in the leather desk chair. "*Well*, I'll let you two talk. Hope to see you soon, Gabe."

"You, too."

"They'd want me to ask--Have you gotten their letters? I know they've written several."

Gabe frowned, eyes darting away. "The mail must be delayed."

"Josh finally got a batch of mail today so maybe yours will arrive soon."

Gabe nodded repeatedly, saying nothing.

"I'll let them know to be on the lookout."

"Thanks."

"Have a good night, Gabe."

"You, too."

Matteo glanced back as he exited his office to see Esther beaming at the computer screen, looking happier than he'd seen her in months.

6

buonanotte

"You're looking very serious," Essie said, peeking her head into her dad's dimly lit office. She stepped inside with some degree of difficulty as the office doubled as storage for the food pantry and various other community donation drives, which had ramped up in recent weeks. Most of the floor space was covered with boxes. Even the tufted leather couch, a donation from the estate of a congregation member, was starting to collect piles. "I don't know how you get anything done in here."

"Have you seen *your* room?"

"That's books–and they are very well organized, thank you very much."

He grunted, tapping out one last sentence on his laptop.

She eyed the computer but had long stopped asking if there were any messages for her. Mandatory's leadership had put a stop to electronic communication with enlistees not long after she was first able to reach out to Gabe, and had to switch to regular mail, which was subject to increasing delivery delays, it seemed. It had been several months since she'd heard from Josh, longer from Gabe.

"If you get nervous during your sermon, just break out with a smile, maybe thicken that Italian accent of yours. A bit of charisma will go a long way."

"I don't have an Italian accent," he said dismissively.

"I-a-don't-a-hav-an-Italian-a-accent-e," she teased, emphasizing each syllable with a hand gesture that made it look as though she were conducting an orchestra.

He smirked, closing his laptop as his notes printed out behind him. "Wish I had you out there singing today. The congregation could use your inspiration."

"Oh, I've got my hands full."

He nodded. "I heard." Patty, the retiree who typically ran the children's ministry, had told Matteo through a rush of tears that her husband forbade her from coming to church after a series of attacks on churches in the region. None were as deadly as Saint Dominic's, almost a year earlier, but nearly ninety people had been killed with hundreds more injured in the other attacks.

"I was hoping at least Joanna was going to–"

Esther shook her head.

"Think you can handle the rugrats on your own?" Matteo asked, rising from behind his ornate wooden desk, trying to keep a light tone to his voice.

"Rugrats?" she said, raising an eyebrow. "The youngest is eight."

"Still."

"Thought I'd go old school with our music today."

"Old school to you is anything not written this decade."

"That is untrue. I know no music written this decade."

He pressed his lips together. It was true. Ever since radio, television, internet became heavily regulated and monitored, he had limited his utilization and relied on the music he had purchased years earlier. She hadn't listened to anything written since she was born, probably a decade or so earlier. "What'd you have in mind?"

"*This little light of mine, I'm gonna let it shine–*" she sang in a gentle whisper.

"*This little light of mine, I'm gonna let it shine,*" he echoed, nodding approvingly.

It was a song he sang to her when she was little. She could see him sitting in the lamp light of her room—she was only four or five so there were substantially fewer books surrounding them. Nightmares had been a regular event for her so there were typically at least two goodnight routines completed most nights. He always asked if she could remember the nightmares and she always said no, even if he was certain it wasn't true.

He tucked the blankets up to her chin. "You know, mi amor. By not talking about what's so scary you make it more powerful. You let it dim your light, but if you shine as brightly as ever, shine a light on all those scary things, they may start to fade away. They'll want to hide from you."

"But I'm not scary."

"To me, you're not. You are the most wonderful, beautiful thing in the world." He had placed a hand gently on her face. "But if I were something that wanted everyone to live in a dark, cold world, guess what?"

"What?"

"They're way more afraid of you than you are of them," he whispered conspiratorially. "As long as you just keep shining your light? They don't stand a chance."

In his crowded office tucked across from the children's ministry, he blinked slowly, smiling. "*Let it shine, let it shine, let it shine,*" he sang softly.

"I thought it was appropriate."

He gave a tight smile. "That it is."

"You should sing, Daddy. During Service? They love it when you play guitar. They'd be thrilled to have you sing." She raised her eyebrows expectantly.

"Maybe I will."

"Really?"

"No, not really."

"But you have a great voice."

"You're biased."

"Okay, you're a bit pitchy at times, but I love when you sing. Plus Jay has an auto-tune effect he can put on your mic."

55

He chuckled, wrapping his arm around her shoulder, kissing her on the top of the head, which was becoming a bit of a challenge as she nearly matched his 5'10" height. "We agreed you'd stop growing."

Essie released herself from his hold, spotting a family approaching the children's ministry classroom for drop-off. "I never agreed to anything," she called in a sing-song voice, disappearing around the corner.

Seven children came to the children's ministry consistently from week to week. The oldest of the group, Michaela, was thirteen. She had spiraled dark hair and fancied herself Essie's understudy. She liked to mimic her gestures and had shown up with a voluminous Dutch braid since that was what Essie sported the previous week. Next was Sam, a round boy with chestnut skin and kind, black eyes, who prided himself on being a comedian. There were twelve-year-old twins, Renee and Thomas. Renee was eleven going on a confident sixteen, who often thought she was too old to be coming to children's ministry. Essie suspected she wanted to have some time apart from her twin, Thomas. Born with spina bifida, he sped around in a sporty wheelchair and frequently ran over toes in the process. His condition could have been addressed and potentially repaired in the womb, but the hospital's Ethics Board had instead made the recommendation for selective termination, which is to say Thomas would have been killed in the womb via lethal injection in the heart, his dead body delivered at the time of his sister's birth. Because this was the official recommendation of the Board, the repair surgery was not made available to them at any facility in the country—unless they could pay privately. Additionally, because his family had failed to follow medical recommendations, they were dropped from their health plan and had been denied public health insurance coverage ever since.

Rowan was eleven, had an unruly mop of blond hair, and was incidentally, quite smitten with Renee. Last, there was ten-year-old Mason, and his sister, nine-year-old Madison.

There hadn't been a baby born to anyone in the congregation, or even in the town, in nearly a decade. People said it was because of the uncertainty of the times and the division in the country, and they reasoned that people simply couldn't afford to have children. They didn't like to talk about the surge in infertility, miscarriages, and stillbirths.

Sunday services had been combined into one service since attendance had been on the decline. People had been relocating in droves, either toward cities, where they could obtain public assistance, or "off the grid," up in the mountains. Her dad liked to focus on the positive, that it had allowed for better participation in the food pantry and attendance at life groups. Both were true. The congregation that still attended regularly was very close-knit.

Essie watched the group of seven children quietly conversing around the front tables and peered out the classroom door out of formality to see if anyone else was coming before she got started.

"Today, we're going to talk about–" Essie jumped up to the front of the classroom, just as she finished pulling on a costume lion head. "Daniel in the Lion's Den."

There were nervous giggles from the younger children, who stared wide-eyed at her.

"*What*?" she said, pacing along in front of the chalkboard. There were four circular worktables spaced around the classroom, each with a bin of art supplies in the center. The children typically ended up grouped at the front two tables and today was no exception. Essie scanned their confused faces. "Be honest, can I not pull off being a lion? I was sorted into Gryffindor, I kind of feel like it should feel more natural than this."

"Try roaring," Thomas suggested, wheeling his chair back and forth impatiently.

Essie cleared her throat and crouched to the ground. Pushing through her toes, she released the loudest roar she could manage.

There was a rush of chaotic voices as the children responded to her performance and provided tips to be more lion-esque.

"Alright, alright, alright. I get it. 'Don't quit your day job, Essie.' Now, I need 3 big, *scary* lions–do we have any volunteers?" She removed her headdress and placed it atop Madison's head. She retrieved two more from the clear tote by the chalkboard and handed one to Rowan and one to Mason. "Next, *oh*, Sam? Will you be our Daniel?"

Sam's cheeks tightened.

"I don't have much of a costume for you—would you like a cloak maybe?"

He nodded.

"Ignore the Hogwarts house crest," she said, eyeing the serpent design apprehensively. "Okay, we also need an advisor to the king. Spoiler: They're kind of the villain."

Renee's hand shot up.

"Well, Renee, there is something to be said for enthusiasm. What I have for you is something that Pastor Matteo said was popular a long time ago. It's called a 'meme.' This was a popular one." She handed Renee an enlarged printout of a woman pointing angrily, then dug out one of a glaring cat, which she handed to Sam. "It works best if Sam, you move to this side."

Renee scowled, trying to suppress a smile.

"Now we need our king."

Michaela glanced around nervously.

"You know what? Don't worry, you can totally pull this off." Essie returned to the bin and tugged out a fake, very bushy beard, and a gold crown.

"Wait, what are *you* going to be?" Thomas asked.

"That'll come later. For now, I'll be the storyteller. Is everyone ready?"

There were some nervous laughs.

"Our story takes place in Babylon, a dry, mountainous land. At the time it was ruled by King Darius." She moved over to stand behind Michaela. "King Darius was a nice enough ruler, aside from having a pit of starving lions for no apparent purpose except to carry out capital punishment without a fair trial but *be that as it may*—King Darius had a team of advisors as kings often do. That team included Daniel, who was a faithful servant of God. Daniel happened to be Darius's favorite. The other advisors included–" She hurried over to Renee. "What shall the name of our villain be?"

"Horace."

"That's thinking on your feet. *Horace* and the other advisors were very jealous of Daniel since he was so adored by King Darius. They concocted a plan and convinced King Darius to write a law that said the people were banned from worshiping anyone or anything but the king. Bending to peer pressure and having no discernible backbone, King Darius did just that."

"So much power, so weak in intelligence," Thomas said, shaking his head.

Michaela's cheeks were red beneath the beard.

Esther gave her a sympathetic pout. "Yeah, I'm sorry, there's not much in this story to redeem you, King. So, *Horace*–" she turned on the spot and presented Renee, "--wasted no time in catching Daniel praying to God. Daniel knew of the law, but he refused to obey. Before the law was put into place, he prayed three times a day with his windows open, right in the middle of the city. Once the law was in place? He prayed three times a day with his windows open in the middle of the city. Oh, there's another meme–or maybe it's called something else–of an owl doing this move–" She whirled her chin around in a circular pattern. "--and the caption reads 'Come at me, bro.'" There was a series of laughs. "That's kind of what I think of when I think of what Daniel did. He wasn't going to let anyone, or anything keep him from worshiping God."

She paused to let the weight of the message sink in. "*Seriously*. There's a law put out saying if you do this, you will be killed and he's like–"

"Come at me, bro?" Thomas said with a grin.

"Yeah, don't use that one with your parents. They probably won't be pleased with me for teaching you that. But *anyway*, Daniel was arrested and as established by the new law, Daniel–" She moved to stand behind Sam, motioning to those playing the lions to move behind her. "--was thrown in the lion's den, where at least three very hungry lions waited."

"Couldn't Darius just change the law he wrote?" Michaela asked, indignantly.

"Oh, he tried. He realized he had been tricked and he tried to stop it, but there was nothing he could do to delay Daniel from being thrown in the den." Esther walked backward toward the box, piquing the interest of the kids. "Darius stayed up *all* night thinking about what might be happening to his beloved advisor. In the morning, he ran down to the lion's den to see if Daniel had managed to survive the night. He called out to him and to his surprise, Daniel called back."

"How did the lions not eat him?"

"*Well*, Daniel said that God had sent an angel, who had told the lions–" She dipped into the box and quickly pulled on a long white wig with an equally long beard and yelled: "You shall not pass!"

The room fell silent.

"Too violent of a series for you–*Lord of the Rings*, if you're wondering. Sorry. That was Gandalf, not to be confused with *Dumbledore*," she clarified, saying the headmaster's name in a high, squeaky voice. She exchanged the wig/beard combination for a tinsel halo, which she perched on her head with a flutter of her eyelashes. "God sent an angel who shut the mouths of the lions so they would not hurt Daniel nad ultimately, Daniel was freed." The halo began to totter, and she tugged it off, placed it on one of the worktables. "*So*–what does this story teach us?"

"That peer pressure is bad?"

"Well, it certainly can be."

"To trust God?"

"Yes. To have faith in God. Always."

"What happened after Daniel was freed?"

"King Darius changed the law and decreed that all people should pray only to the one true, living God."

"Did Horace get thrown in the lion's den?"

Esther smiled nervously. "This story can also teach us about forgiving others."

"That's unacceptable. Horace should have been lion food," Sam declared, shaking his head. "He's sadistic, the lions are hungry, win/win."

"Well, let's be sure not to get on your bad—"

"*Actually*," Thomas began. "It says that Darius had his other advisers, their wives, and their chil—"

"Okay!" Esther interjected.

"He killed their wives and kids?"

"Their kids didn't do anything wrong."

"We aren't going to go into specifics, but the grownup version also teaches us how sin can spread and impact a lot of people and how justice is done on those who don't follow God. But the main message *today* is to have faith in God."

"What about Saint Dominic's Church? The other churches? Weren't those people killed for worshiping God?" Thomas asked, his face furrowed.

Esther felt her body stiffen. "That's true, Thomas. They were."

"Why didn't God save *them*?"

She glanced around the room, grimacing. "That's probably something that's on everybody's mind, right?"

Renee nodded, the tone in the room significantly less jovial than just seconds prior.

Esther sighed, encouraging everyone to have a seat. She pulled one of the chairs from an empty table and sat backward in it, facing the children. "Well, *I'm* not a pastor and I don't know the Bible backward and forward, though I'd like to think I know it pretty well," she prefaced, willing her dad's wisdom to speak through her. "I *have* given this some thought and prayer."

"And?" Thomas said impatiently.

"The world is not anywhere close to being a perfect place. God intended it to be, but He also gave us free will, the ability to make our own choices. Some people choose to do evil. Terrible things happen because people are free to do what they want."

"He could stop it though."

"Yeah, he could. Everything that happens, God has the power to stop, but let's not underestimate free will, guys. Imagine going through life not feeling like you have a choice in anything, being required to stay on a narrow path. It would be pretty restricting. It wouldn't feel meaningful to follow God, right? Because we wouldn't have a choice. At least *I* don't think it would feel very meaningful. It definitely wouldn't be the same loving relationship we have with God. *Think of it*: if we always do exactly the right thing, never do wrong, we don't have the need to speak to God nearly as much, right? He'd feel a bit less like an understanding, loving Father and more like a ruler.

"I think it's more meaningful to God to have followers who *choose* to believe in Him, don't you? I know I'd rather have people who choose to love me and *do*; I wouldn't want that to be something they're forced to do."

Michaela nodded slowly.

"So free will is a good thing, even if bad actions come out of it. But even though bad things happen, God promises to bring good from everything. We can't always see what it is, but I believe it's there because I believe God is good and faithful and always keeps His promises."

"Psalm 145:13," Thomas murmured.

"Thomas, do you have the Bible memorized backward and forward?" Esther asked, incredulously.

"He has an eidetic memory," Renee explained, peering over at her brother.

"So, you're going to remember the whole meme thing and I'm going to get fired?" Esther gave an obvious wink.

"Don't be so dramatic, you don't even collect a paycheck," Thomas muttered with an eye roll.

"It's the principle, Thomas."

"You're only, what, 16?"

"Nearly 17," she said unnecessarily.

Thomas narrowed his eyes. "Are you telling me that you're sixteen and a half? I thought only small children did that sort of thing."

She pressed her lips together. She was 15 the last time she saw Josh and Gabe in person. She pushed the thought and the accompanying sadness away. "That's a fair point."

"*Anyway*, I was just going to say: You're only 16, Esther. You only have the name of a much older person. You don't need to worry about getting in trouble. I'm pretty sure you're universally liked anyway."

She puffed out her lower lip. "*Aww*, Thomas. That's the nicest--"

"Wait for it," Renee warned.

Thomas shrugged. "What? That's the end of my sentence. Have you ever met someone who *doesn't* like her?"

"*Esther*," Sam began, his voice low and uncharacteristically serious. "Do you believe in Heaven?"

Essie smiled kindly. "Of course, I do." She glanced around at their faces, which were much more at ease now. No one seemed eager to add follow-up questions.

"On *that* note, I want to share a song that my dad taught me when I was a little girl." She turned to retrieve her guitar from its stand in the corner. There was mild chatter behind her as she lifted the instrument and pulled the strap around her shoulder. "He's always told me that I have the power to counterbalance any of the bad in the world. And all of you do, too."

There was a sudden clank of metal on the floor behind her and she wheeled around on the spot. A canister was rolling to a stop along the back wall of the classroom. Its presence was punctuated by the slamming of the classroom door. Through the window in the door, she could see a group of masked individuals. There was a squeal of a power drill as they jammed something into the outside of the door.

The outer door was meant to be locked, she thought, confused. Ever since the other attacks, they'd made a point of increasing security. The building containing offices, the food pantry, and the Children's Ministry was locked during Service. Most of the church leaders were armed, as were some of the congregation members.

Her eyes scanned over to the metal canister in the back of the room. It seemed to pulsate with each passing second. *It's poison gas*, she determined silently, her heart seized in fear. She looked up at the basement windows, which were too high to reach and too narrow for most of the children to fit through.

Everything was progressing in slow motion. Her eyes passed over the confused, terrified faces of the children and landed on the door of the supply closet. As her dad had needed to take over much of the maintenance in the building, she knew there was a poorly placed return air vent inside the closet. The vent had been large enough to accommodate an entire raccoon family at one point and ran straight along the classroom to the perimeter wall, with an exit point near the playground. The older children might struggle to fit through, but they might be able to manage. *It's the only option*, she thought, whipping the guitar back off her body as she turned to sprint for the closet.

They'll need something to unlatch the return, she strategized silently, grabbing a pair of kid-safe scissors from the center of the closest worktable.

"Everyone in here *now*," she yelled, throwing open the door. Thankfully, the path to the vent was clear. She turned to the first face before her–Sam–and handed him the scissors. "Get the vent open as quickly as you can. Let the younger kids through first, they'll be faster. Get outside to fresh air, then out toward the park."

"Esther?" a small voice said behind her. Renee was staring at the canister, which had just split open, a thick fog starting to rise into the air.

It was on a timer, she concluded, glancing at the classroom door. Through the small windowpane, she saw the attackers taking off through the outer door. "*Move it*," she bellowed, searching for Thomas, who sat motionless in his wheelchair, staring at the smoke seeping out of the canister with a low hiss.

"Who would throw something in a classroom?" he postulated.

"Thomas, you're going to need some help, okay?" She said rhetorically, unbuckling the strap across his waist. As she lifted him, she was surprised by the heft of his body.

The other children were scrambling into the closet.

"Sam, did you get it?"

There was a pause and then he cried: "I got the screws out; I just can't get the cover off."

Esther made eye contact with Michaela. "Please help him."

Michaela nodded and scurried into the closet.

The fog was rising higher and starting to billow out. Madison, who Esther discovered was clinging to her leg, was starting to cough.

"Don't breathe it in. You'll be out to fresh air soon."

Madison cupped her free hand over her nose and mouth, gazing up at Esther for more reassurance.

There's not enough time, Esther thought in desperation. She started using her body to apply pressure to the kids to push together and move forward into the small closet space. "Everyone inside–*now*."

"It won't come off," Michaela whimpered.

"It's okay," Esther said. "You're all going to be okay. Sam, hand me the roll of duct tape just over your shoulder, please."

"I'll take Tom," Sam offered once he'd weaved his way to her. He wrapped his arms around Thomas as he handed off the tape.

Thomas screamed, trying to cling to Esther.

"Buddy, you need to let go for now."

"*No*," Thomas screeched through gritted teeth. "Don't pretend I'm going to see you again."

The other children looked up, startled.

Esther swallowed, shifting her attention to Sam and Michaela. "Keep working on getting into that vent."

They both nodded.

"I'm going to close this door and seal it up as best I can."

Thomas let out a cry. "*See?*"

"Try to fill in the gap at the bottom of the door when I close it. Use your jackets, anything you can find. Do *not* open this door."

Their faces went blank.

"Do you understand me?"

"If you stay out there, you're *going to die*," Thomas screamed angrily.

Renee nudged forward to comfort her brother, struggling to look at Esther.

"Thomas—" Essie said, but he had turned away and buried his face into his sister's shoulder.

She took one last look at the children and closed the door.

In the quiet of the classroom, she went immediately to work. The gas was starting to tickle at her throat and her eyes were beginning to burn. She tugged out the supply of costumes from the bottom of the storage bin and stuffed them along the bottom edge of the door. She then began the process of sealing the perimeter of the door with duct tape.

As she finished the last side, she felt the gas enter her lungs more persistently, her throat feeling like it was coated in splinters.

I can throw it out the window, she reasoned, staggering between the tables, her head starting to throb from the fumes. She scooped up the canister clumsily in her arms, knowing immediately that she'd made a terrible mistake. She screamed silently as the slowly leaking gas made direct contact with her arms first, causing the skin to immediately blister. As the canister rolled out of her grasp, the gas coated her face, like steam rising out of a dishwasher. She squeezed her eyes shut. Her cheeks, her eyelids, her ears felt like there was suddenly a shallow fire coursing across her skin.

The canister clattered loudly against the floor, but the sound seemed to be traveling through water to reach her. She squinted through eyelashes she was sure were coated with the gas, trying to locate the canister.

Cover it, she thought, eyeing the clear bin she'd been pulling silly costumes out of all morning. She took one stride toward it–it suddenly looked so much further away–and she felt her muscles start to spasm. Her back arched unnaturally, her knees buckled, and she collapsed. There had been a horrifying snap that corresponded with a strange sensation in her back.

From where she lay on the floor, she could see the duct tape start to lose adherence to the wall surrounding the closet door.

You have to protect them.

She propped herself up on her elbows and tried to drag herself forward, tears rolling down her cheeks. Unable to build any momentum, she dropped her gaze to her hands, raw and blistered, and the floor, which was speckled with thick, scarlet blotches she realized were her tears. She blinked repeatedly as she started to lose the ability to see. Her ears had started to shriek, as though pressurized in deep water. She dragged her body across the vinyl flooring toward the canister and summoned all her strength to throw herself over the top of it. The valve of the canister dug painfully into her hip bone, and she could feel the flow of gas absorbing into her abdomen.

And then, all became quiet.

Through the sludge coating her eyes, Esther could see the blurry shape of her guitar. She didn't remember the sequence of steps she had taken to remove it before moving the children into the storage closet, but there it was, lying on the floor. She saw the strap, which one of the church elders had sewn for her. She saw the costumes strewn about–the Gandalf get-up, the angel's halo, the lion headdress, and she thought of the laughter of the children during the story, the smiles from even Renee.

She thought of how she hadn't had the opportunity to teach them the song that her dad had taught her. When she first came to live with him, she frequently had trouble sleeping at night, haunted by the darkness, the quiet, the shadow of memories, and he had been so patient with her. The song and his message had been such a comfort. She wasn't even sure that it originated in the church, but she had always loved the message, the determination of the song. She had hoped to share it with the children so it could help them as well.

She thought of the bedtime routine her dad started with her when she was around three years old. He would sing *Buona Sera* to her as he situated each of her stuffed animals beside her. He would change the lyrics to be more fitting for a young girl–from buying "a wedding ring" to some sort of stuffed animal, or perhaps a storybook. He'd gallop her favorite horse up the length of her bed and supply an enthusiastic neigh when he reached her neck, nuzzling her cheek before getting tucked in under her arm. He'd end the song with a kiss and turn on a sound machine, telling her it was the ocean waves in the town they had sung about. He'd run his palm over her cheek and say softly:

"Buonanotte, Esther Evin. Dormi dolce, mia bellissima ragazza. Dormi dolce."

Every night.

First, he would say the phrase in Italian with dramatic enunciation meant to make her giggle. He would then move whimsically around the room, again to make her laugh, turn on a seashell night light given to her by one of the leaders of the worship choir, turn off the main lights, and return to her bedside. He'd make sure the covers were pulled up just right and repeat the phrase in English:

"Good night, Esther Evin. Sleep sweet, my beautiful girl. Sleep sweet."

Essie gazed across the classroom to her guitar, covered in stickers from road trips they took to visit the Wests. She thought she could hear the squeak of a swing on the playground. She hoped it meant the children had gotten through the vent. In the distance, she could still hear the piano music from the sanctuary being piped into the courtyard.

They don't know what's happened, she thought, feeling her lungs reflexively release their last bit of air. They began to twist in her chest, like a wet towel being rung out.

As she closed her eyes, she heard her dad's voice one more time:

"Sleep sweet, my beautiful girl. Sleep sweet."

7

branch

Annette finally removed her blazer, rolled the sleeves of her dress shirt. Despite checking the thermostat and finding it was set in the 60s, her body was perspiring like never before. She checked her reflection in the wet bar mirror and found her golden brown hair had curled and was sticking out at random, frizzy angles. The color also looked brassy in the hotel room lighting. As offensive as she found her hair, it paled in comparison to the fury she felt toward the deep lines that surrounded her eyes and the creases around her lips. For the past few weeks, every time she looked in the mirror, she had noticed another skin discoloration, another wrinkle. Her short haircut sharpened the angles of her face. She had first gotten her long hair chopped to be chic and taken more seriously, but she no longer saw traces of what qualities she had sought in the first place. She just looked older.

The hallway door opened, and Georgina Moreno stepped inside carrying a tray of coffees.

"Are you doing okay?"

Annette smiled weakly. "Coffee will help. Thank you."

"Ready for the next round?"

She wasn't. She couldn't be, but she nodded just the same. "Is this coffee for Mr. Graham?"

"It is. I just got a house blend. I wasn't sure what he preferred."

Annette shrugged. She didn't look back in the mirror before leaving the room and walking three doors down to room 718, the suite where Luther Graham was staying.

*　　*　　*

"You were about to tell us about the research facility where you worked," Georgina prompted.

He nodded as he sipped his plain, black coffee, which he had brewed before their arrival, extended thanks for her thoughtfulness, but ultimately refusing to drink the beverage Georgina brought. He ran his fingers lightly through his damp hair.

"They were using human fetuses, grown in the lab?"

"Babies. Some of the babies at the beginning were born naturally, by the time the research was shut down, most were being born via artificial womb."

She seemed oblivious to the fact she'd been corrected. "And this was 15 years ago?"

He nodded.

"Wow. It seems like they'd be using this technology more? For premature babies? For pregnancy complications?"

Luther blinked slowly. "Perhaps if their intent was for good."

"This was all before my time in Congress, but I mean, Annette, these were budgetary items that *you* advocated, right? Artificial wombs?" There was little distinction between inquisitiveness and interrogation with Georgina.

"I believed it would be used for good," Annette began, "but unfortunately, I learned too late that it was never the true intent of the technology."

Luther motioned for Annette to continue.

"The idea to use artificial wombs started early last century. In 1924, a geneticist had hypothesized that by the end of the 21st century, the majority of births would be mother-less. An artificial womb was safer, less impacted by biological or environmental factors. Miscarriage rates would drop. Babies facing premature birth would be given a much stronger chance of survival earlier in pregnancy."

"Yeah, that makes sense," Georgina said, a little too enthusiastically.

"When the proposal to try artificial wombs came out, that was what was advertised. The country had just settled in a post-Roe era and the lines were divided again. The anti-choice camp was concerned about what would happen to the babies if the parent or parents couldn't pay for the service? What if they changed their minds?"

"Still using the script," Luther said angrily.

"Excuse me?"

"It's pro-life, not anti-choice, Speaker Gibbons. 'Pro-choice' was designed to stop arguments against it." He looked directly at Annette, daring her to argue.

Annette's shoulders stiffened. She cleared her throat multiple times. "The original scientists couldn't have anticipated the social changes that had occurred. There was so much more draw to it, which sparked a lot of fear and controversy. Something for everyone. For one thing, it offered gender equality, equity. Anyone could have a baby. Career-minded women wouldn't have to face the burdens of pregnancy. Etcetera, etcetera."

"So, the original intent was good," Georgina offered.

"'Good' is relative. just because you *can* do something doesn't mean you *should*." Luther took a long sip of coffee.

"When politicians saw that this wouldn't be a winning topic for campaigning, talk about it pretty much vanished. The wealthy accessed these services as an alternative to human surrogacy and utilized artificial wombs discreetly, and of course they were used in the experiments, but the idea of it being a new social norm disappeared–"

"So *before* artificial wombs," Georgina said, her brow furrowed, "you said the babies were born naturally. Where did *they* come from?"

71

"Many were pulled from foster care. They also took advantage of late-term abortions in the states that had passed laws allowing them. There was a mobile group established that drove around the country, including to states that made abortion illegal. They'd offer free services if the mother signed over her baby 'to science.' That was typically an easy sell for the doctors; they'd been convincing women to donate their aborted babies to science for decades and they weren't exactly regulated for what they told the women."

Georgina stared at him, her mouth twisting.

"Did you have a question?"

"No," she said shortly. "It's just, *women* aren't the only ones who get pregnant."

Luther did not move, did not blink, did not speak.

"Sorry, it's just that inclusive language is so second nature, it just sounds--*archaic*--to hear someone use such dated terminology. That's all."

Luther pressed his lips together. "Are we okay here?"

She gave a quick nod, blinking nervously. "What was the purpose of the experiments?"

"My understanding is that they wanted to increase human resistance to disease," Luther said, motioning to Annette.

"Yes, that was the purpose as it was explained to me. We couldn't take another pandemic. Economically. Psychologically. That was the primary reasoning: to make human immune systems impenetrable."

"So, cancer would be gone?"

"That should have been a tip off, honestly," Annette conceded. "A huge part of the country's economy is healthcare. If everyone's healthy, what happens to pharmaceutical companies? Hospitals? How do we financially support all these extra people if no one's dying of heart disease or cancer, if people can live naturally well into their 100s–"

"So that was never the true intent?"

Annette shook her head.

"Not for *everyone* at least."

"Oh," Georgina said shortly.

Annette looked down and closed her eyes briefly. "I wouldn't have advocated for it had I known."

Georgina turned to Luther. "What did they do? At the lab?"

"They tested immune response. They loaded babies pre-birth with antibody treatments, they attempted to modify cellular structure while organs were still developing to have a more pro-active immune response."

"So, they wanted people to be born with resistance to diseases– that sounds revolutionary."

"From that perspective, it was an easy sell," Annette remarked.

"Was there some sort of adoption program? For after the babies were born?"

Luther frowned. "The real experiment didn't start *until* they were born."

"What do you mean?"

"They tried to enhance the immune response during development. Once the babies were born, they started testing their response to stimuli."

"Stimuli?"

"Diseases, chemicals, pathogens–"

"To see if they were immune?"

"Depending on what was being tested on them, most babies didn't survive very long. They also had complications before and just after they were born, from the 'modifications' that were made to their cells."

Georgina tensed, resituating herself in her chair. "They exposed them to those things?"

"They injected babies with cancer cells, they triggered cardiac arrest, they injected them with active Ebola, smallpox, they poisoned them—wanting to see how their bodies responded."

Georgina swallowed hard. "That sounds—" She hesitated. "You must have been OK with it though--at the beginning, if you worked on the testing?"

Annette recognized her colleague's uncomfortable redirection of the topic.

"I started off being able to distance myself from what I was doing. I was working with the first trimester babies. They were 'specimens.' That's what they told me and that's what I convinced myself. All I was doing was injecting them with 'immune boosters.' I was giving them 'a healthier start.' I didn't know what happened to them after they aged up."

Annette closed her eyes, nodding.

"What changed?"

"I was reassigned to the third trimester lab. From there I discovered the ward they had for children involved in the experiments."

Georgina's eyes widened. "What was that—I mean, I can only imagine what that was like."

"It's difficult for me to describe."

Georgina exhaled, appearing relieved.

"I can show you though."

"Wh—what do you mean?"

"Experiments were recorded 24 hours a day."

"Oh."

"You cannot unsee what I'm planning to show you though."

Georgina glanced over to Annette, eyes widened.

"I think we owe it to our constituents to watch it," Annette said coldly.

This statement appeared to have a distressing effect on Georgina.

Luther raised his eyebrow questioningly.

Georgina nodded quickly and he clicked play.

"*Test Subject S01-24. The last remaining subject from the original batch. We have gone through all the objectives stated in the experiment, so we have been given clearance to try other potential bioweapons. Given our test subject's race and ethnicity, we will use a combination of Zyklon B, a cyanide-based gas, ironically developed by this one's ancestors in Nazi Germany.*"

"They only used descendants of Nazis?" Georgina whispered.

Luther shook his head slowly. "It's because she's Caucasian."

"Just because she's--" Her eyes scanned over the image of the young child bolted down to the table with metal clamps. "They're going to--" She clapped her hand over her mouth.

"*Wakey wakey*," the gritty narrator's voice chimed, stepping into the frame. He pulled up the dirty cloth wrap from over her eyes. Her swollen lids twitched in response to the glaring light. He pulled a device from his pocket and held it next to her side. It made a snapping noise as it made contact with her bare skin. Her body convulsed, but her eyes remained closed. Another snap. Her breathing had become erratic from the shock to her system, from the pain. "*I said wakey wakey.*"

The child's eyes opened.

"Oh, wow," Georgina gasped, "she has beautiful eyes."

Luther and Annette both swiveled toward her.

"That's not important," she defended. "They're just--striking."

The child looked as fierce and determined as any full-grown adult, staring him down.

"*Man, she is giving you the death stare. This could be a meme,*" someone off-camera hooted. *There were several camera sound bursts close to the microphone.* "*When your roommate eats the last of the Cookie Crisps.*"

"*I know speech isn't your strong suit, but it would really make my day if you would say 'Aye, Hitler' before I do this.*" Marcus rolled over a silver canister, turned the knob. He looked back at her, her fierceness giving way to fear. "*You won't humor me?*"

The child did not move, did not blink.

"Fine then." He strapped a mask over her nose and mouth, which immediately fogged with her breaths. "*I'll set the timer for, let's say, 30 minutes?*"

There was a loud clank of a solid metal door, then another as the lock was activated. Left alone in the room, the child started to cry silently, her shimmery eyes creasing and flooding with tears. It seemed she was trying to hold her breath, her mouth twisting around trying to shift the mask from her face.

After a few moments, she stopped suddenly, realizing there was nothing she could do to stop what was about to happen. She closed her eyes, relaxed her body, and took a deep breath.

Georgina winced, tears running from her eyes. "This is *real*? This is part of that video, right? The one they said was a hoax?"

"Does this look like a hoax?"

She looked back at the screen, wincing.

It took less than a minute for the effects to kick in. First, the girl started to cough, then gag. Her body kept wanting to fold itself, but the restraints made this impossible.

"I can't," Georgina said, rising from her chair.

The child released a blood-curdling cry against her efforts to remain silent and her body turned rigid.

Georgina covered her eyes with both hands, her thumbs reaching to press her ears closed.

"She *endured* this," Luther said, angrily. "People you work wth authorized this. You can't close your eyes and make it go away. This *happened to her*."

"Sit down, Georgina," Annette said coolly, though her eyes were brimming with tears, her palm braced across her mouth.

"How can you be so calm about this?" Georgina demanded, cringing as she forced herself to look back at the screen.

The child's body had started to seize, shaking, her eyes now wide open and noticeably darker, her pupils swelled to fill the irises, the sclera red. This image continued for seven minutes, and then her body went limp.

"How—" Georgina's mouth fell open. "How did our society get so evil?"

Luther exhaled, saying nothing.

Annette was still staring at the screen.

"She was in the first group they said? So she was born before the artificial wombs?"

Luther nodded.

"So *you're* telling me that women, *mothers* gave their babies to torture chambers?"

"I doubt any of them knew what they were signing up for," Luther offered, glancing up at Annette, who had stood and was delicately touching her fingers to the screen over the image of the child's hand. "I'd like to believe no parent who donated embryos or newborns to this experiment actually knew what would happen to them."

"Some weren't handed over willingly," Annette said tightly.

"How many?" Georgina asked, lowering herself back to her chair. "How many went through this?"

"Thousands? For this round of the 'experiment'--" he said, motioning to the screen, still showing the same image, though the footage was still running, "they started with 24 newborns. By the time I stumbled upon this room, there was only one child alive."

Annette still stood gazing at the child as the camera zoomed in on her face.

"This little girl lived in a torture chamber. All the other babies had died early on--painful, horrific deaths. She endured that which should have killed her. Over and over again," he said, pointing at the screen. "None of it worked."

"She survived?" Georgina said quickly, her mood suddenly optimistic.

Annette returned to her sea.

Luther lifted the remote and began to fast forward. "If she had a different colored skin, she would have been everything they had hoped to create."

Georgina narrowed her eyes. "What were they creating?"

"An enhanced human. One immune to virtually everything. They would have harvested her eggs and bred an army. They would have added a psychological component, some form of brainwashing–I understand there's such a device they use for Mandatory?"

She opened her mouth to speak, but only a small gasp came out. She clapped her hand to her mouth.

"Can't have super soldiers thinking for themselves."

"They didn't want to use her because she's white?"

Luther gave a firm nod.

"But it's not like they couldn't—" Georgina began, "I mean, there's such a thing as mixed race, if they just—" She shook her head, dismissing her reasoning. "But to reproduce they'd need a male with the same level of immunity. Right?"

"Correct. Unless they were aiming to create clones. In their arrogance, they thought they'd be able to replicate the results–or rather, the scientist in charge thought they would. As I understand it, he had an 'accident' shortly after making that determination."

"They haven't been able to come anywhere near success again. That I can tell you," Annette said, stepping back, her brow lifting.

The men in the video returned after forty-three minutes, according to the timer, wearing full biohazard suits. One stepped to the child and pried off the mask. "*Holy shit, look what it did to her skin.*"

Even with the quality and angle of the video, it was apparent that her face was bubbled and raw.

"*If it did that to the outside, the inside can't be doing so great.*"

"*She's still alive,*" the other observed. "*Body temperature is low and pulse is faint, but she's alive.*"

"*Okay, little sister here is really starting to freak me out. She should definitely be dead right now.*"

Luther scanned the video forward at maximum speed, showing that she remained clamped to the table for the entirety of the recovery. "In the next round, they gave her the drugs used for lethal injections." "*Wait, she survived the gas then?*"

"Yes," Luther said patiently. "This was two days later." He allowed the video to play as Marcus gave the injection, chuckling to himself as he stepped away. The door slammed shut and she was once again, left alone as the effects kicked in. Luther fast-forwarded again.

Georgina tilted her head to the side. "The scars are gone. From the gas?"

Luther nodded. "Her entire body had an enhanced response. That included her organs. The skin is the body's *largest* organ."

Georgina's jaw fell open. "That's incredible."

He took an exhausted breath, advanced the video.

Seventeen hours, six minutes later according to the timestamp and they watched a young Luther step into the room.

"Is that *you*?" Georgina asked, squinting.

He nodded. He could remember the exact smell of that chamber when he came into work: the potent musk of burnt flesh, the nondescript pungency of chemicals, the bitter reek of concentrated urine and feces. They watched him place his hand delicately on her dirty face.

Luther stopped the video.

"What happened to her? After this?"

"The lead scientist authorized the ending of the experiment. They had a new batch of babies, the first born from the artificial wombs."

"But what about *her*?"

He shook his head. "They destroyed all evidence."

"What does *that* mean?"

"Everything went into the incinerator," he said quietly.

"But she was still alive—you said she could withstand anything," she said, insistently pointing at the screen.

"No one's immortal."

Annette looked ghostly watching Georgina's horrified reaction. She swallowed hard, squeezing her eyes closed.

"How long after this?"

Luther sat solidly. "The same day."

"You're saying—what we're looking at here," she said, pointing at the screen. "She died this same day?"

"About 30 minutes later."

"*But*—she did what she was supposed to do. This was the whole point of the experiment—*she did what she was supposed to do*!" Georgina was pleading now, tears filling her eyes. "You're saying they killed her because of the color of her skin?"

"Yes," Annette said quietly.

"They get—like—the *irony* here, right?"

"Apparently not," Luther replied.

"Did you *see it* happen?" Georgina's face twisted, and her eyes narrowed on Luther. She was thinking about what he would have in her place: *Why didn't you help her?*

Marcus had taken his time, as though torturing a two-year-old before burning her alive was some kind of sadistic foreplay. Luther didn't have any defensible reason to keep the child from him. In his heart, he couldn't bear the thought of handing her over to him, but when Marcus returned to claim her, a heavy voice in the back of his mind softly instructed: *Let him take her.*

With no intention to do so, Luther had stepped aside, opening the path to the bathroom.

The image of Marcus slinging the toddler over his shoulder like a sack of rice was one that had haunted him every day since. Luther had promised to protect her, to save her, and he had put up no defense. Meanwhile, the child *had* put up a fight. She had twisted and writhed, screamed at Marcus, as he carried her away.

Luther didn't have to witness what came next to know it was horrific. He had made his way to his locker and retrieved his coat, resolving to never return to the lab. He would have to try for the rest of his days to forget what he had witnessed.

Then the voice returned. *Go to her.*

Luther had been confused but stood and rushed to the door. He found his way to the furnace room without ever being shown the way. The door flew open just before he arrived and Marcus rushed out, unable to catch his breath. He burst through the stairwell door without noticing Luther was there.

Luther made his way inside, the room particularly sweltering since the furnace hatch had been left open. The room was empty aside from a banker's box far too small to fit even a petite child.

Open it.

Luther feared what he might find inside the box, but his heart inflated upon seeing her vivid eyes looking up at him. Marcus had been unapologetic in his delight of seeing this girl burned alive just minutes earlier, as she represented all he hated. Luther couldn't imagine what had sent Marcus running from the room. The only remaining step was to toss the box into the flames.

Luther froze for just a moment before tugging her gently from the box.

"They broke her legs to fit her in the box to toss in the furnace—at the knees so she'd fit," he said, his eyes downcast.

Georgina was captivated, while this detail had sharpened the contours of Annette's face. "Did you—were you the one to—" Georgina asked.

He shook his head. "I didn't see it happen."

Georgina's face fell.

"Did she have a name?" Annette asked, her voice weak.

"They didn't name the babies–probably because it would humanize them too much. It was easier to think of them as 'specimens.' Each just had an ID number."

Annette released a stifled breath, turning her attention back to the toddler on the screen.

"I called her Evin."

*   *   *

"Do you think things can ever be set right?" Annette asked, staring out the window at the cityscape below, the historical buildings, the Congress building visible toward the East. Although it was early afternoon, the sun had barely broken through the cloud cover; a haze always seemed to settle over the city.

Luther was sorting through the remnants of miniature liquor bottles from the night before. No matter how many times he watched the footage, he still struggled to recover emotionally from it and always tried to use alcohol to numb his thoughts. Annette had, as usual, declined to partake. "Nothing that's been taken can be returned so I honestly don't know." He dumped the bottles into the trash can. "I hope there's a way forward though."

"I advocated for the artificial wombs. I signed off on the experimentation."

"It never passed Congress until a few years ago. This was all done illegally."

"It was funded through budget packages I helped write. I helped hide the funding in two-thousand-page documents we knew no one would read."

"You must have believed there was good to be done with the research," he offered. "You didn't even know what the research itself entailed."

"*That* I didn't," she said quietly, not turning from the window. "'Greater good' propaganda. That's even how everyone referred to it–as propaganda. You'd think I would have looked into it?"

Luther placed his empty rocks glass in the wet bar sink and rinsed it out quickly. He stepped behind her, running his palms on her bare arms. She was becoming incrementally thinner each time he saw her, the contours of her body sharpening. "How about we get some lunch?"

She shook her head.

"I can go," he offered, "if you'd rather be alone?"

"No," she said, turning into him. "Please stay."

He placed a hand on her cheek, and she nudged gently against it.

"What time is your flight?" she asked, her eyes closed.

Luther checked his watch. "Three-thirty."

"You should go soon," she murmured. "It'll take you at least an hour and a half to get to the airport with how things are."

He wrapped his arms around her, and she eagerly burrowed into him. "Soon," he agreed.

"You're going to San Diego this time?"

He nodded.

"Georgina thought highly of you. And the video seemed to make an impact on her. Do you think it'll make a difference?"

He cleared his throat. "We'll see. She's always been pretty outspoken, operating by her own rules, so we'll see if that's true."

Annette sighed, facing the window again, stepping out of his hold. Her shoulders resumed their impeccable posture. "I just—I can't stop picturing her—Evin?"

Luther stepped toward his already packed overnight bag, where an unfamiliar wind chime noise emerged. He pulled out the phone to find a single text message notification. As he read the concise message, he felt his head begin to swirl.

"*Luther*?" Annette said, clearly not for the first time.

He slowly resumed an upright position, still staring at the screen. "Sorry, what did you say?"

"What made you choose the name Evin? Does it mean something?"

"God is merciful," he said reflexively, pulling in his breath.

Annette nodded and repeated speaking the name slowly once more.

"I think I probably *should* get to the airport," he said, then decided he sounded too frenzied. "I wouldn't want to be late for my full body cavity search."

She didn't seem to hear what he'd said, her eyes unfocused staring toward the unkempt bed.

He stepped toward her. "I'll call tomorrow."

"*Oh*," she said, startling to awareness. "Safe flight."

It took all of his restraint to wait until the stairwell to dial the number. Due to poor reception, he idled the phone and took the stairs two at a time down to the lobby. He crossed the glistening marble floors, nudged the revolving door more persistently, and spilled out into a steady flow of pedestrians. He weaved through the stationary traffic, tugging up the collar on his coat, and entered the diner on the opposite side of the street. It was densely occupied, every booth, every counter seat taken.

"Luther?" the cook and owner, a middle-aged man with a protruding belly underneath his heavily stained white apron, said as Luther stepped into the kitchen.

Luther held up the phone, his eyes a bit frantic. "I need to make a call, Rick."

"Upstairs." The cook motioned to a younger man to tend to the grill. "This way." He led him just beyond the meat freezer to a narrow stairwell lined with dingy wood paneling. The steps creaked and seemed to bend a bit with each step. At the top was an apartment with high loft ceilings and comfortable-looking leather furniture. "It's safe here. Take your time, Luth."

As the door clicked shut behind him, Luther extracted the phone from his pocket. He stared briefly at the text message again and found it difficult to take a solid breath. With shaky fingers, he dialed the number for Matteo Natale.

8

home

The train station was two miles from the road that led to his family's farm. Josh wasn't sure what he might find when he got there. He prayed silently as he walked that his parents were safe.

As the walk persisted, he found himself thinking about his brother, wondering if he'd been given the same impromptu "respite." He had laid eyes on Gabe only once since the train platform. They had been loaded into different cars since Gabe was a year ahead of him, so their last interaction had been uncomfortable eye contact after Gabe had spontaneously kissed Esther. To Josh, it felt staged for his benefit and/or the benefit of any Service person onlookers.

Essie had looked stunned. Only 15 at the time, Josh felt confident it was her first real kiss.

She had written lengthy letters to him since, mainly detailing their ongoing plan for a goat farm business venture. Since they were kids, they'd been pulling together ideas. Their original plan to raise racehorses was nixed once horse racing was outlawed. They came up with goats once they determined they needed a product to sell and there were too many regulations with cows. Also, Essie wanted no part in the business of slaughtering animals. She had made it clear the goats were to be used for milk, or to be kept as pets. Despite the impracticality of keeping so many goats that would heed no financial benefit to the business, Josh had agreed to her terms.

It was a very real plan; they'd worked tirelessly to find every loophole in regulatory texts and plot out the daily logistics of having such an operation. It was also a source of amusement for them with countless inside jokes. They came up with elaborate back stories for the goats they would acquire, giving them silly names like Goatesque the Destroyer and Vincent Van Goat.

After the train platform, he wasn't sure if there was something he'd missed between her and Gabe. They'd always been friends, but the dynamics seemed to tread more in the brother/sister realm—or at least that was his view of it. *He'd* had the stronger connection with her; she'd always referred to Josh as her best friend and vice versa.

The kiss had seemed to come out of nowhere, though looking back, Gabe *had* been observing Essie with a lot more focused, intense interest during leave after his first year of Mandatory.

Although it was illogical and probably immature, Josh had felt betrayed by Essie, more so than Gabe, for what had happened at the train station, despite her playing no obvious role in it. Gabe had said goodbye first, or rather, he had acted out a mini stage performance right there on the train platform before taking immediate leave.

The incident had then resulted in an uncharacteristically awkward parting for him and Essie. Whenever she left the farm, there was always some antic on one or both of their parts that left them laughing through their goodbye, but at the train, he could hardly meet her gaze.

He hated himself for what he felt—it was like before she had been this unspoiled, Eden-esque paradise and now his brother had constructed a strip mall in the middle of it, claiming her for himself.

He had boarded the train and taken his seat, nagged by the thought that there was something left unfinished, that their goodbye felt incomplete. Though first-year recruits to Mandatory never saw war, some never came home. He hated the thought that their last interaction would be what she would remember of him. He had just stood to remedy this when the train made its initial lurch forward and he was forced to take his seat.

He leaned his head against the cold window, straining to get a glimpse of her or his parents, but the angle was too distorted as the train pulled away from the station.

He wasn't used to leaving her. It was always the other way around. She'd spent entire summers at the farm from the time she was four, along with week-long breaks throughout the year when her dad could steal away from the church while a visiting pastor was in town. As she got a little older, she'd persuade her dad to let her stay out at the farm for weeks at a time without him.

There was always a delayed sadness when she left. The ache in his chest would start long after she climbed into her dad's truck, long after he'd felt the emptiness of the house, the ghost of her presence.

Gabe would never linger outside, moving on to something else the moment after they left, if he hadn't made himself scarce already.

The last time he watched Teo's truck drive away, he had nodded toward his parents, who had just started to busy themselves with the many tasks left to perform that day, and he had started across the field toward the stables. From the pathway, he had an ideal vantage point and could see the entire stretch of dirt road they'd have to take on their way to the highway. He focused his eyes on the right side of the back window, on the passenger side, trying to pick out the shadow of her form. He lowered his eyes to traverse the embankment, then jogged up the hill on the other side, past the stables. His eyes floated back to the truck, first locked into the license plate then moved up to the empty passenger bench. It was then he noticed her arm floating along on the breeze hanging out the back window on Teo's side. She had her chin resting on her opposite arm, staring back toward the farm watching him. It was quite a distance, but just before the truck disappeared on the other side of the white barn, he thought he saw her smile.

He hoped she was doing well. Her last letter talked about how she had taken extra work with the Children's Ministry. It was something she loved, working with kids. Her skill for dramatics and performance helped her bond with them. She mentioned that she was starting to work on plans for the Christmas show. The music team had been trying to recruit her to sing lead, but the idea of singing unaccompanied still unnerved her a bit.

Josh hadn't been given access to write back since her letter arrived nearly three months earlier but he intended to write to her as soon as he settled in at home. He had planned to start the letter during his journey home but found his eyes persistently wanting to close every time his body sat idly for more than a few minutes.

He wanted to encourage her to accept the Christmas show offer. He wanted to tell her that he had never in his life heard such a beautiful, soulful voice, that he believed someone hearing her sing would ignite their faith in the Almighty; it had for him.

Of course, he planned to tone down his rhetoric substantially, be convincing enough about her talent, but stop shy of being blatantly obvious about the fact that he was in love with her and had been for years, that in an unforced moment, he had made a remark to his dad about his intent to marry her someday.

He wondered how different she looked from the last time he saw her, now that she was two years older, if she'd continued to grow her golden-brown hair or if she'd cut it off like she teased her dad she would: "Bright blue mohawk on one side, shaved on the other."

He wondered if things had changed for the church since he'd last heard from her. He'd heard that people were abandoning church altogether. Many churches had been accused of vague crimes and stripped of their tax-exempt status; some officials had been imprisoned. He had heard in some areas there had been faith wars—churches, synagogues, mosques, temples attacking one another. It all sounded like the propaganda his dad had described from when he was younger, designed to divide. It was commonplace for the government and media to emphasize the need for unity and the end of 'hate speech' while condoning and even encouraging destruction and violence. In all the times Josh had visited Essie's church, he'd never heard a word that supported the idea that they were at war with other faiths. At home, they ignored the sensationalized reporting and the cunning speeches, but the news was required viewing at

Mandatory and it became very clear very quickly that many not only watched the news but believed it as well. He had observed Mandatory recruits having rage-filled fits after news coverage of 'faith-based violence,' threatening to rip the heads off all the 'supremist Christians,' even passing through the dormitories to try to identify such individuals among them.

It was too much to think of. It should have been a comfort to be home, a pleasant walk in the moonlight, but he found himself tense. He feared for Essie's safety. He wondered why Teo hadn't sent her to live at his parent's farm, away from the threats faced at the church. Then again, he wasn't sure about the state of the farm. Maybe it wasn't safe there either.

More and more farms were being seized by the government under the privileges established by emergency proclamations declared under the name of "shortages" that began years ago. The public was told that the situation was temporary. There had been messages of unity and "we're in this together" and something about "sacrifices for the greater good."

Talk of shortages had ceased, the public had seemed to have lost interest in the matter, and only those with direct connections with the farms knew or cared that the lands remained under the government's control. His family had been fortunate to retain rights over the farm, but there were strict regulations on their practice, and the taxes were crippling.

His arrival home was unannounced. The day before, there had been some sort of explosion at the compound and leaders had sent recruits home for a "one-week respite." While the term "respite" didn't seem to be a part of leadership's vernacular, he decided against questioning it. He was one of the first to depart, not wanting to risk a retraction of the reprieve. He had spent half a day securing transportation home. With the nonsensical train schedules and transfers, the journey had taken a full day and he had spent the previous night in a station that served as housing for rows of homeless.

He had been reminded of the television show he had watched a few times with his parents that featured a team competition journeying around the world. Teams had traveled through India and his parents had gasped at the conditions, how the ground was a sea of men, women, children, and animals, making it difficult to move around. The conditions had been slightly better where he spent the night, but not by much. He had tucked himself out of the way against a concrete column and a bank of vending machines, which provided his dinner, and pulled his hood up. He was used to sharing sleeping accommodations, but he felt more at ease at the station blending into the crowd of people.

Every three or four steps triggered a throbbing in his right calf muscle. The Service doctor dismissed it as nothing of significance, granting him no reprieve from exercises, but it felt as though the muscle had been ripped in half. He exhaled deeply, determined to walk smoothly as he entered his parents' house. The gravel road made it impossible to walk in silence, the dirt crunching into the hard soles of his boots. Work boots weren't made the same anymore, to protect the foot or to absorb impact. These were made from something deemed carbon neutral and only cosmetically looked appropriate for the functions they were expected to perform.

The grass field looked drier than when he last saw it, but the exterior fences were intact and besides being far quieter than he remembered, the land looked as it should. With the sharp contrast to where he was accustomed, the air felt too still, like at any moment something unexpected would slice through it and fill the void with noise and chaos.

The city was so different from home. The only pleasant smell he had encountered in the city was a Jewish bakery when he first arrived. He purposely planned his routes and walked a little faster to compensate, just to breathe in the smell of fresh bagels, crusty gourmet bread loaves, pastries, and sweets. It was incredible the storefront was still there; it was the only place still open on the block.

All the farm smells came drifting toward his nostrils, overwhelming him with their pungency. They weren't unpleasant to him, quite the opposite since they reminded him of home, but he had forgotten he knew such aromas. The crispness of a fall night had a twinge of pine in the air. Pine made him think of Christmas during his early childhood, his mom's homemade banana bread, thick wool socks, and chilly wooden floors. Their door was constantly opening, bringing in a gust of chilly air, as neighbors, family, and friends made their rounds to wish greetings and love to one another. Some would wear pajamas, others were dressed in their finest clothes, and some of the children would wear newly unwrapped costumes they received as gifts, but there was a comfort, a joy in the separate, but together celebration of the birth of Jesus and the hope the promise of his life meant to people.

A pang of sadness filled him as he wondered if he would get to experience anything resembling that feeling again, if anyone would.

Pine, spruce, and fir were protected, their lumber regulated and taxed. Christmas trees were not permitted to be sold in their full form. Branches had to be removed, the trunk cut, so that the government was certain it was only being used as firewood for heating purposes. Even then, fires were restricted to a few limited days each month with harsh penalties for rule breakers.

Bananas were impossible to purchase due to supply chain issues so there wouldn't be the aroma of banana bread wafting in the air. His mother had said at one time, you could get a bundle for a couple of dollars at any grocery store, but now they were only at specialty marts in the city, along with most fresh fruit and vegetables. Only essential food items with long shelf lives were sent to the less densely populated areas for distribution.

Josh clenched his jaw as he climbed the front steps, his calf screaming. The porch floorboard creaked loudly in the normal spot, but he found the door bolted closed where he would have expected it unlocked before nine o'clock. The side window had a new solid curtain installed and lowered, but through a fold in the material, he could see into the living room, softly glowing with the light from the kitchen. Someone was asleep on the couch, one knee bent upright, neck contorted in an uncomfortable hunch. The hair color was nothing like his dad's, Gabe would be standard issue bald, depending on what program he was in--this man had dark brown waves.

Teo.

He strained to see in the reaches of the kitchen. It didn't appear anyone else was in the downstairs area. Immediately his eyes turned to the stables, the loft where Esther frequently liked to spend time, but the windows were dark.

It was just as he was about to knock on the door that his mother slipped out onto the porch. She closed the door gently behind herself and pulled him to her.

"Oh, my boy," she said, a deep relief in her voice. She kissed him repeatedly on the cheeks, her green eyes brimmed with tears. "You're home." She embraced him again, clinging tightly as though fearful he might disappear.

"Is that Teo?" he asked once she'd released him and stepped back to get a better look at him, wincing when she saw his shrinking midsection, the sharp angle of his jaw.

She nodded nervously and cleared her throat, taking a moment to collect her thoughts. "Josh, something's happened." She ran her hand over his arm, motioning toward the porch railing. Once they were distanced a bit from the front door, she spoke in a low voice. "Calvary Church was attacked." She briefly closed her eyes, shaking her head, tears streaming down her cheeks. "The Children's Ministry—" Her voice broke.

His body tensed. "*Mom*?"

"*Esther*—" she began, her lip quivering. She stopped to gaze out at the night, her hand braced over her face.

His heart dropped to the pit of his stomach. All he could think was: *No. Please, God, no.* This had to be a dream. Had to be. The world could not possibly have continued to exist if Essie was no longer in it.

"She must have had God watching over her. It's the only way I can explain it."

He released a breath but found he needed to steady himself on the railing.

"Oh, *Josh*," his mother cried, placing a chilly palm on each of his cheeks. "I shouldn't have said it that way. She's safe. Esther is safe."

He nodded repeatedly, his eyes closed, as he tried to regain his composure, his throat constricted, his pulse racing.

She spoke more urgently now. "I don't know how. It was just her, Josh. She saved all those children."

"What do you mean? What happened?"

"They locked them in–she was doing the Sunday Children's Ministry lesson. They threw in some sort of bioweapon and then barricaded them in the classroom." She mopped her eyes with the sleeve of her shirt.

"A *bioweapon*?"

She nodded distantly. "It was some sort of gas. Your dad was explaining it–a neurotoxin he said? Something more advanced than what they used in the Holocaust--" She clapped her hand to her face, tears streaming from her eyes.

He tried to process this information but gazing toward the big oak with the wooden swing now dangling by only one side of the rope, he felt only vague relief. Essie liked to spend time sitting on that swing, at least she had when she was younger, leaning far enough back so that the tips of her hair brushed the ground.

He made a mental note to repair the swing.

"She saved all of them, Josh. All the children," she said, swallowing hard. "She shouldn't be alive," she added, matter-of-factly. "Dad said the gas is supposed to kill people in seconds, if that. There's no possible way she should be alive."

Josh let the words absorb into the cortexes of his brain, hoping it would allow him to breathe normally again. *She's alive*, he said silently over and over again.

"So many things happen that make me lose faith, but this reminds me that God has a hand in things." She smiled weakly, taking in the details of his face, which he knew looked worn and older than his eighteen years. He'd been unable to shave during his journey home so his face was covered in stubble. "The heart wrenching part of parenthood is not being able to protect your children from the evil in this world."

"Well, there's a lot of it."

She studied his face for a moment with maternal nostalgia, then furrowed her eyebrows. "There's so much good in it, Josh. I know it doesn't feel like it, but there's *so much* good still in this world."

He took a step forward and hugged her. With his broad stature and thick canvas jacket, his arms seemed to swallow her up.

She sniffled. "I pray every day for a better world for all of you."

"They're staying here? Teo and Essie?"

She nodded, parting from him. "Teo is going back and forth to Wallace."

"After what happened?"

"He says he has a responsibility to everyone at the church. People are lost, Josh. They need their faith now more than ever."

"Didn't the sanctuary get attacked, too?"

"No. They just went after—" She couldn't bring herself to finish the sentence.

The children, Josh said silently, dropping his chin to his chest. He wondered how many people continued to even attend service after what happened. "How often is he making the drive to Wallace?"

"Well, he's been mostly staying there. He's trying to ration gasoline. It's so expensive and difficult to come by these days. We've had him use our store of it that we kept for machinery, but—"

"What about his *daughter*?" he demanded, with more anger and at a higher decibel than he intended.

His mother put an index finger to her lips. "Josh, their relationship–it's changed."

"What do you mean?"

"She hasn't been herself. Since the attack? It's been a few weeks now. She's been distant from him."

"*Why*?"

She shook her head. "People deal with things in unexpected ways sometimes. She's withdrawn. We don't see much of her. She's still the polite, sweet girl that she is, but—she doesn't say much. I've tried—your dad has told me to let her be—"

"Is she upstairs?"

His mom nodded toward the field. Illuminated by moonlight, he saw the elegant shape of a horse cantering across the pasture. It appeared to be the gray Percheron, the large draft horse they used to plow fields and haul heavy loads, with a small figure holding onto his white mane, her golden-brown hair bouncing against her back.

He took one step toward the field before hesitating. "Is dad awake? I should see him."

"He's sleeping," she said, waving off his apprehension. "Go to her."

*   *   *

Bree stopped abruptly, snorting distrustfully in Josh's direction as he approached. It shouldn't have surprised him; the horse had always favored Essie above anyone else.

Bree was born during a summer Essie spent at the farm. He had become ill as a foal and his mother had begun to reject him, forcing him away when he tried to nurse. The vet had indicated they should consider euthanizing him if they couldn't get him stabilized and fed. After the foal refused to eat from a bottle for four days, Josh's dad brought in the vet before sunrise. He intended to have him put down and hauled away before anyone was awake. When they entered the stables, they found Essie asleep in Bree's stall, the foal nuzzled up against her, two large empty bottles of formula resting in Essie's lap. From that day forward, Bree was good-natured with everyone, but was most bonded with Essie despite long periods of separation.

Now there was a fierceness in his eyes, a rigidity in his stance.

"*Woah*," Josh beckoned. "It's just me, boy."

The horse sniffed the air and whinnied, running his hoof along the ground.

95

Essie's face was shadowed; he could only make out the outline of her nose and chin. "*Josh?*"

There was a delay in her reaction. From what he could tell, she was still looking at him. He began to wonder how different he looked after two years at Mandatory, if he was that unrecognizable to her. According to the guidelines, his hair was too grown out; he would require a sheer before going back. The government didn't seem to value muscle preservation in the Mandatories, reserving proteins & complex carbs for the officer ranks so he'd lost most of the muscle tone he had from farm work. He hadn't bothered to shave for the three days it had taken him to get home, which he hoped provided him a more mature look, as opposed to just looking unkempt and scruffy.

Another possibility came to mind: That like with his parents, like with her dad, Essie would maintain distance from him, haunted by what had taken place. He wondered what it would be like to face a shell of the girl he knew. Worse than anything at Mandatory, that was for sure.

She extended her hand low onto the horse's dappled neck and said with gentle firmness: "Bow." Bree's ears twitched slightly, and the large horse folded one leg and straightened the other, easing his chest close to the ground, his back with a cat-like arch. Essie slipped off the nearly 19-hand horse with ease, patting his side.

As the horse resumed an upright position, Josh managed a smile. "As many times as I see that, it's still--"

It was then he noticed how quickly Essie was closing the distance between them, her long, wild hair bouncing against her back, her face lowered, her steps determined. He had barely opened his arms when she crashed into his chest, locking herself around him. He only realized she was crying when he felt the waves of sobs tremor through her back, her icy fingertips trembling against his neck.

He closed his arms around her, the embrace of another person a surreal and overwhelming sensory experience. All the scents he associated with her seemed heightened—morning dew and hay and wildflowers all filled his nasal cavities.

After a few minutes, she started to regulate her breathing and stepped backward. Even in the darkness and with a firm stance of resolve, he could still see the persistent quiver of her lower lip.

"Should we tuck Bree in for the night?" He suggested quietly.

She turned toward the horse, lips pulling up at the corners. "It's a little late for you, huh boy?" she asked rhetorically, her voice constricted.

Sure enough, Bree was more than happy to trek back toward the stable, a bounce in his stride. Essie was quiet, stepping in a tense rhythm with the horse.

"Where did you get his name again?"

She sniffled, glancing at the horse and managing to push through a slight smile. "*The Horse And His Boy*. By C.S. Lewis. It's part of the Narnia series."

"Ah, that's right," Josh said softly. As they walked, he stared at his boots over the grassy hill of his childhood, a very different background than the broken asphalt he was used to. "I never did read those. I remember the movies though."

"The books are a lot shorter than you might expect."

"Maybe we still have the movies? If you don't feel like sleeping, we could watch them?"

"I checked. I think Gabe had gotten them from the library." Her face was neutral, voice flat.

"Has he been back?"

She shook her head quickly.

"Has he written to you?" After the words escaped his lips, he considered that there could have been a gentler way of asking.

She pressed her lips together. "I'm not getting my mail from home anymore, but it's been—" her face tensed. "I haven't heard from him in nearly a year."

"They could be intercepting mail," he heard himself say, regretting those words as well.

They moved in silence as they reached the stable, freshened Bree's trough for an evening snack. He appeared to be the only remaining horse residing in the barn.

Josh glanced around the bobbing head of Bree as he fed. He felt compelled to reassure her further about Gabe, that he was probably desperate to get back as soon as possible, but by the sound of it, he wasn't sure it was true, and even if it was, he didn't feel like extending any goodwill toward Gabe.

The conversation with his mom came to the forefront of his mind as he tidied the stall to have something to do. It seemed surreal—that Essie could have been so near death, surviving against all odds, and yet be standing before him. In the brighter ambient light of the stables, he could more clearly see her face. She looked older, there was no denying it; her features all seemed a bit narrower. He took in the disheveled messiness of her hair, something that she'd never been able to tame, the sprinkling of freckles across the bridge of her nose, her full lips, the shadow of dimples in her cheeks. He was in awe that this was Essie standing just feet before him.

He was home.

"I'm happy you're safe, Essie." He shook his head at his idiocy. "I mean, of course that goes without saying and 'happy' doesn't seem like the right word."

She met his gaze, the manual work easing her tension a bit. Her lips seemed to have a developed a tendency to fall at the corners, but they pulled upward upon meeting his eye. "You, too."

He smiled fondly at her, savoring her presence. Despite the solemn overtone, he couldn't help but feel energized being close to her again. He wanted to scoop her up and hug her. "Were *you* going to turn in?"

She shook her head. "I'm not really sleeping," she said slowly, motioning toward the loft. "Your parents set me up in Gabe's room, but I've been staying out here."

For a brief moment, he felt anger that his parents would have her stay in Gabe's room—*had they presumed they were a couple? They were suddenly okay with premarital cohabitation?*

Two things struck him simultaneously. One: They knew Gabe wasn't coming home anytime soon. Two: She always stayed in Gabe's room. There just weren't that many bedrooms in the house. Gabe typically slept on the bottom bunk in Josh's room when she came to visit, while Teo stayed downstairs on the office Murphy bed.

He gave her a sympathetic smile. "You've always liked it in the loft."

Essie made purposeful eye contact as she stepped around him to hang up Bree's bridle. There was a palpable energy to the air, an uncertainty to her behavior toward him. He wasn't sure if it was the time apart, the simple fact that they were older that had altered things, but there was certainly a building tension in the air between them. "Do you want to come up?"

He nodded, patting Bree's side.

She moved toward the ladder but paused just as she started to climb. "You're probably exhausted. You don't have to."

"Honestly?" he said, placing his hand above where hers rested on the ladder rung. "I'd really like to."

She pressed her lips together and continued her ascent.

It was on the second step, as he pushed his weight through his right leg that his calf muscle throbbed, sending a flash of pain through his leg. He paused for just a moment, then concluded silently that nothing was keeping him from climbing into that loft, even if the descent would likely be more challenging.

The loft typically housed extra bales of hay and other supplies. As he climbed inside behind her, he found there wasn't much of either, probably less than a quarter of the average amount they typically kept on hand. She had managed to construct a cozy lounge area out of hay bales, some utility blankets, and a pillow and comforter he assumed were from

Gabe's room. Next to the makeshift bed were a dimmed lantern and an open backpack filled with books.

"Soon it's going to be getting pretty cold to be staying out here at night," he observed, turning on his heel to find where she had gone. To his surprise, she was immediately behind him, her eyes downcast, staring at his chest. She lifted his stainless-steel dog tags, running her thumb along the imprint of the barcode that, when scanned, would reveal all his identifying information. He reflexively placed his hand on her cheek and spoke her name, intending to say something about what she had been through, show support, ask what happened, how she survived.

It happened slowly and suddenly at the same time. First, she raised her eyes to meet his gaze, her irises reflecting the flicker of the lantern. Second, her eyes narrowed thoughtfully, deciding something internally perhaps? The next thing he knew, she had her arms braced around his neck, he had his arms wrapped solidly around her back, and he was kissing her lips with increasing enthusiasm. He wasn't even sure who closed the distance, who kissed who first; he just knew that her mouth tasted like spearmint toothpaste while her hair, her skin smelled like the night air and open fields. In contrast to all the rough materials and textiles he was so accustomed to, her soft beige skin was a welcome contrast. His senses delighted at the soft warmth of her skin as his hands rested on the small of her back.

It was a thick tear droplet rolling from her cheek to his that caused him to stop kissing her. He found their bodies were pressed together, foreheads leaning into one another. As she released a breathy series of sobs, she lowered herself back onto the heels of her feet. Their bodies parted more than he intended, and his reflexes overcompensated, his arm looping around her as though intending to keep her from falling. The force of his forearm pushed her abruptly into him.

She gasped, her eyes closed, beads of tears forcing their way through her lashes. "I'm sorry," she whispered.

"Essie. Look at me."

Her eyes opened reluctantly.

"Don't apologize for kissing me. *Ever.*"

She raised an eyebrow in a deceptively sportive fashion, but her swollen, bloodshot eyes were now more visible in the light of the lantern. "I didn't. I was apologizing for crying."

Josh wiped the tears from her cheeks gently with his thumbs. "You don't need to apologize for that either."

Her voice was slightly raspy as she spoke: "I'm not crying because I'm sad or angry or scared—I'm *all* of those things, but right now?" Her hand, which had been wedged between their bodies in his effort to keep her close, gently rested on his chest. "I'm just really, really happy to see you."

He took in the details of her face. Her shimmery silver eyes looked more defined, the edges deep graphite, and her chin and jawline had matured since he last saw her. It was surreal that he had known her since her face had the rounded edges of toddlerhood.

She perked her brow again. "You kissed *me*, by the way."

"Did I? It was kind of a blur."

There was a small glint in her eye.

"But it's *you*—of course I would—"

She arched backward, narrowing her eyes. "*Of course* you would? You have never taken *any* action, aside from *just now*, to back up that statement."

He felt blood rush to his cheeks. "You know I adore you."

She seemed to be making a superhuman effort not to smile.

He allowed about three seconds to pass before actively filling the silence. "And while I can't blame him, honestly it still bothers me that it wasn't me kissing you on that train platform. It should have been me."

Her eyes studied him, processing his remark, her facial expression revealing little of what she was thinking.

He regretted admitting his jealousy so overtly. He regretted bringing up Gabe again, worrying her concern for him would dampen the moment, dreading her telling him that she was, in fact, waiting for Gabe, that this had all been a mistake. When she didn't speak for an excruciatingly long time, he started to panic. "Oh God, I shouldn't have said that. Essie, please say something."

She cocked her head to the side, allowing a short silence, and then said quietly: "I love you."

He wrinkled his forehead. "*What*?"

"I love you," she repeated, pushing upwards through her toes to kiss him on the cheek. "I always have, but I'm not sure I've ever said it." She looked at him with a slightly sheepish expression.

"Essie."

"Oh, don't look at me like that." A familiar playfulness had returned to her eyes, a thin veil barely concealing the sadness and fear beneath. He felt compelled to say he loved her in return. It felt as though he'd told her dozens of times, the words bursting from his mouth as he wrote her letters. Then again, she may have just meant she loved him as a friend. She may have said it as a consolation. She may not have meant it as some grand declaration, like what it would feel like if he said the same words.

He was about to speak when he felt her foot slowly sliding up to the back of his knee. It was a move she had been successful using during their wrestling matches. A swift dig of her heel into the nerve at the back of his knee and he would fold like a lawn chair.

Josh acted quickly, sweeping his arms around her waist, denying her the proper angle for the move.

"We don't deal well with sentiment or emotional declarations. I'm trying to lighten the mood," she giggled, her voice muffled against his chest.

"Leave it to you to use big words," he managed to say, struggling to keep hold of her as she wiggled around trying to break free.

"Too bad Mandatory makes you lose muscle tone. I sense this is more difficult than it used to be."

He squeezed more firmly and put her in a fully upright position. She established steady footing but didn't move away, the remnants of a smile still attached to her face.

He traced the contours of her cheeks with his fingertips, smiling lightly. "I love you, Essie."

She smiled. "You *know*, I wondered about that. Your letters aren't exactly sonnets."

Josh exhaled, that single sentence erasing his doubt that her 'love' was platonic. He moved in with intention this time and kissed her again, slower and with more intensity than before.

After a few moments, to his surprise, he felt the pull of her legs guiding him toward the hay bed. Once he felt the straw binding against his knees, however, his mind dead-ended. On one shoulder, the small, but unconvinced voice of his conscience told him that Gabe had some claim on Esther and that he should have a discussion with him before pursuing things. She was probably experiencing some sort of post-traumatic stress; her behavior could be some sort of emotional manifestation. Moving forward with anything leaned a bit too close to taking advantage of the situation.

On the other shoulder was the longing he'd felt for her for so many years, now being set free by the emboldened persistence of her arms, her hands, her lips.

It was during this entanglement of limbs that he discovered an enormous and unexpected supply of restraint. "Essie?" he breathed.

Her fingers were tickling his cheek. "Hm?"

"We have to stop."

She let out a small whimper, then wrapped her long limbs around him, from her angled position on the hay bed. "Just keep kissing me," she whispered, continuing to kiss his lips, his chin, his cheeks, her lips creeping into a smile, tugging him closer.

He felt his senses numbed, his mind blurred, as he was lured back into the moment.

When things reached a noticeably more impassioned point, he pulled away in a much more resolved manner. "Essie, we can't."

She reached for him, but he maintained the distance. She pulled herself to an upright position, her hair speckled with bits of hay. Ordinarily it would be a comical sight, especially with how she seemed unaffected or unaware by it, but somehow now it just underscored his affection for her, and even his desire for her.

He closed his eyes, took a steadying breath.

"Josh?" she whispered in a pleading tone, suddenly just beside his ear. Her warm breath tickled his neck. She placed her palm on his cheek.

He shook his head. "We can't. This isn't the right time."

She sighed heavily, leaning their foreheads together.

Josh kissed her cheek, still focusing his breaths. He gently directed her chin toward him so he could look her in the eyes, though he felt far less certain in his decision the moment he did.

She saw his confidence falter and seized the opportunity, tugging him in for a kiss by the collar of his shirt, running her hands along the back of his neck. Her lips were so soft, her touch addictive. He felt intoxicated by her presence, the smell of the crisp outdoors on her skin. Before he knew it, his hands were running over the length of her body.

Without warning, he broke free and jolted away, standing. The cold loft air immediately surrounded him. He'd been so forceful in this movement, he'd nearly stepped into the ladder opening.

Essie looked stunned—and horrified. Her lower lip quivered. "I'm sorry, Josh. I--" She shook her head, looking back at the hay bed, the lantern, taking in the setting of the loft, and Josh before her. "This isn't--this isn't me. I can't believe I--"

He rushed to her side, sat down beside her, immediately wrapped his arms around her.

"I'm sorry," she said, voice muffled into his chest.

"You don't need to apologize for anything."

"Yes, I do," she said in a higher octave. "What am I *doing*?"

"It's not that I don't want to," he whispered. He explained, in rushed, winded words, why he wouldn't go further; that he knew they were both going through a lot, her especially, that she had always been virtuous about waiting until marriage—as had he—something that had perked her interest--and even though he wanted to, it just wasn't the time to take that step.

She gazed up at him in silence, a longing and something resembling confusion in her eyes. "I just—" She winced, struggling to let her thoughts surface, of tampering with his perceptions of her. What finally emerged was: "I don't really understand God's plan for me."

He frowned, motioning toward the reclined hay stack. "Let's sit back together."

"I won't attack you," she murmured, attempting humor, though her chin sank to her chest. "Josh, I'm sorry," she added in a pleading tone.

"*Hey*," he said, then kissed her tenderly on the lips, allowing her to be the one to conclude it.

When she did, she shifted to allow room for him to lie down, then immediately nuzzled into his arms once he had. She tightened her arms around him. "You're here."

He nodded. "I probably smell. I'm sorry."

"I don't care," she said firmly, nestling herself into the nook of his arm. "But yes, you do," she added teasingly.

Josh took in a deep inhalation of her hair. "You smell good."

She shook her head. "I've been outside all day--"

"What'd you do today?" he asked breathily.

"I swam in the stream, I read under the tree by the stream in the grass, I rode Bree, I made a really aggressive, out of line, out of character move on my best friend that resulted in embarrassment I won't soon recover from--"

"Mm," he murmured, unfazed. "You also told said best friend that you love him."

"I did that. I meant that. But I'm afraid that will be forever intertwined with what happened after."

"Are you taking it back?"

"No," she said forcefully. "But could you forget what I did after?"

He furrowed his brow. "Can I be honest with you?" Without waiting for a reply, he said: "What am I saying? Of course I can."

She smiled tightly.

"*If* these were different circumstances, a different time in our lives-
-"

She lifted her chin, twisting her expression. "What are you suggesting, Josh West?"

"I don't know, what were you suggesting before, Essie Natale?"

She scrunched her nose. "I retract the question."

"Yeah, I thought you might." He grinned. "What was I saying?"

"You were proposing marriage."

"I was not."

She lifted an eyebrow.

He shook his head and kissed her forehead. "To think I've been agonizing about how to tell you how I feel about you."

"You have? Well, I suppose there was that 'adore' moment."

He laughed. "You've recovered from your embarrassment clearly, if you're teasing me."

"Yeah, I'm in a volatile emotional state. I should really cut myself some slack."

"I agree, but does that mean I shouldn't hold you to what you told me?"

"That I love you?"

"Yeah."

"No, I've been in love with you for years. The unrelated emotional devastation is recent."

As much as he savored the playful banter, glimpsing the Essie he'd always known, her honest assessment snapped him back to present, reminded him of the conversation he'd had twenty minutes(?) earlier with his mom.

"You saved a dozen children's lives--" He began solidly, taking pause hearing the words out loud.

"It was seven--"

"*Essie.* Seven children are alive because of you."

She furrowed her brow. "Who told you?"

"My mom."

"She keeps trying to feed me."

"Cake?"

"No, sugar is hard to come by these days. She says she won't bake with the fake stuff so it's been mainly casseroles. Lots of corn and potatoes."

His stomach yearned at the thought of starchy potatoes, creamed corn, or literally anything his mother managed to plate up for a meal. It was a welcome distraction that allowed him to reset his brain a bit. "You surviving the attack reaffirmed her faith in God."

"She said that?"

"Mmhmm."

She paused as she listened to the thumping of his heart echoing in his chest.

"Do you want to talk about it?"

"No," she said quickly, but softly. "Not right now."

He nodded, tightening his arms around her.

"Do you want to tell me about Mandatory?"

He took a breath. "Not right now," he echoed.

A chilly breeze drifted through the stables.

Josh reached for the comforter and tugged it over the top of them. As he settled back in, after making sure she was completely covered, he found her watching him intently. "What's on your mind?" he whispered.

"Josh, I didn't know you were—" her voice trailed off. "Have you always believed in waiting?"

He furrowed his brow. "Would that surprise you?"

"No," she said quickly. "Well, *yeah*, a little. I just thought—you've always been so popular in town."

He sighed. "Money's always been tight. I found I could negotiate a better price if I talked up the ladies at the market."

"By 'talk up,' you mean flirt with?"

He shrugged. "It didn't go beyond that though."

"For the record? Those were not 'ladies,' Joshua."

"I agree. My young ears were not prepared for such lascivious dialogue."

She chuckled, pursing her lips. "That's gross. Impressive word choice. But gross."

"Did you think I was *involved* with them?"

She stretched her arm across his chest hesitantly, like she suddenly wasn't certain she was allowed. "Of course not."

"Liar." He took her wandering hand in his, resting them both on his chest.

"I don't know what I thought. I was pretty naïve."

He frowned.

"You didn't answer my question."

"What question was that?"

"Have you always believed in waiting?"

"No. I mean, I hadn't made a conscious decision when I was younger—until I did."

She wrinkled her forehead. "And when did you make the decision?"

"It wasn't about *waiting* specifically. It was just a decision about how I was going to live my life."

"When was that?"

"I was thirteen."

She nodded slowly.

"As I got older, the other aspects came into mind."

"You mean you were tempted by the lascivious ladies?"

He chuckled. "Not exactly."

"No? I saw some of their behavior toward you."

Josh shrugged. "I realized that nothing I could experience would be worth it."

"Worth what?"

He felt his cheeks tense, his throat constrict. He couldn't say it out loud. He couldn't possibly verbalize his reasoning.

Responding to the silence, Essie propped herself on his chest gently. Her eyes blinked slowly, patiently.

"I knew it wouldn't be worth losing the chance of ever *possibly* being good enough for you."

Her lips widened, her silver eyes brightened, and her eyebrows pulled up into a comically deep slant.

"Say something. You're being too quiet," he prodded when the silence had stretched. "Your eyebrows are saying a lot, of course, but I don't know how to read them."

She smiled tightly and shook her head.

"I didn't think it was possible to render Esther Natale speechless."

She narrowed her eyes but was struggling to suppress her lips from continuously turning upwards.

"God, I missed this face," he said softly, placing his hand on her cheek.

She contorted her facial features in a series of grotesque expressions.

Josh laughed lightly. "All of those, too."

She sighed conclusively, settling back up into the nook of his arm. "I've been thinking."

"About?"

"It might be practical for us to have some sheep at our goat farm. We could use the wool for sweaters and jackets and bedding." Her voice was slightly strained.

Josh exhaled deeply. "I like it. Obviously, we would have to learn how to shear sheep—"

She nodded.

"I'm assuming we have to wash the wool?"

"Probably. Sheep could roll through all sorts of things."

"For bedding, we could just use it as stuffing, but there must be a way to turn wool into—thread I'm assuming?"

"Yes. Must be."

"We'll have to look into it. Probably some special machinery. Second hand would be our best bet while we're getting things started."

"That sounds like a practical suggestion."

Essie was quiet for a few moments, listening to the whistle of the wind through the trees and Bree settling into his stall. He had a ritual much like a dog settling into a bed. He hooved at her bedding from multiple angles then circled twice before lying down with a grunt, the only horse they'd ever owned that laid down to sleep.

"Baa-lthazar," Esther said finally. "He'll be the sheep leader."

Josh smiled and kissed the top of her head, breathing in her hair. "Captain Floof."

She laughed lightly. "Serta."

"Ah. Is that who makes the mattress we're lying on?"

"You should really be sleeping on a real bed, Josh."

He sighed. "A real bed wouldn't have you. House rules."

She smiled into his chest.

They were both silent. Outside the barn walls, the breezed stiffened, signaling an incoming storm, an owl hooted in the distance, and the barn door latch rattled.

When Josh finally spoke, he kept his voice low: "You *know*, I've run it through my head a few times and I'm fairly certain *you* kissed me first."

He anticipated a suppressed laugh, some sort of reaction or denial, but she didn't respond. Her body felt more relaxed, her breathing slower and heavier, a few decibels shy of a snore.

He settled a bit into the hay. "Not important," he whispered.

9

safe and sound

The creaking of the loft ladder woke Essie from a mercifully dreamless sleep. She kept her eyes closed, savoring the closeness, the shared body heat, hating that the morning had come so quickly. She felt Josh release her on one side and gesture to whoever was on the ladder. His heart rate quickened during the interaction; she listened to the tippy-tippy-tap of his heart echoing in his chest, like the clopping of horse hooves trotting down a dirt path. Once the intruder had descended and left the barn, Josh's body relaxed into the hay bed. He gently tightened his hold around her, kissing the top of her head. He took long inhalations of her hair.

"Was that your dad?" she asked quietly.

"It was. He invited us up to the house for breakfast."

She sighed. "You should go."

"What about you?"

She shrugged. By her estimation, it was Tuesday, which meant her dad would still be there. "It's a little complicated with my dad right now."

"Why?"

"With what happened—it's just—"

"Is he being overprotective?"

Refusing to go would require a lot of explanation and her brain quickly scolded her for bringing a dark cloud to the day. His parents deserved to celebrate their son's return without her being resentful toward a man that had given her a wonderful life when really, he owed her nothing. Essie swallowed hard, moving to sit up. "Forget it–I was being selfish. I'll go."

"Ess, wait," he said urgently, reaching for her right forearm. The underside, from halfway to her elbow and covering the entirety of her palm, was covered in jagged, pink scarring. "I didn't see this last night."

Her lips parted, her pulse starting to race. "Yeah, well, you were otherwise occupied. I saw to that," she jested nervously.

Josh sat up, peering at her other arm, which had a single diagonal block of scarring beneath the data matrix tattoo that had been present since he met her, something she was given as a baby at the orphanage where she lived, according to his mom.

"I'm fine, Josh," she said, trying to keep her voice light. "Let's go have breakfast." She stood, moving to retrieve the oversized sweatshirt she had tossed aside in the middle of the night once their combined body heat had created sweltering conditions. As she did, she purposefully tugged her shirt hem down to her hips. It was clear when she turned around that he had seen a glimpse of the scars on her stomach.

He moved slowly toward her. He tried tracing her cheek, her chin with the tips of his fingers in the same manner that had been so effective the night before, but there was a rigidness to her body, a defensiveness to her stance.

He lifted her right hand and kissed her knuckles, meeting some resistance when he tried to rotate her arm. To her surprise, he didn't force the movement. Instead, he released her, took a step back, and tugged off his undershirt, turning his back to her. "This is nothing in comparison, but they weren't intending to kill me."

On his back was a crisscross pattern of raised scars. Some slashes did not bevel the skin too much from the surface, others looked like the wound had initially reached down to the bone, the scar swollen and angry. She counted at least three dozen slashes. She was frozen where she stood, imagining the bite of the whip, or whatever device made the impression, on each strike.

He glanced over his shoulder, and slowly moved to retrieve his shirt. "They're gutless, these people. They do these things to give the appearance of strength and power." He stepped toward her, shaking his head. "It's neither. They're weak."

She stared at him, her eyes wide.

"You're still you, Ess. No matter what they tried to do. You're still you."

*   *   *

From his seat at the farmhouse dining table, Matteo watched his daughter walking toward the house holding Josh West's hand. Their fingers intertwined firmly as they had as children, and they moved as a singular unit. Matteo smiled lightly, getting the feeling of satisfaction out of the way for having predicted the match, though his heart ached a bit, as it always did when he was reminded that she wasn't a little girl anymore.

There was more now, of course, that had been lost.

He had feared Luther's explanation was too detailed, too explicit in describing the conditions that were her world for the first nearly three years of her life. Despite just witnessing his daughter recover from what should have killed her, knowing but not fully allowing himself to understand just how painful it had been for her, he had still felt desperate to protect her. It was overwhelming for him to accept that her childhood, which he had worked so hard to preserve for as long as possible, was over. More than that, he wondered if the years of her childhood he'd been privileged to experience had been an illusion she'd created for his benefit. Her childhood seemed to have been stolen before it had even begun.

She walked alongside Josh, her lips curling up at the corners, but she looked like a ghost of her typical self. There were shadows beneath her eyes, a pale hue to her skin, a heavy grief in the curve of her shoulders.

How many times had he explained to people that grief doesn't always involve actual death?

She couldn't return to Wallace. Everything she had known, the roots she had had been sliced out from underneath her.

Except one, he observed.

For the second time in his life, he felt an almost overwhelming appreciation for Josh.

Matteo slowly rose to his feet as the pair entered the house. The look in Esther's eyes when she saw him was heart-breaking. While just outside, she had been smiling, she was suddenly uneasy, uncertain of herself. Not even when she was three years old did she ever look so lost.

He would have preferred for her to be angry with him, but what he saw in her eyes was a pain that struck deep within her heart. She had initially expressed hurt that he had kept so much from her, but it was unconvincing. Learning the truth about where she came from, and how he ended up raising her had brought into question something that seemed to affect her more deeply: He didn't *choose* to adopt her; the responsibility was thrust upon him, and he acted as Christ called upon him to act. Whether this translated into true fatherly love was something that seemed to be weighing heavily on her mind.

Essie stood watching Josh embrace each of his parents, smiling with a genuine appreciation for the moment's meaning for them. She dropped her gaze when he extended a hand to Matteo. It had been this way since they had arrived at the Wests' home, but the apprehension in her eyes was also now accompanied by a guilt a child would have when facing a parent they feared they'd disappointed. He wanted to tell her that it didn't matter to him if she did something she thought he would disapprove of. He wanted to tell her he was sorry for keeping so much from her, that he was kept in the dark about most of it himself. He wanted to tell her he was sorry for everything that had happened, that he wasn't able to protect her from the evil of the world.

Luther had told him it was the safest option for her to relocate to the farm, that it was best for the congregation to think she was dead. Too many had seen her body. Word would get around and she would be at risk.

It was too much to absorb as it happened. *It was always going to take time for her to process things*, he told himself. Still. It eased something in his heart to see Josh quickly scoop up her hand when he returned to her side, to see how they subconsciously leaned toward each other as they moved.

When everyone had situated themselves around the table, at Sara's direction, Esther found herself seated between her dad and Josh. She appeared so uncomfortable with the arrangement that her eyes brimmed with tears, her neutral facade failing her. It was as though the proximity was causing her physical pain.

Matteo had seen her reach that level of emotion only a couple of times, but he recognized that it was a necessary step. His wife had used the phrase "a good cry" more than once, justifying why she watched the same sad movies over and over again. So, knowing, but not knowing the impact he would have, he leaned toward Esther and whispered: "Buongiorno, mia bella ragazza."

Esther looked up abruptly, her breaths shallow, those wild irises of hers softening. She frowned, thick teardrops starting to fall down her cheeks. He hadn't been in this close of proximity since the day after the attack. Her face had looked raw, the top layer broken, singed and black in some places, glossy and red in others. Even then, new layers of epidermis had already begun to fill in. He had taken frequent glances in the rearview mirror as she slept in the back seat on the drive to the farm, unable to believe the speed at which her skin was healing. Now he could barely see even faded traces of scarring, and at least on the surface, she was starting to look more like herself.

"Ti ho amato fin dall'inizio," he added, his jaw tight, tears filling his eyes.

She furrowed her brow, working through the translation. When she did--*I loved you from the start*--she nodded, her voice tight as she said: "Ti amo, Daddy."

And just like that, she'd flipped the tables and Matteo found himself dealing with an outpouring of emotion.

Josh watched with interest, catching his mom's eye as she placed a casserole dish on the table filled with what appeared to be some sort of scrambled eggs and fried potato bake. His stomach grumbled, but he tried to ignore it. His mom clutched her chest silently, watching Teo embrace Essie. She rounded the table to Essie, unable to help herself, and waited for Essie to sit back in her chair. Like so many times since she'd known her (it was no secret she'd always wanted a daughter), she gathered up Essie's long, golden-brown waves by the nape of her neck, kissing the top of her head.

"I'd be happy to brush out your hair later, if you'll let me?"

Essie frowned, then nodded apprehensively.

"The thought of the tangles has been keeping her up at nights, Ess."   "Luke!"

"It's fine. Yeah, it's gotten a little out of control," Essie admitted. "I swear I brush it."

Josh exchanged looks with his dad, who gave him a quick wink.

Sara released Esther's hair and let it cascade over her shoulders, glancing helplessly at the bits of hay falling to her clean floor. She moved back toward Essie and added: "You are the apple of your dad's eye. You should know that."

Essie glanced up over her shoulder at Sara, then met her dad's gaze, her eyes brightening.

"Must you meddle, Sara?" Luke asked incredulously.

"*Well*, she should know."

He shook his head. "Of course, she knows. Never in the history of the world has there been a dad who loves his child like Teo loves Essie, myself included."

"As his child, I will second that assessment."

"*Lucas*," Sara scolded.

"Josh knows I love him."

"I *do* know that."

"Just not to the level that Teo loves Essie," Luke added with a shrug.

Josh considered this and shrugged, nodding.

Esther released a chuckle, her face stretching into an easy smile for the first time in a long time.

*   *   *

Josh breathed in deeply, crossing the front porch to take in the sight of the green hills, snowcapped mountains in the distance. It was with bittersweet familiarity, seeing as it would likely be one of the last times he'd see them.

The breakfast conversation could only circle casual topics for so long and eventually, his parents shared that they were relocating to a town in the south.

"What about the farm?" he had asked, stunned.

"It hasn't been a business for a while, Josh. We've been holding onto it for as long as we can, but it's time."

"There are weekly attacks on churches," his mother added, looking regrettably in Essie's direction. "It doesn't make the news, of course, but it's happening. It's just not safe anymore."

Essie stiffened in her seat, uneasy with being used as a visual aid, raising her napkin to her face.

"What's different where you're going?"

The parents at the table all seemed to hesitate to give a response.

"We just feel like it's our best chance to get through this—*era* in American history," his dad reasoned, his eyes locked on Sara.

"Are you going, too?" Josh asked Teo, who sat more upright, wiping his mouth with his napkin repeatedly.

"I'm working with churches to help families relocate."

"Is everyone moving to 'the south'? And where is 'the south'? Are we talking Florida?"

"Florida's part of it, yes."

"Is *everyone* moving there?"

"Many are, yes. Some are going to San Diego. A few up north."

Josh was getting impatient. "What's in these places that makes them better or safer?"

"They're Arks," Esther said bluntly, raising an eyebrow at the parental occupants of the table. She wasn't supposed to know. When they first discussed it upon her arrival, they had all agreed it would be too much to put on her and left it at that, never revisiting the topic. "That's what they're calling them. It's catchy," she said with a shrug.

"*Arks*? As in Noah?"

"How does she know about the Arks?" Sara demanded of her husband. "We *agreed*--"

Luke shook his head, nodding pointedly across the table. "She has ears, Sara. I appreciate you want to protect her, but--" He motioned firmly toward Essie, then reeled back his hand when she met his eye. "Sorry, kiddo."

Essie took a steadying breath, briefly making eye contact with her dad. She pushed her chair back from the table, letting the legs groan loudly, and stood, shifting her attention over to Josh. "How about a walk?"

Matteo glanced up at her, his eyes regretful.

"It's okay, Daddy. I know why you didn't tell me," she whispered, patting Matteo's shoulder lightly as she scooted by his chair. She stepped outside without another word.

Essie was leaning against the railing, waiting patiently for Josh to follow. She didn't turn when he pushed open the squeaky screen door. He stepped alongside her, his eyes scanning the fields, the broken swing, the stables.

"You're going to fill me in?"

"I am," she said, turning to descend the front steps.

He moved to catch up and scooped up her hand in the process. He lifted their hands upward and kissed the top of her hand.

She slowed her pace, smiling lightly across at him.

"*You're* going to one of these Arks, right?" he asked as they continued on.

"I am. Unless I finally get my acceptance letter from Hogwarts," she said, scrunching her nose. "I'm starting to think the government intercepted my owl."

He chuckled tensely, then stopped mid-step. "Wait."

She turned on her heel, raising an eyebrow.

He took in the sight of her in the morning sunlight, the farmhouse suddenly looking rather dingy behind her. He stepped forward and wrapped his arms around her. "I love you, Esther Natale."

She buried her face in his shoulder. "I love you, Joshua Horatio West."

"That's not my middle name and you know it."

"It starts with a 'B,' right? Benedict? No wait, it's Arnold? Your initials spell JAW?"

"You *know*," he began, his voice low. "*They* all think I'm the obnoxious one."

"Don't discount the effort involved in keeping them thinking that. It's exhausting."

He nodded, suppressing a smile.

Their pace was deliberately slow as they passed the shade tree that served as the center of the circular dirt drive and climbed the perimeter fence of the main pasture where Bree grazed in the distance.

"'Ark' is symbolic or metaphoric, right?" he asked after they had walked for some time without speaking. "I was never great at grammar or linguistics."

"In this case, it will very much act like an Ark from the Bible. Minus a literal flood that I'm aware of, or a direct order from God to construct anything--again, that I'm aware of. It's also not a boat. And I don't think there's the two of every animal requirement—although, there's some iffiness there. When I read those passages, it seemed like there was more than two of the 'clean animals.' But yes, it's symbolic." She took a deep breath. "There are a few Arks in different parts of the country, strategically placed around key resources."

"Power, water, military, nukes?"

She nodded. "I'm not sure of the exact plan in regard to those resources. Based on what I've heard, there *could* be a plan to commandeer resources from the rest of the country."

"Cut them off, you mean?"

She shrugged. "Luther has more involvement with that."

"Who's Luther?"

She stopped short, struck by the idea that he wouldn't know him. "He's a leader with our side. He's who set all of this up," she said hesitantly, then added: "He saved my life when I was little."

"*Saved your life?*"

She took a breath. "Where I lived before I came to live with my dad? It wasn't safe. If he hadn't gotten me out of there, I wouldn't have survived. I wouldn't be here right now."

Josh squeezed her hand gently. "I hope I get the chance to thank him someday."

She pressed her lips together.

Reading that she didn't want to discuss that particular situation further, he prompted: "*So*, people are moving to symbolic Arks."

"Yeah. The idea right now is to relocate people into these zones for the 'Arks,' just in case."

"In case of what?"

"We reach the point of no return."

"Like Revelations?"

She nodded slowly. "I wouldn't rule it out, but the story of the Ark ends with hope. Well, a lot of death, but hope. I think the idea is that this is not the end of times and everybody outside the Ark isn't doomed."

"Let's go with that sentiment then."

"Agreed."

He sighed. "I should probably hear the details—" He squeezed her hand again. "But I think I'd like to just walk with you for a little while. Would that be okay?"

She gave a quick nod, moving in step with him, and peered to the East toward the rising sun.

"I have to say," he began, tilting his head to the side, "with this vibrant morning lighting, the slight breeze blowing through your hair—" He dropped her hand so he could frame out a portrait with his hands.

"What?"

He cleared his throat. When he spoke again, it was as an Australian narrator: "Look at this beauty of the American West, how she seems to glide across the tall grass of the prairie—"

A smile broke out on her face, though her silver eyes were misty. "I both love and hate you for making me laugh right now."

They didn't speak again about the Arks until they reached the stream where the horse pastures met the cattle land. During the summertime, both species liked to gather around the gentle water, and lie along the riverbank. Without the animals, it was still peaceful, but in an eerie sort of way.

"So, my parents are going to the Ark in the south," he began.

She nodded slowly. "Sounds like it."

"Are you going there, too?"

"I haven't been included in the discussions, but there are concerns about me going to the Ark in the south, as our entire remaining congregation thinks I'm dead–and they're all mostly going there."

"Wait–*they think you're dead*?"

She frowned. "I was told it was easier this way."

"Easier for who?"

Her eyebrows pinched together in desperation. There'd never been anything she'd struggled so much to share with him.

"Tell me."

She started to speak, generating the word "when" repeatedly before finding the task of describing what happened too difficult. She growled and wandered toward the shade tree. "Why do we have to have such horrible topics to talk about?" She placed a hand on the bark and traced the grooves with her finger. When they were children, the boys liked to carve things into the trunks of trees–until she informed them that carving bark damages trees, leaving them more susceptible to disease.

Josh stepped toward the stream, dipping the tips of his fingers in the chilly water. "Did my parents *choose* the south?"

"I think so. Your aunt and uncle are going there."

He shook his head. "We haven't seen them since I was ten."

"It makes sense they want to be close to family. I'm not sure what the travel options will look like if the Arks lock down."

Josh sighed as he took a seat on the grass and leaned against the trunk of the tree. He took in the sight of the empty pastures, the layers of hills and farmland, and the ridges of the mountains in the distance. From his vantage point, he couldn't see the fields of solar wasteland, rows and rows of solar panels long left to decay, couldn't see the high-speed railway grotesquely cutting across the landscape. There was just green grass, wildflowers of purple and yellow, crisp, clear water, and a cloudless blue sky overhead. It felt like it was simply an illusion, a trick of the eye, and it would all dissolve into nothingness before his eyes.

Esther lowered herself to the ground and tucked herself against him. "It's so pretty here," she said softly, reading his thoughts.

His throat was tight as he took in the scenery and breathed in the scent of her hair.

"What I want feels so simple, like it shouldn't be that much to ask," she said reflectively, "but I kind of feel guilty wanting it, given the state of things, like I'm being selfish to think I'm entitled to it."

"What do you want?"

She took a deep breath. "A bit of land with a pretty view, a cozy place to live; a quiet life."

"Am I there?"

"You can be the pretty view."

Josh felt his cheeks tighten despite himself.

"I'm sorry, I meant that in a flirtatious way, but I feel like I missed the mark."

"Yeah, how dare you objectify me."

She smiled tightly. "Nah, being able to appreciate you as a 'view' implies you'd be too far away for me to snuggle with."

He nodded, chuckled to himself. "A bit of land with a pretty view," he echoed.

She nodded.

"That's the plan then," he said, trying to sound confident in his optimism. "Wherever that happens to be."

She nodded, rotating her chin to look at him. "And Bree."

"And–" he began, glancing over his shoulder at the Percheron moving toward them. "Are you always going to be the third wheel, Narnian?"

Bree whinnied as he approached, as though vocalizing some grievance that he hadn't been invited for their walk.

Josh wondered suddenly about the horse's fate. Had his parents planned to transport him to their chosen Ark? Josh had grown up on the farm, been taught to treat the animals kindly, but first and foremost, remember their purpose. *The humans come first*, his father had told him if he expressed sentiment or attachment to the animals. More than once, this had prefaced putting an old animal down, selling them, or more frequently, sending an animal to the local butcher. He wondered what his dad's logic would be about still keeping Bree, despite it being obvious that supplies were scarce and there was little contribution the horse could make to the current operation that would justify the expense, both time and money.

Bree's muzzle tickled Josh's face as he followed Esther's scent, stretching his dappled neck to reach her.

"Hey, we talked about this," Esther laughed as Bree chomped down on her messy knot of hair.

The horse released her and bobbed his head, tapping his front hoof on the ground.

"Yeah, yeah. You're hilarious."

Bree moved toward the stream and took an indulgent drink of water, his white tail swishing.

Josh again thought of questioning his dad about why they'd kept Bree, but as he watched Esther smiling at the horse, he thought of how his mom had described Esther as being very withdrawn since she'd arrived. He imagined she'd spent most of her time with Bree, that workhorse being the proverbial life preserver keeping her afloat. And then he found he could answer his own question, repeating silently: *The humans come first.*

*   *   *

The aroma of freshly baked bread wafted through the screen door in the early evening as Esther sat opposite her dad in the rocking chairs on the porch, a chess board positioned on the small table between them. The pieces were hand-carved by a woodworker in town, Luke had said, one side's pieces made from a pale oak, the opposite from a deep cherry, the board butcher block. Matteo had excused his last error in play, saying he was distracted by the craftsmanship of the board.

When Esther was first learning the game around age 8, she accused him of letting her win on more than one occasion. She had become frustrated with him, scolding him about how he had such little confidence in her being able to win on her own. Ever since, he'd never let her win, but she very rarely lost.

He watched her eyes drift over the board from one piece to the next, her chin resting against her fist.

"Luke and Sara have decided to come to the northern Ark."

Esther moved a bishop to be in the same diagonal as the oak king. "Check. But they're not starting to move people there yet, right?"

"They've started, but it's gradual. They want to be sure we can accommodate everyone–and not draw too much attention."

"But the southern Ark–they could go now?"

"They decided to wait."

"Is that a good idea?"

"Well, none of the Arks are locked down and on 'guard,' so it doesn't make a difference yet. But they decided it was a better long-term decision." His index finger and thumb held firmly to the top of a rook as he reviewed any repercussions of his move besides the intended sacrifice to save the king. He released the piece cautiously.

"I guess it makes sense to wait until Gabe can come with them anyway."

Matteo frowned.

"He should be back in a month or two? Right?"

He exhaled deeply. "He re-upped, Essie."

She froze. "For how long?"

"It's another two years minimum."

"Why would he do that?" she asked quietly without looking up.

"Your guess is as good as mine–probably better."

"I haven't heard from him in a year." Her voice croaked a bit. "He told me he would call in a couple of days."

Bree neighed in his stall and Matteo took the opportunity to let his eyes drift toward the stables.

"He wouldn't just not call."

"I know. It's not like him."

She squeezed her eyes closed. "It was over two years ago," she said in a flat voice. "That drive back to Wallace after the train station?"

After he kissed you, Matteo added silently. The idea of her kissing anyone now turned his stomach a bit, let alone more than two years ago. *She's still a kid*, he thought desperately. The anger he rekindled eased any concern he had for the oldest West brother. "He made his choice, Essie. I don't understand it, but it's what he's chosen."

"What if he didn't make the choice? They're just going to abandon—"

Matteo shook his head and gave her a pleading look. "They're doing everything in their power. There's not much they *can* do."

There was clearly more she wanted to say, her mouth twisting tightly. She crossed her arms, running her palms briskly against them, as though to warm herself. "Did you tell Sara and Luke about me?" she asked, clearly wanting to shift subjects.

"I told them enough. Not much, but enough." Matteo watched her stare at the chessboard, her eyes unfocused. "You should know—before they were under the impression we were going South. They would have never chosen it otherwise."

"What about their family?"

"Everyone has to make their own decisions."

She swallowed hard, nodded.

"Did you tell Josh?"

"I told him enough," she said quietly. A flash of her hand and she had claimed the rook and placed him in the lineup of captured oak chess pieces. "Check."

"You shall be avenged, brave rook."

Esther gave an obligatory smirk.

He started to send his queen forward but stalled. "Or not."

The phone rang inside, and Esther peered over her shoulder through the front window as a square image projected on the empty wall space next to the refrigerator. A skinny young man with heavy beige eyebrows and a sallow face appeared.

"Are you sure this isn't a checkmate?" Matteo asked, frowning.

"You have a few moves," Esther replied quickly, still staring inside. Josh had stepped into the frame of the video feed to take the call. She could hear him providing his name and registration ID, a sixteen or so alpha-numeric combination he had memorized.

"I've verified your identity," the man said robotically. "Joshua O'Neil West, you are required to report to the Denver International Airport this Thursday morning at 9am for immediate deployment and resumption of your duties."

"This Thursday?"

"Yes," the man replied.

Josh reset his footing. It was Tuesday evening. "May I ask where I'm being deployed?"

"You're slated for a 10:30 departure to Los Angeles."

"Is there a return date?"

"Our records show you are committed for deployment until December 31ˢᵗ, though that date is subject to change."

She could see him exhale tensely.

"As a reminder, all enlistees are required to adhere to the dress and decorum policy prior to the resumption of your term. Hair should be no longer than one-eighth inch in length, facial hair of any kind is not permitted." The small man raised his eyes, briefly scrutinizing Josh's appearance.

"I understand."

"This recorded call will serve as documentation of your acknowledgment of your assignment and expectations. Failure to appear at the scheduled date, time, and location may result in a charge of desertion, which holds a penalty of 3-5 years imprisonment, minimum $100,000 fine, revocation of any and all public benefits and health coverage for yourself and all immediate family members. Do you understand these terms?"

"Yes."

"If you have any further questions, you can contact our office by dialing 9-9-7. Repeat the number back." The caller did not lift his eyes from his script.

"9-9-7."

"Have a pleasant evening." The projector screen vanished.

Josh nodded slowly, his hand rising to run over the thick stubble he'd allowed to accumulate atop his head. Sara stepped before him, and placed her hand on his cheek, taking in the details of his face. Her eyes were lined with worry.

"It's two months. I can do two months," he was saying, trying to keep his voice low.

Matteo watched his daughter processing what she'd just heard, as well as their earlier conversation. Even if they relocated within the boundaries of an Ark, the government could still track him down. The punishment for defectors was severe, meant to discourage others from taking the same path. Turning in defectors was heavily incentivized for both private citizens and foreign countries. It was something praised on the news as falling into the 'see something, say something' civic duty.

He didn't have a choice.

Her shoulders sank at the same moment Josh met her gaze.

10

overture

eight months later...

Luther recognized her immediately as she took the end seat at the hotel bar. She had attracted much attention with her long waves of honey brown hair, large doe eyes, elongated limbs--a nostalgic and rare natural beauty. The social expectation now, particularly in the District, demanded an edgier look—streaks of vivid colors, eyelashes that looked like glittery tarantula legs, a contoured bone structure, accomplished by makeup or surgical enhancement. Against the backdrop of bold was an ethereal, natural being.

The women were disgusted and intimidated. The men appeared captivated as though she were a siren humming a melody.

Esther had risen from her bar stool and moved closer when the chair beside him freed. She slid onto the seat, which sparked the interest of several men who were watching her, wondering what appeal this man had that they didn't.

The closer proximity brought her familiar eyes into sharper focus. They shimmered in the light with flecks of white like a mirror of a distant, chilly planet.

She extended a slender arm and grasped his drink. She clinked the ice around in the lowball glass, surveying the amber liquid. She swigged it down in one gulp and contorted her face slightly at the bitterness.

"You're too young to drink that."

"The drinking age was lowered to 16. I'm nearly 18."

"The voting age was also lowered to 16, which I also don't agree with."

"Alcohol, among other things, has little effect on me. I'm guessing you know that."

"All the more reason for you not to drink it," he muttered, ordering another. When the bartender finished the pour and tossed in an additional rind garnish, Esther intercepted the glass and downed the contents. Luther noticed the almost imperceptible scar tissue on her palm that wrapped the glass.

"That was seventeen dollars."

"*That* was disgusting."

"Jesus, Mary, and Joseph, how are you almost eighteen?" he said, the realization hitting him in the chest.

"Better watch that kind of talk around here," she said, raising her eyebrows.

He nodded reluctantly. "Your dad told me you'd be looking for me. That took some bravery to travel all the way to the District."

"Or stupidity," she confessed.

He lifted his eyebrows in agreement. "Yeah, I didn't want to say that."

She shrugged. "Is that why you're drinking? Because you knew I was on my way here?"

"Attempting to drink, more like."

"Wow, that burns going down." Her eyebrows pulled upward at the center in an exaggerated, youthful manner.

"It's whiskey."

"Are you attempting to drink—*ugh*, it's like a pool of lava in the pit of my stomach—"

He chuckled under his breath.

"Isn't there usually a mix-in? Something sugary to offset the–wow, that's still burning–" she said, placing her hand on her ribcage.

"I try to stay away from mix-ins. Diabetes runs in my family."

"I applaud your commitment to your health," she choked. "I'll rephrase my question--Are you drinking lighter fluid because you knew I was looking for you?"

"No, me drinking is a regular occurrence." He waved the bartender over to refill his glass. The bartender, a young man with a thick goatee suddenly seemed uncertain if he should be asking the young woman for identification. "Just one more for me," Luther clarified.

When the bartender delivered the drink, Esther cleared her throat and spoke softly: "I'm sorry about your mom, Luther."

Luther stared at his glass, slowly wiping off columns of condensation. "What we're doing—hopefully it puts a stop to it." He cleared his throat, taking in the surreal sight of Esther Natale sitting beside him. Her hair was so much more vibrant than when he first met her. She had freckles scattered across the bridge of her nose she would have never had in the dungeons of the lab where he found her.

"She would have loved to have seen you all grown up."

She smiled lightly. "I remember she called me 'baby girl.'"

He narrowed his eyes. Essie wasn't even three when she knew his mother and she'd only spent a few days with her. How she remembered that detail was beyond him. "She *did* do that," he said, then sighed and pushed the glass away without drinking the contents. He stood and scanned his wrist on a sensor on the bar. The name Frank King appeared on the transaction screen. Luther glanced around at the spying patrons. "You don't belong here."

She seemed to take notice of the other people for the first time. "People in the District look different."

"Yes, they do." It was then he spotted Annette making her way to the concierge desk.

"You need to move away from me," he said sternly, raising his hand to shield his mouth under the guise of scratching his face.

Esther shrugged on a canvas jacket much too large for her and casually backed away from the bar, checking her watch as she moved into the lobby. She glanced toward the elevator bank, and checked her watch again, clearly trying to sell the act that she was waiting for someone. Finally, she plunked down in one of the oversized chairs.

Annette motioned him to follow her toward a less prominent part of the lobby by the business center.

"Who's the girl?" Annette asked immediately, her eyes panning to Esther. She had applied a significant amount of makeup since he last saw her.

"*Oh*, she thought I was someone else. Some celebrity is supposed to be staying here."

"Well, that's flattering."

"Depends on the celebrity," he replied casually. "I'm also not looking like myself, am I?"

She smiled lightly. "This is a good look," she assessed. "But I prefer your regular face."

He was taken back by her remark, particularly being in a public setting. "You're looking—

"'Provocatively powerful'?" The accentuation on the syllables had afforded him a whiff of schnapps on her breath. "That's what the stylist said. I just finished the second photo shoot for the campaign."

"Ah," he said. She had admitted to never feeling comfortable with having her photo taken so it seemed she had taken his suggestion, though through the filter of Esther's eyes he could recognize that this was perhaps poor advice.

"I'm not the target audience, I suppose."

Her face fell a bit.

"You don't need all that, in my humble opinion," he clarified, peering over her shoulder.

His remark appeared to brighten her mood, but he was too preoccupied to pay much attention.

Esther was thumbing through a digital fashion magazine with confusion. The cover showed a trio who appeared to be clad in outfits made out of duct tape and newsprint. She swiped through the magazine hastily then placed it back on the coffee table with care, as though she thought it might detonate. As she did, a man wearing an expensive business suit sat down exceedingly close to her on the couch, at once placing his fingers on her neck to raise her chin. Esther's silver eyes narrowed as he spoke just inches from her face. He looked like a politician, sporting a trendy, spiked salt and pepper hairdo, at least forty years her senior.

When given a chance to speak, Esther did so calmly, with precise delivery. The man watched her lips with captivated interest at first, but after a few moments, suddenly retracted his hand, a pink imprint left on her skin. The man stood stiffly and took leave, bowing apologetically, wiping his hand on his suit.

Esther briefly made eye contact with Luther before busying herself with studying the tile mosaic on the far wall. She appeared unfazed by the interaction.

Most of what Annette was saying sounded like it was being filtered through water, but she was speaking with a lot of animated hand movements, which she did in the rare instance she was intoxicated. Luther recognized the social cues when she was ending their conversation. "I'll meet you at your suite at 9 then."

He frowned, realizing his occasional head bobbing must have inadvertently accepted an invitation, though checking the time, he wasn't sure if she meant 9 pm, or 9 the next morning.

She pressed her rouged lips together, smiling tightly, and moved along toward the elevators. Her gaze panned curiously in Esther's direction, her confidence faltering.

He waited for Annette to exit the lobby before turning back to Esther, eyeing the front entrance pointedly. She stood just as he passed her, and she trailed slightly behind. He continued out the revolving door. She spilled out onto the sidewalk a few moments later, the door proving to have a bit of a learning curve.

"That's anxiety-inducing," she remarked, glancing back at the door continuing to whirl in a counterclockwise direction.

Luther had drawn his cell phone and spoke into it. "We'll meet at the diner on the corner then?"

"That one there?" she asked loudly so he could hear her over the city noise.

He sighed, tucking his phone back into his jacket. "Be careful through here. Wait until I get there. Keep some distance from me."

He zig-zagged around stationary traffic with determined confidence, crossing to an unassuming diner just across the street, the same one from which he called her dad when he thought she was dead.

Esther watched him from just outside the hotel and surveyed the traffic situation, bumper to bumper through the crosswalk and intersection. She moved with a bit more caution than he had, opting to cross the street with what could best be described as polite methodology, smiling lightly at the drivers as she slipped between the bumpers.

She pushed open the door of the diner and was met with the smell of grease, baked goods, and bacon. She spotted Luther's back in the row of booths along the back wall, as far from the windows as possible, and slid into the bench across from him.

Before she had even considered the menu, he had placed his fist angrily on the tabletop. "I won't do it, Esther."

"Do what?" she asked casually, motioning toward her own face. "How does *that* work?"

He tapped his ear, where she could barely see a clear patch-looking device over his ear canal. "This maps my face and does an overlay."

"That's impressive tech."

"*You* recognized me."

"You have a very distinct gait."

"I was sitting at the bar."

"I was in the lobby when you got to the hotel."

"Well, you took your time approaching me then," he said, shaking his head. He had been sitting at the bar for nearly a half-hour. "Speaking of the lobby--what *happened* back there?" he asked, pointing across the street. "People like him don't take no for an answer. Did you Jedi mind trick him?"

She pursed her lips, leaning forward with an air of excitement. "Are the Jedi *real*? Because we could use their help right now."

"This isn't a joke. You can't be here." His eyes darted toward the front windows and the hotel across the street.

"What's the Speaker's role with the Arks?"

His expression tightened, but he looked in her eyes and found he couldn't feel even mild frustration toward her. "Bluebird."

She narrowed her eyes.

"Her code name."

"*Bluebird*," she repeated slowly.

He nodded.

"Not the bird I would have chosen for her," she said shortly.

He was slightly amused by the scowl that had taken over her face. "What would you have chosen?"

"For *her*? If I'm limited to bird species? Ostrich?"

He considered this. "Why?"

"They're terrifying, nasty, prehistoric-looking creatures. Seems fitting."

He smiled briefly, shaking his head. "Your dad told me you're funny."

"Yep. Hilarious. What does *Bluebird* have to do with the Arks."

Luther took a breath. "I can't share much, but if we succeed the way I hope we succeed, it'll be because of her."

"You trust her?"

He let his gaze drift across the street, suddenly certain Annette had meant 9 *pm*.

"From what I understand, she helped ensure the success of the current regime. She's why places where you rescued me from existed."

He pressed his lips together. "Something I've learned, repeatedly actually, is that God uses very imperfect people to do His work, myself included."

She appeared taken back by his statement, furrowing her brow.

"So, she's a part of *His* work? *His* plan?"

"I hope so."

She nodded. "Do you believe God has a plan for everyone? That he uses people for certain purposes?"

"Yes."

She straightened her posture. "If you knew my *background*, you knew what threats lie ahead, but you didn't know me personally, would you say God's plan for me is to hide away in some bunker and do nothing?"

Luther dropped his shoulders, letting his eyes settle on her. "Your dad also warned me you're good at arguing your case," he said with a sigh.

She raised her eyebrows.

"You're not—I hear what you're saying, but—"

"If there's something my body generates to—*defend itself*—" she glanced around the restaurant to check for listening ears. "Science was never something that interested me much, but from what I've read, if that something can be extracted, it could work like an antidote. *Right?*"

He sat back. "Yes. Theoretically."

"And another attack is coming."

"We think so, yes."

Her eyes narrowed.

"Yes. It's coming. Before we hoped for diplomacy, but this Administration, this Congress--" he shook his head, trying not to give much thought to Georgina Moreno, who was the reason he had to assume a new identity as Fred King and wear a facial overlay. "It's not happening."

"So, an antidote would be—*helpful*."

He said nothing.

"Luth--wait, what's your code name or call sign or whatever? Should I use that?"

"It's safe here."

"What's yours?"

"Moose."

"Moose," she repeated flatly, pinching her face. "Is it the ears? Because they're on the large size?"

He gave an amused smirk. "It was my nickname in high school. I held the record for homeruns."

Her face remained blank.

"In the olden days, there was a really amazing baseball player nicknamed Moose. Traditionally that's how the name was used, as a nickname for someone who was a good hitter."

She frowned. "Okay, so *Moose*, don't you think--no, I'm sorry. I can't say that. I sound insane."

"You can call me Luther here."

"*Luther*, wouldn't an antidote be helpful? Given all that might happen?"

"You know the answer. Yes. Of course, it would be helpful, but—" he lowered his voice. "Number one, we don't know for sure that it would work or if it did, what the extent would be. Number two, I can't do that-- I *won't* do that to you."

"It's not the same as before. I'm asking you to."

He took a deep breath. Having an antidote was an undeniable advantage, especially for extraction teams. In his mind, he tried to separate the little girl he smuggled out of an incinerator room from the young woman sitting before him. He shook his head. "We can't assume there's nothing out there that can kill you."

"I understand that."

"The process, just to test it? Would be extremely painful. You'd be subjecting yourself willingly to torture."

She nodded, swallowing with noticeable difficulty.

"Esther--"

"What's something that was tested on me already? We could start there."

"Ebola."

She frowned. "Easy to get? Concentrated Ebola virus?"

"Not especially. *Well*, easier than it should be, but no."

"What would be more accessible?"

"Batrachotoxin."

"'Trach' is something respiratory?"

"It causes respiratory paralysis."

She stared at him. "This was tested on me."

He nodded, though it didn't sound much like a question.

"How long did it take me to recover?"

"From batrachotoxin, 13 hours I believe, but there's no telling if your system still operates the same way, if you even have the ability anymore."

Her eyes drifted away for just a moment. "It seemed to operate the same way at the church, didn't it?"

He lowered his eyes. "The gas was very similar to something that was tested on you."

She appeared to be absorbing the facts of the situation again. "So, they *really*—" she began, just as the waitress stepped up to the table.

Luther softened his expression as she greeted them.

"We have a limited menu right now," she said apologetically.

"What do you recommend?"

"The soup is actually great. Tomato bisque. We can do a grilled cheese with it."

"Perfect," Luther said. "Two of those. You don't have a gluten, dairy, or nightshade intolerance, do you?"

Esther contorted her face as though he'd just spoken Wookiee.

"Two of those."

"I'd bring you water, but they're regulating the tap and it's been looking iffy anyway. We have some canned juice that's decent. A little sugary."

Luther nodded approvingly. His face turned serious again.

"They're regulating the water?" Esther asked once she'd gone.

"There have been shortages, droughts. They're intercepting food supplies, too."

"There was caviar and lamb chops on the appetizer menu across the street."

"Different clientele."

Esther glanced around the cluttered diner at the scattering of patrons who looked more weathered, less refined compared to the people eyeing her at the bar. The waitress had long, muddy waves. There was a man with heavy stubble and a tattered baseball cap hunched over the table across from them reading a newspaper. In the far corner, a couple sat silently eating, seeming to avoid each other's gazes, appearing to be in the middle of a disagreement. It was a decidedly normal, working-class setting despite its proximity to the elite neighborhoods.

"I prefer this clientele."

Luther had a distant look in his eyes, not joining her analysis. "You don't have to do this."

She swallowed hard. "I have the opportunity to do something that could make a difference."

He studied her face. He could still see the toddler intended for the incinerator standing in the bathroom of that research lab wearing a t-shirt several sizes too large, her eyes gazing up at him with inconceivable optimism, asking him if she could leave with him.

When he'd made his decision and carried her broken body under his coat out of that torture chamber, he'd brought her to his mother's house, where he lived while finishing medical school. He thought she'd be sleeping, but his mother had emerged from the kitchen just as he'd turned the handle to his bedroom. His instinct was to hide Esther from her; it was safest for her if she didn't know what he'd done, but his mother could read his mood even with his back turned.

"*Child*, what's happened?"

Luther turned slowly, the window air conditioning unit airflow sending a chill through him as it hit his tear-stained cheeks.

She peered at the bundled-up coat he carried as he pulled back the fabric. She immediately placed her hand over the child's body, gasping.

Young Esther looked back and forth between the pair of strangers, her eyes full of questions and uncertainty.

Luther moved to the couch, sitting Esther beside him.

His mother gazed at the young girl's dirty face in wonder. She saw her contorted limbs, which sat a little unevenly in their joints. The bones had managed to nearly heal in the two hours he'd spent circling the neighborhood, something he hadn't begun to process.

"Baby Girl?" she said, effectively capturing Esther's attention. "How would you like a nice, cozy bubble bath?" She let her voice rise and fall the way she did when interacting with pediatric patients.

Esther smiled ever so slightly, looking directly into this stranger's eyes, and said: "That sounds nice."

His mother spent the next hour tending to Esther, bathing her, and dressing her in Luther's childhood clothes. She reheated her famous Sunday lasagna and placed a large portion on a plate, situated the girl at the kitchen table with her food and a large glass of milk.

"You eat up now, Baby Girl. I'll be right over there," she'd told her, crossing to Luther as he returned from a shower. She squeezed his arm tightly, taking several moments to be able to generate words again. "No harm must ever come to that child again."

He nodded, peering over at Esther, wondering if his mother had seen scars or wounds he hadn't.

"You're a brave, brave man, doing what you did, getting her out of there."

He shook his head. "You were right, Momma. I shouldn't have gone to work there."

She tightened her hand again. "I was wrong, Luther. God led you there."

"To save her?"

She scowled. "Of course not. She's not the only one, is she?"

"But–there's no way for me to save them all."

"That's probably true." She paused in the way she did sometimes, though he could never figure out if it was to give herself time to think of her next words or to give him a chance to reflect. "You save those you can. Simple as that."

He remembered the silence that followed, how he echoed his mother's words in his head. The task was daunting, impossible probably, but as he determined that turning his back on all those children would never sit well for him, the image of the baby boy he had been working with, designated now for "parts," as though he were a car in a junkyard, came to mind and he felt a calm resolve wash over him.

You save those you can.

"My dad says you chose my middle name," Esther said in a light voice, fidgeting with the sugar packets.

The diner noises swelled around him. "What?"

"My middle name? My dad said that's what you called me."

"Your dad told you that, huh?"

She nodded, smiling slightly.

Oh, how thankful he was for Matteo Natale. Fifteen years earlier, Luther had been desperate to relocate Esther, away from the lab, the city. It had been for her own safety, but also to allow him to help other children. His mother had cared for her while he kept up appearances at the lab, but time was not on his side.

He had received a lead on an agency that operated a group home, but he knew the moment he saw the dilapidated apartment complex with barbed wire fencing and bleak landscaping, that he would never leave Esther there. He had driven over a hundred miles to the group home, but he didn't even get out of the car.

He pulled into a highway gas station, which was attached to a mid-century diner, built to resemble a train car. As Luther filled the gas tank, he found his attention drawn to the diner windows. He remembered wondering what it must be like for the patrons so far removed from the city, not burdened as he was, eating their patty melts and going about their evenings.

He peered over his shoulder to the back seat where Esther was sleeping in a car seat he'd picked up at a consignment store. She was snuggling a dolphin stuffed animal that had been his favorite as a child and any envy he felt toward the diners disappeared. In its place, he felt an ache.

He had actually felt relieved that the group home hadn't worked out. He knew she couldn't stay with him, but it had delayed the pain he knew he'd feel when he inevitably had to say goodbye to her.

All at once, that pain was upon him. He felt his eyes coaxed to a worn burgundy pickup truck parked in the end parking space. The truck bed had a few repurposed boxes, and an antique desk, but what stood out to him was the intricate cross decal centered in the back window.

The tide had been turning for a while in the media about Christianity, media talking heads accusing "Christ worshippers" as being hateful and intolerant, manufactured events and flat-out lies the only evidence provided. Having grown up in a Baptist church, he knew first-hand the warmth and love pouring from church communities, something he missed since living in the city.

He remembered feeling in awe of anyone who would advertise their beliefs so overtly.

It was just after he noticed the decal that the bell rang on the diner door and a young, olive-skinned man emerged. He paused to hold the door open for an approaching couple, nodding kindly to them, then moved toward the truck, shrugging his jacket higher around his neck. Luther had climbed out of his car and gone through the motions of approaching him without a conscious decision to do so.

Matteo was calm when Luther closed the distance between them, slow to react as he listened to the abridged and vague account of what brought him to that moment, of asking a stranger to take and care for this child. As difficult as Luther anticipated the moment would be when he parted from this girl, he had driven away with an empty backseat and felt tremendous resolve and confidence in his decision.

When he went to Calvary Church after the attack, he'd finally had the opportunity to ask Matteo Natale how he trusted what he said so quickly. Matteo had taken a breath, leaned back in the pew, ran a hand through his thick brown hair, and said: "I could feel the love you had for her. Asking me to take her was like entrusting me with a piece of your soul."

At the time, Esther was still recovering in his office and Matteo's brown eyes were burdened with exhaustion. He stared up at the large wooden cross depicting the crucifixion of Jesus above the altar and sighed, the tears that had been brimming his eyes starting to stream down his cheeks. "As it turns out, you gave me the greatest blessing of my life."

Esther placed her hand gently over Luther's wrist. Luther stirred from his memory, resetting himself in the booth. *My dad says you chose my middle name*, he echoed silently to help get his bearings.

He smiled, thinking of the few days he spent caring for her, how her hair had shimmered so brilliantly once it was clean, how wide her silver eyes had become when she tasted pancakes with butter and syrup for the first time. "You weren't with me very long, but you deserved a name."

"I'm thankful my dad's last name didn't start with an L."

He frowned.

"Esther Evin? My initials would have spelled EEL."

Luther pressed his lips together. "My great-great-grandfather was named Evin."

She blinked slowly.

"He was the happiest, most witty, most resilient person I've ever known. He lived to be 104 and he was sharp as a tack until the end. I didn't know if I was ever going to have a family, but I knew if I ever did have a child, he or she would have his name."

She tilted her head to the side, her expression thoughtful and a bit humbled. "I understand I wasn't the only one you saved."

"I had the opportunity to do something that could make a difference," he said, raising an eyebrow.

"*Luther*," she began, her words slow and calculated. "I was processing a lot the last time we saw each other at Calvary–"

He lifted his chin in agreement.

"I know you risked everything to save my life."

The waitress arrived with their meals and noisily placed their plates before them, removing two cans of juice from her apron pockets. "Anything else?"

Luther shook his head and she left.

"*Thank you.*"

He smiled tightly, his eyes misty. "You changed my life, Esther Evin."

She sank a bit in her seat.

"I meant that in a positive way."

"Oh."

He remembered how his mother had panicked when he'd gone back to work at the lab, wondering if she'd been crazy to encourage him to put himself in such danger. After having a stream of consciousness conversation with herself aloud, she'd finally placed her hand on his cheek and said: "I have to let you be the man you're meant to be. Even if it frightens me. I have to have faith that God will watch over you. Because you're doing His work, you know that, right?"

He sighed, looking at Esther with reluctance. "I'll do it. What you've asked. I'll do it."

She straightened her posture, eyes widening.

"We need to get you inside the boundary of the Ark first though. That's non-negotiable."

She nodded, a hint of fear now swimming in her eyes.

He leaned forward and lowered his voice to a whisper. "They don't know you're alive. I'd like to keep it that way. I need you to keep a low profile, even if that means hiding out in a bunker, metaphorically speaking."

She nodded quickly.

"Esther, if they find you—" He let the thought hang, unwilling to complete it.

Esther stared at him, the message registering. Her eyes drifted over to the facial overlay device near his ear suggestively.

"I have a spare you can have."

She took a deep breath.

"You can't tell anyone what we're doing. Not until we're secured at the Ark. Even then—people are unpredictable." He felt compelled to share how he'd observed even the most honorable people falter under even mild duress but decided against it.

"I don't have—" she began, looking away, regretfully. "I don't have many people left. I'm not going to put them at risk. My dad knows–obviously–"

He nodded. "This is going to be difficult for me, Esther. I can only imagine what it will be like for your dad."

"He worries."

"He's your dad. Of course, he does." He smiled kindly. "It's a lot to take on without having support though."

"The only one I would have told—" Her voice thickened.

"Your dad mentioned Josh."

She raised her eyebrows, slightly flustered. "I didn't think he should have gone back--"

Luther shrugged. "I agree."

The impact of those two words was immense. She looked like she might burst into tears. "He thought if he defected, they'd come after his family—"

Luther nodded. They didn't have the resources to send people, but with a few strokes of the keyboard, they could destroy their lives. That is, if they were reliant enough on the government for support, if they had any money in banks or investments, which the Wests didn't. The truth was, the government didn't have the workforce to enforce many threats. Not yet anyway. That was ironically what one of the primary purposes of Mandatory service had been, to "recruit" reinforcement.

"He was only supposed to have two more months and then—"

"Required renewal."

Her eyes were round and desperate.

"I'm already working on getting him pulled. After your dad called to tell me to expect you, I made a couple calls–"

Her breath caught in her throat. "You can do that?"

"We have someone on our side who can pull some strings." It was surprising when he'd found out Josh had been stationed in Long Beach. When Matteo mentioned that he was a part of the required renewals, he had thought the worst, but it seemed Josh's assignment had to do with supply chain rather than pseudo-militia training. The government was using his unit to process shipments from overseas.

Her mouth turned up repeatedly at the corners. "What about Gabe? His brother? He's been gone so long."

Luther lowered his eyes. "Esther, it's tougher the longer they're in." He decided it was better to omit further explanation, that while Gabe wasn't a part of a militia, his role did involve advanced psychological training. He couldn't tell her that it was best if she didn't have any contact with him because with their strategies, using the Sim, they could extract and exploit anything he ever thought, heard, or experienced. Furthermore, based on what Matteo had said about Gabe's change in behavior since leaving the first time, he seemed like too much of a risk to try to pull covertly.

She kept her long slender arms crossed in front of her on the table, her fingers fidgeting. "I have my dad—and I have them."

He hated the idea of telling her no. It was causing physical pain to even think of looking in her eyes after everything she'd been through and telling her she'd likely never see Gabe again.

"If I can, I'll get both of them out," he heard himself say.

11
trial

Luther had insisted on something mild, something with a tried and true antidote that wasn't entirely lethal, for the initial test. He pulled together a basement lab at his temporary housing, a long-term vacation rental, which had come equipped with a leather recliner, big screen television, and kitchenette.

Esther tapped in the code he'd provided and apprehensively entered the basement apartment. She was immediately struck by the newness of the floors—a plank tile meant to look like wood. She pushed the door open further and found the place looked exceptionally put together and contemporary. Clean.

"Luther?" She called out. She half-expected him to appear as an attentive host in a home furnishing commercial, ask for her coat to hang on the wall-mounted coat rack, and offer her a beverage in a solid, but reasonably priced tumbler.

Instead, he emerged moments later from the bathroom looking ill. He barely acknowledged her, sights set on the refrigerator, where he removed a can of ginger ale.

"Nice place."

He shrugged as he took a swig. "The listing said it had a view, not that I care about such things, but that seems a bit of a stretch."

She lowered her backpack to the floor and pulled out two thick, hardcover books. "I brought along a couple of books for you in case I'm not a great conversationalist."

He took the books, scanning the titles. "*Great Expectations* and–" He grinned, raising his eyes. "*Harry Potter and the Sorcerer's Stone.*"

"I'd probably stick with the wizard."

He exhaled deeply, setting the books on the counter. "You're trying to make this easier for me."

She shrugged. "It's just a test. Nothing crazy."

He eyed her over his glasses. "I don't like the fact that I've now come full circle on this."

She said nothing, peering around the room. "Do I get the big chair?"

"Yes. *Although*--why don't you use the bathroom first?" He motioned toward where he'd just emerged.

"*Oh*. Right. How does that work once we've started?"

"I don't know, to be honest. Considering the potency--"

"This was not included in the brochure, Moose."

He looked uncomfortably toward the open bathroom door. "I put some adult undergarments in there."

She squinted. "Well, it's OK for astronauts and racecar drivers, right?"

Of course, the space program and NASCAR were long a thing of the past, but he appeared to decide not to mention it.

Once she was situated in the chair, her hair pulled into a messy knot, she took a few solid breaths, coping with more apprehension than before.

He stared at the syringe of cloudy liquid then looked up. He appeared to be debating asking again if she was certain she wanted to go through with it. He opened his mouth to speak twice but stopped short both times.

She nodded. "I'm sure, Luther."

Luther stepped quickly toward her outstretched arm and secured a rubber tie around it, just above her elbow. He inserted the needle into the exposed vein without a word.

At first, the substance felt cool in her veins. For a moment she thought perhaps he had injected her with something harmless.

Esther knew little about the complexities of science, but she recognized the sensation when the molecules began to interact. She felt her veins stiffen. She felt the foreign substance clawing through her contracting veins with surprising velocity.

In contrast, everything else was slowing down. Her chest rose and fell in slow waves, her eyes shifted with delayed response. She watched as the skin surrounding the injection site retracted, burned with small literal flames, taking on a dead, charcoaled appearance. She was unable to decipher if it was truly happening or if it was a hallucination. She could feel the same sensation throughout her blood vessels as the chemical spread. Sounds became muffled and amplified at the same time as though the noises were traveling down a long tunnel to reach her, but when they did, were shrill and pierced her eardrums.

She looked over to Luther, who she was certain would be panicked by her response. Surely, he'd be furiously administering an antidote.

But Luther was sitting calmly on the dining chair he'd positioned beside her, stroking her hand with fatherly affection.

Surely, he would see her torched skin, the blackened veins? She shifted her eyes back to the injection site and found only a small remnant of trickled blood.

Her lungs felt pressurized, and she made a conscious effort to breathe gently for fear they'd crack. It was then the heat from her blood vessels reached her heart, where it seemed to reach a boiling point, pushing curdles of what felt like burning lava into her chest cavity and down to her abdomen, too much for her to contain. She bellowed out a cry she didn't recognize, grinding the noise between clenched teeth as her body seized, internal organs turned to char. It went on for what seemed like hours. She convulsed involuntarily, her lungs opening and filling with a boiling liquid, drowning her.

"You should be starting to feel the effects," Luther said calmly as he squinted at the vitals monitor.

She made eye contact with him as he readjusted the sensors on her chest. He seemed suddenly struck by something in her eyes.

And then, nothing. There was darkness, stillness, silence. At first, it was a comfort, a relief even, but then she felt anxiety set in. She couldn't breathe. She couldn't see. She couldn't move.

There was nothingness for an exceedingly long period of time--so long that she wondered if this was what death was like. Other faiths believed in something called purgatory, the wait before judgment to determine if a soul was worthy to pass into Heaven. She knew her dad didn't believe in the "flames of judgement," they'd had lengthy conversations about most topics related to faith and the Bible, but she wondered if this was believers of it imagined purgatory to be like, waiting in nothingness until judgement.

It was just as she began to accept her confinement that heat engulfed her. She could almost see the flames surrounding her, never quite touching her skin.

It was when the chill broke through that she felt her senses reactivating. She heard the shifting of fabric before she felt it around her. She felt a warm patch on her face before she concluded that it was Luther's large hand resting there. She heard the trickle of coffee in the kettle before she smelled it.

When she took her first deep breath, she could taste a burnt, scorched flavor on her tongue. She let her eyes open slowly and she silently scanned over her arms, her torso.

Luther placed his hand on her chin and pulled gently upward, shining a pin light into each of her eyes. She waited until he was finished before fumbling desperately for the controller button to lower the footrest on the recliner.

"*Shh*—stay put for a minute. Get your bearings. You'll probably feel weak."

She took a gulp of air, as though breaking the surface of water, her breaths shaky and uneven. She watched him carefully tug the tape from her arm and slip the needle from the IV out of her skin.

"Esther, you're OK," he said reassuringly. "Take it slow."

She waited until the footrest clicked into its starting position before bolting out of the chair. She had been covered with a patchwork quilt she decided he'd brought with him, as it didn't go at all with the aesthetic of the room, which dropped to the floor. She dragged it halfway across the room on her foot before bending and picking it up. She froze, recognizing the blanket from his mother's house, experiencing a sudden, vivid memory of his mom—Loretta, but she called herself LoLo—tucking her beneath it to go to sleep.

Essie tenderly placed the quilt on the side arm of the couch, slow to release her hand from the fabric. Her fingers trembled.

Her chin lifted and she examined the interior of the apartment. It felt like years since she'd first seen her surroundings. She grasped onto a dining chair for support.

"Do you know where you are?"

"The vacation rental without a view," she answered automatically, swallowing hard, trying to establish a steady rhythm to her breathing. "How long have I been here?"

"I figured your system had changed since you were young, though I wasn't sure in what way. Children have faster metabolisms, but then again--" he began to explain.

"So, you're saying it took longer? *How long*?" Her eyes darted to the appliances in the kitchenette. She narrowed her eyes on the coffee machine, which claimed a time of 12:04. She wasn't sure if it was AM or PM due to poor natural lighting.

"You've been here 6 hours."

She nodded, narrowing her eyes. "So, it worked."

He lifted his eyebrows in relief. "It did." He approached her cautiously. "How do you feel?"

Esther realized she was zeroing in on the smell of the coffee brewing. The aroma had dimension--an earthy undertone with a robust, comforting glaze resulting from the roasting process. It had been ground into a fine dust. She could pick up on a slightly bitter burnt taste in the brew as the water seeped through the grounds, dripping into the pot below. "You should use a medium grind instead of fine to cut the bitterness in your coffee."

His eyes darted across the room, but he spoke slowly, somewhat amused. "I'll keep that in mind for next time."

She squeezed her hands into fists, then released them, and rolled her shoulders. "Are you hungry? I could eat," she said abruptly. She started for the door without waiting for an answer, the image of a pizza shop storefront a block away coming to mind.

The stairs proved more difficult than she had anticipated. She tripped multiple times, once stumbling forward and nicking her chin on a concrete step. Finally, she allowed Luther to act as a crutch for her, wrapping her arm around his.

The pizza shop was only still open because it was finals week at the nearby college. The owner said this in justification for their scaled-back menu and to deter them from trying to order a specialty item.

"What do you have ready to go?" Esther asked, peering behind him into the kitchen.

"Pepperoni or cheese. Large only."

"One of each would be fine."

"One for each of you then?" the owner asked, amused, punching a few buttons on the register. One of the teenagers working in the kitchen slid two large boxes across the counter, smiling flirtatiously at Esther, who was hunched over the counter taking long inhalations of the pizza through a gap in the box.

Luther stepped forward and paid with cash, grabbing a few bottles of water from the drink cooler, despite having stocked the fridge with electrolyte drinks. By the time he'd turned back to the counter, Esther had a slice of floppy cheese pizza out of the box and was folding it in half as she wandered out the door, staggering a bit on the uneven sidewalk.

"She's on something good, huh?" One of the cooks said, amused.

Luther grabbed the boxes, stowing the drinks under his arm, and chased her out into the crosswalk, where she was pointing out the shape of the night clouds.

"It smells like it's going to rain," she remarked, taking another bite of pizza.

When they reached the steps for the rental, she turned suddenly, craning her neck, as if she'd spotted someone familiar down the street.

"Do you see someone you know?"

"You know, I bet they took the photo from the top of the steps with a zoom lens toward the mountains." She made a circle with her hand and peered through it as though it was a telescope. She lost interest quickly and took the steps at a brisk, careless pace, though she kept a tight hold on the handrail. He was more than a little surprised when she made it down the stairs without falling. She did, however, collide with the door, unable to hit the brakes fast enough at the bottom of the stairs. Once there, she tapped in the code with casual precision, forehead pressed into the door.

She spilled into the apartment, finally able to stabilize her footing a few steps inside.

"Esther?" She was already plopping onto the couch cross-legged.

"Are you're *OK*?"

"Yeah. Just very, very hungry. For having an Italian dad, I've only had pizza on rare occasions," she said, her eyes wide and unblinking. "Hey, is it OK if we eat over here? I'll do my best not to spill."

"It's fine," he breathed, stepping around and placing the boxes on the coffee table.

She immediately lifted the lid on the top box, threw in her crust, and claimed another slice.

Luther placed a slice on one of the provided plates and sat down on the opposite end of the couch slowly, cautiously. The room had an eerie silence. His brain reeled the possible explanations for her strange behavior. Perhaps there was some chemical reaction in her body, some surplus that was giving her this drunken persona? Whatever it had been, she seemed to have settled considerably, starting her third slice of pizza after retrieving her rejected crust from the box. "So, I guess the next step will be to run another test and extract some plasma while you're recovering."

She was frozen in her reaction, the color draining from her face. She stared at him blankly, the pizza slice hanging loosely in her hand, the grease from the cheese starting to slide downward.

"Essie?"

"You can't tell my dad what we're doing," she said quickly, her gaze intensifying. Her eyes were not their usual bright silver. Her pupils were exceptionally large, but the irises seemed to be speckled with globs of muddy brown.

Luther frowned. "He knows already though, right?"

"I know. Just don't share unnecessary details."

He nodded, hesitating. "Esther, you don't have to do this again."

Her eyes sharpened, the pupils narrowing. "Yes, I do."

"We don't even know if we'll be able to generate anything from your blood."

"But you'll try?"

He sighed. "If you still want me to."

She nodded.

"OK," he said, dropping his chin, and abandoning the uneaten slice of pizza on the end of the coffee table.

She sat back in her seat, blindly taking another large bite of pizza.

"Can you remember what the test was like? You were so quiet."

"*Like being burned alive, drowned, and ripped apart in a space vacuum all at the same time.*"

At one point her heart felt like it would burst from the pressure. She wouldn't have been surprised if he had told her she had been in the wrath of the experiment for days, weeks. The time dragged on seemingly without end--and yet, it had been less than six hours. Her record had shown the same experiment had taken her 13 hours to overcome fully as a baby. She tried to imagine the terror of a child experiencing the same thing for twice as long, but she realized quickly that she didn't want to imagine it.

Against her attempt to block it, she could hear the echo of a scream in her ears--a blood-curdling, shaking scream growing hoarse with desperation, produced in the naivety that someone would eventually come to her rescue. Her brain suddenly made the connection between herself and the photos, the videos that had made the rounds on social media recently of a toddler bound at the waist, knees, and wrists to a metal table, her skinny legs bare and bruised, her face masked beneath a pillowcase, her fingers and toes unfathomably dwarfed in size by the nearby tools and equipment. It was blasted on the televisions at train stations, reporters dismissing the images as a hoax. Some forensic digital experts claimed it to be computer-generated. Politicians matter-of-factly stated that the footage was certified to have been from a Russian hacker, which had allowed them to segue into proposing sanctions against the country. Some claimed it was footage taken from a movie that the government had the good sense to ban, hence why no one had ever seen it.

She knew it was real—and with a paralyzing surrealism—she knew it was her.

Esther shook herself back to awareness, her ears filling with the sound of a delivery truck backing up outside. She dropped the pizza onto the top of the box, brushing the cornmeal bits off her fingers like they were insects. She sat back on the couch, her heart lurching in her chest, and as much as she tried to fight it, found herself choking on sobs.

12
half-life

"I was told I might find a girl named Esther Natale here?" Josh asked, his eyes scanning the labyrinth of a gym.

The racerback tank-wearing gym attendant raised a thick eyebrow. His body appeared to be in a permanent state of flexion, muscles testing the resilience of his brown, heavily tattooed skin.

"She's in the ring."

"I beg your pardon?"

"MMA. We call it Fight Club. Center ring," he said, motioning toward the slightly more illuminated boxing ring that had acquired a handful of spectators.

"Thanks—wait. MMA?"

"Mixed martial arts. You asked about Esther? Young, fine ass Esther, not 90-year-old 2-pound dumbbells Esther, right?"

He chuckled. "The first one."

"Well, that's where you'll find your girl, Bro."

Josh stepped through the free weights and cardio equipment, his eyes fixed on the two forms in the ring. He watched the movements of the pair and focused on the wavy-haired brunette, who seemed to be the amateur, her movements rigid and a bit clumsy in comparison to the fluid artistry of her opponent, whose sleek honey brown hair bounced rhythmically with her motions.

He watched as the opponent beckoned Esther closer. She dropped into a frog stance when she did and swept her long leg in a large circle, causing Esther to trip and fall backward. There were cheers of encouragement and before he knew it, both had rejoined at the center. Esther managed to land a right hook, but her opponent used the leverage she gained by grasping her shoulder at the moment of impact to throw her over her back and fly toward the side of the ring. Her body slammed into the side ropes, the force of which caused her to ricochet backward. As Esther slid across the floor, the opponent leaped into the air, landing in a perfect straddle position over Esther's chest. For a moment it looked like she was going to thrust the heel of her hand into Esther's throat, but she stopped short, and cheers erupted.

The opponent jumped up and bounced away. Josh stepped toward the edge of the ring hoping to catch Esther's attention as she stood, planning to greet her with some words of encouragement. It was as he closed the distance and his vision became more refined that he noticed the girl being pulled to her feet didn't look a thing like Esther. Her face was too round, and her eyes were narrow and brown with short, thick lashes. She was taller than he would have expected based on how the fight unraveled. She was at least a few inches taller than Esther, who he discovered was removing her padded helmet on the opposite side of the ring. She tapped knuckles with a coach, who alerted her of Josh's presence, nodding toward him.

Esther turned quickly, her ponytail swishing with the motion. Her silver eyes brightened in the split second before she bounded in his direction, throwing herself into the cords.

"I didn't think you'd be here until tomorrow," she breathed heavily, her smile wide and genuine as she balanced herself on the cords.

"We got back early. I thought I'd surprise you."

"Well, you did," she said, swinging her leg between the parallel ropes and guiding the rest of her body through.

He offered his hands to help lift her down and she obliged.

She immediately wrapped her arms around his neck. "Oh, I'm happy you're here."

Neither seemed in a hurry to let go, Josh breathing in the scent of her warm, salty skin.

"Oh, I just realized I'm really gross and sweaty," she said, pulling away. "I'm sorry."

"I honestly couldn't care less."

Her smile broadened. "You regained some muscle." She extended an arm to his bicep, one eyebrow jumping suggestively. "A lot of muscle."

"MET training is a lot more grueling than Mandatory. Better food."

She reached up and tousled his hair. "Better haircuts, too," she teased, her cheeks rosy from exertion. "I'm never buzzing that head again so don't ask." She broke eye contact, looking slightly uneasy.

He regretted not grabbing her in their playful way when she touched him, pulling her to him, and kissing her. Oh, how he wanted to kiss her. Now it felt as though the moment had passed. "Your dad called it a pompadour? I'm not sure if that was a compliment."

"You saw my dad already?"

"Yeah, he was at my folks' new place playing cards."

Her smile briefly faded. "Pompadour was a women's hairstyle centuries ago and then Elvis Presley made it stylish for men."

"*Who's* Elvis?"

"You're kidding, right? *All Shook Up, Heartbreak Hotel, Suspicious Minds, Burnin' Love?*"

He furrowed his brow.

Esther pulled up her lip and dropped her voice several octaves. "Thank you. Thank you very much." She broke into a smile again. "Seriously?"

He grinned. "Actually, I know exactly who he is, I was just thinking I could get you to sing. The impersonation was spot on though."

"I feel such regret for him for what his last memory must have been," she said quickly, her face falling. She waved the thought off. "Sorry. So, you're here."

"I'm here."

"That means you don't have other plans, right?"

"Excellent reasoning skills, as always."

"If I wasn't so happy to see you, I might think you're being rude."

"But you're happy to see me."

"And I did hug you whilst being drenched in sweat so I guess we can call it even." She glanced over her shoulder. "Let me go shower off and change clothes? There's a great burger place a few doors down—maybe we can get a bite?"

She emerged from the locker room about ten minutes later wearing leggings and an oversized hooded top, tugging a heathered gray beanie over her damp, side braid. She smiled broadly upon seeing him. "I'm *so* hungry."

"Well, you certainly worked up an appetite," he remarked, turning with her toward the exit. "That was impressive."

A teenage boy, who looked no older than sixteen, with blonde spiked hair and broad, protruding shoulders rolled a sporty wheelchair toward them. "I presume this is the guy I've been hearing about?" One cheek featured a prominent dimple.

"Danny, this is Josh," Esther said with a warning tone. "Josh, this is Danny."

"Hi Josh," Danny said, extending a hand, sizing Josh up as he did. He turned to Esther conclusively. "Yeah, *he's* the guy, isn't he?"

"Don't you have something to bench press?"

Danny grimaced. "I wish. It's leg day."

"Just keep at it. Soon enough you'll have calves like Max." She nodded toward the gym attendant at the front desk.

Danny rolled his eyes. "You're sweet, Essie. A liar, but sweet. Next session at the Nest is Sunday, right?"

"We talked about Friday, right? Friday and then Sunday?

159

He pressed his lips together. "Yeah, I was afraid you were going to say that."

"It's fine, Danny. You know what you're doing."

"I don't like going behind Luther's back, Essie."

"It's not."

"There's a phrase: If it looks like a duck, quacks like a duck..."

"He'd shorten the time between sessions; he's just busy with other things."

"Friday, what time?"

"8?"

"You're sure you won't be busy?" he asked, lifting his eyes briefly to Josh. He turned back to Essie, who was glaring at him. "Fine. 8 o'clock. Weekly plea for you to talk to Luther," he said in a deceptively light tone.

Essie lifted her eyebrows. "I hear what you're saying, Danny."

"Do you though?"

She narrowed her eyes. "Enjoy the workout."

"Get some sleep, Essie. Or try to anyway." He spun his wheelchair toward the weight machines. "Nice to meet you, Josh."

The distinct smell of pine trees rushed to greet them as they stepped into the cool night air.

"Have I met Danny before?"

"No, not that I know of."

"I was thinking I remember meeting one of the kids from the Children's Ministry at Calvary who was in a wheelchair. I thought he was younger though."

"You're thinking of Thomas. He has his twin sister, Renee?"

"Thomas. That's right."

"Both Thomas and Danny are spikey-haired blondes in wheelchairs who lack censors," she said with a shrug. "Thomas is thirteen and Danny's seventeen so a little off with the age."

"What's Danny's story? Was he in an accident?"

"No, he was born with spina bifida, same as Thomas."

160

Josh frowned. "Ah. When did the two of you meet?"

"Me and Danny? When I started working with Luther last year, technically."

"Did you have a non-technical meeting?"

She shrugged. "Actually, yes. I doubt it counts though." She cleared her throat, dug her hands into the pouch on the front of her hoodie, staring at the ground immediately before her.

"I remember you talking about Thomas--most of the people from Calvary headed to the southern Ark though, right?"

"He and his family are the only ones who came up north."

"Oh, really?"

"Yeah, he didn't like the idea of high humidity," she said with a smirk.

"I can understand that."

She sighed as they continued down the sidewalk into the main stretch of town. "It's absolutely beautiful here, but I would love to see the ocean someday. That would have been the draw to the southern Ark for me."

Josh had been deployed for part of Mandatory to the west coast. His barracks were situated on an expansive beachfront that lacked any of the serenity travel stock images claimed. The beach was vast but artificial and littered with trash and cigarette butts, the water was frigid, and the horizon was nearly always hazy. Incidentally, he hated sand as well, how it made everything gritty.

"We'll go someday," he said confidently.

"You think so? With how things are going—" she let her voice trail off. "My dad went to Hawaii on his honeymoon. One of the quieter towns. He said it was really picturesque."

"It's weird to think of your dad being married."

She nodded, reflectively. "You don't remember his wife?"

Josh shook his head. He was four-years-old when Matteo's wife died. Matteo and Rachel had been childhood sweethearts, inseparable according to his dad. No one spoke about her except if Matteo happened to be visiting on what would have been her birthday or their wedding anniversary or the anniversary of her death. He knew this much about her: She was born on June 2nd and died on August 17th, just after her twenty-fourth birthday. Esther was the name she had picked out if they ever had a daughter. The one time he asked how she died, his mom's eyes had become sorrowful, and she had said something vague, that she had been through a lot, and it had taken a toll.'

"I'm glad he's here. Selfishly, I mean. The last time he looked at me that day at Calvary–it kind of haunted me."

Josh furrowed his brow, realizing he knew very little about the sequence of events that nearly took Essie's life. "That must have been a shock for them. You said the congregation thought you had died?"

She nodded lightly. "Renee won't speak to me. His twin sister? She's having a really hard time with everything."

"I may have asked this before, but why did they *have* to think you were dead?"

She sighed. "The attack was traumatizing enough for them. Everyone saw me—" She was only managing to sputter out a few words at a time, trying to string together an explanation. "—in a state— *incompatible* with surviving."

He processed her words for a few moments. "But wouldn't having you be alive be a relief to them?"

"Maybe at first, but there was concern about news getting out about it. I shouldn't have survived what happened. People might question how—"

"They wouldn't just accept that it was a miracle?"

"People tend to want to tell others about miracles. The thought was that I would be in danger."

He frowned, suddenly feeling very out of the loop. "I guess that makes sense."

Her eyes drifted off down the street and they walked in silence. Finally, she sighed, looping her arm around his. "Smells good here, doesn't it?"

"Well, I kind of miss the smell of dust and garbage, but this is nice, too."

She motioned toward the main intersection strung with globe lights. "Restaurant is just down this way."

This version of Esther was unexpected after their last encounter, when he first arrived at the northern Ark. Luther had managed to pull him from his assignment in Long Beach, along with a handful of other enlistees. The group made the journey from California to Montana under the guidance of two intimidating-looking men. His great uncle had been a member of special ops in the former military and these guys captured that essence—chiseled muscles, vague and impressive scars, quiet, unwavering confidence, and as demonstrated when a group of teenagers stupidly tried to mug them during a midnight train station stop, highly skilled at hand-to-hand combat.

The journey took a couple of days, but by the time they had arrived in the town, Josh had not only learned all about the training and purpose of the Mobilization & Extraction Team, or MET, but he had decided to join their ranks.

Esther had reacted poorly to this news, or rather, she seemed highly unsettled by it. All she had managed to verbalize was supportive, but there was an uncomfortably constricted manner to her behavior, her words. It was the first time in his life that he knew she wasn't being truthful with him. There had been palpable tension atypical for any room she occupied, as she tended to have a calming presence.

A year later, she had a different gait. She walked taller, and carried herself more confidently, with a defined, fit frame. She seemed rather content in the setting. So why did his parents seem more concerned about her now than ever?

"Teo is really worried about what Essie's gotten herself involved in," his dad had said in hushed tones mere moments after their greeting. He had limited information beyond that. Something about her having heightened immunity so they were having her test antidotes, but they were afraid of the effects this was having on her. She had fainted when she came over for Sunday dinner a few weeks earlier and never seemed to be available for any invitations since.

"Isn't it pretty here?" she asked rhetorically, tightening her hold on his arm.

The road had a modest collection of diagonally parked cars facing storefronts and restaurants, the sidewalks lined with trees and hanging flower baskets. Beyond the flagpole set at the far side of the street, the pavement appeared to run directly into a mountain.

"I didn't think these places existed outside of books."

"I can't wait to see this place at Christmas," she said, beaming. "I was told that they have lights all along here. There's a living Nativity, too."

He put a mental pin in his interrogation assignment, lured away by her enthusiasm. "I do miss Christmas—and not for the reasons I would have thought years ago. I remember things about Christmas I never knew I noticed."

"The warmth of the decorations, the lights, the smells."

He nodded slowly. "People breathe differently around Christmas. You have to move at a little bit slower pace, breathe in deeper to take it all in."

She took in the scenery as he spoke, pondering his observation.

"Is this the place you're talking about?" Josh asked, motioning toward the lively patio.

She startled, breaking from her thoughts. "Oh, yeah it is. Let's sit inside. It's a little chilly out here with damp hair."

They were seated at a cozy corner booth that had just been vacated. The wait staff were rushing to wipe the table as they sat down. Josh ordered a draft beer, while Esther stuck to water.

He glanced around appreciatively. Most of the tables were filled with people laughing, peering up at monitors showing reruns of games from years prior. He appreciated the liveliness, the general merriment. Outside the boundaries of the would-be Arks, he had started to recognize an eerie excess of breathing room.

Josh watched the bartender scanning through programming options to replace the game that had just ended. He noticed how quickly Essie's eyes shifted to the screen when the State of the Union Address came on, the menacing voice of Samuel Gowon booming through the restaurant. The President was simulating feelings of sadness, reaching behind his vintage half-frame glasses to dab at his eyes. He apologized to the Congressional members in attendance, who fawned adoringly as he motioned behind him to Speaker of the House, Annette Gibbons.

"It's a challenging time for our country, there's no doubt about it," he said, shaking his head. "I've been asked, *Sam*, what gets you out of bed in the morning? How do you–" He paused to raise a dramatic fist. "-- keep keeping on? How do you stay motivated to keep fighting the good fight? To them, I say: the American people." He paused, nodding slowly. "Even when it's difficult, I know the great people of this country are counting on me. They are the reason I chose to get into public service. It's about the people." He paused again, glancing around the room. In a complete mood shift, he peered over his shoulder with inquisitive playfulness. "I'm also so tremendously blessed to have the best woman in the world at my side–to support me, to challenge me, to put me in my place quite frankly."

A few people in the crowd chuckled.

"To inspire me. I am endlessly inspired by this woman."

The camera zoomed in on Speaker Gibbons, who smiled a poised, closed-lip smile.

Josh shook his head as the bartender switched to a hockey game. "Can't stand that woman."

Essie continued to stare at the screen blankly, her brow deeply furrowed, her breaths heavy.

"Ess?"

She jumped slightly in her seat.

He lifted his eyebrows. "Are you okay?"

"Gibbons and Gowon are a couple now?"

"Married. Very hush-hush."

She lowered her eyes, swallowing hard.

"Ess?"

She shook herself to awareness. "Are you staying with your parents?"

He tensed at the sudden change of topic. "For now. I'm going to be traveling for the most part so there's no point in me having a place yet."

"I have my own temporary socialist utopia housing assignment," she said a little flatly. He raised his eyebrows to see if there was more suggestive context to her words, however, her expression matched her tone.

"How will that all work? Money and things? When things go-active?"

She tugged out her hair tie, shaking her damp hair free. It cascaded over her shoulders in voluminous spiral curls. "It's a bit like starting a new country, I guess. I think the idea is that it will take time to get started. It's not really my area."

"What *is*—your area? I hear you've been busy."

Her eyes were fixed on the television screen, now displaying a hockey game.

"Essie?"

"Hmm?"

"What's your area? I hear you've been busy."

She nudged closer to him. "Can *this* be my area?"

Josh furrowed his eyebrows. He knew her well enough to know she was avoiding the subject of her work and he had to agree with his dad that her behavior was just *off*, but the simple act of having her so close was playing with his senses and blurring his thoughts. He turned her chin toward him. She looked uneasy suddenly with this assertiveness, pinching her eyebrows together. He decided against kissing her, pressing his lips together and tasting the oaty aftertaste of his beer instead.

It was then he noticed a looming figure standing before them and they were both startled.

"I don't want to intrude," the man said in a smooth voice. He was not nearly as intimidating as his presence seemed initially. He was a few inches shy of six feet, broad-shouldered, but average build otherwise. He carried a to-go bag and had a kind, tired face. "I'm Luther Graham. We haven't officially met yet, but am I correct in presuming you're Josh?"

Josh stood, politely extending his hand. "Oh. Wow. I've heard a lot about you."

Luther smiled humbly. "You as well."

All at once, it struck him that he was meeting the man who saved Essie's life when she was a child, though in the same moment, it hit him that he had no idea what he saved her from, where she lived, what she was subjected to. He tried to push through his blurred thoughts. "There aren't words to express--" Josh panned toward Esther. "If not for you--"

Luther waved him off. "You're all finished with MET training?"

"Yep. I've been on a few assignments already."

"Not much rest on the road," Luther remarked.

"Not too much."

"Well, thank you for the work you're doing."

"I'm happy to do it."

Luther's eyes drifted over to Essie. "Perhaps you'll have a chance to see the work Essie is doing while you're here." His voice lifted when he spoke her name, something that seemed to catch both of their attention.

"If I can? I don't even know what you've been working on."

Essie narrowed her eyes at Luther.

"Thomas said Friday night was when you're working next?" Josh asked, recognizing the tension that had thickened the air.

Luther frowned but maintained a calm demeanor. "I thought we decided on Sunday night to allow you enough recovery time?"

Josh's heart twisted at the words 'recovery time.'

"Are you feeling up for Friday?" Luther asked rhetorically.

"Yes," she said quietly.

"Josh, can you make it on Friday?"

He nodded. "I don't see why not."

"Well, then that's settled. I don't want to take up any more of your evening though. You two enjoy."

As Josh returned to his seat, he noticed that Essie was sitting more rigidly at the table, taking some stiff breaths.

"So, you and Danny work together?"

"Yeah, he's part of the Phoenix Initiative. Well, he backs up Luther. Usually, he works with the tech gurus of the Ark."

"The Phoenix Initiative?"

Essie helped herself to a swig of his beer and grimaced. "Wow, that is so not worth whatever buzz it provides."

"Buzz?"

"Well, isn't that what alcohol does? It numbs your brain a bit?"

"I suppose that's sort of the feeling. Is that what you're going for? Because this probably isn't the best choice of beverage."

"Sometimes it'd be nice, but it's not an option for me."

"Because of your work?" There was something in how he said the word that sounded accusatory to him.

To Essie, too, it seemed. She stared toward the kitchen for a long enough period of time that he turned in his seat to see what could be so interesting. "My dad said something to you?" she asked tensely.

"It was *my* dad actually."

She nodded. "They don't know anything about what I'm doing, Josh."

"Maybe that's why they're worried."

Their food arrived, but even after the server left, Essie didn't move to eat. She had her arms crossed, her breathing shallow.

"I'm sorry, I'm just feeling off," she said finally. "I'm not sleeping much." She was silent as she picked at the steak fries on her plate, then suddenly muttered: "You know, for being a friggin' orphan, I've certainly acquired several overprotective father figures."

His mouth fell slightly ajar.

Her shoulders sank. "It wasn't necessary for me to phrase it that way." Esther buried her face in her hands, rubbed roughly at her face, then winced. "I probably shouldn't have done that with greasy fingers."

He reached for a clean napkin off the pile and dunked part of it in his water glass, blotting at the shiny section of skin near her eye.

"Thank you," she said, her tone lighter as she took the wet napkin and did a quick, all-over wipe.

Josh took the opportunity to munch on some fries, hoping to tread into some lighter conversation topics. "Well, you've spent a few blissful REM cycles in the nook of my arm. I wouldn't mind helping you get some shut eye."

Her lips pulled up at the corners, her cheeks deepening. "Mr. West," she said in a slow southern drawl, fanning at her face. "You're fixin' to give me the vapors with talk like that."

He smirked. "The accent works."

"Southern phrases are interesting. That one sounds kind of flirty, but I think it just means sweating profusely."

"Would you rather I not stay with you?" he asked, furrowing his brow. "I don't want to presume—"

"I'm already envisioning stroking your pectoral muscles as I try to doze off," she replied, straightening her posture, her lips turning upward persistently. "*That* was flirty."

He stopped mid-chew. "*You* are a pastor's daughter."

"*Through your shirt*," she clarified emphatically, her cheeks tightening. "Honestly, Josh, it would be rude if I didn't introduce myself to your new muscles. I wasn't raised to be rude."

Josh nodded repeatedly, trying to keep from laughing, but ended up dropping the burger on his plate, his throat seized by dueling needs to laugh and swallow simultaneously.

"Drink your disgusting beer," she said, encouragingly.

When he'd composed himself, he reached for her hand. He kissed her fingers. "I'm sorry I was gone for so long. Obviously the time apart has had some ill-effects on you."

169

"I've gotten *real* weird, Josh."

He cringed.

"Weird-er."

He gave a shrug of agreement.

"You should stay with your parents though. It's more proper. They'd be thrilled to have you."

He made a superhuman effort not to look disappointed.

"*Although*, and I'm just arguing the other side, *to be fair*," she said thoughtfully, taking a bite of her burger, the juices dribbling down her chin. "I'd like you to stay with me."

He grinned, pressing a spare napkin against her chin, amused when it adhered to her skin. "My pectoral muscles would like that, too."

"Well, now you're letting your physique go to your head, Josh." She wiped at her face, then grabbed another spare napkin, tucking it into her neckline like a bib. "That's a really unappealing quality."

*   *   *

"You made it," Luther greeted from the small wooden kitchen, just pouring a cup of coffee. He took a sip black, then pinched his face. "I'm out of sugar."

"Yeah, it took me a while to get adjusted to plain coffee," Josh said.

"It's one of those former first-world problems that I'm struggling with the most."

"I'll be right out," Essie said, marching to the bathroom, side-eyeing Luther as she crossed the room.

"Did she explain a bit about the process?"

"She did," Josh said with a sigh. "Still taking it in."

"It's a lot to wrap your mind around."

"She warned me that it can look worse than it is."

Luther stared at him blankly, then said: "Well, *she'd* be the expert."

"How long does it take?"

"That depends on the bio-agent."

Josh gulped, uneasy with the term. "What are you using?"

"Cyanide."

Josh chuckled nervously. "You're kidding."

Luther shook his head. He glanced up to see Esther exit the bathroom. She was not amused by what she'd overheard.

"It's one of the quickest recovery times for you," he offered as justification.

They both knew why he had chosen it: He wanted a brutal scene for Josh to witness so he'd convince her to stop.

Luther led the way to his study where Essie sat automatically in the large leather recliner in the corner, putting up the footrest. There wasn't a need to prepare much at the beginning; Luther had hours before he would need to extract her blood.

"You can have a seat, Josh," Luther told him, motioning to a pair of club chairs. "I'll sit with you in just a couple minutes."

Josh's motions were stiff as he situated himself in a chair. He immediately stood up again. "I'm sorry, is there something I can be doing?"

Luther shook his head silently, turning Esther's arm over so he could do the injection.

"How does it work?" he asked. "Sorry, I don't want to be an imposition."

"It's a lot to wrap your mind around," Luther echoed in a patient tone.

"Yes."

"Cyanide prevents cells from using oxygen to make energy molecules. Heart muscle cells and nerve cells require oxygen to function. When they don't have it, they quickly use all their energy and start to die."

"But that doesn't happen with Essie, right? The antidote stops that process?"

Luther looked up at him over the rim of his glasses. "She experiences the same process of cell death."

"Wait, *what*? Is there a backup I'd the antidote doesn't work?"

Luther blinked slowly, doing his best to internalize his thoughts. "She'll be fine, Josh."

"It's *cyanide*, right? You're injecting her with cyanide."

Luther cleared his throat.

Essie frowned. "Josh, I'll be fine."

Josh's eyes flashed to the syringe. He started to object again, but it was too late. The syringe was already plunged into the inside of Esther's elbow.

The trial run at the basement rental had been the only time she'd successfully restrained the outward physical effects. She had internalized the pain and the bacitractoxin had assisted by causing her body to stiffen. She had done 107 sessions with Luther now and he said her outward physical responses were getting more brutal to watch. She suspected this had something to do with her adding a session per week with Danny's assistance over the past three months. She no longer felt fully recovered before the next session and she felt the effects more intensely.

Hence, it was not overly surprising that within moments of the cyanide reaching her bloodstream, Esther felt her entire body contract. Her chest began to pulsate, and she was having a difficult time breathing. She watched Josh move toward her, his eyes wide and anxious.

She squeezed her eyes shut.

13
first

three weeks earlier...

Esther inhaled deeply as the VR goggles took her inside the West's kitchen. She anticipated the smell of baked goods, pies in particular, but the Ark's version of the Sim didn't yet have the full sensory experience. She had seen this memory enough to know what to expect, but it always struck her with a poignant realization each time that the first pleasant memory the Sim had stolen from Gabe was her fourth birthday.

Gabe had lived nearly six years before even meeting her and, in the time, since there were more days each year that they were apart than together, but still, when the Sim prompted him to think of something that brought him happiness, he had thought of her first.

She celebrated every one of her birthdays, starting at age four, at the West's farm. The idea of a birthday was a foreign concept to her; her dad hadn't even known her birthdate until Luther checked in after she'd been with him for several months and her third birthday had already passed. Had it not been for Sara West's insistence, her fourth birthday may have slid by with little hoopla and Esther wouldn't have minded a bit. Instead, Sara stayed up until all hours the night before, dressing the house with yellow streamers and horse decorations. She had offered to bake a "horse cake," but Esther had been absolutely horrified by the idea of *baking a horse*. Many of Sara's ideas were lost in translation so eventually,

Sara took her husband Luke's suggestion to stop getting input from a preschooler.

On September 2nd, there was a pile of gifts wrapped in glossy paper dressed with an excess of curling ribbon covering the kitchen table when Esther padded downstairs for breakfast. She looked uncertain as Sara rushed to embrace her and wish her a happy birthday, her silver eyes very round. Free from her, Esther smiled broadly upon seeing her dad and giggled when he hoisted her into the air. He kissed her on the cheek, intending to place her back on the floor, but she wrapped her arms around him so he'd continue holding her.

"That's right. It's your *birthday*, isn't it?" Matteo said toward her cheek conspiratorially.

She shrugged.

"And I thought all those presents were for me."

She rested her head on his shoulder.

"Yeah, did you see all the presents?" Sara asked, moving quickly to the kitchen table to show them off like a game show model.

"What are those?"

"Those are your birthday presents."

"What's a present?"

"Presents are surprises people give you. Remember you went to the party for Angela, and we bought her a building set?"

She nodded.

"And *Christmas*?" Sara assisted.

"Of course. Remember all those presents under the Christmas tree?"

"So, we share these?"

"No, these are all for you."

"*Why*?"

"Because we're celebrating that you were born today four years ago."

She twisted her face. "We're having a party *for me*?"

"Yep. We can do whatever you want today," he said with building enthusiasm.

"Wait. So, all of those presents are for me?" she asked again, turning to survey the gifts.

"They are."

"Really?" she squealed quietly, then added: "Are you sure? It's a lot. I'll share them with the other kids at church."

"That's very kind, if you'd like to do that. How about breakfast first?"

Appreciating a consistent routine, Esther asked for her usual eggs and toast as she climbed from Matteo's arms to her normal breakfast spot at one of the island bar stools.

"Sweetie, I'll make you anything you'd like," Sara offered in a cheery, doting voice, leaning across the tiled surface. She eyed the small girl's nest of morning hair, her face longing to brush it. "Would you like waffles? I can make them with fresh whipped cream and drizzle some syrup. I can put chocolate chips in if you'd like?" She raised her eyes to Matteo, who was sliding on the bar stool, to get his approval.

He shrugged. "I think waffles might be a new thing for you, huh Esther? They're really yummy though. I couldn't tell you the last time I had them."

"You've never had waffles, Essie?" Josh asked, perplexed. He finished his swig of orange juice while standing at the open refrigerator door. "How is that *possible*?"

Essie's eyes narrowed slightly at him, but she said nothing.

"Don't drink from the container," Sara scolded.

"I'm finishing it," he replied.

"Mom makes the best waffles, so Essie wasn't missing much," Gabe said from his place behind the birthday presents, rubbing roughly at the corners of his eyes. As soon as Matteo vacated his place to get coffee, Gabe rose to his feet and took the counter spot next to Esther. It was a strange thing to have the perspective of the memory be through Gabe's eyes. Danny described it as feeling like a first-person video game. She couldn't see Gabe (unless he happened to look in a mirror), but she got to see the world through his eyes. At this moment, she saw herself at the age of four, unruly curls framing her soft, youthful face, smiling fondly at him.

Josh rounded the kitchen counter, glaring at Gabe, appearing to be eyeing the stool on the other side of Essie.

"So, everyone's good with waffles?"

"Only if they're chocolate chip," Luke said, flinging open the front door. Gabe had spun around abruptly. His dad was already coated in a layer of dirt, his plaid shirt sleeves cuffed to just below the elbow. There was a rumble as he kicked off his boots by the front mat.

Gabe turned back to his mom. Sara had wheeled around, appearing satisfied to see that her husband's boots were already removed. He walked heavily toward the kitchen and Sara's lips turned upward as he approached.

"For the birthday girl," he said softly, presenting Esther with a small bouquet of yellow and pink wildflowers.

She gazed at them, her eyes brightening, her velvety lashes blinking in disbelief. "Wow. Thank you, Uncle Luke. It's the best day *ever*."

He kissed her lightly on the side of her head, clutching at his chest. "I never thought I'd have such an adorable child call me 'Uncle Luke,'" he said dramatically as he rounded to his wife. "No offense, Sara, but our nieces and nephews better have *fantastic* personalities when they grow up."

She play-smacked him but accepted a kiss, at which point, he pulled a slightly smaller bouquet from behind his back for her.

"It had to be smaller than the birthday girl's," he explained with a shrug. Gabe had turned his attention to Essie, who was taking a long inhalation of the flowers that likely had no discernible smell to them. She held the bouquet to Josh's nose, who had made his way to the other side of her. He smiled sweetly, nodding in agreement that he'd never smelled such nice smelling flowers.

"We'll have to show you the field where these grow," Gabe told Esther, leaning in close. "During certain times of the year it's flowers as far as the eye can see."

She turned to face him, her eyes widened. "Can we go there *now*?"

"Maybe later today if you want."

She nodded enthusiastically, holding the bouquet just under her nose again, her smile tight, her eyes shimmering. "This is the *best* day," she said with a sigh.

"Well, I'm happy to hear that," Luke remarked, placing a hand on each of her cheeks. "Anything I can do to make it better, you just let me know."

"Careful there, Luke," Matteo warned with a chuckle over his cup of coffee. "She'll try and shake you down for a puppy."

Esther grinned. "That was *one* time, Daddy."

"What? You won't get her a puppy?" Luke chided, stepping next to Gabe. He lowered his voice for only him to hear. "I thought I'd get you to help me this morning, but you seemed to have your hands full this morning?"

Gabe's eyes panned quickly to Esther.

"What do you mean?" Sara asked, appearing suddenly over Luke's shoulder.

"Oh nothing," Luke replied, sipping his coffee. He rotated his chin back to his son, let his eyes dash to Esther and back, smiling. "In a few years, it might be a different story, but I believe your intentions at the moment are honorable."

Matteo cleared his throat and raised an eyebrow at Luke.

"Don't worry, Dude," Luke whispered to Gabe. "I'll put in a good word for you with her old man." He held out his fist and waited for Gabe to bump it with his own before he and Matteo moved toward the living area space.

"Here, Sweetie. I'll put them in water," Sara offered, taking the bouquet of wildflowers from Essie and arranging them in a mason jar.

Esther watched the process closely, examining to be sure each stem touched water.

"Is it going to be a little while for breakfast, Mom?" Josh asked, surveying the counters and the lack of prepared foods.

"It is."

"Then I'll be back."

"It's Essie's birthday," she said in a hushed tone.

Gabe lifted his chin toward his mom and brother.

"She's busy anyway," he pleaded, motioning to Esther, who was starting to climb down from the chair.

Sara tossed her hands in the air. "Fine."

Esther glanced up as Josh thundered up the stairs but continued toward the family room. Gabe watched as she retrieved a book from the shelves, and he moved automatically toward the couch. A few moments later, she had climbed up on the couch and was nestled up against him. She eagerly opened the cover and slid the book toward him.

"I thought she was sleeping better," Matteo whispered just over Gabe's shoulder.

"Well, if it makes you feel better? She seemed to be sleeping *very* soundly," Luke remarked with a grin. "Oh, *relax*, Teo. They're kids."

Luke's last words echoed in Esther's ears as she took in the simple joy of the moment. Her arms felt warm—or rather, Gabe's arms felt warm, holding her close as he read to her.

Darkness enveloped her again—and then there was silence, but it wasn't a peaceful silence. It was the sort of silence that wasn't quiet at all. Her heart began to race. She knew what this lull, this lack of imagery meant:

The memory was being deleted.

The way it had been explained to her was that first enlistees would be prompted to remember pleasant memories, triggered by a number of smells, sounds, and images. They were typically given a drug to numb their inhibitions and defenses. The Simulator allowed the full 4D experience of memories and when the individual found themselves in a memory, the brain mapping would begin. The device would allow the memory to play out, mapping out the neurons impacted, locating the storage centers for all the parts that made up the memory. Once enough information was collected, the Simulator would shut off all stimulants, needing the individual's brain quiet for the process of applying electrical surges to those specific storage centers. The process was a lot more technical, but Danny had elected to use "layman's terms" to explain it to Esther. He had tried to liken it to deleting a digital file on a hard drive, but with her limited experience with computers and technology, the analogy wasn't exactly helpful.

The goal of these particular Sim sessions was to neutralize the "feel-good" receptors. In the same way ibuprofen neutralizes pain receptors in the brain, the intent was to neutralize happy memories, so they no longer brought pleasant feelings. Danny had added reluctantly that with some people, the Simulator tended to over-correct.

"Meaning?"

"*Meaning*," he had begun, taking a significant exhalation. "They eliminate the memory altogether and anything connected to the memory."

The playbacks of Gabe's sessions didn't allow for the full experience for her to feel exactly what he felt as the contraption sent electrical pulses into his brain, but she had watched video footage of others during the procedure, and it looked excruciating.

As she waited for the inevitable counter-experience –the operators typically triggered a positive memory or two, completed the neocortex torture, then followed up with some very distressing imagery of civil unrest and a call to action–Esther thought of the exchange between Luke and her dad. She knew, of course, what they were discussing. At home, she struggled to sleep quite a bit. Her dad would find her awake at all hours of the night. At the farm, however, she slept consistently every night.

From the very first trip Esther made with her dad out to the farm, the sleeping arrangements had been the same: Gabe and Josh would bunk together in Josh's room, Esther would take Gabe's room, and Matteo typically slept in the downstairs den. It was nearly impossible to climb the stairs without waking someone, so Matteo wasn't able to check in on her as he did at home. He just assumed she slept better there since she hadn't come to find him, and he hadn't heard her moving around upstairs. If he *had* checked on her, he'd know that days after their initial trip to the farm began, she had convinced Gabe to return to his room to snuggle with her. After a few nights of this, Gabe had fallen into the routine without prompting.

Watching the scene unfold, Esther couldn't remember ever feeling concerned about the situation being put to an end. When Gabe had mentioned that he might have to stay in with Josh if any of the grownups found out, she remembered feeling bewildered. It just made good, logical sense for them to continue sharing a bed if they both slept better. Her mind didn't comprehend any impropriety, not at the age of four–or twelve, when her dad finally did put a stop to it.

The images flashed all around her quicker than in prior sessions, but the sounds, the colors, and the imagery were all the same propaganda. There were protests and random burning buildings, babies screaming, gunshots–then all was silent, and Danny's voice emerged in her ears: "You know the rest by now, right? 'You can make a difference. You can help create a world of peace, equity, prosperity, something else with an 'e' sound–' They talk a lot of 'you' when their whole objective is to make people mindless sheep without feelings, don't you think?" He sighed. "Sorry. I shouldn't have said that."

"Can you show me WG009?"

Danny had his speaker button pressed so she could hear his prolonged sigh before he spoke. "Don't you think you've watched that one enough?"

Esther glared over at the tiny blue light positioned just to the right of her central vision and imagined looking into Danny's emerald eyes.

"Is this helping either of you at this point?"

There was already a heaviness in her chest, knowing what footage awaited her, but she raised her eyebrow at the camera, and a moment later, there was a hum as the session memory loaded.

14
reflection

Esther felt her fingers twitch first. She took in a breath, expecting the aroma of freshly brewed coffee to waft in her direction, but there was an antiseptic smell in its place. Her upper body felt unnaturally cold, despite the weight of a blanket on her chest. Her heart rate felt more rushed than usual, and she had an unyielding need to pee.

Her toes cracked as she flexed the muscles in her feet. When she arched her back, there were a half dozen pops in her spine as it realigned itself. Having bones break and muscles rip as a result of the sessions didn't startle her anymore.

She expected to feel Josh's hand over her own, or perhaps stroking her arm or whispering something reassuring to her, but the room was silent. As her eyes fluttered open, she found the silence was not for lack of company.

Josh had relocated the club chair to be beside her. He was sitting forward in the seat, watching her stir awake. He sighed, stood, and kissed her forehead.

Esther pushed up on her elbows, squinting at her surroundings. "Where's Luther?"

"He left about a half hour ago."

She tried desperately to ignore the urgency she felt to use the bathroom and instead focus on the meaning of his facial expression, but she found her eyes repeatedly drifting in the direction of the bathroom.

"He said you'd need to use the bathroom pretty desperately. I made him give you a lot of fluids."

"My legs aren't fully awake yet," she replied, wincing.

"Here," he said, encouraging her to wrap her arm around his neck. When she did, he scooped his arm under her knees and started across the room. There was a tension she could feel emitting from his pores, his muscles tight.

When they reached the bathroom, she felt the need to dismiss him as soon as possible. Despite the desperate subconscious request of her bladder to not utilize the undergarment during recovery, she feared she had, and her face had a dry, tight feeling, indicating she'd had a nosebleed along with some other unpleasant physical responses.

He was understandably unconvinced that she could manage by herself, but he obliged, gently leaned her against the vanity.

She waited until he left to turn on her heel, pull forcibly at her pants and undergarment, and sit on the toilet.

She emerged a few minutes later, face clean, clothing changed, her legs still tingling awake. Josh was standing, propped against the chair where she spent so many hours of her life. He stared straight ahead, his jaw tightly clenched, lost in his thoughts. She pleaded silently for him to look at her, regretting when he did. There was an obvious lack of sleep in his features, but also a genuine, soul-crushing sadness in his eyes. *Well played, Luther,* she thought but found blaming him didn't resonate very well.

She hadn't prepared Josh for this. She hadn't told him about her body's capabilities, what she'd been doing. He had no idea what he was walking into and that was her fault.

"Do you just get up and go home?" he asked stiffly.

She nodded.

"Are you hungry?"

"Yes, but—"

"There's a cafe close by," he interrupted, furrowing his brow. "Are you okay to walk or should I carry you?"

She chuckled nervously at the suggestion, but his stern expression was unwavering. "I can walk," she affirmed, though she knew it would be a struggle.

They navigated the sidewalk and crosswalk in silence. He said nothing about her unnaturally slow, cautious gait, though he walked on the street side and seemed on alert to catch her if she stumbled.

They were seated in silence. They received courtesy water glasses in silence. Josh spoke a few words to the waiter, asking for orange juice for her, and black coffee for himself, but said nothing directly to her.

"You're making me nervous, Josh," she finally said, once their beverages had arrived. "Please say something."

Interpreting her dropping the menu to the table as a signal that they were ready to order, the young waiter, who had shared in his introduction that his parents owned the diner, returned. "What can I get for you?"

"Ultimate breakfast platter, scrambled eggs, pancakes, sausage, English muffin with jelly, blackberry or grape, if you have it, and could I please get a side of the hash brown casserole?" She spilled out.

The waiter was unfazed and turned to Josh, who sat blinking at Esther.

"Do you really have steak?" he asked.

"Yes, sir."

"Then I'll have the steak and veggie omelet. The hash browns are good?"

Essie nodded enthusiastically as she gulped down her entire glass of water.

"Hash brown casserole. Please." He frowned after the waiter left, sliding his water glass in her direction.

"You *know*, I'd love to share a meal with you and pretend like everything's OK."

She leaned forward. "Incidentally, I don't share food after a session." She immediately regretted her words.

"*Don't*," he said gruffly. "Please don't make light out of what I just saw."

She took a deep breath. "I should have given you more warning about it. I *did* tell you it looks worse than it is."

He raised an eyebrow.

For all she knew, Luther had shared her description from her very first session: *Like being burned alive, drowned, and ripped apart in a space vacuum all at the same time.* She had not intended to say the words aloud.

"I want to respect what you feel like you need to do--"

"But?"

"That was excruciating to watch."

She became unsure of herself, fidgeting and repositioning in the booth. "It looks bad, I know."

"It looks bad because it *is, right*?"

She swallowed. "It's about what you would expect."

He nodded, clearly holding back more he wanted to say, his mouth twisting uncomfortably. "How many times have you been through that?"

He knew the answer. It was part of he and Luther's limited conversation that she had enough awareness yet to hear. "*Well*, each pathogen is different."

He raised his eyebrows.

"120."

His jaw tightened. "It must hurt. *A lot.*"

She gave a small nod.

"I don't suppose I could convince you to stop if I asked really nicely?"

"Are you doing that?"

He released a breath. "*Begging*, actually." His eyes were set on her, wide and disarming. "If I had known before–"

She leaned forward onto her arms, her shimmering eyes glistening with tears. "If you had known before, *what*?" she whispered.

He shook his head. "It doesn't matter now, I guess."

"We're doing so much good with it, Josh."

"Yeah, *at what cost*?" he nearly growled, clearly holding back tears now.

She sat back. "I'm fine, Josh. I'm at a diner about to eat four days' worth of calories, I'll sleep a bit, and then I'll be back to normal."

"In time for you to do another session?"

"I'm *fine*, Josh."

He mouthed the word fine and exhaled deeply. "What I saw, what I watched for *eleven hours*? Wasn't fine."

Essie sat back, keeping eye contact.

"How much of your life is spent doing this?"

"Right now, a lot, but it's important that we do this."

"I know that."

"I'll be taking a break soon anyway."

"Good," he said, but seemed to sense there was a reason outside the territory of acceptable. "Why though?"

"It was my bargaining chip with Luther."

"What was?"

"He's going to send a team in to get Gabe."

"*Wait.*" Josh looked angry suddenly. "You agreed to take a break *for Gabe*. When was the last time you even spoke to him?"

Her chest felt deflated. She turned her gaze to the window, willing the tears burning her eyes to evaporate. "Not *for* him. Luther wanted me to take a break."

"So, Gabe was *his* bargaining chip. Not yours."

Essie snapped her chin back to attention, glaring at him. "I guess it depends on how you look at it."

"I thought Luther said it was too risky to get Gabe?"

"He did."

"But now he's okay with it because he's that desperate for you to stop what you're doing?"

She dropped her shoulders.

"What does *that* tell you, Essie?" There was a bite to his words.

She shook her head, tensely turning to look out the window again. "That I have too many overprotective father figures for having been sold down the river by whatever degenerates share my DNA?"

This hostility toward her biological parents was new, like a big gaping wound she had only just developed awareness. She didn't want to feel it. She had a wonderful dad; she felt like she should just be grateful, but the more she learned about where she came from, the more she felt her anger build and contort.

When he spoke next, Josh made an outward effort to relax his posture, and use a gentle tone. "Have you *considered* the possibility that Gabe doesn't want to be rescued?"

She swallowed hard. "Yes."

"With the reconditioning and mind-warping they do, Ess," he began, wincing a little at the recollection of his only experience with the Sim, things he'd been told by other members of MET. "He may not be Gabe anymore."

"Yeah, but what if he is?"

He sighed, widening his eyes as he turned away.

"*Stop.*"

Josh raised his eyebrows. "Stop what?"

"Thinking whatever you're thinking about him. You're being unfair to him."

"How do you know that? Do you read minds now?"

"Your nostrils flare."

"My nostrils—" he repeated slowly, then lowered his voice. "If he's not Gabe anymore, we don't have a choice. He'd be a threat to everyone."

Esther let her eyes drift toward the clattering and sizzling noises emerging from the kitchen. "Josh, he's *still* Gabe."

"Ess–"

"Listen to me. Consider, just for a *minute* the possibility that I'm right."

He nodded.

"He's still Gabe, but they're making him—" Her voice broke.

"Making him what?"

She shook her head, her jaw tense.

"How do *you* know what they're doing?"

"Everything is recorded. With facial recognition, the software can isolate footage of him."

"Aren't those video data files protected? Tracked?"

"There are ways around that."

He raised his eyebrows.

"Danny's a computer guru and works on Security."

Josh nodded. "He covered when Luther had to leave for a while. Nice guy."

"Yeah, he is."

"He said he was a fellow 'lab baby,' that's why he was allowed to help 'torture' you."

Essie's jaw tightened.

Their plates arrived, but neither moved. Finally, Esther fixed her posture and started drizzling syrup onto her stack of pancakes.

"What did he mean?"

She sighed. "We've had a lot of poor segues in conversation, what topic are we currently arguing about?" She regretted the words as soon as they flew out of her mouth. "I meant that to be funny for some reason, but it sounded very angry."

"Well, you *are* clenching your jaw quite a bit. That's probably not helping your tone."

She gingerly touched her jaw, which ached from the pressure.

When he spoke again, his gentle tone seemed to take less effort. "What did he mean, Essie?"

She sliced through her pancake stack, exhaling deeply.

"It's me, Essie."

She finished loading up her fork, avoiding his gaze. "There's a lot to explain and I can't do it here."

"When we get back to your place—will you tell me then?"

She hesitated, then nodded.

188

His shoulders relaxed and he lifted his fork for the first time, taking in the sight of his food. "Is there something we've been arguing about that we can talk about here?"

"Is there only one gear for this breakfast conversation?" Essie asked, smirking slightly.

*   *   *

Essie's apartment was contemporary but fairly nondescript. The apartment building resembled something from the northeast coastal area with its white siding exteriors and tall, cone-shaped trees. The place had come furnished; nothing inside resembled anything she would have picked. The only giveaway that the apartment was occupied by her was the presence of books.

Essie dropped her keys next to an early edition of *Wuthering Heights,* which had a blood red slash mark over the fore-edge from when the library took it out of circulation. She had a desperate look on her face when she turned around, still slightly unsteady on her feet. "*First* of all," she declared. "Can you just look at me like you do for a second?"

"How do I look at you?" His stern facial expression broke as soon as he met a stretch of silence.

Her lips seemed to click into a smile the moment his expression did what she'd hoped. "That'll do." She closed her eyes, inhaling and exhaling deeply. When she opened her eyes again, she grabbed his hand, tugging him to sit on the couch with her. Josh found an adequate position immediately, but she made several attempts to get comfortable on the boxy teal cushion.

"What have you been told about the church attack?" she asked quietly.

"Mom said it was a biological weapon. Some sort of gas." He frowned, realizing he'd failed to ask even basic questions about how she survived.

She was silent for a moment, piecing together and rearranging the words in her mind. "Any way I try to explain what happened is going to make me sound crazy."

He shrugged. "Try me."

She took a deep breath and then found herself saying: "They rolled the canister inside—the canister that had the gas. It was the size of a small fire extinguisher. At first, I thought it was some sort of prank, but then I heard them jam the door. I had seven kids in my care and when the canister vent popped open, all I could think about was protecting them." Her eyes drifted toward the bookshelves. "There wasn't anywhere to go except the storage closet. The classroom–the windows are too small and too high–"

He nodded.

"I got the kids inside the storage room. There was a return vent that was pretty large–"

"The one with the raccoon family?"

"Recently evicted, yes. I told the kids to open it while I tried to seal up the door so the gas couldn't get to them." It occurred to her as she skimmed over the details that her last glance at their seven sweet, terrified faces would be the last time she would ever see most of them. Three years had already passed; she probably wouldn't recognize them anymore.

"Ess?"

They're all alive, she reminded herself silently. *That's what matters.* She cleared her throat, willing the tears away. "I got the door sealed–the tape didn't stay long, but I had blocked the gap at the bottom of the door.

"I couldn't escape the gas. It was starting to fill the room. I lost control over my body--it started spasming. At one point, I felt my spine snap and I fell to the floor. I could feel the pain down to my bones, in my lungs. I watched the gas cause blistering across my skin." She winced.

"The last thing I remember was my heart racing way too fast--and my lungs wouldn't expand anymore."

Josh gazed at her in shock. She knew why. This wasn't a story a living, breathing, seemingly healthy person could tell. This was an experience, these were sensations someone carried with them into death.

He opened his mouth to speak, stuttering: "I'm just glad they got to you in time."

She stared at him, her forehead deeply furrowed. "They didn't."

His confusion was apparent.

"Josh, it took so long for them to even know something was going on–and then they couldn't get through the door."

"They only targeted the kids," he recalled, swallowing hard. "*Okay*, but if they didn't get to you in time, how are you–?" He reset himself. "Sorry. Please finish what you were telling me."

"They couldn't find a pulse. They tried mouth to mouth. They used a defibrillator. By what they could tell, I was dead."

His face was filled with panic, his breaths quickening.

"Josh? I don't die at the end of this story. I'm sitting right here."

He nodded. "I know. You're sitting in front of me looking--well, very beautiful—and you're very much alive. I just can't–I can't believe I never–I never asked how you survived, did I?"

She shook her head slowly.

"I guess I cared more about the fact that you're alive than the *how* part?" he offered, lifting his eyebrows.

She gazed at him with curiosity.

"What happened? They took you to the hospital?"

"No. The hospitals have been taken over by the national health agency, whatever they're calling themselves. People have been leery of going for years. They refuse to treat you unless you do x, y, and z."

"So, what happened?"

"They declared me dead. We don't have emergency services anymore, but we had a couple doctors in the congregation. My pulse was so low, they just assumed my body was easing into death."

"But–" he protested.

"*Josh?* I'm alive."

He nodded. "Could you *hear* what was happening?"

She took a breath before she continued. "After I lost consciousness, it was just darkness for me—endless dark and quiet."

"Before you lost consciousness though? What was that like?"

"A lot of pain."

"Like last night?" He appeared to regret making the statement so punctuated.

She lowered her eyes.

"After the darkness and quiet?"

"I started to feel my body again. Everything seemed to be happening in reverse, but a lot slower than before. My lungs expanded," she winced as she spoke. "My heart started racing. It took some time for it to slow to normal. When I was able to open my eyes, I was in my dad's office, and it was late at night."

"The attack happened during regular service, right?"

She nodded.

"Your dad thought you were dead for 11-12 hours?"

Another nod.

"Was he there in his office when you woke up?"

"No. I found him in the sanctuary."

"What happened when he saw you?"

"He stared at me. I suppose my appearance *was* a bit terrifying. The scarring was still really raw," she began, turning her palm upward, "Well, it's disappeared now. I was also bleeding out of my eyes, my ears, I think."

He grimaced, touching the place on her palm where the scarring had been. "I'd say you look beautiful no matter what, but that's not a great mental image."

"No, not a great look."

"What kind of gas was it? Maybe the effects were meant to be temporary?" he reasoned.

"Similar to sarin gas, but about twenty times more concentrated."

He took a few solid breaths. "*Essie?*" His voice was a whisper. "How are you alive right now?"

She swallowed hard. "That gets a little complicated. When I found my dad in the sanctuary, Luther was sitting with him."

"You said he saved your life when you were little."

She nodded. "He's also the one who gave me to my dad."

"*Gave* you to your dad?"

"It wasn't exactly a legal adoption." She took a deep breath. "When I was a baby, I was in a government research program called STRONG. I'm not sure what the acronym stood for."

"Research?"

She nodded apprehensively. "Genetics. Something to increase human immune response to disease, poison, pathogens. I was in the program from the day I was born--actually, long before I was born, during my zygote days."

He narrowed his eyes.

"That's an early development baby still in the womb."

He raised an eyebrow but decided against telling her he knew what a zygote was. "You were experimented on as a baby?"

"Sounds like the start of an X-Men movie, right?" She frowned. "And you thought the surviving poison gas was going to be the unbelievable part."

"What was the research?"

"By what I've been told, pumping me full of chemicals during development to make my body have a hyperactive immune response to threats? Something with cellular response."

"Did they use gamma rays?"

"I *do* have a temper." She raised an eyebrow.

"You do not, and I shouldn't joke." He frowned. "Actually, you *do* have a little bit of a temper these days, but I still shouldn't joke."

"It's not a sexist thing, but I'd kind of prefer Captain Marvel's powers from that glowing blue energy core. Turning into Hulk sounds taxing—and it would be annoying to have to constantly have spare clothes."

"There was a She-Hulk somewhere in the comic books. I wonder how she handled that?"

She raised an eyebrow. "I was afraid you wouldn't believe me, but *now* it kind of feels like you believe me and you're making light of it."

He shook his head. "Just trying to keep my calm facade."

"You're doing well hiding your freak out."

"I am?"

"No, you're terrible at hiding your emotions, Josh."

"*You're* really calm about all this."

"The freak out is kind of my baseline at this point–and it's happening internally."

He took a gulp of air. "What you've described is insane and terrifying."

She nodded.

"So, they exposed you to--whatever chemicals before you were born--*then what*?"

"They tested my response to different things—to see what would kill me and what I could survive." She tugged up the sleeve of her shirt, turned over her wrist, and revealed the data matrix code tattoo imprinted in her mid-forearm.

He touched the skin delicately. "I remember seeing this when we were kids. *Wait*, so what I witnessed, what you've done *120 times*–they did that when you were a baby?"

She nodded, watching him tracing his finger over the tattoo.

"How many times?"

She lowered her eyes.

"Essie?"

"A few hundred."

"You know the number."

"I do."

"What is it?"

"718."

"718?"

"From birth to age two years, nine months. Four to six times per week."

He drew in his breath.

The room was silent.

"So, since you're *alive*, that means what exactly?"

She shrugged.

"Are you immortal?"

"No." She answered quickly, but the disbelieving expression on Josh's face gave her pause. "No. I *can't be*. I'm still aging like everyone else."

He frowned. "Did Teo know about this?"

She shook her head. "He knew I was taken from a 'bad' situation, but he didn't know what that meant until after the church attack."

"So, *Luther* took you from this research facility?"

She nodded.

"How did he know your dad?"

"He didn't. He needed to find me a home. He saw the cross decal on the back window of my dad's truck at a gas station and thought it was a sign."

"He saw the cross--" he repeated slowly. "I guess that's not a terrible selection process."

She raised her eyebrows briefly in agreement. "Luther didn't think I was targeted—in the church attack," she clarified. "—mainly because people don't know I exist, but if word got out about what happened and that I survived essentially spooning with a sarin gas canister, there would be—questions. So, he thought it was best that they think I'm dead."

He sat up straighter, uneasy again. "Wait--don't they know you disappeared back when you were two years, nine months old?"

She hesitated. "There was a fire at the lab, so they presumed I was dead."

He grimaced. "You said you were spooning the gas canister—while it was releasing sarin gas."

"Don't be jealous." She twisted her face. "I'm making light of it, I'm sorry."

"Why were you *spooning* the canister?"

"I tried to cover the canister with my body so the gas wouldn't reach the kids, but my limbs weren't working right—bones had snapped, muscles were spasming, it was a whole thing."

He stared at her, his bottom lip parting. "You didn't know about any of this–what happened when you were little? Before the attack on Calvary?"

"*Well*, I had nightmares when I was younger."

"*No*, I mean, you didn't know that you could survive–*spooning* with the canister."

She shook her head.

He exhaled deeply as he slid closer. Esther lowered her eyes as he pulled up the hem of her gray shirt. The soft fabric inched upward, revealing the taut skin of her stomach covered in faded swirls of pink scarring.

"These are being more stubborn to fade," she said, eyes downcast.

He placed his hand delicately against her skin. "Does it hurt?" he asked softly.

She shook her head. "It kind of has a too-tight feeling sometimes, but I like to think that's my six-pack."

The corners of his mouth lifted.

She stared at his hand, a warm contrast to the cool air of the apartment, and found she wasn't taking full breaths.

"The six-pack probably isn't helping," he conceded quietly.

She smiled, relieved to have him play along. "Should I purposely grow a gut to stretch out the skin?"

"Probably for the best." He gave her a light smile. His hand slowly slid away from her stomach, allowing the shirt to fall back into place. He twisted his expression. "You thought you were going to die. When you covered the canister."

She said nothing, chest tightening.

His jaw clenched. "You're not *testing* antidotes."

Essie gave a small shake of her head.

"You generate the antidote. You're *creating–*" His voice gave out. She watched his eyes blankly scan the space between them, replaying the evening's events in his mind. He stood suddenly.

"Please don't go," she said, rising to her feet.

Josh turned on his heel. "Luther wanted me to see it so I would try to convince you to stop."

She nodded apologetically.

He continued stiffly: "I can't stand the thought of you going through that once, let alone all the time, Essie–but I also know that there's nothing I can do or say to stop you."

Her eyebrows furrowed. She felt a flexion of her heart.

"It's incredible what you're doing. I haven't begun to wrap my head around it. You're amazing—*without* this, you're amazing. You being willing to do this?"

"But?"

He pressed his lips together. "But I can't support it." His tone was conclusive.

"What does that *mean*, you 'can't support it'?"

"I'm saying," he began, taking a deep breath, "that you're a big girl." He said this with a rehearsed, well-meaning smile that didn't quite hit the mark. "You can make your own decisions."

Her eyes narrowed. "You didn't answer," she began, choking on the words. "What does it mean–you can't–"

"I'm going to be really busy with MET anyway." It sounded like a consolatory statement for himself rather than some form of reassurance for her.

"And that's okay, *right*?" Her lip was quivering, her hands balled into fists. She had never once raised her voice to him.

"What is?"

"You risking *your life*? That's okay, I have to support *that*?"

He lifted his eyebrows. "You don't support me being in MET?"

197

Her face tensed and she turned away to search for a tissue box. "Essie?"

"You were supposed to be coming here *to stay*, Josh."

He tilted his head to the side. "You knew I was going to have training and missions when I joined MET."

She glared at him as she bent to yank a tissue from the box.

"*Oh*," he said, his face softening. "You meant because I—" He let his voice trail off.

"I thought after the last time we saw each other at the farm—" Her jaw tightened. "I *thought*—"

"What?"

She shook her head, refusing eye contact. "You know what? No. Never mind. *Nothing*. It doesn't matter now."

"Essie, talk to me. Please."

"No," she muttered dismissively. "I think you should go."

"You're going to shut me out, too, now?"

Her chin snapped upward. "*What* did you just say?"

"I didn't mean it the way it sounded."

"I *didn't* shut you out. *You* shut *me* out." She was grinding her teeth as she spoke. "I wanted to share this with you—it's been horrible to go through it alone."

"Then why *did you*?"

"*Because you weren't here*," she shouted in a primal sort of growl.

He stepped toward her, extending out his hand. "Essie—"

"*No*. This is all a little too much for you and you 'can't support it'? *Well*, thanks for that. *Really*. That's very helpful. Why would I share *anything* more with you after this, Josh? *Why*? Just to have you shrug it off and say, 'I told you that you shouldn't do it'?"

"That's not what I meant."

"Well, that's what you said."

"Essie, I didn't sleep at all last night. You'll have to cut me a little slack if I'm not finding the right words right now."

She pressed her lips together, shaking her head, willing the tears back in her eyes.

"Case and point. That was really stupid what I just said."

"Well, you should get some sleep then," she said coolly, narrowing her stare.

"No, we need to talk this through."

"You know, I didn't exactly get any shut-eye last night either, the purgatory-like state isn't exactly restful, and I think I've heard enough." The sadness in her shimmering eyes had given way to anger, as she began herding him toward the door. "I hope I can still count on you for discretion even if you 'can't support' what I'm doing." She hated herself for the condescension, the bitterness in her voice.

"Essie," he said roughly. "Stop. Please."

They stood glaring at each other just inside the front door, Josh's eyes their soft, deep brown and Esther's a wild silver hue.

"If you're worried about me being a part of MET, you could say so."

She tilted her head to the side. "Well, that's *just silly*, isn't it? You're a big boy. You can make your own decisions." She meant to stop there, but then she heard herself add: "You didn't give a thought to my opinion when you signed up in the first place, why would it matter to you now?"

It looked like he'd been shot.

She swung open the apartment door and motioned for him to leave. She was only slightly surprised when he obediently stepped over the threshold. Her heart dropped to the pit of her stomach when he said goodbye and didn't fully profess his love or beg for forgiveness.

She started to cry silently when he didn't immediately beat down her door once she'd closed it to make some bold declaration or wrap her in his arms.

She broke down in sobs as she watched through the front window as he crossed the street and disappeared from view.

15

last

Esther stepped into "Dan Headquarters," as she referred to it, in a daze. The sky had been dark and misty all day and a wind tunnel had formed along the outdoor corridor as she scanned her badge at the door. She was still feeling the effects of the antidote run, her gait sporadically faltering. Mercifully, the lab where Danny and several others studied the Simulators did not require much walking once inside. She took the elevator down to level -8 and found Danny waiting when the doors opened.

"Wow, I never get a greeting at the elevator."

"We need to talk."

She forced a smile. "Are you breaking up with me, Danny?"

It was evident by the look on his face that she would not like what he was about to tell her.

"What is it?"

He motioned toward a glassed conference room to his left and wheeled himself inside. He rotated the chair slowly, seeming to be searching for the right words, raking his fingers through his blonde hair. "*Oh*. Will you close that all the way?" he asked, raising his emerald eyes to the door.

She frowned, pushing the door closed. "Should I draw the blinds, too? Can people read lips around here?" She asked this facetiously, but as the words emerged, he tapped a button and the glass panels that surrounded the conference room turned opaque.

"They canceled the mission to get Gabe."

She stood in silence. Images began to swarm her brain, some from the Sim recordings, some from her nightmares–Gabe holding the limp, broken body of a newborn, its spinal cord snapped, its skin coated in amniotic fluid, Gabe being beaten repeatedly and without end, him smiling lightly at her as he boarded the train, him as a young boy, tucking her shaking body close to his, kissing the top of her head, reassuring her that she was safe.

Her body heaved forward as though someone had just punched her in the stomach.

"Essie, there's a chair. Have a seat."

She clambered into the rolling conference room chair, struggling to take full breaths.

"I'm sorry."

"Why? Why did they cancel it?" Through her shock, she felt anger, anger that Luther wouldn't tell her himself. It was their deal, after all.

"I lied to you, Ess. I'm sorry. When I told you we couldn't access Gabe's most recent Sim session? It's because I was hiding it."

"Why would you do that?"

"I knew if they saw it, they'd cancel the mission."

She clutched her rib cage.

"I knew if *you* saw it–" He began, shaking his head.

Her hand dropped slowly to her side. From what she'd already seen, she didn't want to imagine what could be worse, what would cause Danny to take such measures.

Danny rolled toward her but seemed to decide to provide comfort in proximity rather than through physical contact. "I didn't want them to ruin your memories of Gabe. You shouldn't have even seen any of what you've seen already, but *this*–"

She lowered her chin, encouraging him to complete the sentence.

"You can't unsee things, Ess. I know what we've seen has been–" He stared across the room, wincing.

"What *is it*–does he look awful? Is he messed up mentally from the Sim? Do they have him doing terrible things?"

Danny stared at her sympathetically. "I'm sorry, Essie."

"Answer the questions, Danny."

He took a deep breath. "Yes."

"Yes what?"

"To all of the above."

She sat back in the chair, dropping her chin to her chest, her eyes closed. She was quiet for a few moments. "I need to see it."

He opened his mouth to protest, but she immediately cut him off. "MET has risked their lives and exposure of the whole Ark plan to transport effing *zoo animals* here, but my best friend was deemed unworthy. I have a right to know what they know."

He exhaled deeply, turning his hand over to reveal a small memory card. "While I agree with you on principle, I'm going to ask you not to watch this. It's for your own good. Trust me."

She picked up the card, debating about where she could safely store it, finally deciding to continue grasping it in her palm.

"Essie?" He waited for her to look at him. "It's for your own good. You can't do anything for him. You know that."

She stood and turned to leave. She started to rotate back toward him but thought better of it. "Thanks for trying to help him, Danny," she said, her voice breaking.

"You're one of like a handful of people on this earth I care about, Ess. I know he means a lot to you."

Her back heaved upward as she took a deep breath and she pushed the door open, the windows automatically turning translucent again.

The wind was still unruly, the flags whipping against the flagpole in the courtyard. She kept her eyes lowered, pulled her coat tightly around her torso, and walked quickly toward the faded green pickup truck parked in the first row of spaces. Most of the people being relocated to the Ark were issued housing, but not necessarily a vehicle if they didn't have one since both vehicles and gas stores needed to be preserved. Luther had been the one to issue an exception for her. All the vehicles in the Ark were gas-powered with a combustion engine, most dating back to before the last turn of the century. The truck had the symbol for an apple farm in Washington she suspected had been seized by the government. The woman making housing and vehicle assignments had noted that she was permitted to change the truck's appearance to more fit her taste, but it would be at her own expense.

"What happened to the people who owned the farm?"

The woman shrugged, checking the file on her tablet. "We acquire a lot of vehicles at auctions. Yeah, there's not much information here."

She had left the weathered logo alone and focused her eyes on it as she zeroed in on the truck. She climbed inside and released a breath. For the next several minutes, she focused on converting oxygen into carbon dioxide. Once she felt composed enough, she turned the key in the ignition and directed the truck toward town.

Given the low inventory of food in her refrigerator, Esther thought about stopping on the way to the apartment to pick up some essentials, and some dinner, but any food item she considered immediately brought a sensation of nausea. She drove through the center of town without stopping, even managing to hit the notoriously long main stoplight on green.

Walking toward the downstairs entry of her apartment (Luther had preferred an upstairs apartment for safety but reasoned that downstairs would save her a trek post-session), she looked out across the green space to the pool area. Based on the decorations and the giant number 7 balloon, there was a birthday party going on. Her lips turned upward reflexively at the sound of laughing children, but then she felt the memory card still pressed in her palm, she thought of running around the fields at the farm with the West brothers. She thought of Gabe teaching her how to ride a horse, skip rocks, and suddenly she noticed she wasn't taking in breaths.

She rushed inside, dropped her keys on the coffee table, and started pacing, the thoughts she had blocked out the entire drive racing through her mind.

They canceled the mission.
You will never see Gabe again.
Over and over again.
They canceled the mission.
You will never see Gabe again.

Josh left with MET.
He may never come back.
The last thing you said to him...

She dropped to her knees and started to cry.

The Sim session was the shortest to date. Less than seven minutes in total. As the screen turned black, Esther frantically pulled off the VR headset. She was left standing in the empty apartment listening to the birthday party guests sing *"Happy Birthday to You."* As the guests cheered, Esther struggled to breathe.

You will never see Gabe again.

She folded over, clutching at her stomach.

When she had eventually stopped crying and taken in her surroundings again, the birthday party was over, the sunny day had given way to clouds, and the silence that engulfed her was deafening.

16
upward

Matteo was surprised when he stepped out onto the screened porch and saw his daughter standing at the paddock fence. She had a defeated angle to her shoulders, to the tilt of her head. He made a purposeful bit of noise closing the screen door behind him and she glanced over her shoulder before turning her gaze back to Bree, who was exploring the far reaches of the paddock with the new horse, a Belgian with a shimmery chestnut coat and a crimped blonde mane and tail.

"Bree's got a girlfriend," he remarked as he stepped up to the fence alongside her.

"She's beautiful. I don't remember seeing her last time I was here."

Matteo nodded, sighing deeply. "She just arrived a couple of days ago actually."

"What happened to her legs?" Esther asked, referring to the bandages wrapped around the horse's back legs.

"She was found in a ravine tangled in barbed wire."

"Nearby?"

"Down in Wyoming. A lot of people are letting their horses go free rather than turning them over to the government so some are wandering where they shouldn't."

"I'm in a fragile emotional state. Feel free to edit your story if it involves animal suffering."

"Well, she's safe now."

"She's lucky someone found her."

"Well, most people would have put her—" he stopped short, seeing the horror on her face. "She's very lucky. She should make a full recovery he said."

"Who found her?"

"Josh."

Her entire body tensed. "I thought he deployed?"

"He did. As I understand it, there's a safe house they use outside Cheyenne, and he found her on his way there."

"So he made the drive back."

"Twice. He had to get a trailer, go back and get her, then he drove her here."

This information was clearly having a distressing effect on her. He suddenly wondered how much he should share.

"How long did he stay?"

Matteo cleared his throat. "Not long. He was back with her the same day then headed out that night."

She nodded slowly, struggling to suppress building emotion.

"Do you want to talk about it?"

"Talk about what? The horse or the fact that I was a complete and total bee with an itch to the guy who—" she shook her head.

"I'll talk about whatever you'd like."

She chuckled lightly. "No disagreement there?"

Matteo frowned. "Well, you'll have to give me more context before I can dispute that you were a–what did you call yourself?"

"'Bee with an itch.'"

He nodded. "Is that a euphemism for my sake or the horses'? Because I've heard you say worse."

"You're sassy for a pastor."

"I'm making up for your absence."

She pressed her lips together. "Sorry about that."

"I meant it as a joke. I didn't say it to make you feel bad."

"I know," she said, dropping her shoulders. "But I'm still sorry."

"I'm happy to see you, even if you're a bit of an emotional disaster right now."

Her jaw dropped and she fanned out her arms. "I'm trying to turn being a mutant human into a positive thing here."

"And also coping with the collapse of the country," he added, helpfully.

"Well, we all carry that burden—"

"So just the mutant human thing. Absolutely *nothing else* you're dealing with at the moment."

She sniffled, inconspicuously trying to wipe her nose on the sleeve of her flannel shirt. When she turned back toward the field, Matteo presented his handkerchief, which she accepted gratefully. "I don't normally do that. The cold air out here sets me off."

He gave a low grunt of acknowledgment and raised his eyebrows toward the mountains. "I'd appreciate it if you wouldn't refer to my daughter as a 'mutant.'"

"I'm clearly being facetious."

"Are you sure about that?"

"*Well*—what else would you call me?"

He exhaled deeply. "A miracle."

"I am the result of Lord knows how many babies being tortured to death," she scoffed. "I am *not* a miracle. I am the reason they are dead."

He froze momentarily. "Are you out of your mind?"

She considered this and shrugged. "Possibly. But it's true, isn't it?"

"Hell, no it isn't. Is that what you really think?"

She twisted her shoulders uncomfortably, frowning as she stared blankly out at the horses. "I've thought it. I haven't said it out loud before though."

"How did it feel? Saying it out loud?"

"Wrong."

"That's because it is."

She swallowed. "I know it's not my fault what happened to them."

208

"Baby, you went through the *same* torture. The difference is you survived it, only to be tortured again and again. Those other babies? They went home to Jesus. Way too soon, but they were saved—but *you*?" His voice constricted, tears filling his eyes.

Esther turned abruptly and collided into his chest. "I'm sorry, Daddy."

He enclosed his arms around her, stroking the back of her head. They stood in silence for several minutes, her breaths slowly deepening.

"Does she have a name?" She asked softly as they started to part, motioning to the Belgian horse.

"Hwin."

She swiveled her neck to look at him. "H-W-I-N?"

Matteo gave an affirmative tilt of his head. "It seemed like an unusual choice, but Josh seemed sure about it."

Esther smiled weakly as Bree jogged toward the fence line, having just realized she was there. He raised his nose in the air as though following her scent, whinnying. Hwin was following eagerly, blonde mane blowing gracefully in the breeze.

"I doubt she knows her name yet if you wanted to pick something else."

She shook her head as Hwin curiously sniffed her hands for signs of treats. "It fits her."

"Is it an acronym?"

"No," she sighed. "The protagonists from *A Horse and His Boy* are two talking Narnian horses, one named Bree, the *other*—"

"Hwin."

Her lips tightened at the same moment tears began to stream from her eyes again. "That Josh West is something else."

He exhaled, otherwise providing the space of silence.

After a minute or so, she spoke, her voice raspy. "Sometimes I feel like he cares about me—that he loves me—"

When she gave no indication there was a second half to her sentence, Matteo broke his silence: "You only feel that *sometimes*?"

She did not roll her eyes or blush the way he expected, just the opposite. Her expression showed her exhaustion, emotionally and physically. She looked on the verge of tears again. "But *this*? Naming her Hwin as some sort of gesture after telling me he doesn't want anything to do with me? It feels mean. Like it's not a kind gesture, like he's doing it to make me feel bad."

Matteo tried not to jump to defend Josh, which was made easier when she suddenly walked back into his arms, hiccuping on tears.

"I'm sorry I'm unloading all this on you."

He squeezed his arms gently around her again, indulging a bit in the moment, opportunities for fatherly affection growing more infrequent. "You never have to apologize for coming to me with this stuff. I wish you had come to me sooner."

She nodded. "I know what he's doing is important and it's really selfish of me," she said, her words distorted by her frequent sniffling. "But I feel like he abandoned me, like I must not mean that much to him."

Matteo held her tighter, stroking the back of her head. He remembered worrying about her lack of emotional expression when she first came to live with him. She wasn't able to sleep at night, probably haunted by nightmarish images of her life before, but she relied only on herself in the early days. She didn't come to him for reassurance or validation. She simply remedied the situation for herself the best she could manage. Once he learned what she went through those first three years, he understood: She had no one to comfort her when she was living through hell; insomnia on its own probably seemed quite manageable in comparison. This became something of a character trait for her: she was very adaptable, accepting of inconveniences and change. In hindsight, perhaps she just never let her struggles rise to the surface for the world to see. It wasn't a tremendous surprise that having her world turned on its head had pushed her to the point she could no longer hide her struggles. Her need for support was so obvious, so desperate, it felt palpable. He couldn't imagine that Josh wouldn't feel it.

"Josh found out what you're working on with Luther? Is that what some of this is about?"

She gave a noncommittal shrug. "He doesn't want to spend time with me if I keep working with Luther. Because spending time with me would equate to supporting what I'm doing—Which. He. Does. *Not*."

He swallowed, trying to divert his thoughts from his daughter in excruciating pain by choice.

"But it's no skin off his nose because he's *very* busy with MET. He won't have a free moment to worry about what I'm doing."

Matteo narrowed his eyes at the horizon, finding it difficult to suppress his anger. "He really said that?"

"He said he knew there wasn't anything he could do to change my mind, but he couldn't support it, buuuuut, and I quote: 'I'm going to be really busy with MET anyway.'"

His heart twisted in his chest.

This sort of statement sounded as far from something Josh would say as he could imagine, but it was also not in his daughter's nature to exaggerate things. She was a stark contrast to the female melodrama he recalled from when he was a young man. Then again, he'd never seen her so unraveled.

It didn't matter that Josh probably meant what he said as some sort of ultimatum, trying to force her to take action that was likely in her best interests. What mattered was that his daughter was suffering, had probably been struggling silently for quite some time, and the one she needed to be there for her, had, in her eyes, abandoned her.

Her body had turned rigid, and she was balling her hands into fists. "I thought maybe he'd have a little more to offer. He finds out I'm a mutant—sorry, '*miracle*,' and he's like: Wow, that's crazy. Good luck with that."

Matteo took a deep inhalation of her hair, which had been recently washed. The coconut scent swept into his mind's eye a Hawaiian beach, a sunset, calm waves, and the smell of sunscreen still wafting in the air.

He shifted his chin to allow better airflow. He couldn't think of Rachel right now.

"I know it's a lot to take in, but you'd think someone who cares about you to maybe ask—'you're volunteering to be injected with poison twice a week—is there some deeply rooted psychological, emotional hole you're trying to fill? Let's talk this out.'"

"Can *I* ask that?"

"You did, in your own way." She took a steadying breath. "I just thought he cared about me."

Matteo understood: It probably never occurred to Josh that she needed support; she had never been the sort to ask for it. She probably didn't ask it of him, even during their argument.

But then a nagging thought came to the front of his mind: She *had* asked for help from a very young age, just not from Josh.

She had always, always, always gone to Gabe. She had dealt with not being able to sleep on her own when they were home. At the farm, she relied on Gabe. She had let him see her struggles. She had sought comfort from him. After what she went through, she shouldn't have trusted anyone. And yet, after knowing Gabe less than a day, she had put her trust in him.

Had his distrust of Gabe stemmed from some dormant jealousy from all those years ago? Had he misinterpreted Gabe's behavior after all? Perhaps he had been more perceptive when it came to her emotions and that was why he was so protective of her as they got older?

Maybe Josh was insensitive to her needs? He should have known with all that was happening, with all she was going through, that she needed him there.

He's only 20, Matteo reasoned silently, trying to keep from saying too much or making any rash judgments. *I pushed her toward him. I made her believe he was a better fit for her than Gabe, but what would Gabe have done in Josh's place?*

Matteo lifted his gaze to the darkening clouds over the hills. *How was she coping without Gabe these past few years?* He had considered that it

212

was difficult for her without him, but had he ever checked in with her? Maybe he'd severely discounted Gabe's importance in her life.

"You are not alone in what you're going through."

He felt her twist a bit, disagreeing silently, but she said nothing in return.

The sky grumbled in the distance, the clouds looking increasingly foreboding.

"I should get these two inside with the others before the storm hits."

She backed away, took in the sight of the sky, and nodded. "Probably a good idea," she said reasonably, wiping at her cheeks.

"*Esther.* It's okay to not be okay, you know."

She turned on the spot, pressing her lips together. "I'm *not* okay."

He knew he prompted her to say the words, but he hadn't anticipated how hearing them would affect him, and found he needed to support himself on the fence. "You have people you can rely on, talk to, cry to. You don't have to go through anything alone."

Her eyebrow was not convinced.

"You have me. You have Luther. You have Sara and Luke." He felt compelled to encourage her to pray, to talk to God, but she hadn't been to church in three years and whenever he suggested she join him for Sunday service or Wednesday Worship, she was never available.

"I have *you*, Daddy. Luther is only going to get busier. As it is, I only see him for the sessions. Sara and Luke know nothing about what I've been doing *and*–" Her voice broke. "I have you," she said conclusively. "I'm incredibly lucky to have you–but I don't have 'people,' Daddy. Not anymore."

He shuffled his boot against the gravel ground.

"He should be here," she said desperately, raising her eyes to the layers of hills and pastures in the distance. "*He should be here.*"

Matteo nodded. "Gabe would love it here."

Esther's chin snapped in his direction, her eyes wide. She nodded quickly, turning and ducking through the rails of the fence. Bree rushed

213

forward to nuzzle her. "Is this your new buddy?" Esther asked affectionately, trying to stifle a cry.

He accepted her change of focus for the time being, committing himself to circle back to this conversation once they were safely inside. "I assume Bree will just follow you like a Labrador?"

She gave an obligatory smile and clicked her tongue, starting toward the barn.

Once they'd fed all eight horses and secured the barn, a wall of rain was approaching from the fields. Together they jogged back to the house.

"This is a nice place–the house is cozy, you've got a lot of space, the horses–" She observed, shaking off her jacket inside.

He shrugged. "Can't complain." His clothing, his boots, and the calluses on his hands made him look the part, but he felt a little out of his element.

"Don't take this the wrong way, but it's a little surreal. It's almost like you're a little kid playing make-believe."

"I don't pull off the cowboy look?"

She pressed her lips together, moving to wash her hands at the sink. "Do you think there will be a chance for you to be a pastor here?"

He nodded, taste-testing the chili simmering in the slow cooker. It was lacking in salt, so he shook the canister over the pot. "You know the old church downtown, just around the corner from your place?"

"I do."

"It opens for services this Sunday. I'm going to be one of the pastors."

"Oh *wow*. That's great, Daddy."

Matteo shook some hot sauce into the pot and stirred the chili. "I won't be the lead pastor or anything–"

"But still. I'm excited for you. *And* I'm excited for the congregation–they're lucky to have you."

He glanced up at her. She was putting on the best smile she could manage, her inner turmoil still apparent in her eyes.

"Are you going to take care of the horses *and* work at the church?"

"That's the plan. I'm more or less the fill-in at the church."

"Until they get to know you."

His cheeks tightened.

"I guess when you pull so many churches into one area, it's going to produce a bit of clerigical competition."

"*Clerigical competition*," he repeated slowly.

"You all should compete like on those old singing competition shows."

He shook his head, chuckling to himself.

"It's got to be a lot just taking care of all those horses," she pointed out, temporarily lost in thought. Her eyes appeared locked on the lopsided ceramic planter she made for him when she was six or seven. It was covered with bright painted swirls, housed a small juniper bonsai tree, and was the solitary item in the protruding window box above the kitchen sink. "What if *I* took over with the horses at some point? Or would I need to petition in front of a council or something?"

He furrowed his brow as he took down two turquoise bowls from the open shelving. "Is that something you would want to do?"

"It would be tough keeping up with all of it right now, but I wasn't planning to do the lab rat thing forever."

Matteo winced. "Well, that's an equally comforting and disturbing statement."

"That was tactless. I'm sorry."

"Is it accurate?"

"*Oh*, not at all. I'm treated infinitely better than a lab animal."

He ladled scoops into each bowl. "Well. Hallelujah."

Esther crossed the kitchen and retrieved two bottles of beer from the refrigerator.

"What do we have here?"

"I'm old enough to drink, plus three years."

"Is the drinking age really sixteen now?"

She nodded.

"I don't agree with that *at all*, but I'm being silly. You're a responsible girl. Would you like to have a beer with me?"

She placed one bottle back. "I was just messing with you. Alcohol has no effect on me."

He frowned. "Is that right? How'd you figure that out?"

"Wouldn't *you* try drinking if you were in my shoes? It's all a part of my mutant–my special, 'miracle' powers. Luther thinks my body just metabolizes it really fast." She placed his beer at the seat adorned with his tropical seat cushion and a fruit drink at her place, with the elephant print cushion. Her face relaxed as she took in the familiar sight of the cushions.

"How much longer do you think you'll be working with Luther?"

She twisted her expression. "Maybe another couple weeks, if that."

He nodded, his brow lifting. "I've actually considered that this wouldn't be a bad place to start a goat farm," he said lightly as he placed their bowls at the small breakfast nook, which served as the primary dining space.

"*Uff*, you're really fulfilling the role of Italian papa and mama, aren't you?" she muttered with an indignant scowl.

"It's something you've talked about doing for a long time."

"*No*. It's something *Josh and I* talked about doing." She took a swig of the fruit drink, pinching her face. "I'm sorry, Daddy. That disgusting swig of high-fructose corn syrup was not blessed."

He folded his hands. "Bless us oh Lord for these gifts we're about to receive. Please watch over us and those we love, especially those far away. Guide us in your way. In Your name we pray. Amen."

Esther stirred her chili, taking a deep breath. "Do you believe God doesn't give us more than we can handle?"

Matteo sighed, pondering her question. "Yes and no."

She lifted her eyes, surprised by his response.

"God gives us opportunities to grow. For example, someone with very little patience might be given the chance to learn to be more patient. So you could argue that the person wouldn't have been able to handle the situation at the start, but because of the experience, they expand their capacity for patience and are therefore able to handle the situation."

She pressed her lips together.

He watched her stare at the contents of her bowl for a prolonged period of time. "I was wrong about Gabe."

Her eyes lifted from her bowl to the plant in the center of the table.

"I'm sorry. I understood he meant a lot–means a lot to you, but I don't think I really understood how much."

She nodded without looking up.

He replayed their conversation in the truck after Gabe kissed her; he was certain she had confirmed his assessment that Josh was a better fit for her. But no, he had done most of the talking in that conversation; she had provided silences. She had refuted his claims about Josh having feelings for her, but she had done something that made him believe she had feelings for Josh–hadn't she?

She was quiet for a few minutes, during which time she did not consume one drop of chili. It was when the rain started to peck on the tin roof that she finally spoke. "Have the Wests given up on Gabe?" Her voice was thick and strained.

The good feelings generated just minutes earlier by the thought of his daughter finally being done with the experimentation had dissolved into the chilly, damp air. It was replaced by palpable energy radiating from his daughter of sorrow and helplessness. Matteo exhaled but found it difficult. "He stopped responding to them, Ess. He wrote a letter telling them he had accepted a permanent position with the Department of Public Health and that was it."

Her jaw tensed.

"Obviously they want to do something, but they don't even know where he is at this point."

Esther stirred her chili absentmindedly, peering out at the rain. "He's in Denver."

His eyes widened. "How do you know that? Did he write to you?"

She shook her head, still staring out the screen door.

"Is Josh's team planning to get him?"

She flinched slightly at the mention of Josh. "No."

"A different team?"

"No," she said, her teeth grinding. She dug around in her pocket and pulled out the handkerchief again, turning her face away.

He held back from asking his follow-up question if she was planning something, mainly because he didn't want to put the idea in her head, and in the likely event the idea was already in her head, he didn't want to inadvertently give merit to it.

"It's *just*–" Her voice cracked, and she wiped roughly at her eyes.

Matteo allowed quiet to fill the house.

"It seems like they're waiting for him to act, to come home on his own, like he up and joined a traveling circus and they're just waiting for him to get through the phase."

"Who?"

"Luke and Sara."

He lowered his chin to encourage her to continue.

"What if he *can't*?"

"If he's being held against his will, you mean?"

"He *is*. Being held against his will."

"Luther knows this?"

She nodded quickly. "What *if*–" She swallowed hard. "What if expecting him to break himself free is as unreasonable as expecting me to break out of the lab on my own when I was a little girl?"

Matteo dropped his spoon in the bowl, the image Luther had described from when he first found her in the lab invading his thoughts. Ever since he had shared details about the lab, he'd found the images intermixing with his own memories of her. He'd think of her sweet, dimpled toddler face beaming at him–and then he'd think of people clamping her to a cold, metal table. Torturing her. He'd see her sitting on her window seat reading and suddenly he'd imagine the pain she experienced when they broke her bones to stuff her in a box bound for the incinerator.

"Don't look at me like that," she said, rotating back to the table. "I can't go anywhere, and you know it. I'm an 'existential threat,' remember? Plus, if they caught me and picked up where they left off? I couldn't put you through that."

He closed his eyes, oddly grateful for her remark. "Luther could send in a team though?"

"He won't."

He scratched at his stubbled cheek. "Maybe there aren't any safe options, to get him, I mean?"

Esther shook her head angrily.

"I've heard they're using mind control, Essie. Gabe might not–" He raked his fingers through his dark hair, reading the tension building in her shoulders as a cue not to finish the sentence.

"I wish people would stop saying things like that. I *get it*— it's easier to think that way, that he's not really himself anymore? It makes him seem like some sort of animal?" There was a venomous bite in her voice.

He froze but heard himself say: "Sometimes people cling to a lie, not because it makes them feel 'good,' but because if they don't believe the lie, they'll be overwhelmed by the truth."

She was silent, processing his words. "Who do you think is believing a lie? Me or them?"

He pushed his bowl away. When he failed to respond, leaving them sitting in a deafening quiet, she widened her eyes, insistent he give an answer.

"They haven't seen what you've seen," he conceded reluctantly. He released a breath. "Luther cares about you. He knows what Gabe means to you. If there was a way–"

"*Does* he? Know what he means to me? You're *my dad* and you just admitted that you didn't know what he means to me. You were even *aggressively* trying to convince me Josh was a better romantic choice just hours after Gabe kissed me."

"If I was wrong—"

"That's not what I'm saying." She slanted her eyebrows incredulously, her eyes welling with tears. "You thought that kiss at the train station was romantic."

"It wasn't?"

She shook her head patiently, her demeanor suddenly more resolved, more like herself.

"What was it then?"

She blinked slowly. "Just trust me when I say that it wasn't romantic? Not for me, not for him."

Matteo thought of the scene. He had been standing next to Luke and Sara, having already said goodbye to both of the boys. Esther was accompanying them to the loading platform. Josh had stopped to zipper something on his bag. Esther was holding Gabe's hand as they continued up the ramp.

Matteo remembered how grown up they all looked suddenly, even Essie. Sara had insisted on doing Essie's hair and had wrapped her head with golden brown braids. Her short overalls provided a youthful balance—Luke had teased her about looking 'just so gosh darn precious' as a means of lightening the mood, something that had earned him a hard stare from his wife.

Gabe had been speaking quietly to Essie as they trudged up the passenger ramp. When they reached level footing, he had turned suddenly and given her a gentle kiss on the lips.

It hadn't been the impassioned kiss Matteo had invented in his mind. He had visualized a naive Esther being stunned by the assertiveness of the kiss, but as he pulled the memory into his mind's eye, he remembered it had actually been quite brief and she had hugged him after. Gabe hadn't looked pompous or victorious as they embraced; he wasn't seeking out Josh's face to gloat, the brothers having developed a sibling rivalry over the years. His eyes were tense with fear as he whispered something in her ear.

Gabe had released her first, kissed the top of her head, running his hand over her braids, and set off, avoiding looking back.

"I don't understand—why would he kiss you—"

She took a breath. "There was a group of kids in town who liked to tease me. They liked to question my faith, accuse me of being secretly promiscuous since my best friends were boys. What a scandal for a pastor's daughter."

Matteo's heart started racing.

"Sometimes they took things too far. They'd grab at me, try to kiss me, touch me–"

"They did *what*?"

She waved him off. "They never ended up—nothing happened beyond that."

"This was at the market?"

"It's the reason Gabe and I veered off on our own. Josh didn't know. He chatted with some of them, but he didn't know how they treated me. They're why I stopped going into town. Gabe had me promise before he left that I wouldn't go there alone."

"You had mentioned girls who flirted with Josh, but–"

"They egged on the boys in their group to go after me. A couple of the girls did, too. They'd record videos on their phones–"

He wasn't taking full breaths. "They *grabbed* at you?"

She nodded stiffly. "As naive as I was, I confided in Gabe that I was afraid that one of them would steal my first kiss." Her eyes were very round.

"Essie–"

"They probably would have taken more than my first kiss if they had the opportunity," she said quietly, frowning deeply, "but I—"

Matteo exhaled suddenly. "*That's* why he kissed you."

She smiled weakly, her eyes brimmed with tears. "Before he got on the train he said: 'Now you know your first kiss came from someone who loves you.'"

He looked into the desperate, swollen eyes of his daughter, and could feel her devastation square in his chest, making it difficult to breathe. He dropped his gaze to the tabletop and stared at the silverware holder for an exceedingly long period of time, replaying moments he'd observed between Gabe and Esther, now through a new lens. "I've been so unfair to that boy."

"And he's still Gabe," she said with a small shrug. "They see what they're making him do and they dismiss him as a lost cause, but he's not. He's still Gabe." Her lower lip quivered. "And they're going to kill him. The second we lock down? They're going to kill him."

Matteo stood and in one fluent motion pulled her to stand and wrapped her in his arms. "Mia dolce ragazza," he whispered quickly. "Ti amo così tanto e mi dispiace così tanto che tu debba passare attraverso questo. Voglio così tanto togliermi il peso dalle spalle. Mi dispiace tanto. Ti amo e mi dispiace tanto." *My sweet girl, I love you so much and I'm so sorry that you're going through this. I want so badly to take the weight off your shoulders. I am very sorry. I love you and I'm so very sorry.*

Her body seemed to melt into him, her full weight leaning into his chest. "He's still Gabe, Daddy." The tears were pouring from her eyes, soaking through his shirt. Her words were becoming garbled as she repeated: "He's still Gabe."

They both heard the rumble of a truck, and the crunch of gravel outside at the same time. Esther startled from his grasp, her eyes wide.

"It's Luke and Sara," he said, swiveling his chin to the drive leading to the house.

"I can't see them," she said, shaking her head fearfully.

"I can send them away. We were just going to have dinner and play cards."

"No," she said quickly, her posture straightening.

"There's a bedroom down the hall," he offered.

She nodded.

"Wait, you're just going to hide out in there?"

"I worked last night. I could really use some sleep."

He doubted she had any intention of sleeping. "You'll stay the night? The roads are so dark–"

She kissed him lightly on the cheek. "I don't need to be driving anywhere." Her shadowed eyes watched the screen door nervously.

"Esther, honestly, they'd understand."

She shook her head and padded off down the hallway. The bedroom door had just clicked closed when Luke and Sara greeted him from the screen door.

"Whose truck? We're not interrupting anything, are we?" Sara asked delicately, her eyes prowling the house.

"Come on in." He pulled open the screen door and Sara entered first, clutching a tray of cornbread wrapped tightly in cellophane. She pecked him on the cheek, laser-focused on dropping the pan in the kitchen before taking off for the bathroom.

"Soo, whose truck?" Luke asked, peering around the small living area.

"Oh, no one's in the bathroom, right?" Sara asked, taking a quick sidestep from the door.

"No, it's free."

She still seemed fearful she might walk in on someone, turning the handle cautiously and peering around the door before fully committing to entering.

"Is someone else here?" Luke asked provocatively, nudging his friend in the gut.

"Would you stop? It's Essie."

He said her name softly, but they could still hear Sara gasp in the bathroom. "Essie's *here*?" she squealed.

Matteo gently hushed her as she repeated herself through a crack in the door, the toilet still mid-flush. "She's sleeping, Sara."

Luke dropped a six-pack of beer on the counter and peered down the short hallway. He lowered his voice to a whisper. "How's she doing?"

There was nothing that came to mind that Matteo could share about her: Not the information she had shared about Gabe. He couldn't share that she was allegedly stopping the work she was doing; he hadn't been able to share the details of that with them to begin with. Finally, he came up with: "She came out to see the new horse."

This didn't seem to please Luke, his brow furrowed.

"What's going on?" Sara whispered, scurrying toward them, wiping her hands on her jeans. Matteo made a mental note to take the bathroom towels out of the dryer. She took in her husband's expression.

"Essie came out here to see the new horse."

"What new horse?"

"That's not the point," Luke grumbled. "She came out here to see a *horse*?"

"It seemed like an excuse."

"Of course it was. She's going through so much," Sara said, giving her husband a threatening look. "How is she?"

"She might take over here, if I'm needed at the church."

"Oh, she'd be *great* out here. Does that mean she's quitting whatever they have her doing?" she asked excitedly.

He nodded.

"Oh *good*," Sara said, clapping silently. "Stop with that scowl, Luke."

Luke busied himself investigating the chili, lifting the lid on the crockpot and giving it a stir.

"Is she feeling alright? It's awfully early for her to be asleep."

"She worked last night."

"Oh, no wonder," she said, nodding, though she had no knowledge of the work she was doing. "Should we set things up on the porch, so we don't disturb her?"

"That's not a bad idea anyway. It's so nice with the rain," Luke observed.

"I knew I should have brought my extra sweater."

Luke rolled his eyes. "It's not cold, Sara."

"It will be in an hour."

"I've got extra coats. Essie wouldn't mind if you borrowed hers."

Sara let out a laugh that sounded like a hoot. "Bless you, Teo, for thinking I could fit in her clothes, especially in my condition."

"What condition is that?"

"Sara, no one but you can tell that you've got a belly."

Matteo panned back and forth between them. "*Wait*, are you saying–"

"I'm pregnant!" she exclaimed, then repeated the sentence in a whisper. "Four months."

"She was very excited when she finally got the house organized. Took me entirely off guard," Luke explained. "I always said if she'd just relax, things would happen." With all that had transpired, Matteo had nearly forgotten how for years, they had tried to have more children after Josh.

"Ignore him," Sara said, beaming at Matteo as he stepped forward to hug her.

"You could have done so much better than my best friend is all I'm saying," he whispered.

"That's Essie humor rubbing off on you," she said in a sing-song voice, tapping his chest as they parted.

Matteo raised his eyes, peering down the hallway. The light appeared to be turned off in the bedroom, but with the echo and the way Sara's voice carried, he had no doubt she had heard the news. It would only solidify her thinking that they had given up on their oldest son. He had to admit, without knowing the conversations and the tears they'd shared with him, he could understand why she would have that impression.

It can be tempting to shield children from grief, he could hear himself say during the parents' group at Calvary. So many couples had faced infertility, miscarriages, and stillbirths, not to mention the high death rate in the country. *Don't do it. If you don't show them how to cope with loss, they'll never learn for themselves. If they don't see that you're sad, they won't know it's okay to be sad. They might also interpret that you just don't care as they do and that's dangerous, isn't it?*

Luke and Sara were on their way home by 9:30 pm, as they, like Matteo, rose around 4am each day. They lived only two miles down the road; it was one of the things he enjoyed most about the new living arrangement.

Matteo washed the dirty bowls and utensils, set them to dry on the rack, then secured the door locks. Each time he checked the spare bedroom door, the light was off, leaving him to believe she had somehow managed to sleep. When he had finished tidying the kitchen and replaced the towels in the bathroom, he went to check on her.

She didn't even pretend to be sleeping.

"Daddy, can we please just talk in the morning?" Her voice was low, muffled, and barely recognizable.

He crossed to the bed, intending to move the tissue box closer to her, but found the box empty on the nightstand. He was fairly certain it had never been used. He retreated to the bathroom and returned with another box. "Wake me up if you decide you want to talk, OK?"

She nodded fiercely, pulling two tissues from the new container and covering her nose.

He kissed the top of her head. "Buonanotte, Esther Evin."

"Daddy?" she called just as he reached the door. "Pregherai per lui?"

Will you pray for him, he translated silently.

"Ogni mattina e ogni sera e ogni momento intermedio." *Every morning and every night and every moment in between.*

She sniffled in the darkness. "Ti amo, Daddy."

"I love you, Esther. Più di quanto ne sai." *More than you know.*

17
faith

Gabe sat in the waiting area on the second floor, staring at the snake plant situated next to the elevator bank, wondering if it was real or artificial. The wait for a Mandatory training Sim session was estimated to be longer than two hours from the time he arrived. Something about "enhancements" to the program was causing a bottleneck. His stomach grumbled loudly, causing one of the other waiting enlistees to glance up, out of annoyance based upon his expression, his thick eyebrow scowling.

Gabe leaned back in his chair, wishing he'd eaten before signing onto the waitlist since the cafeteria would likely be down to ration bars or 3D-printed mystery foods made from recycled food paste by the time he got there. He just needed something that would fill the void in his stomach enough so that he could fall asleep.

A shattering of glass jolted him to attention, and he whipped around to look into the atrium. At the basin, just behind the security desk, strewn across an Adirondack chair in a decidedly cheerful shade of yellow, was the body of an enlistee from his year.

Preston.

When he arrived at Mandatory, he had a mane of sandy hair, a strong build, and was a source of positivity and reassurance in his group. In their orientation sessions, they had gravitated toward one another. Preston reminded him of Josh with his humor and wit. They had parted ways once they were assigned to different sectors, Gabe moving into the medical team, while Preston moved into civil management.

The security officer was now examining Preston's body, peering up at the balcony from which he'd fallen. It was then Gabe noticed the angle of his limbs, jutting out from their sockets loosely, like a marionette puppet that had been dropped. While before he had the appearance of landing in a reclined position, his face turned upward, Gabe realized he could read the name of the surf company on the back of his t-shirt.

Preston had a twin sister named Olivia. He had agreed to take her years of Mandatory so she wouldn't have to report.

He pulled in his breath.

Keeping her safe and away from this place was Preston's primary motivation. He wouldn't do anything to put her at risk.

An additional security officer had appeared, taking in the scene. Together, they strategized how they would transport the body. After attempting to hoist him by the legs and shoulders, only to have the spine fold, they decided to lift the entire chair.

"West298?" came the snippy voice of one of the Simulator operators. "Sim Program Start."

Gabe swiveled his chin toward the source of the voice and stood without conscious decision to do so. He proceeded stiffly toward the door that led to the Simulator Theaters, thinking not of the young man who he had once considered a friend now sprawled lifeless across an Adirondack chair being hauled away by security guards.

His thoughts were decidedly blank as he followed the mole-looking woman with round glasses, his mind making only superficial observations, such as the temperature of the hallway, the volume level of each of the theaters they passed before reaching the one assigned to him.

*   *   *

The next morning, Gabe was back to work at the public health clinic. He had just wrapped up giving a pre-employment exam and was inputting his notes to forward to the orientation coordinator. There was an uneasiness in the air since he'd come back to the lobby area and he found himself picking up on ambient noises he typically had no trouble blocking out— the whirring of the air conditioner, the flickering of the overhead lights, the muffled, nondescript sound of crying.

"They say your people are going extinct."

Gabe turned his attention to the source of the voice, Deidre Chauncey, the lead social officer in the clinic. She raised her red eyes at the young woman sitting across from her, who was a stark contrast. Deidre had the vague appearance of a comic book villain. Half her head was shaved with a psychedelic circular pattern on her skull, like crop circles. The other half was feathered and dyed a dull black. She maintained a blunt edge of bangs across the entirety of her forehead. The stubble on the shaved half of her head, along with the light tint of freckles on her cheeks indicated she had once had naturally strawberry blonde hair. She appeared to be tattooed on every part of her visible skin. Three tattoos tended to stand out to him: the Communist flag, a clenched fist, and an American flag burning in a bonfire, which appeared to include the broken cross of Jesus as kindling. If her appearance wasn't intimidating enough, she had also subscribed to a recent trend where people had eye injections to change the color of their irises. She had chosen to have hers dyed blood red. The effect was incredibly eerie.

The young woman sitting across the desk from Deidre was radiantly natural. She looked a year or two younger than him. Her golden-brown hair poured over her shoulders in bushy waves. Her face appeared washed but was free of any of the thickly coated makeup that was so popular in the city, her skin a medium tone and soft, despite the harsh industrial lighting. Her features were defined but delicate, nose petite and rounded, lips pale but full, and dimples in her cheeks visible as she must have been literally biting her tongue. She blinked slowly, saying nothing in return.

"Are you a mute?" Deidre asked sharply as she forced the young woman's hand across the desk to complete a finger prick blood test, the primary method used for identification.

The young woman frowned at Deidre, but when she spoke, her voice gave a cool: "No."

"They say your people are going extinct," Deidre repeated, glaring at the girl's arm turned upward on the counter. She was motioning to something, but Gabe wasn't able to see what it was with Deidre's shoulders in his line of vision. He suspected it was a tattoo of some kind. Tattoos had become popular, not only for bodily mutilation, as was the case with Deidre but also for the identification of specific societal groups. Originally it was just used for convicted criminals, but a number of years earlier, there had been a push to brand individuals who didn't comply with government mandates, "for simplified identification." The initiative was short-lived, disappearing into thin air without a mention on the news, but he had heard about an uprising that took out several government buildings as a result of such programs. He suspected there had been similar occurrences elsewhere. A tyrannical government doesn't just stop doing something they hailed as brilliant for no reason.

He walked to the counter behind Deidre's desk pretending to look for a pen. From this angle, he could see that the underside of the young woman's forearm appeared to be covered in an intricate design—he could see a tree, as well as other objects he couldn't decipher. The pattern outlined a very defined cross. It was inked by a much more talented artist than whoever had branded Deidre's skin, that was for sure.

"What people would that be?" The young woman challenged delicately.

The blood test beeped, and Deidre checked the small display reading. "Fertile women," she said in a chilly voice. "Many are choosing Purity as the responsible choice."

The young woman withdrew her arm from the table, body rigid. Her brown eyes lifted away from the officer sitting before her and found Gabe, widening as they did.

She seemed like a distant dream, details he vaguely remembered, but couldn't reclaim no matter how he pulled and grasped for them.

Deidre glanced over her shoulder to see what had caught the young woman's attention, snickering to herself. "Young women should enjoy themselves, don't you think, Emily?" She arched an eyebrow condescendingly. "Or does your 'God' not permit that?"

The young woman dropped her gaze back to the officer.

Deidre made a clicking noise with her tongue as she scanned the computer display. "You've never sought aid until today?"

The young woman gave a small shake of her head.

"Highly unusual."

"Emergency supplies are running low." Her voice had a pleasing tone that drew him closer. He tilted his ear in her direction, thumbing absentmindedly through a file folder.

"What's a current address for you?"

"It's a few miles out of the city. There aren't any road signs anymore."

Deidre narrowed her eyes, exhaled through her nostrils, and scrolled through her screen. "The only thing on record for you is your birth information."

Emily shrugged and looked up at Gabe briefly, but the sound of sobbing behind her caught her attention. An older woman was being wheeled toward the exam room at the end of the corridor. Her body was hunched forward, probably from osteoporosis or malnutrition and she clutched a brass photo frame in her hands. It appeared to be a faded family photo. By the look of it, she and her husband just had one child.

"The doctor says this is the best thing, Mom. It'll just be like falling asleep," her son reasoned.

She shook her head fiercely without looking up. "It's not time for me, Frankie. It's *not my time.*"

Her words echoed in Gabe's ears after the exam room door closed.

Gabe had observed three "assisted releases," but hadn't yet performed one. As a way to market killing the elderly, or near elderly rather, there had been a wave of commercials put out from the Department of Public Health with the message of opportunity, of "choosing dignity." Given the state of the country, the food shortages and the shortage of "prime age" people to pay taxes, it was depicted as the responsible, "selfless" thing to do. It struck him how Deidre had phrased "purity" in the same way. Semantics was everything. Wordsmiths could make even the most inhumane, barbaric practices sound desirable. Sterilization became "purity," medicated suicide (or in the case of the woman taken into the exam room, medicated murder) became "release."

Most completed the "release" procedure out of a clinic setting, voluntarily (allegedly), but he had heard of resistant patients being brought in with less consideration than a stray dog being euthanized. It seemed most of the new medical programs used the word "choice" in their messaging but provided very little of it. It's not so much a "choice" if you're provided no alternative.

The woman let out a wail from behind the door--a heart-wrenching plea to her son, who quickly exited the room and made his way to the front door.

"Just do it already," Deidre groaned. "This is why they should just knock them out at the curb."

Emily, who had appeared close to tears before, now stared blankly toward the exam door, barely breathing. It appeared to be taking an extraordinary amount of restraint to keep her in her chair. When she looked back at him, her eyes were bloodshot and brimmed with tears.

He couldn't help but notice a sliver of silver in her right iris. He narrowed his eyes. *It's a glitch.*

It happened quickly: A flash across his vision of a girl smiling over at him as they walked side-by-side across a field.

Stop, he scolded silently.

The social services officer cleared her throat. "West, is there a problem?"

He turned to her, his face pale. "No."

"Emily Seger needs a pre-aid exam."

He nodded, glanced across the lobby. "OK, which one is she?"

"Right here," Deidre said, annoyed.

"*Oh,*" he said, frowning into the face of the young woman sitting on the other side of the desk. *It's not her,* he told himself silently. "Emily?"

The young woman looked up, her breaths shallow.

"I believe Exam Room 3 is open," he began, motioning toward the room. He inclined his head toward his patient, waiting for her to follow. When she had risen to her feet, he began to lead her toward the exam room, two down from where the older woman had been taken.

Something deep in his chest began to ache. He thought of the life being ended. He could almost feel the woman's presence fading away as the medicine slithered through her veins and seized her heart.

Holding open the door, his mind reeled the images of death he had witnessed that most times, he was able to block out. Just that morning on his walk to the clinic, there had been a teenage boy strewn across the debris and garbage. He looked like he hadn't had a solid meal in years.

As he turned to address Emily, he found Deidre was also in the room. She swiftly retrieved a paper gown from the exam table and tossed it at Emily. She then positioned herself in the corner, arms crossed, watching her.

"First time food rations is just a basic physical--vitals, reflexes?"

"With her history unknown, she poses a significant public health risk. She needs a full exam followed by the Purity procedure."

Gabe narrowed his eyes. "Is this a new policy?"

"That's not your concern, *is it?*"

He shifted his attention to Emily, who looked startled by Deidre's presence. He thought of the girl from the memory, her golden-brown hair whipping in the breeze. She was laughing, her mouth wide open and smiling, the area around her eyes incredibly expressive.

It's not her.

"*Gown,*" Deidre ordered, raising her eyes at Emily.

"The Purity procedure is still voluntary, isn't it?" Gabe was surprised at his nerve to challenge her. The words had flown out of his mouth reflexively, but he knew better.

Deidre cleared her throat. "Special circumstances allow for mandatory compliance. This includes any individuals identified as posing a public health risk."

Emily looked back and forth between them, her eyes uncertain.

"It *sounds* like you're challenging my authority, West." Deidre said lightly.

Gabe lowered his eyes and shook his head. "You can change back here," he offered, motioning to the changing area at the far end of the room.

"No," Deidre said, her grating voice echoing against the walls. "She can change *here*. If you're uncomfortable, West, you can leave. It's important to make sure that she doesn't try to conceal anything."

He wanted to argue that this girl wasn't a threat. He wanted to demand to know what Deidre thought she could be concealing. He wanted to yell at that vampire-eyed woman that she wanted to sterilize this girl because of her faith and her faith alone. He had the strong desire to rip Deidre apart, limb from limb. He could imagine himself doing this quite efficiently.

He took a breath. He knew better, but as he glanced over his shoulder to see Emily beginning to slide her jeans down her legs, he felt his jaw tense.

Deidre appeared to be thoroughly enjoying herself, not waiting for two breaths before asserting: "*All* of your clothes."

Emily took a steadying breath and removed her shirt and undergarments, which looked cleaner than most patients that came into the clinic. She also lacked the usual odor. Just the opposite–her hair carried traces of pleasant smells that brought to mind visions of grassy fields and blue skies.

He swallowed hard. "I'll bring Emily back out when we're done," he offered to Deidre. "Busy lobby out there."

"I'll stay," she said lightly. "I haven't gotten to see a Purity procedure in a while. It's amazing how efficient the whole process is."

Seeing the twisted joy in the woman's blood-red eyes caused him to step to his right and inadvertently become a human shield, blocking her view of the young patient. An onlooker would have thought the officer had a weapon aimed toward them.

To his surprise, Emily moved around him, the paper gown tied as best as she could manage. For a brief moment, their arms brushed against each other, and then she willingly climbed onto the exam table, the paper rattling loudly beneath her.

There was something wicked to the normalcy of denying a young woman the chance to bring life into the world, even the current one. He'd performed the procedure dozens of times, but he had been able to distance himself emotionally. Many of the women were desperate to acquire food and supplies to support the children they had so they didn't seem to be fully absorbing the impact of the procedure. Admittedly, it was easier to feel okay with sterilizing a woman who'd already had a child or two. The younger ones tested his resolve.

Gabe took a few solid breaths. Questioning or criticizing government authorities was a crime. He knew the consequences if he refused to comply with orders.

He followed the protective motion his body had taken, acting as though his posture was the natural progression to step toward the counter, where he picked up the tablet. "Let's actually have you come over to the scale, Emily."

Deidre couldn't say he wasn't following procedure, but he was hoping that if he could manage to drag out the examination, the officer might get tired of waiting and be forced to leave.

The paper crinkled and he sensed her presence behind him. He reset the scale and directed her to step onto it. He inputted her weight in her chart. "Have you gotten a recent height taken?"

She shook her head.

He asked her to turn around and moved in close to adjust the measuring stick to touch the top of her head. She was two inches taller than he initially guessed, her eyes in alignment with his nose.

He inputted her height into the device. "Let's do a quick eye exam, if you want to step over here."

There was a rattle of the scale as she lost her balance stepping down. In one fluid motion, he thrust the tablet into his opposite hand, rotated, and caught her. She collided into his chest, grabbing onto his shoulder in the process. Her hair smelled like fresh cut grass and warm rain.

"I'm sorry," she whispered.

"You have nothing to be sorry for," he said professionally, though he found himself searching her eyes. She felt so familiar, but her facial features and her eyes were foreign to him. Both were too plain, too ordinary.

"Is it a good idea for me to have something in my stomach before having the procedure?" she asked after passing the eye exam with 30/20 vision.

Gabe was pleased she had the same idea as him to test Deidre's resolve to stay in the room, but he was alarmed by her implied acceptance of the procedure to be performed.

"You'll get your supplies after. You can eat something then," Deidre snapped impatiently.

"Actually, current recommendations from the DPH—" The words spilled out of his mouth.

Deidre rolled her eyes, putting up her hand to stop him. "When did you eat last?"

"Two days ago."

The officer turned on the spot. "Fine. Get her an apple and a glass of milk or something. Better than having her vomit, I suppose. I'll be back in a few minutes."

Once she had gone, leaving the exam door wide open, Gabe took a full inhalation finally. "You don't have to stay. There are safer places to get food outside the city." His voice was restrained, nearly a whisper. "She can't stop you. Just walk out."

"*Gabe*," she said softly, a single syllable startling him more than a gunshot.

The moment their eyes met, he froze. Just moments earlier, he swore her eyes had been a muted shade of brown, but now he was staring into a shimmering sea of silver.

These were her eyes.

"*Gabe*?"

The color in her eyes appeared to shift and returned to the muddy shade of brown he had seen in the lobby. He shook his head, chuckling bitterly to himself. "I should have known."

She looked startled.

"This isn't real. You—" he pointed at her. "*You're. not. real.*"

"Gabe? It's me." Her eyebrows drew upwards in an innocent, disarming way...*like her.*

"You're not taking her from me," he said in a low voice, scanning the room distrustfully. "You can't—" He took a steadying breath, released her arms, and moved toward the door. "I'll get you something to eat," he muttered.

It's AI, he told himself. *She's not real. They're trying to make you think of her so they can erase her. She's not real.*

He left the hallway door ajar while he crossed to the supply of food rations.

As he waited for the clerk to process the aid bag, he attempted to keep his mind clear. *Don't think of her, don't think of her*, he pleaded, though the images kept trying to push their way to the front of his mind: *Flowing hair glowing in the light of a sunset. A joyful giggle. Giving her a piggyback ride when they were children. He could feel her tucked in perfectly to the nook of his arm.*

No. He had to stop.

He tried to force his mind to go blank. If they couldn't trigger the memories, they couldn't take them.

They had never used this method of extraction; it had never felt this targeted. He twitched his face, trying to feel the weight of the Sim sensors, but he felt nothing. The clinic still had its stale stench; there was no low hum of the Sim system.

"Best we can do today," the clerk, a young man with pale ivory skin said, handing him a satchel of cans and some random pieces of fruit. "We're supposed to be restocked Friday, if she wants to come back."

Gabe saw her sitting behind the leather-wrapped steering wheel of the farm's pickup truck, biting her lower lip as she focused on timing the press of the clutch with moving the shifter. She had released a series of expletives as the truck made a grinding noise when she shifted into the wrong gear. The expression on her face was both sheepish and frustrated.

Please don't take that one. He tries to think of a memory for which he was willing to part.

They only take it if it makes you happy.

He couldn't bear the thought of parting with what he estimated were the most recent memories. Instead, though he ached at the thought of not being able to summon the memory again, he chose the one of her at the age of seven, propped against the tree in front of the farmhouse, a thick leather-bound book in her lap, her fists propping up her cheeks, her eyes closed. She tended to fall asleep mid-day, especially if her nightmares the night before had been relentless. He found his mouth pulling up at the corners; she really was adorable as a child. He regretted this choice. Surely there was a different memory, but his mind panicked. At any moment, the memory would vanish, and he would be left stunned as the image dissolved from his brain, a hollow ache in his chest.

Any moment.

But it was still there. He became bolder, the memories filling him with warmth. It had been so long since he had allowed himself the luxury of indulging in happy memories. He could feel her climb under the covers of his bed, tucking herself in against him after having a nightmare once his dad had put a stop to them sharing a bed.

He waited.

Her unearthly silver eyes, how they brightened when she smiled.

Her sitting at the kitchen table at the farmhouse swimming in one of his distressed old t-shirts. She had started stealing his t-shirts from a young age. When his mom asked about it, he always said he let her have them so she wouldn't put a stop to it. He wasn't sure what it was, but there was something incredibly satisfying about having someone *want* to steal your t-shirts.

He sighed. He couldn't remember her name. He knew she would liken the Sim operators to Dementors in *Harry Potter*, sucking out any happy memories, leaving behind only misery and hollowness. He knew she might even slip into a British accent and quote one of the characters describing them.

But he couldn't remember her name.

He turned toward a muffled sound over his shoulder.

It was the son of the older woman who had been released. He was sitting in the row of empty chairs, leaning over his knees, muttering something softly over and over again. As Gabe drew closer, he heard the words: "I'm sorry, Mom. I'm so sorry."

When Gabe returned to Exam Room 3, Emily had moved back to the exam table, her brow tense.

"Very slim pickings today," Gabe said, trying to keep his tone light. "I hope green apples are okay."

She nodded, accepting the netted bag. She looked indecisive, not quite committing to sitting fully on the table. He kept seeing her eyes dart over toward her clothes, up to the door.

"I'll finish the rest of the exam while you eat, if that's okay?" he said rhetorically. The sooner he got through the exam, the sooner he could face the pain that concluded each Sim session, the sooner he would know what damage he'd caused by letting his guard down, the sooner he could return to the solitude of his room.

Her brown eyes were very round as she watched him wheel over a blood pressure stand. She didn't break her gaze as she removed an apple from the bag and took her first crunchy bite.

239

He had to give them credit. The shape of her eyes was spot on. The color, however, was wrong and her face looked too rounded. She was far too young for crow's feet and her nose wasn't pug shaped.

He stepped toward her, turning over her unoccupied hand. The tattoo was now clearly visible before him. He hadn't been able to get a good look at it before, but he let his eyes follow the design, the intricate flowers, the leather-bound books, and the tree that helped create the silhouette of the cross. His eyes fell upon a shading of some kind hidden in the design. As he looked closer, he saw that it wasn't shading at all. It was a data matrix code.

They pulled it from the memory by the tree, he decided quickly. He then realized the tree featured in her tattoo seemed to be modeled after the one in his memory.

He took a breath, allowing himself the freedom to explore the accompanying thoughts, knowing the memory was doomed to be erased anyway.

He remembered asking his mom about a data matrix code tattoo on the girl's arm. His mother had dismissed the question, saying it must have "just been something they did at the hospital." He had only asked to see if she knew, or if she would tell him. He had long suspected the images, sounds, voices from the girl's nightmares were more or less memories. They were just too vivid for them not to have happened.

Knowing what so frequently haunted her dreams, it was especially sweet to see her sleeping peacefully.

"You're a southpaw," he observed, his mind stalling on the memory by the tree, the way the girl pursed her lips as she slept, the sizable hardcover book in her lap. He had taken quite a bit of pride in how much she loved reading, having been the one to help her to learn in the first place.

He placed two fingers gently on her wrist but found the tremor in his hand was keeping him from getting a good read of her pulse. The silky beige tone of her skin, her ease with his touch, was so familiar, so real, and her skin was luxuriously warm against his chilled fingers.

"How could you tell?" Her voice was strained.

He frowned. "You're eating with your right hand, but you have more calluses on the fingers on your left hand. You must write or sketch a lot."

She examined her left hand, then raised her silver eyes, eager to make eye contact.

"Your knuckles look like they've seen some trouble."

She ran her fingers over the scabs along her knuckles. "You should see the other guy."

It was just as he processed her words that his heart lurched in his chest. *Her eyes are silver.*

He took in a breath. Filling his senses was freshly cut grass, open fields, wildflowers, and hay.

He was certain the aromas weren't actually permeating the air of the dingy government medical clinic, but they filled his naval cavities all the same. Baked casseroles. Oatmeal raisin cookies. Coconut. Vanilla. Citrus. A wood-burning fire. A fresh Christmas tree.

"Gabe," she beckoned softly.

As Deidre swept back into the room and the cold air reached his cheeks, he realized tears were streaming from his eyes. Emily was watching him closely. He released her arm, rotating away from Deidre's watchful stare.

"Almost done?"

"Just finishing up," Emily said, presenting the apple. "Were you able to find milk?"

Deidre glared at her, seemingly in shock that this girl would have the audacity to respond to her. "Before you do the sterilization," she said, rotating her chin slowly to Gabe, "I'd like you to do a pelvic exam."

Gabe cleared his throat, straightening himself. "Why?"

"We need to be thorough, don't we?" In his peripheral vision, he could see Deidre tilting her chin toward Emily as she said this. He imagined with her blood-red eyes; she would look more sadistic than usual.

"If you're not up for it, I'm sure Dr. Warren would be. Ms. Seger has not received *any* preventative care. It would be irresponsible of us not to be thorough."

He quickly considered his options, avoiding letting his eyes linger over Emily. There was no way he would be able to spare her a pelvic exam, but Dr. Warren was far more comfortable with the idea of infringing on a woman's autonomy. He seemed to quite enjoy it. He turned his chin toward Emily, allowing eye contact.

"I'll make it as brief as possible," he whispered, furrowing his brow apologetically.

Emily glanced across the room to Deidre, a flash of anger on her face.

"Excellent. Let's get started then, shall we?" Deidre said with faux propriety.

Emily was still finishing her last bite, holding the apple core awkwardly in her palm.

"Here," Gabe offered, taking it from her hand and tossing it in the trash bin. He returned to her side, turning his chin away from Deidre again. "Will you consent to the exam?" he asked delicately. "A pelvic exam is used to identify any abnormalities. It *is* recommended for regular checkups."

Emily didn't seem to be taking full inhalations but gave a quick nod.

He went to the sink, washed his hands, and pulled on a pair of procedure gloves. "Do you have any concerns you'd like to address today?"

When she didn't verbalize a response, he turned on the spot and found her looking increasingly uneasy, her chin lowered.

"Emily?" The name sounded foreign and unnatural to say aloud. She shook her head.

"What brought you in?"

There was hesitation to her reply. "Food."

Deidre scoffed angrily. "You should be thankful to *have* food at all. It's such a strain to feed the people *in* the city, let alone having Rurals come begging."

He clenched his jaw, avoiding eye contact as he raised Emily's feet into the stirrups and directed her to move to the base edge of the table. He sat on the rolling stool, clearing his throat. "A bit of pressure," he warned, inserting the speculum and beginning the exam.

Deidre moved directly behind him, peering over his shoulder. "You can't see anything like *that*," she scoffed, pushing the gown so it receded to Emily's waist and left her exposed from the abdomen down.

Gabe tried to focus on what he needed to do. It seemed to be the only way to end the situation for Emily. After following the textbook process for the exam as quickly as possible, he reported: "Everything appears normal and healthy."

"Is she intact?"

He froze, a wave of fury pulsating through him. "Excuse me?"

"We have to report it. New DPH guidelines for those receiving the Purity procedure. Efficacy statistics, I believe."

He lifted his eyes to look at Emily, but she had her face turned away, chin tucked to her shoulder. "Yes."

"Yes what?" Deidre asked, mockingly.

"Yes, hymen is intact."

"Of *course* it is. Such a virtuous faith," the officer said silkily.

Gabe took a breath, knowing an outburst from him would likely lead to Dr. Warren taking over the exam. "Where are we documenting that for DPH?" He tried to make his tone sound inquisitive.

"Oh, it's not *really* documented, I just wanted to confirm my suspicions. Slide a few fingers up there, West. You don't find them tight like that very often. I might have a rummage around, too. Do the honors myself."

Gabe gently covered Emily with the gown. "That should complete the exam," he said, pushing his rolling stool away.

"Just the procedure then," Deidre said lightly, her lips pulled up at the corners.

No, he thought desperately, removing his gloves and discarding them in the wastebasket.

"We wouldn't want to take any chances should she suddenly decide to abandon her principles," she added in a taunting voice.

His eyes panned from Deidre to Emily, who was silent, staring intensely at the far wall.

Deidre narrowed her eyes. "We can't allow unregulated breeding. We spay *dogs*, do we not?"

Gabe took a breath, hating himself, hating Deidre, hating what the world had become.

It was then he noticed Emily clenching her left hand into a fist. Her body was tense to the point of pulsation, primed to attack. He moved quickly to her side, and placed his hand gently over her fist, stroking the delicate skin on the top of her hand, which seemed enough to distract her. He gave an almost imperceptible shake of his head, and she unclenched her fist.

He released her hand and stepped across the room.

The serum was stored in a cabinet marked with an outline of a lotus flower. He removed tubing and a syringe from the shelf. The syringe itself was nondescript apart from an identical laser engraved logo on one side. He held it in his fist as he crossed the room, finding Deidre had stepped alongside the exam table, staring down at Emily. In his mind, he saw himself dropping the procedure supplies, and throwing Deidre against the wall. He'd never thought of himself as being capable of hurting another human being, but he felt adequately desensitized to it at this point. He'd thought repeatedly about killing Deidre since he started at the clinic. The thought of her collapsed on the floor in a pool of thick dark blood brought him a peaceful feeling, like the world was all the better to have her gone. Unfortunately, there were so many more just like her.

He swallowed his anger and moved back to the end of the exam table. "Emily, we'll make this quick, okay?"

Emily was staring intently at the place where Deidre's hand rested beside her as if it were a flame threatening to burn her.

"*Oh,* don't forget *the gloves,*" Deidre said, her voice lifting, smiling tightly at Emily.

Gabe again felt increasing pressure to get Emily through the situation as quickly as possible, perching himself on the rolling stool. He pulled on a fresh pair of gloves, shifting hands with the supplies. He then attached the tubing to the Luer tip, deciding against narrating the procedure. He inserted the narrow tubing into the vaginal opening, guiding it several inches inside. When the method was taught to him, it was explained that it was the same method used for intrauterine insemination, which had been made illegal a couple of years earlier. All human reproduction now required monitoring by the Bureau for Public Wellness or an individual and any conspirators would be disqualified from receiving health insurance or public assistance.

Deidre turned Emily's wrist with such force that he thought she may have broken it. She examined the intricate cross tattoo, her fingertips slithering across the underside of her arm. To an onlooker, it might appear that she was comforting her—if only they didn't pay attention to the firmness of her grasp. If only they didn't pay attention to the expression of alarm on Emily's face.

"This might sting as it makes contact."

Emily was holding back tears, her jaw tight, but she didn't break eye contact with Deidre.

Gabe applied pressure to the plunger and waited for all the liquid to make its way through the tubing. The entire procedure took less than 60 seconds.

"*Awww,*" Deidre said, puckering her lips and placing her palm on Emily's exposed abdomen. "*No babies for you.*"

Emily squeezed her eyes shut as Deidre moved toward the lobby.

"Let us know if you need anything, Emily," Deidre added in a sugary sweet voice, the door clicking solidly behind her.

The exam room was filled with an eerie silence. Emily's face was braced as though in pain, tears rolling down her cheeks.

"I'm sorry," Gabe breathed, adjusting the gown to cover her, but found the limitations of the paper material provided very little modesty. He stood and removed his lab coat, placed it over her. The action took him by surprise.

It took a few moments for Emily to look at him.

He removed the tubing, then the speculum, and pulled out the bed extension over the stirrups. She immediately pulled her legs toward her chest, seeming to want to get as far from him as possible. He gently adjusted his lab coat over her knees to better cover her. Gabe lowered his eyes as he moved to the sink. He ran the faucet, staring briefly at the lotus engraved syringe, still full, in his palm.

The action had come so naturally, without premeditation. Surely the Sim operators would see it. They would know what he had done.

He glanced briefly over his shoulder at Emily before emptying the contents of the syringe down the drain. He discarded the used supplies into the medical waste bin, including the syringe that had been filled with a saline meant for IV flushes. Unlike the lotus solution, which bubbled on contact as it traveled into the ovaries and caused egg stores to disintegrate, the saline would simply feel cold as it was absorbed into her body.

When he returned to her bedside, her silver eyes stared at him questioningly.

His eyes jumped pointedly to the back corner of the room and the camera mounted to the ceiling. "You'll be sore as the medication takes effect. I've been told it feels like severe menstrual cramps. Do you *feel that*?" he asked, lifting his eyebrows pointedly.

She frowned and gave a quick nod. She started to sit up, trying to keep some control over the gown placement. Her eyelids blinked slowly, the lashes thick and dark against her silver irises.

Gabe studied her face, a furrow on his brow. He held out his hand, guiding her to stand.

She pushed off the bed and allowed him to assist her to the curtained area where her clothes were folded on the small bench seat. He walked to the barred window, assessing the camera angle from below.

"Let me get that for you," he said suddenly, stooping down and quickly moving to keep the camera from seeing that there wasn't anything on the floor he was retrieving. As he stood, he grasped her hand and pulled her just to the limits of the camera's vision. The nearest microphone was several feet away on the ceiling. "You need to get out of the city."

She nodded, setting her eyes on him intensely. "So do you."

He moved closer to her ear, taking an indulgent inhalation of her hair. He intended to tell her he hadn't done the procedure, but instead, he heard himself say: "Lasciami qui." *Leave me here.*

18

the world outside

Safe in the locked cab of the old pickup truck outside the public health clinic, Essie took several deep breaths. She squeezed her eyes shut, pushing thick tears out through the lashes.

"What have you done?" she demanded of herself. "Stupid, *stupid* girl."

She had felt so certain of her plan when she started. Now, everything was worse than before.

She was haunted by regret: She had betrayed Luther. She had left without saying goodbye, not to Luther, not to the Wests, not to the friends she'd managed to make in town, not to her own dad. She had been so preoccupied with what she had set out to do that she hadn't processed that she had a high probability of being killed.

But Gabe's alive, she reasoned, though she knew she was no closer to getting him out of the city than before.

She glanced in the rearview, startled when she saw the face of Emily Seger. She reached behind her ear, pressed the translucent button, and watched Emily's face dissolve and reveal her own, looking more terrified than Emily had with the same expression. She blinked a few times, confused to see her own silver eyes staring back at her. The lenses had irritated her eyes from the moment she put them in. *They must have fallen out*, she concluded.

She was utterly exhausted. It had been two days since she left and the only sleep she'd attempted was parked just off the main highway behind brush so the truck wouldn't be seen by any military convoys that traveled at night. Her larger concern had actually been refugees traveling on foot who might look to ransack supplies from the truck, or the truck itself. Ultimately, the only sleep she'd managed was in the parking garage outside the medical clinic when she first arrived in the city. All 15 minutes of it.

She took a deep breath.

Her mind kept replaying the last antidote run with Luther a week earlier. She had awoken startled, which was typical. The end of the recovery process often felt like being trapped underwater for too long and finally breaking the surface of the water, gulping down air. What was *not* typical was that she was hooked up to two separate IV drips—one fluid, one blood. Luther was sitting at her side. He straightened his posture when he saw her eyes open, stroking her arm.

Once he'd watched her heart rate return to normal, he asked how she was feeling.

They had performed the antidote runs in the study at his cabin, built in the 18th century. It was helpful to have a layer of soundproofing with the thick wood beams, as some of the serums they tested had caused her to cry out as they took effect in her body. The air in the room that morning was more tense than even after those sessions.

"I feel tired, like normal. *Why?* What happened?"

He exhaled, working up the courage to say what needed to be said. "It didn't work."

She was stunned. The words sounded foreign; she repeated them silently over and over to try to make sense of them. "But we've done this combination before."

"I know," he began. "I've noticed some fluctuations with your body's immune response in the past few sessions. I was surprised when you said you hadn't felt a difference in your recovery."

Her jaw tightened. She had been lying about her recovery, even after she had confessed needlessly to him about Danny running additional sessions with her to further build the antidote inventory. The truth was that even after cutting back to weekly sessions, it was taking her far longer to shake the effects. It had gotten to the point that she was no longer feeling full strength before undergoing the next run. "Maybe we just need to space out the sessions more?"

He narrowed his eyes.

"I've probably been overdoing it. I've been doing higher-intensity workouts. If I dial that back and space out these sessions a bit maybe--"

He shook his head.

She sat up, ready to make her case. "Luther, I can do this. I just need more rest, that's all--"

"You're not hearing me."

"No, I am. I understand you're concerned for me--"

"Essie, you were *dying*." His voice bellowed against the walls. The words echoed like cathedral bells in her ears. "You need to stop. *All of this*." His expression was firm and bordering on desperate.

She used the recliner chair controls to sit up, suddenly struck by the need to use the bathroom. "I don't understand. How can my immunity just switch off?"

Luther stared at her, suppressing something behind his eyes. "Maybe God is telling you that you've done enough." His face softened. "You have been so brave, so selfless, so giving of yourself to this. Maybe He's telling you you've done enough."

It felt like she'd had the ground crumble beneath her, and she was in a free-fall. "What if I took a break and we tried again with something-- mild." The word was absurd considering the concoctions they'd tested. The most benign serum would kill the average person within minutes at most.

"Esther, even if this isn't permanent? Even if your immunity comes back?"

"Will it?"

He shrugged. "I don't know. I *hope* so, but not so you can pick up where we left off here. Esther, I need you to hear me–Even if it comes back?"

She lowered her eyes. "You won't do the sessions."

"I can't watch you go through this anymore. I can't. I'm probably being selfish here, but it *physically hurts* me watching you. I know it's nothing compared to what you go through." He shook his head. "I went into medicine to help people–'Do no harm.' I've been fighting to stop people who have done the very thing I'm doing to you."

Essie swallowed hard. There was a sweeping relief to know she wouldn't spend so much time in pain or physically exhausted, but there was also a vast emptiness, an uncertainty threatening to swallow her.

"We're very close to being able to synthesize the antidote. That's been the goal for me since we started. It was never for you to continue doing this indefinitely."

This statement stirred something in her and she sat silently in her seat, trying to process what she was feeling. She had told her dad she would only continue with the sessions for a few more weeks. That was two months earlier.

"I loaded you with a lot of fluids. If you're feeling steady enough, you should probably scoot to the bathroom."

It was as she stood at the sink in the small, rustic bathroom that a thought came to mind. She stood with her hands beneath the faucet staring at her reflection, analyzing the viability of the thought. It took only a minute or two for her to connect the dots and work out some of the logistics for her mission to retrieve Gabe.

Luther had been adamant that she stay put in the small town. He realized the risk of having her venture too far--if she was discovered, she could be experimented on again, weaponized, harvested for her eggs, bred. What Luther was trying to use for good, they would not. They had carried out genocide on their own people and were plotting another round. They wouldn't blink at the thought of developing something with her unwilling assistance to further their cause in a more elegant, concealed manner.

251

Luther had gone so far as to say that discovery of her was an existential threat to the safety of everyone targeted by the government.

It was different now.

She made eye contact with her reflection and said softly and calmly: "If I'm like everyone else now, I'm no longer a threat."

Esther reached to the backseat for her hooded sweatshirt and tugged it on. She felt chilled, despite the warm day. Gabe seemed to recognize her, seemed to handle her with more gentleness than a complete stranger, though truthfully she wasn't sure if that was his bedside manner with everyone. He had been defensive of her as much as he could be, but he had still performed the procedure.

Even if she still had her immune response, it had never been tested in the context of that procedure. She felt an ache in the pit of her stomach, her breaths shallow and uneven. The procedure was designed to disintegrate all egg stores. Chemical sterilization in a simple, quick outpatient procedure. The efficiency of it when paired with the finality of the results boggled the mind.

On her last night in the Ark, she'd dreamt of a cabin set on wide open acreage, smoke billowing from the chimney. She was sitting on the porch swing, her breaths slow and easy. One hand rested on her swollen, rounded belly, the other was entwined with tan, muscular fingers.

Esther gulped down a breath, trying to focus her attention on the internal workings of her body. She had become so in-tune with every organ, every muscle, every blood vessel, how they were all interconnected. She was confident she'd be able to recognize anything unusual, but as she let the silence stretch, there was nothing that seemed unusual, no triggered response, no pain.

She decided to let go of her concern about the procedure and assume that Luther had lied. He had been trying to stop the sessions from the beginning. It would make sense that he would take more determined action to get her to stop. It was logical. Her immunity wouldn't just stop after nineteen years. *The simplest answer is often the correct one*, she reasoned.

She took another deep breath.

Her plan had always been to test the waters and observe Gabe before extracting him from the city, but if she was being honest with herself, she had naively thought the sight of her, even disguised, might have triggered a more dramatic response, that the rest of her hair brain scheme wouldn't be necessary. She had considered not using the facial overlay, thinking it best to go as herself, but Danny had warned that she needed to change her appearance so she wouldn't be tracked as easily by surveillance. The contact lenses were meant as a way to block covert retinal scans but had been more trouble than they were worth. They had stung her eyes the entire time, and as she examined her appearance in the rearview, checking the corners of her eyes, it seemed they had fallen out with all the rubbing she had done of her eyes.

I should have gone as myself, she concluded.

It was with reluctance that she powered on the phone.

He spoke in Italian, she thought desperately, watching the phone come to life.

Leave me here. Did that mean he was unwilling to come with her no matter what she did? Did it mean he'd given up?

No, it made sense. Given all she'd seen of his sessions, she knew he was feeling hopeless. At one point during the exam, it seemed he thought she was part of the Sim.

She shut down the thought and focused on the phone, which was working through its startup prompts. Danny had set up the device with minimal applications. Esther had never used a phone before so he kept instructions as simple as possible. There was only one application she needed to access. The icon featured the two gender symbols abstractly twisted together in a knot pattern.

Danny was the author of this portion of the plan; the nature of it turned her stomach. Initially, they'd discussed adding her to the security clearance under the guise of being an employee, janitorial perhaps, since they were granted clearance to the dormitories where Gabe lived. Once

Danny had taken an evening to consider this plan, however, he had concluded that they needed a different angle.

"You don't fit the profile for janitorial staff."

"Why?"

He detached his monitor from its stand and presented her with the staff photos of the janitorial staff that worked at the complex.

Esther had trouble taking a full breath as her eyes gleamed over the images. There was variance in the ages and appearance of each person, but all of them shared one common characteristic: a thick scar in the middle of their necks. The scars were beveled and blotchy, each wound appearing to have been mended with the same sloppy carelessness. "What happened to them?"

"Laser cordectomy."

She furrowed her brow.

Danny was thoughtful for a moment. "Will you just take my word for it? That it won't work? The facial overlays don't cover the neck and it's not like they allow a turtleneck with the uniform."

"They removed their vocal chords?"

He blinked affirmatively.

"*But*–Isn't that a little barbaric?"

He raised his eyebrows. "Esther, look where *we* came from." He lifted the device, quickly flipped screens, and presented the monitor again. "I *do* have a plan that I think is more feasible, but it would be very much out of your comfort zone." The gender knot logo was present at the top of the page. He cleared his throat. "This is where our conversation shifts from disturbing to disturbing and awkward."

She didn't want to give too much thought to the next stage of the plan. She simply opened the app as Danny had instructed. He would be alerted to the sign-in, then he would ensure her medical clinic records were paired up as required, and her enrollment would be finalized. "It works a lot like rideshare apps back in the day."

"I don't know what that means."

"*Oh*, I don't often think where I grew up was tech-savvy." He cleared his throat. "Years ago when people needed to get somewhere, they could open an app and request a ride. It basically served as a middle person to collect the money, make sure the drivers weren't felons."

Esther applied the concept to what he'd described and winced. "So the app is like a pimp."

"*Where'd* you learn about pimps?"

"I read a lot. Not everything is Shakespeare."

He smirked.

"*So*, once my enrollment is set up, you'll have Gabe's account request me?"

"It doesn't allow for that. Requests go into a queue, matching requests with certain desired characteristics. I'll have your account claim the request."

"So, you signed Gabe up for an account?" She probed. This felt like too intimate of knowledge and threatened to tarnish her view of Gabe, but she didn't retract her question.

"Every enlistee is automatically provided an account. All 'encounters' are covered–as a 'benefit.'"

"How wholesome."

"I guess for some it would be an incentive, but I think the idea is that given the intensity of the program, having an–*outlet*–is mutually beneficial."

Esther lowered her eyes.

"He hasn't used it. If that helps?"

She shrugged, even though it did settle something internally.

In the pickup truck, Esther eyed the bag that held the required uniform for the role she was assuming. She hadn't dared try it on, deciding to wear it once would be enough.

The phone shook rapidly in her hand. Once, twice, five times in short succession. On the screen were several notifications. The first confirmed successful connection with her public health records. The second congratulated her on activating her account. The third confirmed an "encounter" with West,G-298WE4BPH476U for that evening at 7 pm. The fourth made several suggestions for active requests she could also claim with a reminder that she could only be compensated for a maximum of three encounters per 6-hour time period. The fifth was a direct message from a user called PROXY5829511. Esther pondered the screen name, wondering if the number held some significance, or if it was auto generated if there were at least five million proxies in the app. She tapped on the message.

"*Angler nearby. Contact?*"

Esther stared at the message, her heart clenched in her chest. Danny had tried to convince her to recruit help for her mission, namely Josh. She had been adamant that he not be involved, but she had been truthful as to why, not wanting Danny to get the wrong impression: Her voice kept breaking and she had to start and stop several times, her eyes burning. "I can't live in a world where Josh is dead," she said quickly, conclusively.

Danny had winced, staring at her incredulously, and said: "You know he feels the same way about *you*, right?"

She selected the keyboard icon and tapped out a response, struggling with phrasing something that would get her message across, but be safe from AI monitoring and flagging. She then powered down the phone. She would need to sign into the app again later to allow it to confirm her GPS location, but for now, with hours until she was scheduled to arrive, it felt safer to keep it turned off.

With an enormous exhalation, Esther slid out of the pickup truck, pulled on a baseball cap, and tapped the small button near her ear twice. She checked her reflection in the side mirror, finding the overlaid mapping had replaced her face with that of a thirty-something year old woman with deeply dimpled cheeks and an abundance of freckles. Her face was kind and maternal and reminded her a bit of Sara West, had it not been for the enormous slash marks across the woman's face. The marks were crudely healed, rising from the surface of her skin.

"Juliet," she said aloud, taking in the details of the woman's face. She dropped her gaze and directed her feet out of the parking garage and into the mid-day city. Her main objective for the afternoon was to test the route from the housing complex where Gabe lived to the interstate train route, confirm the timing of the light rail, and check for changes to the train schedule. Her second objective was to keep her nerve, clear her mind of the inner turmoil doubting the plan, scolding her for her tactics, her gutless flight from town before anyone could stop her.

She succeeded in her main objective but failed miserably to gain any resolve in the second.

She exited the train station and was retracing her path back to the light rail route when she felt a looming presence on the back of her neck. Her eyes shifted to the far reaches of their peripheral vision to check for someone approaching her, but no one was there. She found most of the city suffocating, but the air felt particularly uneasy in this part of the city. Most of the buildings weren't being utilized for their original business purposes anymore. There were traces of abandoned revitalization efforts: small manufacturing structures featuring dilapidated signs for restaurants and movie theaters, a tall office suite building converted to apartments now missing the left half of the bottom twelve floors, the hole rounded and symmetrical, like a giant bowling ball had rolled through the neighborhood. The rest of the building had the appearance that it might totter over at any moment.

There were people residing in the rubble of the buildings, camping in the parking structures. She had seen a few people scurrying through openings in fencing, some with full gallon jugs of what appeared to be very questionable drinking water or very weak liquor. Others carried dead rodents and other small animals. On her walk to the train station, she had desperately tried to avoid looking too closely at a creature being dragged down the sidewalk by a man with bushy, tangled hair and tattered clothes. As always seemed to be the case, it was the details she avoided the most that her brain captured vividly: the floppy ears, the curly tan fur, the ballerina pink collar with a heart-shaped name tag, the now grayed tongue hanging out of the slightly ajar mouth.

Esther dug her fists further into the sweatshirt, quickening her pace. She'd need to walk this street just one more time, but then she'd hopefully have Gabe with her. There'd be a more pressing need to move quickly; she wouldn't have time to consider the surroundings, the haunted ambiance of the neighborhood as she did now.

A chill ran up her spine as she reached the intersection. She just needed to cross to the light rail station built in the median. It would arrive within two minutes, and she'd be on her way back to the clinic. She could finally get the plan underway.

She stared helplessly at the crosswalk before her to the place on the pavement where she needed to step next, but she couldn't move.

The building burned down, she told herself impatiently, but her breaths were becoming more and more constricted as she lifted her gaze to the large building set at an angle on the lot across the street. It was at least fifteen stories high but was dwarfed by the surrounding structures. The outside was dingy concrete with a vertical lined pattern and protruding rounded windows. The building extended out over a front driveway that appeared to have once featured a valet station, but two of the columns had already crumbled. An outline on the tower spelled out the name "Glory Hospital," with only the O and R in Glory remaining.

She followed what she imagined the sight lines to be from the upper windows and frowned. She considered the angles of the other sides of the building and started heading west until the football stadium came into view on the far reaches of the city just beyond the freeway loop. Peering back toward the dilapidated hospital, she scanned the rows of copper-colored windows reflecting a muted sunset. It took a few minutes of focused searching for her to locate the window with the strip of tinting peeled diagonally across the glass.

Although she couldn't be certain how often it took place, she remembered observing the outside world through that strip of glass. The copper tinting blended everything into a dichromatic color scheme, but through the clear glass, she could see the shades of the sunset, she could make out the shape of stars at night. She remembered seeing an endless line of headlights on the freeway and hearing the roar of the crowd at the football stadium. There was a pungent smell in the room she couldn't ignore, like expired meat and stale bodily fluids.

There were other children in the room at times, but she had learned it was best not to interact. Most were very young and spent their time in the room lying on the mats staring glassy eyed at the ceiling. It was difficult to block out the crying and screaming, the rattling in the lungs of a child actively dying, the squeak as they took their final breath.

Esther could feel the phone in her pocket. She thought of contacting Josh. A simple message to him and he'd sweep her out of the city. It wouldn't be a perilous journey being this far on the outskirts. She imagined his arms closing around her, how satisfying that embrace would be. She held onto that sensation for a few indulgent moments, then exhaled, releasing her grip on the phone in her pocket.

She switched off the facial overlay and stepped across the street.

19

simulation

The Health Services Government Housing was centrally located in what was once the hot spot of the city. High-end retail stores and attractions, including a professional basketball arena, were now abandoned in the surrounding blocks.

The housing project was initially heralded for its innovation, mainly because it converted an under-utilized parking garage into housing for thousands of people, each in cubby-sized accommodations with an average square footage of two parking spaces. Since the existing structure was utilized, it took little more than the installation of massive glass panels and internal separators slid into place like a drawer organizer to complete the project. This particular downtown structure was the first of its kind so much care was taken to have it initially look like its architectural rendering, including horizontal wood paneling along the bottom floor, designed to warm up the otherwise cold exterior. Additional structures of its kind were not so carefully executed. Once businesses folded and buildings were abandoned, their structures crumbling, the government was far thriftier in housing Mandatory enlistees.

Esther glanced up at the logo etched over the doorway--cupped hands holding the medical logo–as she stepped through the automatic door, conscientious of the clomping of her boots on the concrete floors. She tried to appear confident, or at the very least, not overly uncomfortable, with her ensemble--a bright yellow vinyl dress, cut diagonally from shoulder to armpit across her chest, cut in an uneven, fairy-like pattern at the thigh. It was zippered from top to bottom, for simplified access (as it was explained to her) and finished with a pair of gray leggings and knee-high zippered black boots. The dress featured a hood that shielded her face from onlookers and framed her chopped royal blue wig.

The uniformed officer at the front desk took in her appearance with curiosity, tilting his bald head to the side. "Haven't seen you here before. You new?"

She nodded reluctantly, sweeping her fake bangs across her forehead. She placed a business card before him on the desk. As she understood it, women in her job role were meant to speak as little as possible.

He typed the name into his computer on his left. From her angle, she could see Gabe's official enlistee photo pop up. His stare was neutral, void of his usual warmth, and appeared to have been taken recently.

"*Wow*. This is a first for him." He added the identification number from her card into the digital visitor log for Gabe and slid it back across the counter, along with a key card. "That'll get you in his cabin so you can--do what you need to do. It looks like he'll be done with training at 7." The man stood, bracing himself over the counter with a heavily tattooed arm, taking in her full appearance. "I really don't understand the uniform. It's doing you *no* favors, not that you need them."

She retracted a bit.

"Oh, I'm harmless, sweetheart. It's interesting though that the same people who once upon a time advocated for privacy rights now watch and listen to our every move--and if that weren't enough, require us to wear our labels right out there for the world to see." He motioned to the uniform.

She wrinkled her forehead, reading his name badge. "What are yours, Troy? Your labels?" Her voice was raspy. The air in the city had dried her throat, making her feel perpetually thirsty.

He sighed, displaying his wrists. Wrapped around each wrist were groupings of tiny tally marks. Hundreds of them. "Kills. I wish I could say they deserved it."

"Why then?"

"Orders. Survival."

She raised her eyes. "*Your* survival?"

"There were thousands like me. Christ-followers turned into murderers." He nodded regretfully, pulling up his sleeve to reveal a hastily executed cross tattoo. "They couldn't leave it at that. Had to make it so even if you tried to pray for forgiveness--" He simulated folding his hands in prayer. The tally marks were clearly visible.

He flipped his wrist over when a small group of official-looking people in crisp business attire emerged from a room to his right. The group collectively took in the pair of them with judgmental glares, two women in the back whispering and motioning to Esther. The air seemed to have been vacuumed from the space, the only noise the clicking of expensive footwear echoing against the cold floors and glass panels.

Esther turned her chin away in the submissive way expected of her, raising her eyes to check Troy's expression. When his shoulders eased, she stood straighter.

"Don't be surprised if they summon you."

"Pardon?"

"They have their own source--younger and not voluntary--but a few of them seemed interested in you."

She swallowed hard.

He patted the key card, still sitting on the counter. "Just a warning? The boys tend to be a little more aggressive on nights after Sim training."

She took the card and tucked it blindly into her tote.

"This week has been 'Upgrades' or 'Enhancements'? Whatever that means. There's been I don't know how many brawls and at least six or seven suicides." He shrugged. "I don't know how long you've been doing this, but just be careful."

"You should keep praying, Troy," she whispered.

He nodded. "Yeah, maybe I should. We all should." He scanned her face and took another regretful look at her outfit, shaking his head. "Room 5812. Elevators up to 5, take a left then a right, take it all the way to the end."

Esther nodded in gratitude and continued past the counter to the elevator bank. In the center of the building was a glassed atrium of sorts. Rather than removing the parking garage ramps, they had been preserved, the inclines now filled with plants, vacant brightly colored benches, and Adirondack chairs. She had a full view of the feature on the elevator ride, as the vehicle ascended briskly in the elevator chamber.

The doors opened on the second floor to a rowdy atmosphere—the dining hall based upon the sound of plates and utensils clanking. She quickly lowered her chin, encouraging the fabric of her hood to fall over her face. Two men were waiting to board and went temporarily silent upon seeing her.

"They'll automate *her* out of a job soon," one whispered after boarding.

"I guess I'm old-fashioned, but I don't want to screw a robot," the other said, frowning apologetically in her direction.

"*Her*, on the other hand?"

"You're an asshole. She has ears. She can hear you." The man on the right turned and stepped toward her. "Sorry about him."

"I was just saying the same thing as you--I'm not looking for a human substitute. It's like all the substitutes out there for meat and sugar? Just give me the real stuff."

His friend shrugged in agreement.

"I was sure the living wage would solve everything and ensure no one has to sell their bodies."

"Not everyone qualified for a living wage."

"I was being *sarcastic.*"

"I remember them trying to claim that less than 97% of people would qualify."

" 'Qualifying for a living wage *couldn't* be easier—' simply register for an account, complete a full, invasive examination, get every vaccine we're short on participants for, get chemically sterilized, and sign away all your constitutional rights—"

"Give up privacy, give up freedom, ba-da-bing, free money."

Esther relaxed slightly, gave a slight nod.

"You agree?"

She lifted her eyebrows.

"She didn't say that," the shorter one said, eyeing the dome overhead camera pointedly.

His friend nodded. "Sorry, my mistake."

The elevator stopped on the fifth floor and the man to the right stepped back to allow her to pass more easily. "Do you need help finding a room? This place is a bit of a maze."

She shook her head and turned to the left without a glance back. She felt only slightly more at ease in the empty corridor, keeping to the center to keep her loud boots positioned over fluorescent, generically patterned carpeting. The hallway seemed endless as she passed door after door. It was unfathomable that there were adequate living quarters beyond the tightly spaced doorways.

Finally, she found the room and tapped the key card against the lock, pushing open the heavy door.

The space was as small as she had imagined but extremely tidy. The sheets were pulled tightly across what appeared to be the most uncomfortable mattress imaginable. The pillow was crisp and looked like it had never accommodated a sleeping head.

As a child, Gabe's room had been devoid of unnecessary possessions, but the only attempt he'd made to make his bed was haphazardly tossing the blankets in the general direction of his pillows, with varied success.

As she turned around to examine the room, she could find nothing that identified him as the occupant. She didn't immediately see any signs of surveillance, but with the small living quarters and narrow walls that separated each room, she reasoned that they had decided if something was going on, they'd know about it. She stepped toward the window, which mercifully had an outward-facing view of the dark skyline. In the skyscraper across the street, she could see a family gathered around a fire. A similar glow could be seen in several other windows.

She remembered traveling to the city once as a child and staying on an upper floor of a modest hotel. She had sat on the window seat, forehead pressed against the window, and watched the ant-sized cars moving along the streets, the vast park in the center of the city, and the glow of lights as the sun set over the horizon. From those heights, the bustling city had managed to look serene.

She watched a door open on the side of the Peace Bureau just down the road, peace agents emerging with full riot gear. They fell into formation, creating a barricade line down the center of Colfax Avenue. This type of presence, once reserved for volatile situations, was now a daily occurrence to fulfill the agency's mission of keeping the peace. They appeared at sunrise, dispersed throughout the day, then reassembled at dusk, preparing for the night ahead and enforcing curfew. Danny had been sure to educate her about their protocols so she was sure to be off the city streets before 7.

The door opened suddenly behind her. Gabe stepped inside without looking up and closed the door quietly behind himself. His eyes were lowered as he slipped off his shoes. He immediately dropped to sit on the bed. He clasped his hands together, his breathing strained and heavy as he bent down over his knees, face buried against his fists.

Esther froze.

Through heavy gulps of air, she could decipher one clear phrase he repeated over and over again: "Forgive me, Jesus. Forgive me, Jesus. Forgive me, Jesus."

She could only imagine what he had faced in the Sim, what was done to him, what he had to witness, what they had him do. Despite this, her heart swelled in knowing he still turned to Jesus for comfort.

She whispered his name, but his abrupt movement would have indicated she had shouted. He stood, eyes wide. He took in her outfit, wincing a bit, as though the color, the material, the hemlines that left little to the imagination were causing him physical pain.

He pressed a button on the wall-mounted console and an instrumental melody began to play, his bloodshot eyes darting to a small camera dome above his shoulder that she had missed. He pressed another button and the overhead lights turned off, leaving them to rely only on the light supplied by the streetlamps outside. He inched toward her. When he stood immediately before her, he pulled the wig hastily from her head.

"Your name isn't Emily," he whispered in a desperate, almost accusatory tone. "*Is* it?"

Esther gave a small shake of her head.

Gabe moved into her, nudging her to angle toward the window. As the light illuminated her face, he narrowed his eyes. He reached for her cheek, startled by the slight current at the surface of her skin.

She slowly reached up and touched the button behind her ear.

As the overlay vanished, he studied her face with intense interest. He focused on one detail at a time: first, her eyes. His own became very round upon seeing them in better light. Next, her nose, his mouth turning upward as he ran his thumb gently across the tiny cluster of freckles on the bridge, only visible in close proximity. Then he took in the rest—her chin, the subtle dimples in her cheeks, her mane of golden-brown waves, currently matted to her head and full of static from the wig.

"*Gabe?*"

He pulled in his breath. "Please tell me your name." He added, blinking slowly: "I'm sorry, I should remember it."

She felt her mouth tighten, felt the indent of the dimple in her cheek, the tears forming in her eyes. "I'm Esther," she whispered.

People tended to pull a face upon being introduced to her. Most remarked that Esther wasn't a name that belonged to a girl as young as her. Gabe didn't have this reaction. His face reflected deep relief, like finally getting to scratch a hard-to-reach itch. He exhaled deeply, his lips curling at the corners. "*Esther.*" He placed a hand on her cheek, his eyes glossy. "I don't know if I should wish for you to be real or not."

"I'm real, Gabe. I'm here."

He shook his head, his eyes not breaking contact. "You *shouldn't* be. It's not safe." He frowned, running his thumb across her lips. He immediately repeated the motion in the opposite direction, unsuccessfully trying to wipe off the deep rouge color. "*That's* not working."

"It's supposed to be long-lasting. I don't usually wear it."

"Good." He allowed a light smile, his round, brown eyes gentle. "I *know* you," he said more insistently, as though trying to recall a stubborn vocabulary word.

She nodded, her throat tight.

"This *isn't* the Sim?"

"No. It's not the Sim."

He took a sharp inhale. "I've tried so hard to hide you from them."

She felt her nose start to burn and tried desperately to hold back the tears she felt welling in her eyes. "I know you have, Gabe."

He leaned forward, rested his forehead against hers. "I'm not worth what you're risking being here."

She sighed. "Agree to disagree."

"*Esther,*" he said, seeming to savor the name as it crossed his lips. He leaned in close to her ear. "I'm sorry for what happened earlier." His voice was barely audible.

She gave a small shake of her head. She didn't want to think of it. She didn't want the knowledge of what had happened to tarnish her view of him.

"I didn't do it. The procedure? I didn't do it."

She felt her body tense, relax, then tense again in close succession. "*What?*"

"I used saline," he said with a shrug. "I couldn't--"

They both heard when the camera clicked to attention. Gabe instinctively leaned into her, blocking her more fully from view. "They look in on proxy visits," he whispered.

She released a breath. "Oh."

"We *don't* have to–" He gave her an apologetic expression, much like he did before her exam. His thumb stroked her cheek. "I don't—I should, but—are we siblings? Friends?"

Esther pushed through her toes, leaning close to his ear. "Friends." She could feel him nod slightly. "It just has to look believable?"

He leaned his cheek against hers. "Is that okay?"

She pulled in her breath and gave a tight: "Yes."

Gabe began with light pecks on her cheeks, being strategic to keep her shielded from the camera. He placed both hands on her face, sliding his index finger to reactivate the facial overlay.

She followed his lead to kiss every inch of his face except his lips, wrapping her arms around him, wishing she had let her hair down to create a veil over the side of her face.

He strained to extend his arm far enough to untuck the covers of the bed. It was as he eased her onto the mattress that they heard the camera click again.

They both froze.

"Does that mean it's off?" she whispered, slightly out of breath.

He frowned. "That's peculiar."

"Do they usually–"

"Well, I don't have any personal experience–" he said, briefly making prolonged eye contact. He ran his fingers along her neck, the edge of the facial overlay, furrowing his brow.

"Are you sure it's off?"

He frowned. "Stay here," he whispered, sliding off the bed. He moved quickly to retrieve a nearly empty roll of electrical tape from the wardrobe. He climbed up on the corner of the bed and secured it around the dome camera.

"All clear," he said, still in a whisper. "The music should muffle things, but we should be as quiet as possible." He turned on the reading light, craning the adjustable neck to diffuse the light off the wall.

"They won't suspect anything?"

He sat tentatively at the edge of the bed. "If they do check, they'll probably just assume there's something wrong with the camera."

She slowly sat up; a bit more preoccupied with the immodesty of her clothing than she had been initially.

"Please take that outfit off," he said, then chuckled lightly. "I *mean*--I'll get you something to put on, but–"

"I would prefer to wear literally anything else."

Gabe smiled lightly. He quickly retrieved a heathered gray t-shirt with the Bureau of Public Wellness seal over the left chest and a matching pair of sweatpants.

She resisted making a joke asking if he had anything in a different color. Instead, she stood and excused herself to the tiny airplane-sized bathroom. When she returned, she had pulled her hair into a simple side braid and was practically swimming in his clothes. She looked years younger with her washed face. The rouge on her lips was much lighter as she had clearly put some effort into trying to scrub it off, the skin around her lips a bit irritated.

"I didn't even hear the power sander." He made a circular gesture to his face.

She raised an eyebrow toward the camera.

"Still clear."

She nodded.

"Should we talk?" he asked softly, motioning to the bed, which he had re-made while she was out of the room.

She shook her head.

"Sorry, I didn't know what your plans were." He furrowed his brow.

She took two strides toward him and collided into his chest, wrapping her arms around him. There was a moment of hesitation before his hands slid instinctively to embrace her.

*   *   *

269

The beds at the housing complex were designed to accommodate one small to medium-sized adult so it took an awkward rearranging of bodies before Esther and Gabe had finally settled in with her resting in the nook of his arm. She had tucked herself in close, her hand resting on his chest. They were silent as they took in the presence of the other, the music playing on. Esther ran her fingers along the pattern on his t-shirt, occasionally drumming along with the music.

In the quiet, Gabe's mind chased the shadow of a memory. A church with a wood plank wall. A spotlight. The girl lying in his arms singing, her delicate hand raised in worship, her golden-brown hair cascading over her shoulders. He was captivated by her passion, her beauty, her joy, and longed for the moment her silver eyes would open again, glistening in the spotlight.

He tightened his arm around her and kissed the top of her head. As he took in a deep breath, his eyes fell upon the tattoo on her forearm. He reached out and gently turned her left arm upward. He let his fingertips delicately trace the outlines of the design—the flowers, the tree trunk, a very large horse, a stack of books. He smiled lightly. "I have dreams about you–but you don't have *this* tattoo."

"It's new."

"It's beautiful." He focused his attention on the pattern hidden in the design. He knew this wasn't the first time he'd seen it.

"You have dreams about me?"

"Quiet dreams. Peaceful dreams. Nothing provocative," he qualified further, his eyes focused back on her arm.

She smiled lightly.

"Holding you when we were little and you had nightmares." He saw her skin shiver and decided it wasn't necessary to elaborate. "I also have dreams about holding you when we *weren't* so little anymore. Although those might *actually* be dreams."

"Not necessarily," she murmured. "So, what you mean to say is that all your memories of me are non-provocative yet in a horizontal position?"

"Such as this, yes." He pulled the blankets up to her neck, seeing goosebumps starting to form on her skin. "Sorry, they don't believe in heat."

She tugged down the sleeves of the sweatshirt, her body tensing. He suspected this meant she wasn't confident in something she was about to say. "*Gabe?*"

He had been called "West" for so long and with just indifference that "Gabe" sounded foreign to him, but he liked the breathy tone she used when she said it.

"I need to tell you about the plan before I go."

"What do you mean, *go? Now?*"

She nodded.

"You can't go."

"I have to." She didn't sound convinced.

"Go where? Curfew will have started by now; they'll have officers everywhere."

She twisted her neck to check the window. "Why can't I follow the most basic of plans?" She squeezed her eyes shut, clearly sorting something out internally. "We'll go through the plan in the morning so it's fresh."

"What plan?"

"To go home." She flinched a bit at the word 'home,' her eyes round and regretful.

"Esther, I *can't* leave."

"Why?"

"They have my parents. If I leave–"

She pushed herself onto her elbow. "Oh my God, Gabe. I forgot to tell you."

"*What?*" His heart clenched. "What happened to them?"

"Your parents are safe."

"*How?*"

"They never had your parents. That was the Sim."

He felt his entire body deflate. "That wasn't real?"

"No."

271

He rubbed at his face roughly, the images of their torture flashing across his eyes. "You've seen them? You know for sure that they're safe?"

She nodded.

"What about Josh?" He asked hesitantly.

It had been a day like any other, walking the twenty blocks to the clinic when he looked up to the sky and saw a body hurtling toward the concrete. It was a surreal moment when he recognized the person as his brother, his brain absorbing this information lightly, with an eerie whimsy, like "*Oh*, it's Josh. That's weird. I hope he doesn't want to chat because he'll make me late for work." When Josh's body made impact with the concrete, the force caused a vibration in the sidewalk. His body was contorted in directions incompatible with life, his eyes wide and vacant. Everyone around him paused momentarily, then continued on their way. Jumpers were common.

Gabe was about to continue on as well, but then he heard the sound of children's laughter. It seemed to be drifting in from a different street, echoing off the buildings. He closed his eyes and he saw Josh, at maybe 5 or 6, running. He saw a young version of himself chasing him. By the look of it, he was trying to spray him with the garden hose. He opened his eyes and stared into the lifeless face of his brother.

It was the first Simulation session he recognized for what it was, but the Sim's AI brain mapping had made the determination to leave him with the entirety of the memory, even the glimpse into his past. Not because it was being merciful, but because it made the image of Josh strewn across the concrete more haunting.

"He's safe."

He blinked slowly. "It was so real."

She nodded.

"Have you experienced it?"

"Only a few times though."

"A few times can be a lot."

"For me it was different. I experienced the Sim so I would know what it was like."

"What do you mean?"

"It wasn't a part of required training."

"You *chose* to experience it?"

"I knew I wouldn't understand what it felt like unless I experienced it for myself."

He narrowed his eyes. "What did you see?"

"My biggest fears. It seemed to zero in on those."

"It does that," he reflected, noticing a small collection of freckles on her jawline shaped like the peak of an ocean wave. "Did it have you do anything you would never do normally?"

She kept her gaze steady. "I killed someone."

Her bluntness unsettled him. "Why?"

She furrowed her brow. "He was going to kill my dad and I panicked. I knew it wasn't real, but I–had to choose which one I was going to have to see die and--"

"You didn't actually--" he tentatively began to offer.

"I know." Esther shook her head. "But I *love* him. The man who was going to kill my dad? I love him."

Gabe stared at her, focused on the welling of tears on her bottom lashes, the fear and regret in her eyes. He knew what she was feeling, how even knowing it was a simulation wasn't much of a comfort. He knew how those simulated images seemed to be more readily absorbed into the brain, how it seemed that even one experience in the Sim could destroy a dozen happy recollections. "Every session in the Sim erases more and more of the good memories," he whispered. "I think that's why I only have traces of you left."

This statement struck her pointedly. She placed her hand on his cheek, delicately stroked his skin with her fingertips.

Gabe tilted his head to the side, taking in the brilliance of her silver eyes. "I tried *so* hard to keep them from taking you."

She furrowed her brow, moved closer still, and kissed him. First, just his lower lip, then she eased upward, kissing his upper lip. There, she paused, waiting, her breaths shallow.

"Essie," he whispered.

Her brilliant eyes widened.

He felt his mouth pull into a smile, his heart inflating in his chest. "I call you Essie, don't I?"

She nodded.

He braced her cheek in his hand, tucked his thumb behind her ear, and smiled. *This can't be real*, he thought desperately. *But please, let me have this. Let me keep this.*

As though triggered by the positive feelings, images began to flash before his eyes in crisp, cinematic detail. He doubted time would ever help to fade the images of tiny, bloodied bodies and violent injuries he had inflicted. He could feel their struggle, twisting away from his hands, his tools. He could feel the snap of spinal cords against the palms of his empty hands, their bodies going limp. He could smell the metallic odor of blood, the musty stench of bodily fluids filling the room.

"*Gabe?*" she beckoned, inclining her chin.

He startled, blinking repeatedly.

"Stay with me. Push those thoughts away."

He frowned.

"You thought your family would be in danger if you didn't do those things. It's not your fault. You would never do those things."

He shifted away, eyeing her distrustfully. "You said this wasn't the Sim."

"It's not."

"How did you know what I was thinking?"

She swallowed hard.

"You *know* what I've done?"

Her hesitation answered his question.

He nodded, pulling his hand away. "I can't–live with myself for it. I can't go home knowing what I've done."

"*Gabe*," she said, her voice shaking, her face stern. "*No*. Don't *ever* consider doing that ever again."

"Doing what?"

274

"Throwing yourself off the building."

He narrowed his eyes. "How do you know that?"

She frowned regretfully. "The Sim sessions are recorded."

"You've *watched* my Sim sessions?"

"Some."

He continued to glare at her. It would be justified to feel betrayed, she had imposed on an experience far too personal to share, but instead, he felt shame, along with a sense of bewilderment that she knew all those things he'd done and she had still come here, she had still kissed him.

He had to refocus his brain on the experience she had mentioned. He remembered feeling hopelessness. Prior sessions had focused efforts on compliance and contained propaganda meant to garner support. It had been so blatant it would have comical, if not for the effectiveness. He'd walk out of the Sim session mocking them internally, but by the next day, he'd find his thoughts more focused, their tactics, their ideology more palatable. The "Upgrade" session seemed designed to vacuum all hope from his soul.

"I knew it was the Sim. I wasn't going to actually do it," he said softly, his eyes lowered. "I just wanted to end it. *The session*. I knew what they wanted from me so I did--what you saw."

"Look at me," she whispered, waiting for his eyes to lock into hers. "*You* jump? *I* jump."

He felt his body tense. It sounded like something people said, but didn't really mean, but looking into Essie's silver irises, he felt her sincerity, he felt the weight of responsibility for her well-being.

He shook his head. "Never again," he agreed.

She nodded, assessing her options for lying back down.

He laid back, patting his chest. As she settled against him, he took a steadying breath, cautiously rested his hand on her back. "Do you have a plan for getting out of the city?"

"We'll leave first thing in the morning."

"I have a tracking device implanted in my arm."

"I have a plan for that."

"Surgically remove it in my sleep?" he asked, surprising himself by joking for the first time in what he suspected was years.

She seemed equally surprised. She lifted her chin, resting it on his chest. She gave a light smile. "Fortunately for both of us, no. We just have to wait until the last possible second to deactivate it."

He placed his hand on her cheek, smiling lightly. "You're so beautiful."

She scrunched her nose. "Well, I'm no Deidre."

His face fell.

"I shouldn't have mentioned her. I thought it would be funny, but it's not. She's legitimately terrifying."

He pressed his lips together. "I'm sorry about today."

"It was her, Gabe, not you. You would never hurt me or put me through any of that."

"But I did put you through that."

"Because you had to, Gabe. If you didn't, she would have—"

He shrugged. "Still."

"I'm fine, Gabe. I'm right here. I'm fine. Tomorrow morning we're getting out of here."

He took a deep breath and nodded. "Essie?"

She lifted her eyebrows.

"You look like you haven't slept in days."

"I don't sleep a lot."

"Maybe you should try to get some sleep?"

Esther pressed her lips together. "I'm afraid to sleep. I'm afraid that when I wake up, you'll be gone, and this will have all been a dream."

"I don't know if it makes you feel better, but I feel the same."

She blinked slowly. "I'm here, Gabe."

He smiled. "I'm here, Essie."

20
lay it down

Esther knew she needed to sleep. It was mission-critical that she sleep, but she found herself trapped in her head, terrified of what could happen the next day. Gabe could be killed, and it would be her fault.

The best-case scenario still meant they had a long, treacherous journey ahead. There were too many unknowns, too many what-ifs. She was haunted by the fact that if they succeeded, there would be so many people who had been left behind. What would become of those who weren't invited to the Arks? The majority didn't agree with the policies of the current government regime. They simply didn't have a choice but to comply. She somehow didn't feel right about them being abandoned, left vulnerable to what was to come.

In the darkness, listening to Gabe's breaths echo in his chest, she felt genuine fear. If she were honest with herself, she would admit that she had considered that Luther had lied to her to get her to stop the sessions. In that case, she had been reckless with the lives of millions of people. The *other* possibility was that she truly no longer had heightened immunity and had put herself in the middle of a cataclysmic event, modern genocide, and she might not have a way out.

When Gabe performed the sterilization procedure and she felt none of the discomfort he had described, she had felt tremendous relief that Luther had been wrong, or that Luther had lied. Either way, she thought she had a safeguard in place so she could somehow escape death's clutches if put in that situation. She had focused on that. She could see the steps that would get Gabe to safety without putting anyone else at risk.

She had to get Gabe to safety for any part of this to mean anything, to justify the risk.

Then the realization struck her: Gabe believed if he did *not* follow orders, his family would be tortured. Deidre had ordered him to do the sterilization. He didn't. She found herself overwhelmed with the implications of that act of defiance.

He didn't think he would be caught, she reasoned. It's not like he outwardly refused a direct order.

She tried to gently settle into his arm, which was challenging to do comfortably for either one of them. He had lost the bulk of his muscle from all the manual labor required on the farm, his overall frame now gaunt and bony. She watched his chest rise and fall, breathing in the warmth of him beside her. The city held a smell that seemed to latch onto everything, and she resented its presence on his clothes. Beneath it, she could smell a soap of some kind, but it was synthetic, like an antiseptic spray.

She was about to give up on the idea of sleeping, concluding there was no use in her staying the night--someone in her implied line of work would certainly leave in the middle of the night and he could certainly use the space she was occupying--but she hated the very idea of leaving him there. More than that, she imagined stepping into the ungodly city alone, making her way to the truck, while avoiding peace officer questioning, and she felt tremendous fear and emptiness. She agonized over her decision to wait until morning. Surely, she could have found a way to exit the building with little detection in the late evening. There was never a better time to leave than with someone like Troy at the security desk. Morning was a fool's choice.

It was then, as she silently scolded herself for being so selfish, that she felt his arm tighten around her. His right hand settled over hers on his chest, his fingers stroking her skin. Though his body lacked any bulk, muscular or otherwise to make the arrangement more comfortable, his touch was gentle and familiar. She focused on watching the delicate motion of his fingers and surrendered to its lulling rhythm.

She slept in short waves, startling awake with every noise. It was about a half hour before sunrise when she eased herself out of bed and retrieved the outfit and wig he had found so offensive. She retreated to the small bathroom, used the toilet, and quickly pulled the items back on. Without the freshness of makeup to mask the shadow of exhaustion under her eyes, she found the look far less convincing. Anyone watching her on a security camera as she left wouldn't think twice about her appearance though. Just another day at the office.

There was a light tap on the door and she found Gabe standing on the other side looking vaguely like himself at a younger age. Never a morning person, a requirement for his family's line of work, she recalled him trudging downstairs at the farm, hair sticking in all directions, a dull tint to his skin, and hazy brown eyes.

"Oh *no*," he said, his eyes squinting into the vanity light, his morning voice thick and groggy. "Not this look again."

She gave him a small smile, her ears picking up the tickling of a jazzy melody. He had drawn back the curtains, but being on the west side of the building, the room was still dimly lit. Glancing up at the dome camera, she saw he had removed the electrical tape. *Just as well. This way they'll see me leave*, she thought. "Just until I can get a change of outfit." *I knew I should have brought it with me*, she thought sternly. *Stupid, stupid, stupid.*

"What's the plan?"

"Go about your normal routine, then hop on the eastbound light rail out front at 7:32. Third car."

She could picture how it would unfold: he would board at 7:32 just outside the housing complex. She would step on at Booker Street three minutes later. The odd numbered cars had dummy cameras due to budgetary constraints so getting onto the third car was essential. She would have the pocket-sized device that would clone the tracker. She would deactivate the one in his arm. They would exit at the next stop, and switch to an odd-numbered car heading in the opposite direction. The tracker clone would continue toward the clinic. With three traffic signals, and two stops, including the hub station, which had a lengthy delay to allow attendants to change shifts, they would have at least eight minutes before his tracker would pass the clinic. They would stay onboard for four stops before arriving outside the dilapidated hospital. They would easily reach the road leading to the interstate rail line before anyone thought to question his whereabouts. They would be aboard the 8 am train with minutes to spare.

She sighed. "I better go."

"I'll see you in a bit then."

She hesitated, wondering if she should give him the device in case something happened to her.

No. If he's searched, he'll be killed for having it.

She gave him a small peck on the cheek and moved to the door. "7:32," she repeated.

He nodded. "Essie?"

She peered over her shoulder.

"I love you. I don't remember everything, but I do remember that."

Her eyes panned up to the camera as she spun toward him. She grabbed a fist full of his t-shirt, sidestepped into the bathroom, and tugged him inside, out of view of the camera. There, she turned off the facial overlay, threw her arms around his neck and hugged him. "I love you, Gabe."

He tightened his arms around her. "Please be real," he murmured.

Essie took a step back, grabbed hold of his hand and placed it over her chest. "Do you feel that?"

He took a deep breath and nodded.

She pushed through her toes, kissing his lips gingerly, but conclusively, turned, and left.

She took the stairwell, knowing she'd be picked up on camera, quickly descending to the side street exit. It was just as the door began to close that she heard a crisp, grating voice come over the building intercom to say: "Sunrise weekday program start." Esther watched the door creak closed with a sinking feeling in her stomach.

*   *   *

"Canary, what's your status?" Luther's voice was tight, rigid.

She had called Danny, wanting to strategize a new plan, and while she already felt on the verge of sobbing, the sound of Luther's voice was pushing her further to that point. "I'm fine."

But she wasn't.

She really wasn't fine at all.

Gabe had missed the light rail.

He had proceeded on his normal walking path to work. At first, she justified that walking was a part of his routine so he could have automatically proceeded down the street. It would look suspicious to turn around when he realized his mistake.

Esther watched him approach as she waited for the light rail on Booker Street, where she planned to board. Their plan could still pick up from there if he simply boarded the light rail with her.

Instead, she watched as he walked mechanically past her, even as she actively tried to make eye contact. He had paid little attention to anything around him, his eyes downcast.

She had intended to chase him down, but one of the clinic staff members had fallen into line next to him, the same despondent look on his face.

"Where are you?" Luther asked, sounding distracted. "We'll get a team to you."

"No. Bronco isn't secured yet."

"You need to get out of there. It's not safe."

"I'll secure Bronco within the hour." She stared through the windshield, taking in the stillness of the parking garage near the clinic where she'd moved the truck. She couldn't believe how quickly the day had slipped away as she frantically tried to pivot in her game plan. She'd spent nearly five hours in a state of shock, her thoughts frozen, her muscles stiff. She hadn't allowed herself to think that this scenario was possible, and she was now dealing with the consequences.

Luther's voice was closer to the microphone when he spoke again. "Bronco is part of phase one."

"All the more—" she began, knowing that in his role, he'd of course be involved in the dispensing of the vaccine. Then her brain zeroed in on the discrepancy of word choice. *Stage four was the vaccine–what was phase one?*

"They're going to kill him."

Esther felt like she'd been shot. She wasn't processing things. Her brain was derailed by the brashness of his statement, choosing to abandon speaking in code.

"The first phase is to eliminate non-compliance in their ranks. Bronco didn't make the cut. That's why they switched his Sim programming. They wanted him to do it himself."

Esther stared across the parking garage recently emptied of tents of the homeless. The government had announced on the news that they were provided housing. No one questioned this. The media had applauded these humanitarian efforts, touting how homelessness rates had fallen to record lows. No one questioned the presence of train cars previously used for cattle being used to transport dead bodies from the city. The news turned a blind eye. They originally used mortuary and laboratory incinerators. School kilns in a bind. Eventually, they determined that it was more pleasant to not burn multitudes of bodies within city limits. The haze had been in direct contradiction to their clean air initiatives. There had also been complaints about the smell.

Of course they wouldn't hesitate to kill Gabe. Deidre seemed primed and ready.

She felt the tears in her eyes. "He was *still*–he remembers me." She gulped. It wasn't a lie, but it wasn't the full truth either.

"*Canary.*"

"He remembered," she shouted, her voice breaking. "*Yesterday.* He remembered me yesterday. Even this morning—*he knew me.* But then–"

"Sunrise program?"

"Is it--did they--?" The words caught in her throat. "Am I gone? Did they erase me--just like that?"

"It helps to start the day with a blank canvas. Fairly blank at least. They do brain mapping throughout the day, solidify it in the Sim session, and then they trigger the reset in the morning."

She tried to steady her uneven breathing, flipping open the driver side visor so she could insert color contacts into her eyes. The extra tears helped situate them with less irritation.

"Kiddo, you've done all you can." Luther's voice was gentler, apologetic. "Please get back here. Embarkation imminent."

"When?"

"On the 25th. No one in or out." It was a week away but having a deadline so finite with so many potential things that could go wrong--she shook the thought away.

"I'll be back in time."

"*Canary.*" His voice was laced with parental authority.

"Is Angler at the Swamp?"

There was a delay. "Canary, you need to come back."

"Is Angler at the Swamp?" she repeated.

"Yes. I can send him to you? Do you have transport?"

Essie remembered war footage where a soldier was dragged through the streets until he was nearly unrecognizable as a human being. He wasn't responsible for what they charged him with, but he represented what they hated. He represented the enemy. She imagined that happening to Josh and was suddenly desperate to keep him as far from these people as possible.

"Canary, what's your location?"

"There's not enough time. Tell him Bronco will meet him at the Swamp."

There was a pause followed by a long exhalation. "I'll tell him then I'll check in with Angler at 1800."

She nodded, choking on a sudden wave of emotion.

"Canary, you said Bronco would be there. What about you?"

She couldn't see herself in the scenario of Gabe making it out of the city. There would be complications now. The truck would be a better option, rather than the train. There was plenty of fuel–she filled up the tank already. There was a backup in the truck bed. She just needed to get him to the truck. "I love you, Moose."

"Essie?"

"I'm sorry," she said, then immediately removed the battery from the back of the phone. She took a deep breath, checked her reflection, and dropped out of the pickup truck.

She had changed into normal clothes —jeans, a simple navy shirt, which prominently displayed her tattoo, choosing to forego a hoodie that would have covered it, and hiking boots. She was unyielding in her determination and felt her gait take on a motivated stride toward the front door of the clinic.

*　　*　　*

The clinic was revving up for the new vaccine booster rollout. Despite performing all the tasks of a doctor, Gabe had been given no role in the preparation that was occurring throughout the day in several high-level meetings. Instead, he had been assigned to perform inventory. Supplies were being cataloged and shifted to other storage facilities to make room.

With clinic calendars closed and a skeleton crew working, many partaking in training and staff screening appointments, the new age playlist of harps and what sounded like a didgeridoo was much more prominent than usual as he moved around the back corridor of the clinic.

He wasn't sure what prompted him to peer in the direction of the waiting room since no one should have been there, but when he did, his eyes fell upon a young woman sitting in the chair closest to the staff hallway. She sat reading, her eyes lowered to the book before her, looking decidedly casual. Her hair was wavy and wild, a vibrant shade of golden brown. He imagined in the proper lighting, it might have hints of red. Her simple shirt did little to cover a cross tattoo that appeared too detailed, too carefully executed to be government issued.

She glanced up, sensing eyes upon her. Her eyes were a dark, dull shade of brown. They widened upon seeing him. He felt an energy, a magnetic pull to her.

After standing motionless for a few moments, he took notice of the boxes that filled his arms and nodded toward her, hoping she interpreted his hand gesture to mean that he would be right back. He would have called out to her, but he thought that might alert Deidre or someone else about her presence.

The back hallway had been stacked with boxes of the new vaccines and testing supplies that were awaiting space in the storage room. This had caused Deidre to be particularly adamant in her directing him to clean things up. Despite this, she had been in a distinctly good mood all day, remarking about the progress he had made with an unusual sort of adoration.

"Out with the old," she said in as cheerful a voice as he had ever heard from her, as he tried to maneuver to the loading dock.

"Speaking of old," he began. "I set a box back here of what I think is saline, only there's no expiration date or anything printed on the vials."

"Where is it?"

He pointed her toward the small box.

"*Where* did this come from?" She seemed to have a distinct interest in the solution.

"One of the exam rooms. They were next to the saline flush vials." As he spoke, the image of one of the vials in his palm flashed through his mind, combined with a startled expression on the face of the young woman in the waiting room. He frowned.

"You're right. These *are* old. I thought we were out of them, actually."

"They look like saline flushes. Are they not?"

She raised an eyebrow, then shrugged. "It was part of a former public health initiative."

"Oh."

"Never mind. There'd be no point in telling you."

He frowned.

"Almost done with the rest?"

"Last box."

"Nice," she said and continued toward Reception, palming the vial.

The outdated supplies took up the front portion of a rental moving truck. He placed the box on top of the stack but resolved he needed to seal the boxes to avoid being scolded by Deidre. Once they were stacked again, he hurried back inside.

The inside of the clinic was much quieter than the outside traffic and once the door closed, all sound seemed to be vacuumed out of the space. He blinked, trying to get his eyes to acclimate to the clinic lighting. He stepped toward the waiting area, preparing a neutral, but friendly expression for when he saw the young woman again. He tried to anticipate how she might look at him, but when he opened the automated door, he found an empty waiting room and no sign she had been there except for the presence of the softcover book she had been reading.

The cover was unexpected. It featured a green cartoon alien face holding up its hands by its nonexistent ears sticking out its tongue. "The Hitchhiker's Guide to the Galaxy," he read aloud, releasing a light chuckle. "'*If you want to survive out here, you need to know where your towel is,*'" he recited from memory. He blinked, seeing a flash of imagery before him—a large tree set before a farmhouse. There was a swing hanging from on the tree's wide branches, and a girl swaying herself back and forth absentmindedly with her bare feet. She was holding something in her hands. He heard himself speak as he approached her, though his voice

286

seemed to be traveling through water. He could smell the dewy grass, the freshly spread hay. The sunrise was just starting to provide some relief from the chilly morning. His voice was still muffled, but he seemed to be singing to her. She raised her chin, smiling broadly, and closed the book she was holding, the same paperback book he now held in his hands.

He moved quickly toward the staff hallway, nodding to the desk attendant. "I thought I saw someone come in? Do I need to see her?"

"She's in Exam 8," Cecil remarked, glancing up from her computer. "Deidre was going to get started with her."

His heart lurched. "What's she here for?"

"Oh, she was complaining about nausea from the sterilization you performed yesterday. She asked for you, but Deidre came out and decided to see her."

He felt his pulse starting to race and turned toward the left bank of rooms in the back staff hallway. Dr. Warren was just emerging from Exam 8, casually drying his hands with a paper towel and checking his watch.

"Hi Dr. Warren--"

"Hey, West. I've got your staff screening this afternoon, right?"

"I believe so."

Dr. Warren raised an eyebrow, following Gabe's gaze to the door. "I thought there was a patient who came in?" He frowned. "I may have seen her yesterday?"

He tapped the tablet screen. "Emily Charlotte Seger. I've rarely had such a small patient file." He swiped left and right, but the singular consult note remained stubbornly stuck on the screen.

"I just wanted to be sure that everything is okay?"

"Oh yeah. Just got her set with the new vaccine, actually. Figured I'd save her a trip later."

"Cecil mentioned she was having side effects from the Purity procedure?"

"*Yeah*, I'm not worried about that." He pinched his face and picked at something by his nostril. "Anomalies are something I've dealt with many, many times, West." He patted him roughly on the shoulder. "Pretty girl though in any case."

Gabe wasn't sure what to make of the doctor's remarks but was distracted picturing the girl's face, those large oval eyes. "Should we schedule her for a follow-up after the vaccine?"

"No need," Dr. Warren said, glancing back at the door. "She's all set. We're recommending people lie still for about 30 minutes for this one though. I guess it makes a lot of people woozy." He dropped his voice to a conspiratorial whisper. "Best to let her be."

Gabe nodded slowly, motioning toward the waiting area. "Not many patients here today."

"No, we have some administrative meetings before the rollout, so they blocked scheduling. Just walk-ins. You can handle those, right?"

"I just finished inventory. Made some room for the new supplies." Gabe tried to seem casual, suspecting that his behavior was being scrutinized.

"Excellent. Appreciate your diligence, West."

"Did you make it out to the course over the weekend?"

Dr. Warren chuckled. "Fit in 9 holes--ran into the Director of D.O.P. Can you believe that? Nice guy. Lousy golfer. You golf?"

He had explained his limited experience with the game to Dr. Warren several times. "Not much."

"They had a surprisingly good brunch at the Club. Never been a fan of snow crab though. I don't want to work that hard for a bite of food. Know what I mean?"

Gabe nodded but didn't even know what a snow crab looked like.

Dr. Warren smacked him on the shoulder. "Well, I have a meeting I'm late for. We'll get your screening out of the way as soon as that's over. Sound good?"

Gabe gave an affirmative tilt of his head, then watched the doctor stroll toward his office.

There had been no fewer than seven emails detailing that the latest batch of vaccines would be launched on the 24th. Emphasis had been placed on the precision of the timing to allow for a coordinated nationwide rollout. Knowing this, it struck Gabe as particularly strange that Dr. Warren had opened the case early. There was an eerie manner to the way he had referenced her when he used the term "anomalies," subconsciously brushing his palms together, as though ridding himself of germs.

Gabe listened at the exam room door for coughs, a scuffle of the privacy curtain, anything to indicate she was okay. Finally, he pushed open the door, prepared with the story that he'd simply stepped into the wrong room. Inside, he found there was no one to provide an excuse.

He threw open the door that led to the waiting area and found the main entrance door was just floating closed. The waiting area was void of people. Even Cecil must have gone on break.

He stepped out onto the sidewalk in front of the clinic, scanning the road for signs of Emily. The city streets had previously been lined with tents and shopping baskets and old appliance boxes serving as supplemental housing, but they had been cleared, seemingly overnight.

It was then he noticed he was still holding the softcover book she had left in the lobby. He examined the cover, once again amused by the art. In his mind, he returned to the farmhouse, the tree, and the girl, that smile of hers, the shimmery reflection of her silver eyes. He peered over her shoulder to the book, held gently in her hands, but he was drawn to a shadow on her arm.

A restrained cry from the bus shelter 20 yards away drew his attention. He could see the hem of blue jeans at the gap at the bottom. When he moved around the front of the shelter, he could see that she seemed to be having difficulty staying upright, leaning heavily into the advertisement for a law firm that had been recently cleaned of graffiti.

"Miss, are you okay?"

She jabbed something into her leg, discarding the empty syringe into the trash can, her face braced in desperation. "Gabe, we need to go," she said forcefully, turning abruptly toward him.

She moved quickly, but in a stiff, unnatural pattern, like at any moment, her legs would give out. She took the sidewalk around the corner from the clinic, checking over her shoulder to be sure he was behind her.

She quickened her pace, pointing toward an alleyway. She struggled to make the turn, scuffling into the brick wall of the next building. She couldn't seem to take in a full breath. "*Arm*," she said before he'd reached her.

"What?"

"There's a tracker in your arm," she said through gritted teeth, glaring at his left arm, which he presented. She held a device that resembled a small remote control and used it to scan his arm, finally settling over his wrist. Her hand trembled intensely. A light on the device turned green and she pulled a chip from the end. She changed the settings and held the device again over his wrist. After blinking a few times, the light turned red. She exhaled, changed the settings again, and scanned his wrist. Nothing.

She repeated the process over her upper arm, where he assumed she received the vaccine and the device found nothing. The shaking in her hand intensified.

She glanced around the alley, relieved when she saw a garbage truck at the next intersection. It appeared the driver had stopped off at the corner market.

"Throw this in the back of the truck."

He did as he was told and jogged back to her. Her face had turned a ghostly white and there was sweat dripping heavily from her forehead. "I think you need to sit down. You shouldn't be moving around yet."

"Gabe, if they catch us, we *die*," her voice was strained, but forceful. She made eye contact with him for the first time. He didn't recognize the dark hue of her eyes, but he knew her eyes were familiar to him before yesterday.

He nodded. "Where do we go?"

"The parking garage across the street."

Gabe checked around the corner to make sure they weren't followed, then they sprinted to the shadows of the garage. She directed him to the gas-powered pickup truck.

"You're driving," she instructed, flinging open the passenger door, which had a logo for an apple orchard painted in gold over the forest green base coat. She had already turned the key in the ignition by the time he reached the driver's seat.

Her breathing was labored as she leaned forward, letting the air conditioning blow directly into her face. "You can't go back there," she growled, pulling down the sun visor and opening the mirror. She quickly removed the contact lenses from her eyes and shook the sizzling discs off her fingers to the floor. She squinted her eyes as she turned to look at him. Her eyes were neither the dark hue from inside nor the silver color he had seen in his memory. They seemed to be slowly dissolving from metallic to brown and were being overtaken by her dilating pupils. They widened, questioningly. "You know that, *right*? You *can't* go back there. If you go back, they *will* kill you."

The revelation that his work colleagues were planning his death did not penetrate the cortex of his brain the way it probably should have. It just wasn't that outlandish of a claim. He found his mind more concerned by the fact that her facial structure seemed to have changed drastically from inside the clinic.

"*Gabe*," she demanded. "Promise me, no matter what. You don't go back there."

He nodded and heard himself say: "Okay." When he dropped the softcover book onto the bench seat, she stared at it as she tried to force breaths through her diaphragm.

"Interstate 25 North." She nodded toward the windshield, and he pushed the accelerator, heading toward the opposite side of the garage from where they had entered. "I have the coordinates for a safe place we can go, but you can only use *this* to direct you there," she said, ripping the inside title page from the book. He'd seen enough patients to know the pain was blurring her focus. "No phones, no asking for directions, just *this*."

"We should get you to the hospital."

She gave a sideways glance as she tensed back into the bench seat, her body starting to shiver.

"What's happening to you?"

She shook her head. "No matter what happens in the next 8-10 hours, I will be fine." She winced. "Do *not* take me to a hospital. Do *not* give me any medical treatment." She shook the paper toward him, which he took. As he drove, he noticed she had written directions neatly above the book title. "*Promise me*."

He focused on the road ahead. "Just drive to the place on the paper?"

She nodded. Her eyes panned over to a park filled with broken playground equipment, rows of occupied tents, and heaps of uncollected trash spilling out of receptacles, which looked like they hadn't been emptied in weeks. She dropped her head back to the headrest.

"What happened back there?"

"The doctor—I've lost feeling in my limbs so I can't air quote 'doctor' properly--the one with the creepy predator smile?"

"Dr. Warren."

"When I wake up? Remind me to drone his ass." She pulled in her breath, balling her hands into fists, curling her toes.

"What's doing this to you?"

Her eyes turned glassy, the lids started to drift closed, and her breathing slowed.

"He said your name is Emily?"

She wavered, wincing, and slowly lowered her upper body to rest on the backpack set in the center of the bench seat. "*Esther*. My name is Esther."

"*Esther*," he repeated, the name unexpectedly satisfying to his brain. "Promise me you're going to be OK."

She peered up at him driving, taking notice of his proper ten-and-two hand placement, the crease between his thick eyebrows, the tension in his narrow jaw. "I promise. It's going to be okay," she said softly, her eyes closing.

21
angler

Josh sat in the wooden rocking chair on the weathered porch watching the last bit of sunset give way to night over the trees surrounding the lake. He focused on taking deep breaths, not allowing worry to take over his thoughts.

She would be there soon.

There was simply not a future he was willing to imagine that had any other scenario. Since Luther's call, he had tidied up the inside of the cabin and rummaged around the pantry to try to find the most appetizing emergency food items, finally finding pancake mix. He had opted to fish to round out the meal and to give himself something to do until she arrived.

He'd managed to keep himself busy but had been obsessively checking the horizon for signs of a vehicle on the dirt road leading to the cabin throughout the afternoon. Now he had little to do but wait.

Luther had been sparing with details, but then, it didn't sound as though he had much information, and it wasn't easy to communicate when trying to do so through coded messages. What he gathered was that Essie had done what Josh feared when he learned she had left the Ark boundaries. When she reached out to Luther, things were not going well, but she had been insistent that she and Gabe would reach the safe house. It was strange to speak about Gabe, particularly with call signs. He wasn't sure who chose Bronco for Gabe. He suspected it may have been Essie.

Josh had been surprised when he first made it to the Ark and learned he already had a code name used for the mission to retrieve him from his Long Beach assignment.

Angler.

Chosen by Essie, he assumed it cited his enjoyment of fishing, which he did frequently, especially when other meat became too expensive. She had grinned when he mentioned it and he immediately knew he missed the joke.

"What else does Angler mean?"

She lowered her eyes.

"Essie?"

"Have you ever heard of an anglerfish?"

"No–"

"They live way at the bottom of the ocean. They have a light bulb looking thing to lure in prey?"

"The crazy giant demon looking fish?"

She smiled.

"*That's* what you picked for me?"

"Well, it'd be good to have an intimidating call sign," she said, defensively. "The anglerfish is absolutely terrifying."

"Well, *dear heart*, most people haven't cracked a biology textbook and learned about terrifying creatures that live in the depths of the ocean. Especially in land-locked states."

Her face had fallen. "*Oh*. We can change it."

"No, I'm branded Angler forever."

She had been thoughtful for a moment, then her eyes widened excitedly. "Did you know they produce a bacterium that creates that bioluminescence that attracts their prey? Isn't that fascinating?"

Literally no one associated the name with the creature, but people did get the impression he enjoyed fishing a considerable amount more than he actually did.

She should have been here by now, he thought, staring toward the highway hidden on the other side of thick forest.

"Maybe she got lost," he reasoned aloud. *After all, she's never been to the safe house.* He exhaled. "Do you think I should have shaved?" he asked Fenway, his young German Shepherd partner, who was preoccupied watching ducks float across the lake. "I haven't seen her in a few months, she may not recognize me."

The dog cocked her brown head, intensifying her stare.

"You're right. The long hair/beard is sort of a package deal."

Fenway turned her head abruptly, hearing the truck on the dirt road before the headlights were visible through the trees. Josh stood, retrieved his pistol from the porch railing, and slid it into its holster.

Luther had been vague about details, or he simply didn't have any. She had gone to get Gabe and hadn't been having much success, something related to a complication with the Sim.

Luther had mentioned that the Arks had obtained access to Sim sessions, but he'd told him while Josh was in shock observing Essie as she recovered from cyanide. The significance of what Luther had shared hadn't really sank in. Apparently, they'd cloned the technology so they could be better prepared for that sort of warfare. While Luther wouldn't share exact details of Gabe's sessions, he described them as intense and heartbreaking, and he worried about his emotional well-being. He also revealed that Essie had gained access to the sessions through a friend of hers who worked with the technology division.

Danny, presumably.

He also revealed that she'd taken on the Sim herself.

"What happened in her sessions?" Josh had asked, then thought better of it. "It's too personal, probably," he said when Luther had sharpened his look.

He called for Fenway and they ducked into the shadows next to the porch steps. He didn't know what to expect from the truck pulling up the dirt drive. There was still the possibility that Gabe was truly no longer an ally. She could have been captured and was being forced to show the way.

The truck creaked to a stop right in front of the steps. In the darkness of the night, Josh couldn't see into the cab. He had intentionally left the lights off in and out of the cabin so he'd have the opportunity to assess the situation. Anyone who stumbled upon it would think the place had been abandoned for years.

The driver's door squeaked open, and a lanky man slid out, stepping noisily and indecisively toward the cabin.

"Maybe the key's under the mat," he said aloud, glancing over his shoulder as though anticipating a response.

Josh listened for Essie but heard nothing over the sound of Gabe scuffing his shoes against the pine needles and dirt.

"Get *back*," Josh bellowed in his gruffest voice, flipping on the spotlight, and popping out of the shadows. The spotlight lit up Gabe's face and the entire cab of the truck, where Josh could see a crumpled heap topped off by a tangle of golden-brown hair.

He signaled to Fenway and the Shepherd sprinted to Gabe, baring her teeth and forcing him away from the driver's door. Meanwhile, Josh hurried around to the passenger side.

"*Essie?*"

She was strewn over the bench seat, propped up in the middle by her backpack serving as a pillow. He pulled the hair back from her face. She'd had a pretty severe bloody nose, long dried. Her skin was coated in a layer of sweat, her face had a sallow, lifeless appearance. Josh lifted her wrist and checked her pulse, which was slow, but present.

"She's been unconscious, but stable for the past hour," Gabe offered, peering over his shoulder.

"*What happened?*" Josh demanded. He had to repeat himself when Gabe didn't realize he was speaking to him.

"She came into the clinic where I work and one of the doctors gave her the new vaccine."

Josh eased her into an upright position. "They weren't supposed to roll that out until the 25th," he said, placing a hand on her cheek, indented by the zippered compartments of the backpack.

"He opened the box to give it to her."

Josh did a double take of her arm, turned upward in her lap, the elaborate cross tattoo. He ran his fingers across it, frowning. "What prompted him to do that?"

Gabe tried to look in through the windshield. "I'm not sure."

"You said she's been stable for an hour. What was she like before that?"

"Erratic body temperature, pulse, seizure-type behavior." Fenway growled as Gabe tried to approach the cab. "She said not to give her medical treatment. It sounded absurd to me, but I felt compelled to listen to her. Look, could you call off Cujo?"

"Fenway, release."

The dog whimpered and jogged around to the passenger side, jumping up to sniff Essie's jeans. Gabe moved to the driver's side door. "She said she'd be 'okay' in 8-10 hours."

"She said that?"

He nodded, frowning upon seeing her bloodied face. "Oh, I didn't realize she had a nosebleed. I didn't want to disturb her once it seemed like she was actually sleeping."

"She got the vaccine around 3?" Josh asked, furrowing his brow as he did the calculation.

"That's right. Is this typical? Dr. Warren said patients are just asked to lie down for 30 minutes–maybe she had an empty stomach?"

Josh was no longer listening to his brother. By her recovery estimate, she'd be awake between midnight and 2 am. He studied Esther's face, glancing down at his watch.

"She *will* be OK, right?"

"Yeah," Josh replied, stroking her arm. When he noticed Gabe watching him, he frowned. "*What*? You don't like the beard? The hair?"

"*No–*" he said, shaking his head. "It suits you."

His brother had never once issued him a compliment. "'It suits you,'" Josh repeated in a mock tone, then noticed for the first time noticing how gaunt Gabe's face had become.

Gabe's mouth fell ajar, looking confused as to how to respond. "I'm Gabriel West, by the way," he said, extending his hand cordially.

Josh narrowed his eyes as he accepted the handshake. "Josh. Your *brother*."

"*Josh*? No," he said slowly. "You can't be. You're—."

"Taller?"

"Dead."

Josh pondered this and lifted his eyebrows. "Well, I must look *really* good for a dead guy. Could you get the door?"

"Mom and dad–are they–?"

"They're safe."

Gabe's breath caught in his chest.

"You two didn't have a chance to talk, I take it?"

"I don't know," he began, hesitating. "I don't *think* so?"

Luther had mentioned the morning reset, but Josh thought bringing it up might take some time to explain. "Will you get the door? Turn the lights on? I need to get her inside."

Gabe nodded and moved quickly toward the cabin. Just as he found the light switch, Josh brushed by him, carefully carrying Essie into the cabin. He crossed the open, rustic kitchen to a small living room area, where he slowly lowered her to the green plaid couch. He immediately became busy, retrieving medical supplies from the bedroom located just off the living space.

"She said no medical treatment."

"I'm giving her IV fluids. That is the absolute *minimum* I'm willing to do. She can be angry all she wants when she wakes up." *She does anger really well as it turns out*, he added silently. He switched on the vitals monitor and adjusted the pulse oximeter on her finger. He moved quickly down the hall to soak a washcloth under the bathroom faucet.

Crouching beside her, he went to work, gently running the towel over her face, starting with the parts that were just covered in sweat and grime, working his way to the areas streaked with blood and other bodily secretions.

299

The monitors beeped that they had made their initial readings and he looked up. He was thoughtful for a moment, nodding distantly.

"Did you go into the medical program, too?"

Josh's mouth tightened, but he was focused on collecting the supplies he needed to start her IV. "Not exactly." He winced as he forced her right hand into a ball and inserted the needle into the translucent skin on the back of her hand, where her veins were clearly visible. He securely taped the IV to her skin and stroked her forearm. He adjusted the flow, waiting until he saw the fluid dripping through the tubing, and then exhaled deeply. "You're sure it was the new vaccine they gave her?"

"That's what Dr. Warren said."

The monitors confirmed Gabe's earlier assessment, her vitals stabilizing, and her body temperature only three degrees over the normal range. She had a naturally slow resting heart rate, lower than world-class athletes, Luther said. Early in recovery, her heart rate would spike and cycle in and out of extreme levels. After the initial response, her heart rate would typically drop to around 10-15 beats per minute as her cells began the healing process.

"She says she's going to drone strike him when she wakes up."

"Is that right?" Josh's mouth pulled up at the corner. "Not a great guy, I take it?"

Gabe shook his head but did not share in the amusement, lost in thought. "Can she *do* that?" Gabe asked, watching his brother skillfully take a blood sample and place it on the side table. "The drone strike thing?"

"She might know some people." Josh pulled the coffee table closer and sat lightly on the edge, readjusting the pulse oximeter. "You're sure the vaccine was given 3 hours ago?" The question was rhetorical. It correlated with what Luther said, as well as the driving time to the cabin.

"Positive. Why?"

Josh placed a palm on her cheek, moved to her forehead, then pulled the blanket off the back of the couch and covered her.

Gabe twisted his face in confusion.

It didn't make sense. Esther had experienced every type of pathogen, every known bioweapon. By now she knew her precise recovery times. Perhaps she overestimated on purpose? Maybe she initially thought the vaccine was more powerful than it was. But then again, the "weakest" test she'd performed with Luther, the most benign deadly pathogen they'd tested on her–still took more than six hours for her to fully recover, and here at three hours, she seemed on the verge of a full recovery.

"They may have done the Purity serum as well."

Josh looked up abruptly.

"It's chemical sterilization."

"I know what it is," he retorted sharply. "Why would they do that?"

"It's become standard for anyone who comes in. If they're getting aid or getting other care, it's pretty much a prerequisite."

Josh was glad for a solid sitting surface. He stared into Essie's face, his eyes beginning to burn. It seemed logical that if her body could fight off any other threat, it could also be immune to chemical sterilization, but he couldn't shake the uneasiness he felt. His stomach, his heart wretched. He took a few solid breaths before saying slowly: "If they intended to kill her, I doubt they'd waste time or supplies doing that." He took two additional stabilizing breaths.

"They meant to *kill her*?"

Josh looked pointedly at Essie, then back to his brother. "Yes."

"Did she have some sort of antidote?"

He exhaled. "Something like that."

"I did see her injecting something into her leg."

Josh peered up at him. "Before or after the vaccine?"

"After. She was having trouble walking when I found her."

Josh raised an eyebrow, pondering an explanation to provide to his brother. "Maybe an immunity booster to help metabolize whatever was in the vaccine."

Seeing that Gabe seemed to be accepting this explanation, he decided to change the subject. "Would you grab the blanket from the

301

bedroom just down that hallway? Her body temperature is dropping a little fast. Probably the fluids."

Josh remembered how Luther had extracted her plasma as she recovered, how he did this right as her body seemed to be in its most vulnerable state. He thought of draining so much blood from her body, making her have to fight that much harder, even now once her body had stabilized for the most part and it churned his stomach. He checked the monitors again: Low-grade 101.7 fever, mild tachycardia, and no apparent distress.

She had told him that at some points during recovery, she had awareness of what was going on around her. With her vitals steadying, he wondered if this was one of those times. He placed his palm against her cheek.

Before he had time to say something to her, Gabe had returned with a quilt, looking confused. "Did she come to the clinic *for me*?"

Josh closed his eyes. "Yes."

"She said they were going to kill me."

"This *afternoon*, based on what I've been told."

Gabe's eyes widened. "They were going to kill me today?"

"Yes."

"Sooo," he began, processing this information. "She risked her life to save me."

Josh hesitated, not comfortable with confirming this information like it would relinquish something to his brother. "She did."

Gabe's eyes became very round. "Why would she *do that*?" he breathed. There was a long period of silence, which Josh dealt with by tucking the quilt around Essie, dimming the lights in the room, and starting a fire in the wood stove in the corner. When he'd settled again on the edge of the coffee table, Gabe spoke:

"How do we know her?"

Josh released the breath he had held in his chest and glanced regretfully toward Essie, hoping she couldn't hear after all. He snapped his head back to Gabe. "You're messing with me right now, right?"

"No."

"Gabe, this is *Essie*," he whispered.

"She told me her name. Wait–it's Essie, *not Esther*," he said thoughtfully, nodding.

"You remember now?"

"Well, yes and no. I remember a girl I think was her, but when she was little."

"Essie's dad has been best friends with Dad since they were kids. Do you remember Uncle Teo?"

"Uncle Teo," he repeated. "I don't think so? Wait. Uncle Teo is a pastor."

"Yes."

"He adopted a little girl when he moved to Colorado," he said slowly, as though translating a foreign language.

"Yes. *She's* that little girl."

Gabe nodded. "*Okay*, that makes sense. Was *he* killed?"

Josh narrowed his eyes. "No. No one's dead–*well*–lots of people are, but–" He shook his head in disbelief.

Gabe's eyes drifted to Esther. "He sang songs to her in Italian when she was little," he murmured quickly.

Esther's bottom lip parted slightly, her chest rising and falling in a slower, more noticeable way, correlating with a decrease in her heart rate, which was hovering around 64.

"So, you *do* remember?"

"No," Gabe said, a bit flatly. "I know *those* things, but it's like I read them somewhere. I vaguely remember what she looked like as a little girl, but I don't remember anything between that little girl and–" he motioned to Essie, his head tilting to the side. It was like he was taking in the details of her face for the first time, his eyes suddenly focused and intrigued. "*Essie*," he said softly, his mouth curling up slightly.

"You okay?"

"Yeah," Gabe said incredulously. "Have you ever had a wave of good feelings just wash over you?"

Josh furrowed his brow. "I have."

"I haven't felt that in so long," he breathed. "When I saw her earlier? I felt alive for the first time that I can remember." Gabe's eyes were locked on her, his lips continuously pinching upwards. "Just looking at her, I feel it. That wave of good?"

Josh swallowed hard, stroking her arm gently as he rose to his feet. He grabbed the blood sample and stepped around Gabe to the kitchen.

He wasn't sure how Esther had managed the endeavor of rescuing Gabe, but he wasn't comfortable with how transfixed his brother was with her now. He tried to focus on running the tests on her blood, but he didn't trust his typically steady hands that he now saw were tremoring to handle the sample and he wasn't keen on the idea of obtaining a second one.

With a clear pathway now before him, Gabe crossed to the couch. He cautiously placed his hand on Essie's shoulder and whispered something too low for Josh to hear.

"We should probably let her rest," Josh said suddenly.

Gabe nodded, briefly resting his hand over her arm. His face was filled with relief as he turned toward the kitchen, a drowsy smile on his face. "That tattoo of hers?"

"Yeah?"

"*She* did that? It wasn't government issued, right?"

Josh narrowed his eyes.

"The cross?" Gabe clarified, motioning to his left forearm.

"Uh–yeah," he replied.

"Wow," Gabe said, impressed. "That's either really–ill-advised– or–" His voice trailed off.

"Or?"

"Audacious," Gabe said softly, savoring the word. "In the best possible way."

Josh glanced across to Esther, surprised to find Fenway already squeezed between her and the back of the couch. "Fenway, you're audacious in all the bad ways." Fenway lifted her ears then settled her muzzle on Esther's knee.

"The pup's really attached to her," Gabe observed. "Is she hers?"

"No," Josh began, "they've never met before today."

Gabe glanced over at the Shepherd and chuckled lightly. "She seems to have the same effect on dogs that she has on people."

Josh stared at him. "Are you hungry?'

"I should be. I don't remember eating today."

"You look like you haven't eaten in *several* days," Josh said, eyeing his brother's emaciated arms, the excess of shirt fabric around his midsection. "Come on, I'll get you something. Essie and our mother would both have my hide if I didn't feed you when you look like that."

"Actually? I don't know if I *can* eat—my mind is preoccupied."

Josh exhaled, eyes panning to Esther.

"I don't want to impose," Gabe said, motioning toward the living room. "I saw the stairs on the way in—is there a place to lie down upstairs? I'm assuming you're staying close to—Essie."

"That was my plan. You can take the bedroom upstairs."

Gabe craned his neck around the corner, looking for the stairs, then turned on the spot. "Josh?"

Josh tilted his head so he could see around the metal light fixture hanging over the table. His brother looked far more serious than he had a few seconds earlier.

"I feel a little better about the world—knowing that you're still in it."

The brothers stood in silence, staring at one another. Josh tried to summon his ill feelings about Gabe: He was condescending, he was boring, he always did things just a little bit better than him—but as he looked at Gabe, he saw his dad's eyes, his mom's smile, and he knew what joy it would bring them to have Gabe safe.

"You too, Brother," Josh said, smiling tightly.

22

self-destruct

Luther had broken the communications protocol to make contact with Josh. The crackle of the radio caused a shockwave up Josh's spine.

"Angler, status?"

Josh scurried across the room and picked up the receiver, taking a seat at the kitchen table. "Canary & Bronco secure. Bronco says Stage 4 is underway."

"Say again about Stage 4."

"Canary was the preliminary in Stage 4." His eyes drifted across to the couch. She hadn't yet regained consciousness, but she had a more relaxed look as though she'd slipped directly from recovery into sleep. Fenway was still wedged between Essie's leg and the couch and didn't seem keen on moving anytime soon. "Canary is stable. Still silent."

"How long?"

"9 hours."

There was a long pause, then: "Still within parameters."

Josh watched Essie's exhales causing a fluttering of some loose strands of hair by her face. "Honestly, I think she went right to sleep. She's been stable since 18:00."

"That would be--unusual. You're certain about Stage 4?"

"Yes. Tests confirmed."

Luther exhaled deeply into the radio. "Is Bronco a security risk?"

Josh's eyes panned to the stairwell. "No."

"We dispatched The Musketeers to your location to help on final approach."

Josh shook his head, feeling a bit better about his own call sign, as he checked his watch. "ETA?"

"Six hours."

"Is embarkation moved up?"

"Unclear. Just watch your six and get here as soon as possible."

"Copy that." Josh rubbed at his eyes, the exhaustion finally setting in. He turned down the volume on the receiver and examined the road map lying open on the table. The map was ten years old, so he was trying to plot a course along roads that still existed. Road maintenance and infrastructure had not been a priority item so many were now undrivable or otherwise hazardous. He also had to consider the roads frequented by the government's new military agency, UNITY, and therefore were best avoided.

The trek to the Ark border wasn't particularly long; he'd done it dozens of times but given the circumstances and the consequences of any misstep, he was being meticulous in his planning.

It was a short time later that the excited shuffling of Fenway's paws on the hardwood floor startled him awake. He lifted his head from his forearm, feeling a crick in his neck. In a surreal sight, Essie stood in the doorway from the downstairs bathroom, some healthy color returned to her cheeks.

He exhaled deeply, rising from his chair. "Your call sign should be the Hulk, you know. I'm not sure what this Canary business is all about." He stepped toward her, noticing as he closed the distance that her lower lip was quivering.

"Yeah, inject me with poison and in ten short hours, I'll be barely mobile. Very Bruce Banner-like." Her voice was uncharacteristically shaky.

He wrapped his arms around her. "I'm sorry I was such a jerk the last time we saw each other."

"Me, too."

"You don't know how to be a jerk. *Honestly*. It's the one thing you're pretty terrible at."

He could hear her breaths tightening as her body trembled against his. "I meant I'm also sorry you acted like a jerk."

He chuckled, kissing the top of her head.

"I'm sorry for yelling at you and kicking you out of my socialist apartment."

"I'm sorry for letting you kick me out of your socialist apartment."

"Yeah. What the hell, Josh?"

"I literally didn't know what to do."

"*This*. Doing this would have literally defused the entire situation." She tightened her arms around him.

"Well, see, *in my experience*, wild animals don't appreciate being restrained."

"I'd pinch you, but then you'll flail and I'm depending on you for balance right now."

He took a deep breath.

"I'm sorry for not telling you I was leaving."

"Yeah, that wouldn't have gone well," he said softly. "You're safe though–that's all that matters to me. But please don't do that again?"

"I didn't see my dad before I left." The words were strained, her voice barely recognizable.

He squeezed her gently.

"I left without saying goodbye." She tried to actively steady her breathing, but then burst out with a gasp of words: "How could I do that to him?"

He started to step away, but she clung tighter to him. "Essie, *listen to me*," he whispered. "Are you listening?"

Her head bobbed slightly against his shoulder.

"In just a few days, we will set foot in a place that is beautiful and safe and free. Everyone we love will be there. Thanks to *you*, everyone we love will be there."

She started to cry again. "It was stupid of me to go."

"Yeah. Yeah, it was. But you did it, Essie. He's here. He's safe."

She was silent, still trembling. The tightness in her body told him she was holding back from saying more. "I probably smell like city and grime–"

He sighed, kissing her temple. "And sweat."

"I forgot about the sweating part. That can be pretty pungent."

"Uh-hm," he said, burrowing a kiss into the top of her head. "But you know what? I don't care. Do me a favor?"

"What?" she replied, her voice muffled.

"Please don't put your life in danger again."

She nodded silently.

"I don't have any interest in existing in a world you're not in."

She growled softly, then started to pry herself away. "Danny told you what I said."

"No. What did you say to Danny?"

"He *told* you."

He hadn't spoken to Danny since the night of the antidote run and she seemed to read this in his expression.

"*Oh.*"

He lowered his chin, trying to make eye contact. "You do know that you mean more to me than anything else or anyone else in this world. *Right*?"

She frowned, diverting her eyes to things on the countertops.

He decided against forcing the conversation; it wasn't the time for that. He gave her another kiss on top of the head. "I knew you'd be hungry but keep expectations low."

"Oh good gravy, is that—pancake mix?"

"Keep low expectations."

"*Oh.* Emergency 'griddlecakes,'" she read. "I didn't know the word 'pancakes' was trademarked?"

"Even so, in a shocking turn of events, there *is* maple syrup."

She parted from him and shuffled into the kitchen, grasping at the counter. "How do I love thee, dear maple syrup, let me count the–" She made a complete one-hundred-eighty-degree turn. "Maple is spelled p-l-e. They spelled it p-e-l. I think it's an I can't believe it's not syrup situation."

"Oh, wow. I didn't notice that."

She shrugged. "I'm still excited. But first, I need to use the bathroom again."

"I may have overdone it with the second bag of fluids."

"I am *not* a camel, Joshua."

"I'll get the pancakes cooking if you want to take a shower, too," he offered as she waddled down the hallway.

"I'd be offended by the suggestion, but I just got a whiff of my underarm."

He smiled, despite a heaviness settling into his chest.

She returned a short while later wearing his sweatpants and a band t-shirt that once belonged to his dad. He had slipped them inside while she was showering.

"You make surprisingly subdued entrances. Based on what I know, I visualize a phoenix bursting into flames and being reborn from the ashes."

"I thought I was the Hulk? You know, smash, smash."

"Yeah, well, you *are* the Phoenix Initiative, right?"

She nodded, narrowing her eyes. "*So,* every time I enter a room-- *flames?*" She fluttered her fingers for dramatic effect.

"Hair flowing–kind of a cool image." He checked the pancakes on the griddle, deciding they were too pale yet.

"I think that visual is copywritten," she said, retying her damp hair into a top knot.

"Damn Marvel, they own everything."

"I could go back and try my entrance again. Make it more *theatrical?*"

He grinned. "No, I'm actually impressed you haven't fallen over yet. Speaking *of,* please sit."

She moved slowly to the table and lowered herself into a chair. "A bit off-kilter yet."

"Yeah, I regretted sending you for a shower."

"I used the bench seat."

"Good."

"It felt a little like *Flashdance*."

He frowned.

"If you knew the movie, you'd think that was *hilarious*," she murmured. When she reached up to scratch her neck, his eyes followed the tattoo on the underside of her arm.

"That's new."

Her expression remained fairly neutral. "I got it after the last time we saw each other."

"I figured that."

"It made an impression in the city."

"I'd say so. They opened the box of vaccines specifically for you."

"There was a sadistic social officer who had it out for me." She frowned. "Although, it *may* have also been because I showed up as 'fertile' in their little scan test. The tattoo and my fertility status seemed to equally offend her." When she saw his confused expression, she continued. "If you want food rations, you have to establish medical care at one of the government-run clinics. To get care at those clinics, they do a finger prick test each visit."

"They're killing anyone who's fertile?"

She turned over her wrist. "I think there's other criteria, which I also met."

His jaw tightened.

"Plus, I wasn't supposed to be fertile."

"Why?"

"Because she had fast-tracked me for sterilization. Gabe did the procedure yesterday."

Josh glared at the griddle, the bubbling batter. "*He* did the procedure?" When she didn't answer, he raised his eyes. She was watching him with an indiscernible expression.

He took a slow, steadying breath. "So, your body—fought it off?"

"He used saline instead of the serum."

"*Oh.*" He nodded, clearing his throat. He dropped his gaze to the pancakes again, unclenching his fist from around the spatula.

"He remembered me yesterday--to some degree."

Josh nodded without looking up.

"They erased me this morning. Or yesterday morning I guess it is now," she murmured, clearing her throat. "They map all the positive memory locations during the day, during dreams—then, in the morning—" She snapped her fingers. "Gone." There were tears welling in her unblinking eyes. Her lower lip quivered.

The room was unbearably quiet.

"He's safe, that's what matters," she said quickly, nodding along with the words, like a rehearsed mantra.

"He remembers you," he said softly.

She shook her head. "He's safe. That's what matters."

"Essie, *trust me.* He remembers you."

Essie pressed her lips together, saying nothing.

"Objectively? Your tattoo? It's pretty incredible. And I'm not what I'd call a tattoo guy."

She took a seat at the kitchen table, allowing the clumsy segue. "I couldn't look at the lab tattoo anymore."

He nodded, moving the pancakes to two small plates.

"I started having flashbacks a couple years ago from when I was there. I started having panic attacks. Have you ever had one of those?"

He shook his head, deciding against drawing a blatant connection with her doing the antidote sessions and the flashbacks beginning.

"It felt like I was drowning. It was happening a lot and it would come out of nowhere."

"That must have been excruciating."

"That's when I got into working out and MMA. It helped. I wasn't having them nearly as often. One day though, I looked at the tattoo and I couldn't breathe. I felt like I couldn't escape what had happened because it was staring me right in the face."

He had spent the better part of an hour staring at the tattoo while she slept, tracing the lines with his fingertips, getting lost in the flow of the design, examining the intricacies. "Did you design it?"

She described how during a particularly rough recovery period, when even sitting upright on the couch felt daunting, she sketched the intricate cross. "I wanted to represent all the people that mean the most to me. Admittedly I intended for it to be much smaller than it turned out."

Carrying the plates to the table, Josh's eyes tried to focus on her arm. "I guess I didn't get a real good look at it." He decided the small lie wouldn't cause any harm.

She laid her arm across the table. "My dad's guitar," she said, pointing to the instrument hidden against the bark on a tree. "The tree swing at the farm." She pointed to a sunflower. "Your mom's favorite." Her finger followed a twisting branch. "Here are the wildflowers by that lake near your house." There was regularly a small mason jar on the kitchen table filled with them that his dad picked for his mom. She slid her finger upwards. "I had to put some books in here because, well—you know me. The top one is—"

"Your dad's Bible."

She smiled lightly. "I can smell that leather cover just looking at it, that suede page marker cord?"

Josh stared at the whimsical twists of the vines, the leather cowboy boot modeled after the pair his dad always wore, the horse curled up like a sleeping dog. "Is Bree wearing a hat on his back?"

Her cheeks reddened. "For you."

"I've never worn a hat like that."

"Steve Irwin did."

He narrowed his eyes.

"The Crocodile Hunter?"

He tried to resist the urge to smile.

"There's a few other things," she concluded, starting to slice into her pancake stack.

He leaned his chin into his fist, watching her. "Does it help? To see this instead?"

She released a deep exhale. "I have a difficult time understanding why I went through what I did as a baby. It feels like there should be a purpose to it. I get overwhelmed. I start to question why God let it happen, where was God during all of that? Every time I look at this though? I remember everything He's given me in my life since then." She took a deep breath. "Before I'd look at my arm and feel haunted by what happened. I'd feel angry. Now I look at my arm and I feel gratitude and love--and hope." She nodded conclusively, shoving her fork full of griddle cakes into her mouth with a smile.

"I should have been there for you, Essie. I'm sorry I wasn't."

Her eyes creased, her cheeks full of food.

After a prolonged silence, he motioned to her plate, and she continued eating.

Sitting in the yellowed light at the kitchen table, Josh watched Esther devour three stacks of griddle cakes and an entire grilled trout. She was eating with such gusto she had to stop to catch up with chewing—and breathing. She closed her eyes as she gulped down another cup of water, clearly savoring how it soothed her dry throat. Finally, she leaned back in her chair, slowly opening her eyes again. "*What?*" she demanded playfully, catching him staring.

"I was just thinking how you eat like a very cute, but very ravenous bear."

"Bears eat less carbs." She sighed, appearing sedated from the large meal. "I'm going to regret that last stack when my brain finally processes how much food I just ate."

"Probably." He patted a watchful Fenway on the head. "You could go lie down for a while, get some more rest?"

Essie nodded.

"Can I ask you something first, though?"

"Sure."

"Why was it so important to you to go after Gabe? I mean, we all wanted to get him, but—clearly it was risky."

"Risky in what way?" she asked, her brow deeply furrowed. She took a sip of water, raising an eyebrow.

He exhaled, shaking his head.

She leaned back in her chair and said quietly: "It wasn't something I could live with—leaving Gabe behind."

Josh nodded slowly. There was more he wanted to know, he realized. His mind raced, wondering what she felt toward Gabe at that moment. If things had changed for her with Gabe back in the picture. Why did she have to be the one to go? Did she consider him before she left? Did he even factor into the equation?

"My reasons for going were selfish."

He chortled lightly. "Many things you are, Esther Natale. Selfish is not one of them." He lowered his eyes, bracing himself for what he was about to verbalize: *You love him.*

She narrowed her eyes. "Sorry?" She tilted her head inquisitively.

"I didn't say anything."

"I know. What is it you want to say, Josh?"

He shook his head. "It seemed sudden. You up and leaving the way you did?"

She winced a bit, straightening her back. "I couldn't go before because if I was captured and they figured out who I was, I'd put everyone at risk."

He frowned.

She sighed, resigned to the fact that more explanation was necessary. "When Luther said I wasn't immune anymore, I figured there wasn't anything keeping me from going."

"Luther said *what*?"

"In the last antidote session? He said it didn't work, that he had to revive me."

"As in, you were *dying*?"

She gave a small nod.

Josh narrowed his eyes. In the five conversations he'd had with Luther, a couple of extensive lengths, he hadn't mentioned a word about this. "So, did you bring the antidote with you? Gabe mentioned you injected yourself with something after they gave you the vaccine."

"I couldn't risk carrying the antidote."

"What was in the injection?"

"Epinephrine."

He narrowed his eyes. "You were afraid of inadvertently consuming shellfish? Or something you're *actually* allergic to?"

"No," she said with a weak smile. "I thought it might be useful if I got into a pinch. A burst of adrenaline to the system might come in handy. With how things played out, I knew I just needed to get Gabe to the truck and on his way here." A yawn overtook her suddenly and as she set her gaze on him again, her eyes were impossibly tired. "I hoped the adrenaline rush might give me enough time."

His mind tried to absorb this information. He glared at the tabletop, their short stack of dirty dishes in front of an unoccupied seat, trying to sort through his thoughts. He was silent as the realization hit him. He closed his eyes, took a slow breath in, and said: "You weren't planning to make it here alive, were you?"

When she gave no response, he opened his eyes to find Essie hunched forward, her chin to her chest, her breaths deepening.

23
light

16 years earlier...

The aroma of popcorn had just begun to waft into the family room. Usually, Gabe and Josh were only given one movie night a week, but their parents had offered one on a rare Sunday on account of Uncle Teo being in town with his newly adopted daughter, Esther.

"It's a little traditional of a name, isn't it?" Gabe had heard his dad say when he went to retrieve three juice boxes from the refrigerator.

"It was the name Rachel had picked out for a girl," Teo said quietly.

"That's sweet, Matteo," Sara West said, starting to brew a fresh pot of coffee. "Rachel would love that you did that. Her name is Esther what though?"

"Esther Evin Natale. The man who took care of her before had called her Evin."

Luke leaned back in his chair. "She and the boys seem to be getting along well."

The adults all looked up in unison to watch the three children stacking pillows and stuffed animals on the air mattress.

"Skinny little thing."

"We're working on that. She's not picky with food so that helps. She's liked everything I've made for her."

"Are her taste buds working?" Gabe's dad jested.

"I'm a fairly decent cook these days."

"Any behavioral or cognitive issues?" Sara asked. "Considering all the trauma—?" She let her voice trail off.

Gabe glanced up. He'd recently learned the word 'trauma'. They used it on a medical show his parents watched after he and Josh went to bed. Typically, the person who had been through it was badly wounded and bleeding. He looked over at Esther, whose only wound was a splinter from the barn ladder.

"She won't sleep at night."

"Is she afraid of the dark?"

"Yes."

"Well, that's pretty common. Does she have a nightlight?"

"She does. I was reading about trying to get her energy out so she falls asleep, that it might help."

"And?"

"One day I took her to the zoo, we worked in the garden, she helped me stock the church's food pantry--still didn't sleep at all. She finally fell asleep as the sun came up. She'll sleep during the day."

"I wonder if wherever she was before, if there was a reason she became nocturnal? Maybe a danger at night?" Sara asked, her hand clasped to her face.

"How does that work out for you?

Matteo shrugged. "During the week it works out okay. I can get some things done and Trish just works out of the living room if I need to go down to the church. That way she's there if Esther wakes up."

"She doesn't try to wake you at night?"

"We're just getting to know each other. She plays quietly in her room or flips through books. One night she was outside watering the plants."

"Those petrified twigs are plants?" Luke chided.

"So, she's afraid of the dark, but she's not afraid of being outside at night? You did tell her not to-"

"Yes, Sara. I told her to stay inside."

Luke sighed. "Well maybe that will change if she has to be awake during the day in order to play with these two."

318

Matteo nodded.

"What happened? I mean, do you know anything about her history?"

"He said she was abused, kept isolated from people; she was never outside."

"Ever?"

He shook his head.

Gabe, who had been eavesdropping, looked over at Esther, who was focused on the movie just starting. Josh was propped up on the opposite side, tossing large handfuls of popcorn into his mouth. He didn't seem aware of the conversation happening across the room.

"I remember reading about a study done years ago where young babies and children were denied basic affection. They developed an aversion to it. Any physical contact caused them a lot of discomfort. Their pain receptor readings were equivalent to a third-degree burn," his mom said, regretfully.

"You can't tell she has a PhD in Psychology, can you?" Luke teased.

It was in the next moment that Josh had offered Esther his small elephant stuffed animal to snuggle with, to which she had thrown her arms around him, and kissed him on the cheek.

"Daddy, look!" she exclaimed, clambering onto her knees to show Teo, clutching it to her neck. "Josh said I could snuggle with her."

All three adults stared at her, their mouths ajar. Gabe's mom had her hand braced against her face.

"Un dolce elefantino per una dolce bambina," Matteo said with a smile, then translated in English: "A sweet little elephant for a sweet little girl."

Esther beamed at him, taking in the faces of those in the room. "Sono felice qui." With that, she settled back into her pillow, nudging closer to Josh.

"She speaks Italian?"

"She's learning–really quickly. I sing to her in Italian sometimes and she asked me to teach her." Gabe peered over the couch at Teo, who was wiping tears from his eyes, though his face didn't look remotely sad.

Esther rotated back to Gabe at that moment, encouraging him to scoot closer. She held out the elephant for him to see, then clutched it to her chest, smiling tightly. Not satisfied by the distance between them on the air mattress, she tugged at his arm. By the time the first musical number began, all three children shared one pillow and they were tucked under the same oversized blanket.

* * *

Based on the positioning of the moon in the purple western sky, it was just before sunrise. When Gabe woke initially, it was startling, both because he felt alarmed that he'd slept in and because he didn't recognize his surroundings. It was quiet all around him, which wasn't unusual, but it was a different sort of quiet than what he was used to. Typically, there was silence in that cold, concrete building, but he could feel the presence of humans all around. It was confining. Waking at the cabin felt entirely different. The stillness was peaceful, and his surroundings were open. Having arrived in darkness, he didn't have the chance to look at the landscape, so he took the opportunity to examine the view from the upstairs window.

There was the truck he'd driven there just below, the dirt road canopied by pine trees over rolling hills. Birds were starting to chirp to each other in the branches, geese were honking over on the lake, and the purple sky was starting to give way to orange.

He moved into the upstairs bathroom, a time capsule to vintage 1980s decor. He had become accustomed to auto-flush toilets, sensor-triggered faucets, and hand dryers. It was nostalgic to turn the faucet on manually and wipe his hands on a loop-strung hand towel. He hadn't felt fabric so soft in a long time. Most of the materials used in the city were made from recycled synthetic materials not meant to spend so much time in contact with human skin. Everything was too slick, too scratchy, and made a considerable amount of noise. He moved the turquoise towel between his hands repeatedly, savoring the feel against his skin, letting his eyes drift upward to his reflection in the rectangular silver gilded mirror.

He knew he had seen himself in reflections in elevator doors and the sea of windows on the building exteriors, but his appearance confused him. He'd aged considerably since the last time he felt like he'd gotten a good look at himself. The mud color of his uniform did nothing for his appearance, washing him out even further. He stared at his reflection so long his face no longer made sense; it was all just overlapping shapes.

A fragrance reached his nostrils and he found himself searching for the source. He lifted his hands to his face, discovering it was the hand soap and the scent, according to the label, was apple cranberry. It was rich and pungent, and he immediately thought of holidays at home. When he was young, his mother spent the entire weekend before Thanksgiving and then again for Christmas, slicing up apples from their orchard and baking pies. Most of the town bought her pies for their holiday dinners. He closed his eyes and breathed in the scent again, picturing the farmhouse starting to come alive with twinkle lights and gradual additions of decorations. He remembered sitting on the oval rug in front of the fireplace, playing with trucks with Josh. Their dad, exhausted from the day and belly full, would be sleeping in the recliner, while their mother would be playing Christmas music softly through the kitchen speaker, using a pizza cutter to slice lattices of dough, every so often wiping her flour-coated hands on her red and black buffalo plaid apron.

When he opened his eyes again, he feared he might find himself standing back in the cold, steel gray interior of the Health Services Government Housing complex. He exhaled deeply upon seeing the cozy bathroom around him, but as he caught his reflection again in the mirror and glanced down at the drabby uniform, he was suddenly struck with the urge and need to change into different clothes that might spark a memory of home. He peered toward the bedroom and the dark wood dresser wedged under the steep ceiling pitch.

When he reached the top of the stairs sometime later, showered, shaved, and wearing an outfit he imagined a lumberjack might wear, he felt renewed. His descent echoed this, which was met with a glare and a waving of his brother's arms. Gabe stopped abruptly.

"Essie's sleeping," Josh whispered, measuring up his brother's appearance as he quietly descended the remaining stairs.

"She's OK?" Gabe asked, his body tensing.

"Yeah. She was awake for a while, but she was pretty wiped out."

"I guess she has an excuse."

Josh raised his eyebrows. "*Yeah.*"

Gabe recognized that Josh seemed far more uneasy than the night before, but it didn't make any sense. He wondered if they'd argued during the time she was awake. "Did you find out what was in it? The vaccine?"

Gabe slid a sheet of test strips toward him. "I didn't know the test went this dark."

"What was in it?"

"This is just a bulk test kit, but a lethal dose of opioids seems to be the main player."

"Can you test how much?"

"Lethal, Gabe. It takes less than a salt grain of some of this stuff to do the job."

"And they're putting it into vaccines."

"Honestly, I thought they'd do something more sophisticated."

"What do you mean?"

"The government isn't even *trying* to hide what they're doing this time. It's like they've determined they have enough power at this point that criticism has no impact."

"Has this happened before?"

Josh sighed. "Last time they used the tests."

"*What?*"

"There was distrust after the government exploited a pandemic that hit a couple decades back. People rose up against mandatory vaccines, vaccine passports, 'emergency proclamations.' So, when the next big, scary virus came along, they did things differently to accomplish their goals. They didn't mandate *vaccines*. They mandated *testing*. In order to get government assistance, to travel, to enter a hospital, to go to school, to have a bank account, people had to get tested every two weeks."

"I don't understand."

"The test was a lot like a tuberculosis test where they inject a small amount of serum under the surface of the skin. For some, they used something benign. What they injected for others was a very small time-release pouch. Those selected to receive it left feeling fine. They died within 12 hours. Their test would then come back positive for the virus."

"So, the virus was a hoax?"

Josh nodded. "Manufactured. They used the pandemic to create opportunities for election manipulation among other things. Because of the discontent of the public with everything they had done, the amount of fraud they were having to do was starting to create division in their own party."

"So, they killed off people who wouldn't vote for them?"

He shook his head. "They killed off some of their own party members first. The ones who opposed their hostile takeover mostly, but they did have a few 'sacrificial lambs,' though using that phrase to describe *any* of those—" He took a breath, noticing his voice had intensified as he mimicked the intensity his dad sometimes had when talking about the state of the world. When he spoke again, his voice was low and measured. "Their thought was that this would make it look less suspicious. Once the public accepted that the virus was 'legitimate and deadly,' it was open season."

Gabe winced. "And I woke up in such a good mood."

"That's not typical I take it?"

"No."

"*Well*, we have a tough couple of days ahead, but we'll be safe where we're going."

"We're not going home?" The expression on Josh's face carried a lot of grief so he retreated quickly. "Forget I asked."

"The phrase 'home isn't a place' has become really popular, if that helps you."

Gabe shrugged.

"I agree with the sentiment, but I do miss the farm a lot."

"Home is the people you love," Gabe interpreted, his thoughts distracted.

"Mandatory made you philosophical huh?"

"Not remotely. Or not intentionally." He frowned at his brother. "Essie felt like home. When I saw her in the city?"

Josh stood, retrieved the test strips and tossed them in the trash, suddenly anxious. He craned his neck to see that the bedroom door was still closed.

"You should get some sleep, Josh," Gabe said with a tilt of his head.

Josh shook his head, tidying up the kitchen quietly. "There's still pancake batter if you're hungry?"

Gabe perked his eyebrows, stepping into the kitchen space. "*Well*, that sounds good."

Josh retrieved the batter bowl from the refrigerator and placed it by the griddle. "You have like three days to bulk up so Mom doesn't flip out."

He smiled lightly. "I look that bad?"

"I don't know, you were always pretty ugly."

The brothers worked side by side in the kitchen in silence.

Gabe cleared his throat once he had slid his pancakes onto a plate and sat down at the table. "Will you join me?"

Josh shrugged, sitting down across from his brother with a mug of instant coffee. He watched Gabe drizzle the syrup over a stack of perfectly symmetrical, perfectly scaled pancakes, cutting them into a grid pattern.

"*What*?" Gabe asked when he noticed him staring, his fork loaded with a beam of pancake layers. When Josh shook his head, he took the bite, grunting appreciatively. Grid section by grid section, he consumed every last morsel of his breakfast. He had been so thorough, mopping up any stray syrup, that the plate looked virtually unused when he pushed it away.

"How do you feel this morning?"

Gabe leaned back in his seat. "Strange."

Josh nodded slowly, unable to read enough from his brother's face to gain context into his vague response.

"Hopeful, but strange," Gabe added, peering around the cabin appreciatively. "It's nice here."

"I know it's a little rustic for you."

Frowning, Gabe took a sip of water. "*Is* it?"

Josh cleared his throat, glancing over his shoulder to the hallway and back. "*So*, what do you remember?"

"I don't know, to be honest."

"You don't know."

"Everything kind of gets warped with what you see in the Sim."

Josh scratched at his forehead, anxiously glancing around the cabin.

Gabe eyed him quizzically. "I don't remember you being this edgy. Didn't I used to be the serious one?"

"It's not him, it's me," Esther said, appearing suddenly in the hallway.

Josh jolted out of his chair, whirling around on the spot.

"Good *Lord*," Gabe remarked, grinning at her. "*You're* responsible for this behavior?"

Fenway scurried down the hallway, looping around Essie's legs repeatedly, gently herding her toward the kitchen.

"*Release*, Fenway."

The dog rushed over, laid down obediently across the threshold into the living room, eagerly awaiting his next instruction.

Essie gave Josh a side hug and patted him on the chest as she stepped into the kitchen. "Does anyone belong to that stack of pancakes?"

"I can heat them up for you," Josh offered, reaching for the plate of extra pancakes, moving stiffly toward the kitchen. "You probably need more than baked goods in your stomach though. I was planning to go fishing when you got up."

She dropped herself into Josh's vacated seat. Her long hair was pulled into a messy knot on top of her head, strands poking out in all directions. "Don't be alarmed. Despite how I may look, I have *not* been playing in electrical sockets. I forgot to pack a hairbrush and the comb in the bathroom is forever lost in this nest of hair."

"I think I saw detangler conditioner in the bathroom upstairs."

"There is a *second* bathroom? I did not think this place was that spacious."

"It's nice, isn't it?" Gabe observed, glancing around.

"It is," she said, peering over her shoulder. "A little rustic, but it suits Grizzly Adams over there."

Josh's cheeks pinched upward. "I knew I should have shaved."

"No, leave it. The church might need you to play Jesus in the Easter production." Her cheeks reddened.

"*Oh*, you weren't kidding," Gabe said, reaching a hand toward her hair.

"What?"

"The comb."

She untied her hair, trying to sort through the thick, tangled mess. "Can you get it?"

"You just have so much hair."

"Yeah, I know. It's a problem."

After making a small effort to pry it out, Gabe frowned. "Maybe leave it for now? You could try to wiggle it out in the shower."

"Both West boys tell me I need a shower in less than 8 hours. I don't think my self-esteem can take this." She waved her hands. "Alright, it's going back in the nest for now," she declared, looping it up into a bun.

"*Essie,*" Gabe said proudly, like a kindergartener who just learned a new vocabulary word.

"*Gabe,*" she said with a sleepy smile.

"I had a dream about you."

Esther rested her chin on her fists. "I'm listening. *Wait.* Josh is present. Should we cover his ears?" Her eyes lifted briefly to Josh, who stared intently at the griddle and did not look up.

"Approved for all audiences."

She narrowed her eyes at Josh before resuming her primed listening position.

Gabe described the scene in the farmhouse living room: the movie, the popcorn, the stuffed elephant Josh gifted to her. The more details he provided, the wider her smile.

Suddenly she dropped her hands to the table. "You remember *Gelato* and you didn't remember *my name*?"

"Gelato?" Josh asked, frowning.

"That's what I named the elephant you gave me."

"Wait, was that a memory or a dream? I didn't remember that."

Essie's cheeks tightened. "A memory. A distant memory, but a memory."

"It's a *start*," Josh offered, his face brightening as he took in Essie's reaction.

"Will you let *me* do some fishing?" she asked.

"You'd like to?" Josh asked.

"Do I have to be the one to–you know–?" She made vague gestures that seemed to relate to baiting the hook.

"I'll handle the bait," Josh said grudgingly. He delivered her warm stack of pancakes, which immediately received the bulk of her attention. "We'll have a few more mouths to feed. Luther is sending Miles, Corey, and Gunner."

Esther looked up, fork braced at her mouth.

"Who are they?" Gabe asked.

"Ess, you remember Miles, of course."

She glared at him.

"He's toned it down," he said reassuringly. "Okay, that's a lie. He's obnoxious."

Gabe furrowed his brow. "*Who* are they?"

"They do what I do--or *have* been doing. Helping to get people to the safe zone. Miles and I were friends when we were kids."

"Oh, I think I remember Miles. Tall kid, blonde hair?"

"Unnecessarily mean?"

Josh shook his head. "You intimidate him, Ess. That's why he acts that way."

"I am *not* an intimidating person."

"Depends on your perspective."

"I wish Luther hadn't done that," Esther muttered as she stuffed a bite into her mouth.

Josh leaned against the counter, crossing his arms. "He wants to protect precious cargo."

Gabe glanced across the table. Esther scratched at her eyebrow as she chewed. When she caught him staring, she shrugged. "I don't know why you're looking at me. He means *you*. I'm clearly too much of a drain on food supplies."

Josh chuckled as he retrieved Gabe's empty plate.

24

company

"I'm convinced your dad named you Esther so if you ever went on dating apps, guys would swipe right past thinking you were some 80-year-old woman."

"Oh I'm sure that's what my dad, the pastor, was thinking when he named me—how I would be perceived on dating apps."

Josh smiled as he washed his hands at the sink.

Miles, Corey, and Gunner had arrived right on schedule in the late morning, but they had collectively decided it was best to spend the night and start fresh the next day, since none of them had gotten adequate sleep.

"My parents met on a dating app," Corey reminisced. "Those were the days, huh?"

"Which one? Like Christian Mingle or like Tindr?"

"I don't know—what difference does it make?"

"It makes a lot of difference."

"On which app would you find Esther over here?"

"Well, *this* girl doesn't need a dating app."

Essie raised her hand. "First of all, thank you—*Gunner*, was it?"

Gunner smiled lightly through his thick beard.

"Second of all, what's a dating app?"

Miles widened his eyes. "Oh *wow*, you really were sheltered growing up, weren't you?"

"Maybe?"

"People would go into this app on their phone and post their photo, a bio, then they'd be paired up with compatible matches."

"Oh, like a rideshare app?" she asked.

"You don't know dating apps, but you know the term 'rideshare'?" Miles asked.

"*Anyway,* so it gives you compatible matches."

"Or matches who lived in reasonable proximity."

"Let's face it. Dating apps eventually became places to hook up. I remember when the government first started promoting a legitimate *prostitution* app. It was then I knew we had entered the end of times. Or, you know, Biff had stolen the time machine and was running the place."

"Dude, they still have it. All the Mandatory enlistees get access to it."

Josh turned on his heel. "Wait, for *actual*—"

"Yeah. The prostitutes all wear the same yellow pleather mini dress situation. Well, I guess they don't call them that—I think the accepted term is 'proxy.'"

Gabe inclined his chin toward the group while Esther had become very interested in something outside the window.

"Do you see something out there?" Josh asked, moving behind her, trying to match her vantage point.

She raised her chin. "Just looking at the lake."

He lifted his eyes to the windows which mainly reflected the interior activities and furniture. The lake was barely perceptible in the darkness. "You okay?" he whispered.

"Mhmm, just tired."

He rubbed lightly on her shoulder, then took a step back. He leaned against the kitchen counter, crossing his arms. "So why the outfit?" he asked the group.

"There's very much a labeling thing going on. It used to be that labels were bad, but then they started to want to box everybody in," Corey explained. "You can pick your pronouns, pick from dozens of genders and sexualities, but *stay in your lane.* Kind of a similar idea with occupations, religion, etcetera."

"Are there *only* female prostitutes?" Gunner asked.

"Have something to share with the group, Gunner?"

Gunner narrowed his eyes at Miles. "No."

"What would the male ones where? Yellow pleather suit?"

"That would have Man in the Yellow Hat vibes," Josh remarked.

"*Ew.* That image is impeding on memories of a beloved children's book series and character and it's honestly making me a little uncomfortable," Esther said, leaning back in her chair.

"Do *you* have something to share with the group, Esther?" Miles asked.

"No, I'm good."

"You and Amnesia over here coupled up for a minute, didn't you?" Miles asked, causing Esther to readjust in her seat.

Josh looked up abruptly, ready to come to her defense, but she tightened her lips, composed. "I don't see how that's any of your business, but no."

"But you *kissed*, right? Your *first* kiss. It was a big dramatic moment?" Miles had an accusatory tone.

"Was *I* your first kiss?" Gabe asked suddenly, his face kind.

She glanced over her shoulder at Josh. "I did couple up with *that* guy-- or are you only interested in things that happened 4 years ago?"

Miles perked his eyebrow at Josh. "*Really?*"

She glanced around at their eager faces and ran her fingers through her hair as she stood and turned on her heel. "Well, since you gentlemen didn't wait for me to eat while I was taking my second shower of the day, I'm going to get myself some food." She picked up a glass from the counter and took a long sip of water, peering up at Josh over the rim. "Is this my plate over here?"

He nodded, holding up his palm to Miles behind her back, giving a menacing look. "We have more potatoes, too, if you want them."

"I *would* like more potatoes. I'm a Carbivore on my dad's side, as you know." She met his attentive gaze briefly.

"*So*, what are the sleeping arrangements here?" Miles asked pointedly, releasing a wide yawn.

Josh stepped around Esther rather than speaking over her. "There are bunk beds, plus a trundle bed upstairs."

"What the hell's a trundle bed?"

"It's a mattress that slides under the bottom bunk. Then there's a small bedroom downstairs, and the couch."

Miles considered the options. "Well chivalry's not dead yet. I'll take the private bedroom."

Esther, who had just shoved a large number of potatoes in her mouth, smirked, looking a bit like a chipmunk loading her cheeks with acorns.

"*Esther*, dear, feel free to join me."

She choked down a large chunk of potato, but by the time she had cleared her throat enough to speak, Miles had stood and was approaching her. He put his plate next to the sink and placed his hands on either side of her face. "I'm sorry for my behavior," he whispered. "I'll do better."

She raised an eyebrow. "The good news is you can't do any *worse*."

"*Oh*, he certainly can," Josh murmured.

"I'd refute that, but I'd be lying," Miles conceded, releasing the counter. "Who's doing watch tonight?"

"I will," Josh declared.

"Can't let you do that. You didn't sleep last night. You will be useless to us unless you get some shut eye."

"You go in the bedroom with Esther," Gunner suggested in his low, gravelly voice.

"Essie's a good Christian girl, what are you doing?"

"I'm fine bunking with Josh," Essie said quietly.

Miles turned to her. "You're a good Christian girl, what are you doing?"

"You don't think she can resist Josh? Look at him. He looks like a terrorist composite sketch," Corey chided. "No offense, Josh. You're usually very handsome."

Esther took her final bite of food, turning with her plate toward the sink.

"Do I look like a terrorist composite sketch?" He whispered covertly. "You said I could play Jesus!"

She waved at her face, trying to expedite chewing, cheeks tight.

"Should I shave?"

She twisted her face. "I'm sorry, can you repeat the question?"

"Fine, fine, I thought I could pull it off, but the jury has spoken."

"Hey *Josh*, before you shave–?" she asked, swallowing hard. "Can we maybe talk outside privately?"

He set his drink glass down abruptly, nodded, and motioned unnecessarily toward the screen door.

*   *   *

"I can't leave you unprotected out here," Josh said angrily, justifying his return from the tree line, where he'd made a hasty exit just moments prior. He took a seat on the rocking chair next to Essie.

She didn't look up.

He was preventing his chair from making the rocking motion, sitting rigidly upright. "I won't do it, Essie."

She gently stabbed another potato and calmly drew the fork to her mouth, having been unable to resist filling another plate before coming out to the porch.

"I can't even consider doing that."

"I understand. It's a lot to ask."

"'A lot to ask?' I'd sooner give up one of my vital organs."

She frowned.

"Yeah, I know that's not a possibility and makes no sense. Essie, the truth is: I can't stand the thought of a world without you, let alone if *I*–" His voice caught in his throat. "If I'm the one who saw to it."

She moved her plate to the deck to her right and leaned back in her chair. "I'm sorry to put you in this situation."

"*Dammit*, Ess, I thought you wanted to come out here to—"

She raised her eyebrows.

"Why do you want to sleep in the same room? What was *that* about?"

"Are you not comfortable sharing a room with me?"

"Of course I'm comfortable with it."

"The upstairs bedroom has three beds. I presumed that Gabe wouldn't be doing patrol?"

"Yeah, no. I'm not giving him a firearm."

She turned her chin toward him. "*So*, Gabe will occupy one of the beds upstairs. The Three Stooges will probably switch off doing patrol, I'm assuming?"

He nodded, choosing not to correct her purposeful mix-up.

"That leaves the couch and the bedroom. *I'd* stay upstairs, but–"

"*That's* not happening. They're good guys, but–*no*."

"I knew you wouldn't let me take the couch." She shrugged. "You need a good night's sleep, Josh."

He shrugged. "Excellent reasoning skills, as always."

"Plus, I wasn't sure if we'd get a chance to have this conversation otherwise."

His body tensed. "*That's* the reason you wanted to stay in the same room? To ask me to shoot you?"

"Only if we're captured," she reasoned. "You're also delightful to snuggle with."

Her remark had its intended effect. He stumbled a bit over his words. "You expect *snuggling* from me after asking me to shoot you?"

She gave a weak smile. "Probably not."

"That came out like I was teasing, but I'm not. And the answer is no, *absolutely* not."

"I'm sorry, I found the answer vague. No to snuggling or no to shooting me?"

"Not the time to be joking, Essie," he said in an annoyed, sing-song voice.

"I regretted it as soon as I said it, Josh," she said in, mimicking his tone.

He sat angrily, picking at splinters on the cabin wall.

"You have a cyanide pill," she pointed out, eyeing his collar fold.

"I'm *not* giving you one."

She narrowed her eyes. "It wouldn't kill me," she replied flatly. "*That's* the point."

"I knew that," he said, rubbing at his tired eyes before remembering the dirt on his fingers from the side of the cabin.

"I know you know that. You've been up for what? 36 hours?"

He shook his head furiously. "The answer's still no."

"They would find some way to weaponize me, Josh—or my DNA. They'd create bioweapons."

"They have those already."

"They'd breed me—or they'd take my eggs and grow mutant babies in artificial wombs. It'd be like Jango Fett with all the clones except I wouldn't consent to it. Remember that scene in the prequel? It was chilling."

"Points for the *Star Wars* reference, but *still*, no."

"They would torture me."

His skin flinched at her words.

"What I went through with the antidote runs with Luther? It was incredibly painful. The process, the recovery, it was brutal. Every run there was a point that I prayed for death as an escape."

Josh raised his chin and saw the tears welling in her eyes.

"And *that* was with Luther doing everything to keep me as comfortable as possible. What would it be like if the person using me as a lab rat doesn't give a shit about how I feel?" She cleared her throat. "I'm scared, Josh. Literally terrified of what could happen. Everyone would be safer if I wasn't with you guys, if I–*ended* things here."

"Are you talking about suicide?" he asked, his teeth gritted. "Essie, *your dad–*"

"He couldn't be told how it happened."

"*No*. Don't you *even–*"

"Selfishly, I want to see him again. I want to live, obviously, but I at least want to see my dad one more time."

"You will."

She pressed her lips together. "If I die, it's final. If I'm captured, it'll make it so much worse for him, Josh. For everyone. You know that."

He dropped his chin mournfully. "How can I kill you?" he whispered.

"On the farm, you put down horses because you didn't want them to suffer."

"Yeah, but *those* were horses."

"And I'm your goat farm partner," she said softly.

He hunched slightly and released a breath, as though being struck in the stomach.

"I'm sorry, Josh. I'm sorry to put this on you. It's not fair. I would have never done this if I knew–"

He stood, then held out his hand. When she accepted it, he pulled her to her feet and tugged her in for a hug. "Just so you *know*, I'm putting you under house arrest when we get to the Ark," he muttered, kissing her forehead. "I know that sounds like something the other side would do, but it's not up for debate."

"Can I still ride Bree?"

"Yes."

"Hwin?"

He paused, tightening his lips. "Yes."

"Can I go hiking?"

"Yes."

336

"Can I go to church? I really need to go back."

"Absolutely."

"This house arrest doesn't sound too bad."

Inside, the quartet of young men was starting to get raucous.

"They're playing poker," Essie observed, peering over Josh's shoulder into the kitchen window. "We should go inside before Miles exploits Gabe's memory issues." She broke free, moving toward the screen door.

Josh bent down and picked up her empty plate, following her inside.

"Look who's the poker king," Miles professed, showing off the table before him featuring a pile of folded money and random comfort items being used as currency.

"Are you *playing*, Gabe?" Josh asked his brother.

Gabe shrugged. "I guess I don't understand the game like I thought I did."

Essie sighed, gathering the dirty plates at the corner of the table.

"You can try to win it back for him, Proxy," Miles taunted, his eyebrows jumping.

The stack of plates made a loud clatter as she put them in the sink.

"Do you consider yourself a Card Shark, *Proxy*?"

Essie turned on the spot, a nondescript smile creeping across her face.

"Why are you calling her that?" Josh asked, trying to read her facial expression.

"Well, we were talking to Gabe and he's under the impression she's moonlighting as a proxy."

Josh was about to reprimand Miles, but Esther stepped in front of him and patted his chest gently, moving toward the table. "I could go for some poker."

"Do you have *cash*?"

She reached into her pocket and pulled out a money clip. There were at least thirty bills in the stack. She dropped it on the table and took a seat next to Miles.

Miles smirked, raising his eyebrows. "I'm not seeing as many *dollar* bills as I would have expected."

Esther tightened her lips, her voice silky. "That's strippers. And dollar bills? Really?" She clucked her tongue in a disappointed manner. "What kind of Proxy do you think I am?"

There were some light chuckles around the table.

She leaned forward, raising her eyebrows at Gabe. "Short-term memory coming back?"

"I shouldn't have said anything. I'm sorry."

She shook her head. "It's fine."

"So, *wait*, that was a legitimate memory? You being a–" Miles stuttered.

"It was. What are we playing?"

"Texas Hold 'Em."

"That's the one where you're trying to get 21, right?" Esther asked facetiously, lifting her cards.

"Wait *up*—Esther just admitted to *working as a prostitute* and everyone's okay with this?" Miles asked, his tone lacking any sense of jesting.

Corey shrugged. "It's her business."

"Actually, it *wouldn't* be her business because the government runs the proxy services." Miles raised his eyebrows pryingly at Josh. "Did *you* know about this? Surely you have an opinion?"

Josh cleared his throat, his eyes resting briefly on the back of Esther's head and her unruly hair, the detangler conditioner and the only brush available at the cabin doing little to detangle it.

"She saved my life," Gabe said suddenly. "She didn't *act* the part of a Proxy. She barely *looked* the part." He twisted his face, speaking softly toward Esther directly. "I mean that in the best possible way."

Her lips pulled up at the corners.

Corey did a modest raise. "*So,* why a Proxy?"

"Not many ways into the housing complex where Gabe's been living," she said quietly.

"*Wait,*" Corey began. "So, you snuck in there to save Gabe *on your own?* You're not MET. Why didn't MET handle it?"

"The mission to get Gabe was canceled," Josh said, giving his brother a regretful look.

"It *was?* Why?" Gunner asked.

Esther glanced up at Josh.

"Because it was deemed too risky."

She cleared her throat, scanning the counter for a cup. Josh handed her his water glass, which she took appreciatively, taking a long sip.

"And yet, *here you are,*" Gunner said, nudging Gabe on the arm.

Gabe gave a half-smirk. "Yeah."

Miles nodded, pressing his lips together. Unable to contain the words any longer, he finally burst out with: "So you *wore* the Proxy outfit."

She rolled her eyes. "Oh, *Lord.* The outfit is required. I basically looked like *Coraline,* but like, older, after the psychological distress of her childhood caught up with her and she needed to turn tricks to pay the bills."

"Who's Coraline?"

"It's a horror film masquerading as an animated children's movie. Are you going to look at your cards there, Miles?"

Miles lifted his hand and called.

Josh stepped into her peripheral vision. "Is that the one with 'Other Mother?'"

Esther tossed in a bill to cover the call. "Uh-hmm."

"Yeah, that was terrifying. What was the outfit?"

Gunner folded.

The flop revealed an ace of hearts, a ten of spades, and a three of spades.

Corey checked.

Miles tossed a vintage-looking twenty-dollar bill into the center.

Esther raised ten. "Shiny, hooded yellow pleather dress, boots, short blue wig."

Corey called.

Miles called.

"That would be quite a sight seeing you with blue hair," Josh said, shaking his head.

"*That* would be a sight? The *wig*?" Miles mumbled.

Esther smirked, her eyes lifting briefly to Gabe. "It was pretty ridiculous."

The turn presented ten of diamonds.

Corey checked.

Miles tossed in another twenty.

Esther thumbed through her money clip, wrinkling her nose, then took care in finding a twenty to call.

Corey frowned at her, then called.

The river was the ace of clubs.

Corey released a reflexive groan, then checked.

Miles smirked and bet twenty again.

She sighed. "I'll raise you whatever's left here," she said, examining the money clip. "Maybe 200? And I'll throw in the Proxy get-up."

Corey tossed his cards toward the center of the table.

Miles narrowed his eyes at Esther. He glanced up at Josh, who was leaning against the counter, eyes fixed on the center of the table. "Will you *model* my winnings?"

Josh jolted to attention. "Honestly, I didn't think I was your type, Miles."

Esther grinned. "You'd probably look better in it than me."

"I'm going to pretend you didn't say that."

"Yeah, it felt wrong. Please never wear it."

"What do you say, Ess? Do a little fashion show for us?"

There were suppressed mutterings of "Miles, you're such a jerk" and "You're going to get your ass kicked," but Esther didn't flinch. She simply inclined her chin ever so slightly and said: "You know *what*? Win or lose, you can have the outfit, Miles. Maybe someday you'll have someone special in your life who doesn't mind participating in some twisted role-playing, and *she* can model it for you."

There was a sportish roar around the table.

Josh felt his cheeks tighten.

Miles tossed his cards away as though they burned him. They landed face up on the pile of money–the ten of clubs and a seven of hearts.

"Good decision," Esther said, starting to pull her winnings toward her.

"What'd you have?" Corey asked.

Essie shrugged, rising from her seat, her hands busy organizing bills. "I think that'll do it for me. *Miles*, remind me in the morning to get the Proxy costume out of the truck for you. It's rubber-esque so you don't have to worry about ironing it or anything."

"You can't go to sleep *now*," Corey pleaded. "No one else can get Miles to shut up."

"I definitely need good sleep. Sleep and calories keep the mutancy at bay."

Josh rotated his chin abruptly in her direction.

"Mutancy being tired and hangry?" Miles muttered.

"Am I acting hangry? Do I need to eat more?" she asked frantically.

Josh chuckled to himself.

"You ate a whole fish and about five pounds of potatoes," Corey observed.

"*Wow*, Corey. I expected judgment from Miles, but not you." She gave him an almost imperceptible wink.

"So what do you mean, 'mutancy'?"

"Just that I was a part of the government's zombie development program. I'm surprised—*Josh*, I thought you would have told them. Innocent, platonic first kiss story, yes. The government developing zombies—*eh.*"

Corey raised his eyebrows. "The government is developing zombies?"

341

"She's lying, brainless," Miles said with a roll of his eyes.

"Well, they're *not* anymore. The program ran for a few years, but there were too many incidents."

"Incidents?"

"Well, *yeah*. This was years ago when I was a baby."

"When you were a *baby*–"

"Yeah, they tested on babies because they're easier to contain." Her voice was silky and even.

"You're so full of it," Miles muttered.

"*Josh*? Was I or was I not raised in a government genetics lab?"

He wasn't entirely sure he felt comfortable with the direction of the conversation, but there was only one truthful answer. "She *was*, actually."

Miles narrowed his eyes.

"Why do you think I'm so worried about food supply? We can't risk having Ess run out of food. It could trigger an attack," Josh added, smirking.

She rounded the table. "I can't think of that happening again," she said, shaking her head.

"We should probably be honest with them about the risk. Food supplies are pretty low, and you have the appetite of a grizzly bear, as they've seen tonight."

Miles shook his head as he got to his feet. "Such weird people."

Her move was so quick, so unexpected, that Miles released a squeak of fright. With a jolt of her body, Esther had blocked his path, her silver eyes wide and searching. She was doing some shallow breathing and her body seemed to be pulsating as though straining to resist temptation. She tilted her head to the side. When she spoke, her voice was eerily flat. "I think your arm will meet my nutritional needs for now."

He stood there, frozen. He flinched when he noticed her hands grasping his arm.

She smiled.

"Oh, *shit*."

"I'm sorry, that was mean."

Gunner and Gabe were both laughing, sitting back in their chairs. Josh was smiling broadly.

"That *scared* you? It wasn't even good acting," Corey remarked.

"She *wasn't* blinking. And her eyes are that crazy, silver, disco ball color? It was just this pair of dead eyes staring at me."

"Well, that's rude," she muttered.

"And wouldn't they be *undead* eyes?" Josh added.

"You *know*, Miles, if you're scared, you can take my spot in the bedroom. Josh will protect you."

"Josh will be *sleeping*," he corrected.

Esther nodded, twisting her mouth. "*Well*, Corey can't stand you and you've been rude to Gabe so your best bet for protection is probably Gunner."

Gunner grunted.

"Y'all suck."

*   *   *

"So, what'd you have?" Josh whispered as he closed the door to the small bedroom. "Two pair?"

Essie peered over her shoulder, pulling back the bed covers. "Pair of aces."

Josh paused, grinning to himself. "Well played. Remind me to never play poker with you."

There was an insistent whimper at the bottom of the door, a loud sniff.

"Knock it off, Fenway," Josh said in a gruff tone.

"Does she normally sleep with you?"

"She's not whimpering for *me*."

"Did you want to let her in?"

"There's no way the three of us are fitting on that bed. She can be on guard duty tonight."

343

Essie slipped around the bed and dropped to her knees as she cracked open the door. "You're a good girl, Fenway. I'll see you in the morning." She kissed the Shepherd on the head and eased the door closed again.

When she turned around, Josh had slid off his shirt, retrieving a new one from the dresser. She stopped in her tracks, a confused expression spreading across her face.

"What's wrong?"

She shook her head. "Nothing." She quickly busied herself with adjusting bed blankets and retying her hair on top of her head. "So, who named her Fenway?"

"I did. I found her when we did a mission to Boston, just outside the ballpark. Her mom–"

Esther turned her chin toward him, her face braced for what he was about to say.

"Fenway was on her own," he corrected, pressing his lips together, eyes wide. He let his gaze drift back to the door, the shadow of paws at the bottom. "*Fine*, she can sleep on the floor in here."

"Yeah, I'm sure that's what's going to happen."

The Shepherd bounded up on the bed and reared up to kiss Esther, whimpering wildly.

"Let her be, Fenway," he said as the dog nudged repeatedly into Essie's stomach. "I'll call her down here so you can get tucked in."

She nodded, climbing under the covers once Fenway had jumped down, taking care to leave as much room on his side as possible.

"Fenway, *stay*." He had to correct the dog two more times before he made his way to his side of the bed. Once he was also under the covers, he noticed Essie had turned on her side, facing away from him. "Essie?"

"Yeah?"

"Are you okay?"

"I'm fine. Just tired."

"Why are you all the way over there?" he asked, taking in the sight of the empty covers between them. "I thought you wanted to snuggle."

"I want you to get a good night's sleep," she replied, her voice constricted.

His mind reeled their last encounter at the Ark, how she'd glared at him with such disdain, such hurt. He had hoped that their greeting here, the exchanges they'd shared, had all but nullified that encounter. He thought given the circumstances, given all that had happened, that things were okay now. Josh considered pulling her toward him forcibly but thought better of it. He thought of demanding to know where they stood, but that seemed needy and unfair given the state of things. She was probably still shaken up from her time in the city.

He thought of thanking her for saving Gabe, but he found he still couldn't process the risks she took. He couldn't say the words just to say them; she'd see through it; she'd know he was being insincere.

Josh watched her adjust her pillow beneath her neck.

You are the bravest, most selfless person I know, Esther Natale, he said silently.

Her shoulders pulled towards her ears as she took a deep breath. With a great sigh, she turned further away.

25

worthy

Esther could tell by Josh's very first movements as he woke that he was tense. When she stirred from a dreamless sleep just before dawn, she had found herself tucked in beside him, her arm stretched across his chest, his arms wrapped around her. The pure joy that had existed in her unconscious state quickly dissipated. All she could feel was anxiety threatening to suffocate her. She couldn't be in his arms. She couldn't allow herself to feel everything her heart was aching to feel. It wasn't fair to him. It wasn't fair to make this more difficult.

It had taken substantial stealth effort to slip from his hold without disturbing him. She had first taken in the details of his face. The thick, imposing beard made this more difficult, but she gazed at his deeply tanned skin, his full eyelashes, and the thin scar that seemed to "part the seas" of his left eyebrow. When she was younger and early teen hormones were just starting to hit her system, she remembered daydreaming about how handsome he was. She had felt so much. All those emotions, all those feelings felt so alive within her, like they would burst from her mouth, shoot out the ends of her fingertips.

She still remembered how she felt, from when she was young and from more recent times being close to him. She could feel the rush of emotions, as though it were a tangible thing in front of her. But as she gazed into his face, she could feel all of that being pulled inward, compressed into the folds of her heart.

She had been positioned in a cliffhanger position on the opposite side of the bed for a few minutes before he stirred fully from sleep. She had sensed his eyes peering over at her, pulsing into her back. She heard him release a short puff of air and then he abruptly turned and dropped his legs over the side of the bed.

"I know it doesn't mean as much saying it now," he said softly. "But I have never *not* wanted to be by your side. I have never *not* wanted you or needed you."

Essie swallowed hard. It was taking tremendous effort not to release an audible sob, not to allow a tremor in her back. She sat up, wishing she had left her hair down so it could serve as a veil so he wouldn't be able to see the expression on her face. The determination. The lack of tears.

"I just can't think about any of that right now." Her tone was far colder, her words far more dismissive than she intended.

In the corners of her peripheral vision, she watched his chin fall to his chest. It wasn't in anger. This was worse: It was in despair.

*   *   *

The group was already packed and assembled loosely around the kitchen when Esther emerged from the bedroom. There was a palpable uneasiness in the air that hadn't been there the night before. Surely some of it was natural nerves, but there seemed to be something more.

Josh sipped his coffee, leaning against the sink. Corey nervously fiddled with the zipper on his backpack. Gunner's eyes were very round and gazed at Esther with the admiration of a loyal canine. The actual loyal canine wasn't even paying attention to her, having been caught up gnawing at an inch on her hindquarters. Miles was staring at her with the wonder of a child in a sweets shop.

"*Okay*, what's going on?" she asked, petting Fenway, who had satisfied her itch and was now circling her, herding her toward the kitchen.

"*Essie*," Miles began, his tone melancholy, his voice unrecognizable. He stopped short when Gabe came inside, checking around for anything else to load up into the vehicles.

"Hey, Bro," Josh said, picking up a sleeping bag and tossing it toward him.

Gabe smiled brightly at Esther after catching it. "You look very beautiful this morning."

The normalcy of the greeting was like a breath of fresh air. Her cheeks tightened. "*You* look a bit like GI Joe today," she said, taking in the look of him in tan camo pants and an olive-green t-shirt.

"I was going for Steve Rogers, you know, before the Vita rays?"

She chuckled, stepping across the room to hug him, complicated by the presence of the sleeping bag. "You're probably too tall for Stark's Vita rays machine. You're going to have to earn those muscles back the old-fashioned way."

He kissed her on the side of the head and turned to the door to take the sleeping bag out to the truck.

Esther raised her eyebrow at the remaining four men.

"I'm sorry I teased you about the whole proxy thing," Miles said grudgingly.

Esther froze, letting her eyes drift from Miles to Gunner to Corey and back to Miles. She turned on the spot and glared at Josh. "*What* did you say to them?"

Josh released a breath. "They needed to know."

"*What*, Josh? They needed to know *what*?"

Miles took a step toward her. "If it weren't for you, none of us would be alive. Not to mention Amnesia outside."

"*Don't–*"

"I'm sorry. I won't call him that anymore."

Essie glared at Miles and his newfound meekness. "*What* did you say, Josh?"

"That you tested the antidotes as they were developed. You allowed yourself to be exposed to different things to make sure the antidote worked."

She wasn't blinking as she released the air trapped in her chest. "All four of you have *used* the antidote?"

Josh nodded. "We had an eventful trip to Chicago."

She narrowed her eyes, thinking of the fact that he'd just admitted her almost died, that her fears about him never coming back were nearly realized.

"You don't need to know the details."

She locked eyes with Miles, who looked like he'd been crying. Each of the men had similar expressions, but Miles looked the most shaken.

Esther lifted her eyes to Josh, whose face was rigidly blank. "You told them, so they'd feel like they owe me, *didn't you*?"

"We *do* though, right? If not for you, we probably wouldn't have had an antidote. We'd probably all be dead," Corey remarked.

She tensed her jaw. "You don't owe me *anything*." She pressed her lips together, threw her hands in the air, and walked out the front door. "Wow, *this* is what you want to see: Highly-skilled mercenaries reduced to puppy dog eyes."

Stepping into the spotlight of the morning sun, Esther's eyes burned as she approached the truck.

"What happened?" Gabe asked.

"Nothing," Esther muttered, shaking her head. "Did you sleep?"

He shrugged. "The first night was much quieter. I think Miles has sleep apnea."

"His charm continues to multiply."

"Essie?" His eyes flickered as he spoke her name, and his mouth flinched at the corner.

She turned to him with a sigh.

His eyes still looked muted, but there was a bit more energy behind them. "You really *are* an angel."

Not hearing what she expected, she laughed under her breath. "Even my pastor father wouldn't call me an angel, Gabe."

He smiled, undeterred. "You're what kept me alive when I was there—memories of you, dreams of you. I started thinking of you as my own personal angel."

She placed her palm on his cheek, taking in the details of his face. She smiled widely.

"*Hey*, Deadpool," Miles called, jogging down the porch steps. "Want to ride up with me?"

There was a brief delay before Essie curled forward and started to laugh. "Oh, thank you, Miles, for bringing levity to the moment."

Miles shuffled his boots in the gravel, coming to a dramatic pause. "*Wait*, is that sarcasm, or did I do something right for a change?"

She moved forward and threw her arms around Gabe's neck. "I want to hug you so hard right now, but I don't want to break you."

He pulled her closer, breathing in the scent of her hair. "You smell different than the last time we did this."

"I smell like Josh's shampoo. Sorry."

"I am *not* responsible for the bathroom products. They were here when I got here," Josh said, carrying a cooler bag toward the truck cab, eyes directed forward.

Esther released Gabe, smiling at him fondly, then turned to Miles. "I was being totally serious before, and I'll give you a hug to prove it."

Miles startled. "Really? *I* get a hug? I thought maybe those were reserved for those involved in this--" He drew a triangle in the air with his finger, discreetly motioned to Gabe and then Josh.

She narrowed her eyes, shook her head. "I needed the humor in the moment so thank you." She stepped toward him.

"I haven't hugged anyone in a really long time. I'm kind of nervous actually," he declared, gesturing erratically with his hands.

She tilted her chin to the side and raised an eyebrow. "I'll be gentle, Miles."

As she put her arms about his shoulders, he giggled under his breath. "I'm feeling so many things." He wrapped his arms around her back, squeezing gently. "Is it okay that I squeeze?"

She nodded into his shoulder, tightening her hold.

"Oh, it's *so nice.* You have a surprisingly muscular build, I wasn't expecting that, but your skin is so very soft."

"He literally never shuts up," Corey remarked from across the driveway.

Esther stroked his back lightly with her palm, kissed his cheek, and took a step back.

Miles was left standing with his mouth ajar, his eyes dazed. "I *totally* get it now."

"Oh, no," Corey said, resituating a 5-gallon jug of gasoline in the bed of the truck.

"Oh, I'm *not* attracted to her, no offense. You're more of a little sister type that I just want to give a brain duster to," he said, making a kneading motion with his fist into his opposite palm. "But you've got something."

"Excellent. I'll add that to my dating app profile."

He grinned. "I'm surprised Josh only said you were an 8."

Josh slammed the back row door on the truck. "I didn't understand what you were asking me, Miles."

Esther tapped Miles's shoulder. "What's an 8?"

"It's a rating system. On a scale of 1-10, how hot a girl is."

"And I'm an *8*?" she said, her mouth falling open.

"I *know*, right? On a normal, good day, not where we're wearing rose-colored glasses that you saved our lives–"

"4 or 5 at best."

He nodded. "That's a *little* harsh."

"You think?"

He shrugged. "But I was surprised he rated you an 8 at peak level of infatuation."

She pressed her lips together and shook her head.

"*Right*? Because if you're not getting rated a '10' at that point—"

"*I'm never gonna be a '10.'* You know, if I gave a darn about such archaic, objectifying ratings systems, that would be really damaging to my self-esteem, Miles."

"This is why people left technology and social media."

"Am I to understand the two of you are going to be a comedy duo for the duration of the trip?" Josh asked, rolling his eyes.

"Well, *there's* an idea," Miles mused.

"You know, I think we just see what happens. We don't want to push things too fast, force the dynamic."

Miles waggled his pointer finger back and forth between them. "It's like we're of the same mind."

Esther's face was frozen with a smile watching Miles stroll to the driver's side of the Wrangler and climb inside. At that point, her expression fell, and she spun on the spot to look at Gabe. "I feel like I should be worried."

Gabe nodded. "I mean, I don't know him very well, but maybe do some personal reflection."

26

souls

"I don't like this," Miles said, his voice carrying a sense of urgency.

"It's not that far."

"Then it won't hurt anything to lay low and wait for this to pass through the town."

Esther leaned forward, looking through the front windshield. "We need to go."

A group of darkly clad people in costume masks were just turning down the road. The leader, who wore a realistic skull mask, pointed toward the truck with a very loud chainsaw.

"*Oh* yeah, that's nightmare fuel," Miles said with a deceptively comical overtone as he threw the truck into reverse. He spun the steering wheel hard right before shifting back into drive. "It's going straight up horror flick in the real world, boys."

There was a bit of nervous hooting in the cab as the tires peeled away from the madding crowd. Josh whipped his head to the back window in time to see the group stop mid-step and start to turn back. Beside him, Essie started percussive drumming on the back of the bench seat, softly belting out the lyrics for *Danger* Zone. She glanced over at him. "Too soon?"

Miles laughed. "*Girl*, of all the singers you could have possibly chosen, you channeled *Kenny Loggins*?"

"'*Danger Zone*' seemed to fit, although it was admittedly a bit on the nose. I didn't think '*House at Pooh Corner*' was appropriate though."

Josh stared across at her.

"Oh, I don't know. I might enjoy some simple reflections on that silly old bear," Miles said, taking a sip from his water bottle, looking up to the rear view."

"Y'all have a sickness."

"Well, I'm sure agonizing over what just happened is a *much better* coping mechanism."

"Alright, that's fair."

"Glad we consolidated into one vehicle. How's the pooch?"

Fenway sat up, wedged between Essie's knees, looking distraught. Essie rubbed at the Shepherd's lowered ears.

Miles peered over his shoulder and smiled at the dog. "What do you say, Essie?"

"About?"

"Do you know the lyrics for '*Pooh Corner*'?"

"Where are we going, Miles?" Josh interjected.

"We'll try the next town." He glanced over his shoulder, fanning out his hand. "*Proceed.*"

Essie pursed her lips. "Fine." She sat up straighter as she started to sing. The tension in the car eased after the first stanza, particularly once Miles started providing backup vocals. By the time the song ended, they were all smiling.

"My grandparents used to take me to a bridge near their house and play Pooh sticks," Miles reflected after the song had ended, smiling at Esther in the rearview.

"My dad and I did that, too."

"What's poop sticks?" Corey asked.

Miles shook his head. "You find a stick and drop it over the bridge on one side, then you go to the other side to watch the stick come out the other side. It's called Pooh sticks for, you know, Winnie the Pooh."

"What's the point?"

"Man, I feel sorry for you. It's a simple wonder of childhood."

"I just don't get it."

"Don't take this the wrong way," Esther began, "but, Miles, you seem too emotionally stunted to have experienced such an endearing childhood memory."

"Maybe it's because I knew such innocent times that when reality hit, it cut me a lot deeper."

"Wow. That's--" She puffed out her lower lip. "Maybe I've been too hard on you."

"Yeah, I was just messing with you. I'm really just an asshole, Essie."

She twisted her expression, narrowed her eyes upon his reflection in the rear view mirror.

"What about you, Essie? You pack a punch with your dark humor—what's your origin story?" Corey asked.

"Well, I got my most psychologically damaging memories out of the way very early. I actually think it made me appreciate childhood more."

"It's like the Benjamin Button thing."

"Is that a storybook bear also?"

"No, it's this movie about a man who starts off old and becomes younger. Eventually the love of his life is caring for him as a baby."

"So, he dies as a baby?"

"Yeah."

"That's a disturbing thought. Was this a good movie?"

"Actually, it has a sort of creep factor doesn't it?"

"This looks better," Miles remarked as they pulled into a quiet, albeit dilapidated town. The main road was made up of clusters of buildings, most of which were ransacked and graffitied. The town had the appearance of once being considered historic, with its architectural trimmings and ornate town signs and streetlamps. There was a central square, overgrown with wild grass and weeds, littered with trash, where a large stone statue that appeared to be a military or historical figure, had been pulled down. The head was crushed, the body spray painted with several profane accusations.

"I once saw a horror movie that started in a place like this."

Esther gazed out at the storefronts, her eyes scanning the second-floor windows of the weathered brick structures. There was a ghostly presence in the town, like the sights and sounds of the formerly bustling town were still fading away. She breathed slowly, willing the anxiety building in her chest away. "Miles, stop."

He slammed on the brakes.

It took a few short seconds of surveying the scene for Esther to jump out of the cab. She ignored the protests of Gunner and Corey asnd moved toward the sidewalk. Under the wooden awning for what appeared to be a former ice cream parlor lay a young family, their bodies riddled with bullet wounds that had nearly severed body parts—a husband, wife, a son and daughter who both looked to be around ten, and two younger elementary school age girls. They hadn't died long before their arrival, but they were already being swarmed by flies, and Josh shooed away some feral cats who were chewing at the dad's arm.

Esther checked for a pulse on the oldest daughter, then stroked the girl's cheek when she found none. She glanced over at the mother, who was face down, slumped over one half of a rolling suitcase. The contents were strewn over the sidewalk and curb; probably all their worldly possessions that whoever had done this didn't want.

It was then Esther noticed the cloth wrapped around the mother's back, how it protruded around the side. She gently lifted the woman's elbow and gasped.

"Help me turn her over," Esther said softly to no one in particular.

The baby was silent, her doe-like brown eyes glassy, her face a ghostly white. Her body appeared stiff and unmoving. The only sign she was alive was the pursing of her dry lips.

The men turned the mother enough so that removing the baby from the material was less of a struggle, but it was still challenging. Josh helped tug the fabric to the side, so Essie could slide the infant out. She immediately pulled the baby to her chest once she was free.

"I'm so sorry, Little One," she whispered, stroking the baby's back rhythmically. "I'm so sorry."

The child tucked her body tightly against Essie's chest. Essie started to stand, but caught sight of a small photo book next to the suitcase and motioned to Josh. He retrieved the book, inconspicuously wiping off the beet red flesh splatter on the cover. He began flipping through the pages, suspecting she was hoping the baby's name would be provided in one of the captions.

A few moments later, he cleared his throat. "Her name is Vivian," he croaked, rising to his feet. It was just as he stood that he noticed fresh blood on the gravel before him. His eyes followed the trail to where Esther stood facing the sunset.

There was a gentle melody drifting over the scene. For a moment, Josh thought perhaps it was the truck's radio turned at a low volume. Then he recognized the same lyrics Essie had been singing in the truck at a slower, more lulling rate.

One by one, the young men each turned toward Esther, silhouetted by the beams of orange light. She cradled the infant against her, singing quietly into the baby's tufts of dark hair.

There came a light squeak from the bundle, a wheezy gasp, and Esther's shoulders sank. Still, she continued to sing. She finished the song, her voice becoming hoarse by the end.

Miles reached her at the same moment as Josh, scooping the lifeless bundle from her arms, the fabric soaked in crimson blood. She kept her arms extended even after Miles had taken the baby, her face pinched in sorrow. Her shoulders heaved and she released a sob that echoed across the field as she turned toward the horizon and the setting sun.

"WHY??!!" She demanded from the sun, from the billows of orange clouds. "Why are you letting this happen?! Are you not all powerful? Aren't you supposed to be a loving father? WHAT FATHER ALLOWS THIS?! " Her voice cracked, releasing an agonizingly desperate shriek as the air caught in her lungs. "WHY DIDN'T YOU SAVE THEM?"

Josh moved to wrap his arms around her, but she sidestepped his advances.

"*No, I want to know,*" she cried, breaking away. She paced a small section of the field, as though challenging God to a fight, but she said nothing more, dropping her chin to her chest.

Josh could now see the entire front of her shirt, her chest, her arms were coated in the baby's blood. He wouldn't be able to grab her without covering himself and he felt like that would be more traumatizing for her.

The sun suddenly burned brighter, breaking through some cloud cover. Out of the corner of his eye, he could see the sun reflecting off the still surface of a small lake. He strategized the quickest route to it and without another thought, took a quick step toward her and swept her up over his shoulder. He was sure it was quite a sight as she was putting up strong opposition to whatever his plan was. The tall grass around the shore was thick with prickly spurs, which was the only thing that got her to stop flailing. He tugged off the hiking boots she had managed to slip on in the truck, tossing them aside. After clumsily forcing off his own boots, he began to tread into the lake. When the chilly water reached his upper legs, he slowly lowered her off his shoulder, easing them both into the water.

She had gone quiet on the shoreline, no longer struggling, but as he lowered her into the water, she had let her body go limp, her cries silent and somehow more sorrowful. He supported her in the water, keeping her torso submerged. He watched the blood dissolve from her skin, her clothes, into the dark water. Her arms were sunk at her sides so he didn't need to worry too much about washing them, but he noticed a large smear of blood across her cheek. With his left arm looped around her, he scooped some water into his right palm and brushed his fingers gently over her skin. On his third pass, she made eye contact with him, her brow creased severely, her breaths deepening.

He checked her skin one last time to be sure the blood was gone and resecured his right arm around her. There they stayed, kneeling on the rocky lake bottom, staring at one another, dusk falling across the valley.

He felt her shift her knees, unsettling the water around them. She collided clumsily into him, wrapped her arms around his neck, and buried her face into his shoulder. There she settled, giving no indication she planned to leave the lake or his embrace.

27

orion

The amber-colored bottle had just made its second lap around the campfire, arriving in the hands of Esther, who gripped the wide neck, staring into the flames. The orange light danced across her idle face. Miles, who had situated himself next to her on the tree trunk bench, eyed the bottle longingly.

There had been a mild, melancholy inebriation around the campfire throughout dinner. There hadn't been much conversation. They had heated a large can of chili, but most had ended up in a bowl for Fenway, an act they regretted with her first bout of flatulence.

The collective desire seemed to be to drink enough to fall into an alcohol-induced sleep, waking several hours away from the events of the early evening. Gabe and Corey had already fallen asleep, gentle snoring drifting out from the tent.

Esther lifted the bottle to her lips and drained most of the remaining liquid down her throat, wincing as she did. "I'm going to bed."

"Good night, Essie," Josh said softly.

She offered the bottle to Miles, who was visibly disappointed by its light weight. She rose to her feet, tousling his mop of sandy-colored hair before crossing to the cab of the pickup truck.

"I guess the two of you aren't *spooning* tonight," Miles remarked once the cab door had closed, swallowing the last of the bourbon. He gave Josh a salute with the bottle.

Josh lowered his chin regretfully. "I'm on night watch, Miles," he grumbled. "And even if I *weren't*—" The image of Essie holding the baby as she took her final breaths, Essie's screams of anger, of desperation repeated constantly in his head. The entire time he'd known her, she had been so enduring, so unbreakable. There had always been a glimmer of her tenacity, her determination, even on bad days. Wading into the lake, he'd gazed into her eyes and found none of her wild spirit, not even a trace of the rage she had shown earlier. The silver irises still shone as brightly as ever, but he found only exhaustion and hopelessness.

"Tragedy is part of the world we're living in. And all the more reason to spoon the ones we love," Miles remarked, lifting his eyebrows.

"You're becoming quite the philosopher."

"What's the deal here? You're angry with her?" Miles asked, narrowing his eyes.

Josh shook his head. "Of course not."

"Well, you'd be a prick if you were angry with her after what she just went through. I meant *before* that though. At the cabin. You were angry, I could tell." The decibel of Miles's voice was rising.

"It wasn't anger."

"*Well*, whatever it was, it strongly resembled anger. You know what it was like? It was like the spoiled brat kid who doesn't get what he wants even though he called 'dibs' so he has a temper tantrum. You never told me you two 'coupled up.' What the hell?"

"I don't know what I was thinking not sharing that with you."

"What happened?"

"I went back to Mandatory."

"And then? You got to the Ark like a year ago? What's been happening since then?"

"It's complicated, Miles. She's going through a lot."

The sounds of the flickering flames and the owls hooting in the chilly forest air filled the void between them.

"Do you think *I've* got a shot with her?" Miles asked, swallowing a burp.

"No."

"Probably right. I'm too self-centered to treat her the way she deserves."

"You've really taken to her."

"I know, *weird* right? She's not even my type."

Josh rolled his eyes. "What's your type?"

"I don't know, but I didn't think it was her." He scrunched his nose. "I think we're better as friends. We're on a good path. I feel a connection."

"Well, you did sing karaoke together."

"Those *are* the ties that bind." Miles twisted his expression, released a sigh. "Essie's a good girl. I shouldn't have given her shit for the proxy thing."

"She's going through a lot right now, but I doubt she took it to heart."

"She's not that sensitive?"

Josh shook his head. "She understands people." The words glided out confidently, but he found himself repeating them silently, wondering if he could elaborate further than that, if his current knowledge of her stretched far enough.

Miles's voice broke through his thoughts suddenly: "I was thinking when we get back, maybe—*maybe* it'd be nice to go out with a good girl for a change."

Josh lifted his eyes from the dancing flames to the truck cab and back to Miles. "Listen, this is probably a *terrible* idea, but could you be on watch for like the next five minutes?"

"Five minutes?" Miles raised an eyebrow toward the truck, then shook his head. "Your girlfriend drank all the booze though. She's probably passed out."

"Do me a favor? Don't call her that. There's enough shit going on, she doesn't need to worry about being in some ridiculous love triangle situation, *which it isn't.*" His spine cracked twice as he stood. "Oh, and she doesn't feel the effects of alcohol. Her body metabolizes it too fast," Josh said, parroting Luther.

"*What*? Is that from the antidote stuff?"

Josh shrugged.

"Wait, so she *can't* get drunk?"

"Nope," Josh said, handing off the rifle.

His shoulders hunched forward. "Well now I know how Jack Sparrow felt when that British chick burned up all his rum."

Josh arrived at the truck quicker than he anticipated. He peered into the side window, pushing up through his toes. Inside was the glow of a flashlight. Deciding opening the door might startle her, particularly with the rattly squeak of the hinges, he took a step back, lightly gave a tap-tap-ta-tap-tap, then waited.

The truck teetered as she changed positions. He saw her hand first, completing the pattern with a tap-tap on the glass. She pulled the door lock, and then the door squeaked open.

She had her legs folded beneath her, gazing down at him with very tired, very swollen eyes. She said nothing, asked nothing about what he was doing. She sat resolutely, waiting to see what he would do next.

"Permission to come aboard?"

She nodded, sliding backward across the bench seat.

He reached for the hand hold and pulled himself up on the sidestep. He tugged the door closed and nudged closer to her.

Silence filled the cab of the truck. His heart was beating so wildly in his chest that he was certain in the quiet she must be able to hear it. He took as full and steadying of a breath as he could manage. "I love you."

Her eyes did their best to widen, despite their swollen lids.

"I'm not saying that as some big romantic proclamation. It's not the time for that and we've never really had the chance to figure that stuff out, have we?"

She gave a small shake of her head.

"The 'I love you' wasn't some *claim* on you, nor does it quite sum up what I feel for you. I'm sorry I haven't been there for you the way you've needed. I didn't—I didn't know *how* to be what you needed. I don't even know if I can ever be what you truly need, but I love you and I'm here for you. I wish I had the words to express what you meant to me. It's just when I *try* to put it into words, and I *have* hundreds of times, I end up with the same phrase, over and over again: I love you, I love you, I love you."

Essie smiled lightly, tears welling in her eyes.

He furrowed his brow. "Whatever you need me to be in your life, I'm in. No matter what."

She leaned forward suddenly and swept her arms around his neck.

*   *   *

All of the young men noticed the change in Esther the next morning. She moved about the camp singing softly under her breath, occasionally raising her voice as she passed by one of them in a faux serenade.

Her mood was contagious.

Everyone took longer inhalations of morning air and moved with greater motivation.

Miles paused next to Josh as he secured the storage bin in the bed of the truck. "That is an *intoxicating* girl."

"You're still mad?"

Essie drummed her fingers along Miles's back as she walked by, his body subconsciously arching toward her.

He stopped himself short. "There's lots of single ladies at the Ark, right, Ess?"

She grinned.

Miles cleared his throat loudly, redirecting his feet back to the supplies they had left to load.

With the hidden stores of fuel at the campsite, they had plenty of gas to make it to the Ark, but the group collectively decided to stop off at a diner to pick up some breakfast for the road.

"We should just eat here," Gunner suggested as they piled around one of the front booths waiting for their order.

"We *have* diners, Gunner. We need to keep moving," Miles said impatiently. "This is stupid."

While everyone else had started to let their guard down, just a mere three hours to go until they were securely inside the boundaries of the Ark, Miles had stiffened suddenly. He sat on the edge of the booth seat, swiveling his neck almost constantly to check for threats.

Corey smacked Gabe's arm absentmindedly. "Do you have any coins?" He had been mesmerized by the miniature jukebox mounted to the wall at the end of the table.

"This is like really vintage technology, Dude," Miles scoffed. "Do you even know any of the songs?"

"Yeah, as a matter of fact."

"'*Why do you build me up Buttercup–*'" Esther began to sing softly, smiling at Gunner, squeezing Miles's arm.

The corner of Miles's lips pulled up despite his tense mood. "Who *is* this on the facial overlay? She's cute."

"She's CGI."

"Is she based on someone though?"

"I wondered that myself," Gabe remarked. "Who's Emily? She had a government ID number."

Esther swallowed hard, furrowing her brow.

"We should just go. There's no reason we need to eat now. This is stupid," Miles muttered, tapping his foot.

"The food should be out any minute," Corey offered.

"I'm going to go check the perimeter," Miles muttered, rising to his feet. The bell hanging on the door jingled as he made his way outside.

"I'm going to use the restroom before we head out," Esther said quietly, sliding out of the booth.

"Our restroom is out of order," the waitress said as she arrived with two bags of carryout boxes. "We're sharing with the mechanic next door. Just tell them I sent you over."

Esther checked her name tag. "Thanks, Brynn."

"I can come with you," Josh offered.

"I think we can keep some mystery between us," she retorted with a smirk. "Miles is out there anyway."

"I think there's one or two more bags to go, but they should be out any second," Brynn said.

Josh peered over his shoulder as Esther walked out of the restaurant. Through the front window, he saw her tighten her arms over her chest. The prior day had felt unseasonably warm for December, but the morning seemed to be doing all it could to propel them toward Christmas. "I'm going to go give her my jacket," he announced.

"What a prince," Corey remarked.

"Let her use the weird public bathroom in peace, Josh."

"Here you go," Brynn said, appearing from the kitchen with the remaining bags a few seconds later.

While Corey, Gunner, and Gabe lumbered behind with the to-go bags, Josh jogged across the parking lot, intending to preheat the truck.

There was a stillness in the parking lot that caused Josh to pause just as he reached the truck bed. He turned slowly. The mechanic was busy under the hood of a newer sedan. The gas station was abandoned with signs indicating they had run out of fuel.

Then he saw it: the door on the side of the mechanic's shop with the restroom symbol was swung open.

A tight scream came from the back of the building, followed by a crash of bottles, and Josh took off running in that direction. Miles made it to the alleyway between the buildings just after Josh did. They reached the barbed wire fence on the other side in time to see a hooded man inject a cloudy substance into Esther's neck. She twisted and writhed, reared backward, and seemed to be making the challenge of dragging her into the back seat of the black sedan intensely difficult.

Everything seemed to trudge in slow motion. Miles beat manically at the fencing then disappeared to find a way around it. Meanwhile, Esther's wild eyes locked on Josh. She lurched her right shoulder forward, her stare widening, and he knew what she was telling him to do. He unholstered his gun and took aim.

28

blessing

The shaking of tree branches against the window startled Esther awake. Her body tried to coax her back to sleep, but the glow of a full moon in her eyes refused to grant her such an escape. Immediately she was filled with fear and anxiety, emotions she was familiar with. She couldn't remember a single thing about the dream she had awoken from, but she felt the contrast of it now. It was like being bundled cozily in a blanket and then suddenly being dumped into an empty, frigid night.

There was not one detail left from her dream, not one thought, feeling, or place she could climb into and curl up in for solace. She sensed, even in the disorienting stillness of the night, that the dream was as unreachable to her as the outside world was now.

Once she determined the burly man who she assumed had carried her inside was still in the room, she had squeezed her eyelids tighter, deciding she would pretend to sleep until he had to leave the room to use the bathroom or something. She was several minutes into this arrangement, trying to pick out subtleties in smells, fabrics, and air humidity, seeing if this gave her any hint at where she was being held.

He exhaled deeply. "I have instructions to stay with you until you wake and have something to eat. The sooner you stop pretending to sleep, the sooner you can get rid of me."

She turned over slowly, finding her limbs were stiff, but working; bursting out of her supine position to try to escape was probably not the most realistic plan. She opened her eyes.

His appearance matched his deep, resonating voice. He sat casually in a wingback chair, wearing dark wash jeans and a simple charcoal Henley shirt, his long leg crossed perpendicularly. He filled the large chair with his broad physique; an inch or two of extra width would probably have made it more comfortable.

The soft light from the table lamp revealed the dark espresso skin of his face and illuminated his almond-shaped brown eyes. He pressed his lips together and raised an eyebrow.

Esther sat up slowly, assessing the state of her body as she stretched the muscles. Her pants were ripped at the knee, from the struggle, from getting stuck on the fence or scraping along the ground. The skin beneath was bandaged neatly.

"You put up a good fight, kiddo," he said, his lip curling up at one side. "Even after getting hit with a tranq. I was impressed."

She narrowed her eyes.

"I'm sorry about that, by the way."

Her eyes drifted toward the window, hearing a howling just outside.

"Wolves. They've become unruly since there isn't much livestock around anymore."

Exterior spotlights were activated, revealing a perimeter surrounded by forest. A layer of dried pine needles covered the wispy grass outside. The air felt chilly but dry.

"We're about an hour west of Spokane."

Esther slid her attention toward him.

"I'm Demetri," he offered, uncrossing his legs and sitting forward in his seat. He smiled in an indiscernible way.

She let her eyes drift around the room a bit. From one scan, she had identified several decorative pieces she could use as weapons. There was an antique letter opener on the desk in the corner closest to her that seemed to be the best option.

The room was not very large. Based on the vaulted ceiling and wood plank walls, it seemed they were inside an A-frame house. Based on what she'd gathered about the man sitting across from her, he didn't decorate it, with its simplified florals and baroque furniture. Her eyes fell on an ornate handheld mirror on the dresser beside him, also an excellent weapon if she could manage the distance to reach it, as it would be easy to grasp and probably weighed more than a brick.

"You're safe here. I won't hurt you. You don't need to be sizing up weapons."

She turned her attention back to him abruptly.

"*Although* now that I know your skill level, maybe I should have tucked away a few things." He appeared to be debating removing the items but seemed to think better of it, exhaling deeply. "I'm under guidance to keep you here, but that's for your safety. Between wolves, bears, and military convoys—"

"Guidance from whom?" she asked, her voice strained and raspy.

"She speaks," Demetri replied, smiling kindly. "Don't worry, no one I'm associated with wants any harm to come to you."

"That wasn't my question."

He furrowed his brow. "No, but it's as much of an answer as I'm able to give."

"So, I can leave?"

"If you choose to leave, I will help you get safely to the Ark."

She gave him a confused expression, knowing she was probably meant to deny its existence more convincingly.

He flickered a smile. "You weren't trained in interrogation situations."

"Is that what this is?"

"No," he said softly.

"You're from the Ark?" she reasoned, narrowing her eyes.

"Yes."

"Why weren't we notified--"

"Through Luther?"

Her eyes instinctively assessed her exit point through the window. She could visualize herself tucking her head and crashing through it.

"Not a good idea. It's bulletproof glass."

Her jaw tightened as she set her eyes upon him again.

"Decisions had to be made quickly when you popped up on radar."

"What radar?"

He took a breath before saying: "I don't think my answer will set you at ease."

"Probably not."

"When you went to the clinic, you received an injection."

She refocused almost instantly on making her face neutral, but she knew he'd seen the flash of panic in her eyes.

He continued, his lower eyelid twitching. "It contained a microchip."

There was a jolt in her chest. "It's deactivated now?"

"Yes," he said with a reassuring tightening of his lips.

She tried to keep her breathing steady, methodically scanning the room, but her lungs continued to constrict, and her anxiety was only growing now that she knew he was lying to her. She focused her eyes down at the blanket, continuously forcing slow breaths. "Have we met before, Demetri?"

He gazed at her, shaking his head. "Not exactly."

"Did you go to Calvary?" The question came out in a tight gasp as she was having trouble taking in breaths.

It was clear he did not know to what she was referring.

"Did I meet you at the Ark?"

"No."

"Glory Hospital?"

He blinked slowly, then nodded.

She swallowed. "You said you don't plan to hurt me?"

371

"*No.* I said I *won't* hurt you."

Her jaw clenched. "That's why your voice sounds familiar."

Her remark had a profound impact on his composure. He dropped his gaze. "There isn't an excuse good enough for what I did to you."

"I didn't ask for an excuse," she said quietly.

"It was the only job I could get, and I needed to provide for my family. My daughter--" his voice caught in his throat. "My daughter had special needs and my wife needed to stay with her. At that time there just wasn't any decent paying work."

"So they paid you well?"

He furrowed his brow. "In the end, it didn't make a difference for my family."

There was something to the slant of his shoulders, the furrow in his brow that compelled her to trust what he had promised. "You said your daughter *had* special needs?"

He nodded. "Cerebral palsy. She got an upper respiratory infection and had to be hospitalized. The clinical 'board' decided that she would never live a normal life. She didn't meet their threshold on their tests for a positive prognosis, so they refused to treat her."

The pain he was experiencing was palpable.

"She really just needed an antibiotic. We tried to take her from the hospital, and they refused to let us. They brought in police--or whatever they're calling them. The news called us *diabolical* for trying to force her to live when she was so 'incompatible with life'." He shook his head, his eyes brimming with tears. "They 'released' her while we were locked out of the hospital. They stopped her heart and praised themselves for their compassion."

Demetri raised his eyes. The dim table lamp by the door provided just enough light to see the shimmer of tears on his cheeks.

"What was her name?" Esther asked, her voice tight.

He wiped at his eyes roughly. "Salana."

Sun, she translated silently. She took a breath. Her brain struggled to process who the man was before her, what he had witnessed, what he had done. Under different circumstances, she should have been angry, and terrified, but she found herself feeling compassion for him. "I'm sorry, Demetri."

He shook his head. "You had no part in what happened to her."

"I'm still sorry. That's an unimaginable thing to go through. No one deserves that."

He raised his eyebrows, staring at his hands. It appeared that it caused him physical pain to try to make eye contact with her. "I still hear your cries at night."

She narrowed her eyes, struck by his remark. Something was validating about being in the presence of someone who was there, who understood what had happened to her as a young child, even if he played a role in it. They had both suffered, but she sensed his pain far exceeded her own. *I hear them, too, sometimes*, she said silently. *The other babies, too.* She desperately wanted to change the subject. "How is your wife doing? After what happened?"

He released a hard exhale. "When we got word of what they were doing, she tried to break past the guards, and they shot her."

Esther was silent, unsuccessfully holding back tears as she imagined his wife's desperation, the horror of the situation.

After a few moments, Demetri leaned forward, resting his elbows on his knees. "I should never have done the things they asked of me. Words cannot express how truly sorry I am."

She gave a small nod. "Me, too."

"I'm grateful to have gotten to see you now," he said with a slight smile, looking up at her finally. "After what happened--I always prayed you'd be able to still have a childhood."

She thought of her dad's bedtime routines, singing in the choir at church, swinging on the wooden swing at the farm, giggling during wrestling games with Josh, listening to Gabe read to her, and nuzzling into him at night. "I had a wonderful childhood."

He released a breath, pressing his lips together.

"Are the people I was traveling with safe?"

"Oh. *Yes*. I was supposed to tell you that, I'm sorry. They're staying at a safe house until I bring you to them."

She shook her head. "They should have gone on."

He gazed at her with a nostalgic fondness. "You must be hungry."

"I was about to have a diner breakfast prior to my kidnapping," she remarked in a sporting tone that even surprised her.

His eyes widened, uncertain.

"*Yes*, I'm hungry," she said quietly, retreating from her nervous humor. "Thank you."

He nodded. "I'll see what I can find."

Esther dropped her feet to the rug, glancing around for her shoes.

"I took them off when I bandaged your leg," he said, standing reflexively to retrieve the boots from under the bed.

She slid her feet into the boots but didn't tie the laces, peering up into his soft brown eyes. She stood, taking his arm to steady herself. He was a half-foot taller than she would have guessed. She pinched one-half of her face upon meeting his confused expression. "You know, I don't think any of my chosen weapons would have done me any good."

Before he could respond, she had started moving unsteadily toward the door.

A short time later, she sat at the breakfast bar in the kitchen finishing her third full glass of water with an appreciative sigh. The cabin had a high-end rustic feel to it, with touches of nature displayed in contemporary, stylish ways. The appliances were the only form of technology in sight. Esther slid her fingers over the wood pattern of the counter, a live oak, highly polished piece.

Demetri slid a plate before her and took her glass to refill it. When he returned, she was staring at the food. He dropped his chin to get a better look at her face. "I thought you said you were hungry?"

She nodded slowly. "I am. It's just so *colorful*."

"There was a lot to work with," he conceded. "It's a lot of berries and fruit so I basically just sliced them."

"What's *this*?"

"The only meat that was defrosted was lox."

"Lox?"

"Smoked salmon. I made a sort of open-faced breakfast sandwich. You've got whole-grain, bakery bread toast, over easy egg, salmon, and avocado slices."

She pressed her lips together, thoughtfully. "*We--*" She began, motioning to the sandwich. "--are going to need a few minutes alone."

Demetri smiled, turning to clean up. He heard a loud crunch as she took her first aggressive bite. The crunch was followed by an appreciative groan. "Is it okay?"

"It's like my taste buds have started a conga line."

He chuckled, wiping his hands on a towel. "I'll take that as a yes."

The low hum of the garage door suctioned all noise out of the room. He turned on his heel to find Esther stalled in mid-chew, her eyes wide and against her best efforts, terrified.

He gave her an encouraging nod, waving for her to continue eating, but she abandoned her plate immediately, sitting taller on her bar stool, forcing the food down her throat.

Through the solid door, they could hear the ignition turn off, the garage door close, the driver's door open, and shortly after, close. There were five beeps of the lock key code and slight stickiness of the weather stripping at the base of the door before their host was in view.

Esther felt her breaths thicken as she sat stiffly watching Speaker of the House, Annette Gibbons, step inside. "I'm sorry it took me so long to get here. There was an issue at the airport." She shook off her coat as she said this. She stopped mid-step upon seeing Esther, her mouth pulling into an indecisive smile. She moved to speak but was distracted when Demetri stepped into view.

"What issue?"

Annette stuttered a bit. "*Oh*. Protestors burned it down."

"*Well*," Demetri replied, raising an eyebrow at Esther. "That *is* an issue."

"We were diverted to a private airstrip previously used by farmers for crop dusting I think it's called? I'm not sure what that is exactly. Something with fertilizer or pesticides?" She waved her hands in the air, signaling her intention to change the subject. "Oh *good*, I was hoping you'd eat while you were waiting."

"Just started," Demetri said.

"*Oh*. That looks tasty. Don't let me keep you from it. Eat. Eat."

Esther's eyes shifted to Demetri, who stared incredulously at Annette. The Speaker caught the exchange and reset herself. "I've been so eager to meet you," she said, her face expectant. "It's Evin, isn't it?"

Esther frowned. "Evin is my middle name."

"*Oh*. What do you prefer to be called?"

"My name is Esther."

Demetri's eyes widened.

Annette tilted her head inquisitively. "That's quite old-fashioned, isn't it? Is it a family name?"

"It's from the Bible," Demetri interjected.

"*Oh*. Is there a story for Esther in the Bible?"

"She has an entire book in the Bible," Demetri replied. A disbelieving smile emerged on his face. He cleared his throat and spoke slowly when he continued. "Esther was a beautiful young queen who risked her life to save her people from genocide."

Annette turned to him, questioningly, but he was still gazing at Esther.

"Friends call me Essie." She winced. "I'm not sure that applies *here* though."

"No one here is going to hurt you," Demetri stated solidly, raising his eyebrows. "I promise you."

Esther nodded stiffly.

"*Esther*—" Annette began, having trouble committing to the name. "I'm sorry, I've just always known you as Evin."

The logical conclusion was that Luther had told Annette about her but referred to her only by the name he had given her. The question percolating in Esther's mind was how much he had shared that information, and why. "How long have you known about me?"

"Luther and I started working together six years ago."

"He told you about me six years ago?"

"*Well*, he enlightened me to some situations I was unaware of, one being the research lab." Her face became darker. "He shared videos from when you were a child. Not just the ones that made their way around social media some time ago."

"He did."

"Yes," Annette replied.

Esther studied Annette's face, which had turned tense.

"Have *you* watched them?" Annette asked, a bit too enthusiastically. The question seemed to be motivated by nervous pressure to fill the silence.

Demetri grimaced, while Esther subconsciously assessed her exit points. "I read you were sexually assaulted as a college freshman," she replied calmly, her eyes panning back from the garage door, having decided she could make a break for it to the car. Even if there were guards, at least she'd have a motorized vehicle. She'd just need to grab Annette's purse, which likely contained the key fob, and ditch the car in the forest before they could track her.

"Well, *yes*," Annette stuttered.

"Do you still remember details about it? How it felt, sounded, smelled, tasted?"

Annette froze. "Yes."

"Do you still think of it, have nightmares about it?"

"Occasionally, yes."

"If someone told you they had footage of it, would you feel the need to watch it?"

Annette's mouth fell open. "*Oh*. I see your point. I'm sorry. I just thought with you being so young—I hoped—thought—you wouldn't remember."

"I described the lab for Luther. Apparently, my memory is pretty accurate. *The dungeon-like rooms, the copper-colored windows that always made it look dark outside, the gym mats covering the room where babies choked on their own vomit, went into cardiac arrest, or stared brain-dead at the ceiling? Yeah, my memory's rather vivid, Annie.* Esther took a few deep breaths, trying to dislodge her clenched jaw. She decided against sharing that she'd stumbled upon the hospital where the lab was located that same week, that the experience had brought back a tidal wave of memories she'd forgotten existed in her brain.

"She remembered *me*," Demetri added.

"*Oh*," Annette said airily. It was clear the moment the connection registered. "Oh, I didn't--I'm sorry--that must have been alarming for you."

"Between the tranquilizer, the sleeper hold, was it?" she asked Demetri, who gave a half nod. "That was a new sensation for me—being kidnapped, recognizing my captor, and you showing up, *yeah*, you could say I'm pretty on edge today." She took a breath, shrugging. "I guess it could be worse. I had one of my traveling companions promise to shoot me if I was captured so I *could* be nursing a bullet wound—*or dead*."

Annette's eyes were wide, her nostrils flaring in the way Esther had seen on television. "Doe in the headlights" was how Josh's dad had described the expression on several occasions, though Essie disliked the mental image of that. She'd figured out, from a limited viewing of Annette's speeches, that her eyes stopped blinking and widened when she was attempting to be tactful, afraid of letting something slip. "Why would you want them to shoot you?" she asked slowly.

She turned over her arm, and ran her finger the length of the cross, stopping over her dad's leather-bound Bible. "I was raised loving Jesus. I don't have anything to fear in death, but I have a lot to fear if I'm thrown back in a lab, Speaker Gibbons."

Annette frowned. "You don't need to call me that–" She waved her hand before her face, trying to shift the conversation. "*Well*, I'm thankful he didn't do what you asked."

"It was a lot to ask," Esther murmured, closing her eyes as she pictured the expression on his face when she'd made the request, the torment behind his eyes. "Does he know I'm safe?"

Demetri nodded slowly. "Luther was in contact. Yes."

As Esther opened her eyes, she found Annette staring blankly at the countertop.

"Luther knows where I am?"

Demetri briefly touched her hand. "He does." He lifted his eyebrows reassuringly and took her plate, placing it in the refrigerator. "You'll get it back," he said quietly, seeing her concern for the sandwich.

It occurred to Esther that she had failed to make the connection between Luther and Demetri. Now that she had something other than limited amounts of soy in her body, her mind felt a bit sharper.

They had both worked at the lab, but what was the overlap? Based on Demetri's story about his daughter, it sounded like he worked at the lab long before Luther. It had also sounded like he worked there after. As she wandered through the lab, the details all aligned with her memories, from the unforgiving spotlight lamps over the cold metal tables to the submarine-style door, the functional purpose being to provide the ability to pressurize the testing room and seal it off so none of the toxicity escaped. What perplexed her was Luther's explanation that her removal from the facility was not detected because of a fire that destroyed the lab when there were no signs a fire had taken place.

"Would you like to sit in the living room, Esther?" Annette invited, carefully taking a seat on the brown leather sofa.

"Did you help Luther?" Esther asked Demetri quietly over the counter. "Saving the children?"

He nodded, almost imperceptibly.

Esther thought of what a risk this had been for him, for his family. How he had suffered so severely even after helping to save so many lives.

She eased herself off the bar stool, reluctant to take a more relaxed seating arrangement, hesitant to add any distance between herself and Demetri, who was tidying things in the kitchen. She assessed the options and selected one of the plaid high-back chairs.

Annette tilted her head. "Those chairs used to be in my father's office. I loved to play on them when I was young." She motioned to the small table between the chairs, which contained a small round picture frame. Not wanting to divert her attention too much, Esther strained to see out of her peripheral vision, which didn't afford a very clear look at the people in the photo, but she assumed it was a portrait of Annette with her father.

"I sat here because I thought they looked how I feel," she blurted out.

"*Oh*? How's that?"

"Out of place."

Annette pressed her lips together, gazing at her with captive interest. "I guess they don't entirely go with the whole aesthetic?"

Esther did a quick assessment of the other furniture and decor, then shrugged.

"I guess I'm just sentimental about them. I was very close to my dad when I was young. It devastated me when he died. I've thought about having the chairs reupholstered, but—"

Esther shook her head. "I like them as they are."

Annette smiled nervously, tilting her body forward. "I suppose you're wondering why you're here." She took a deep breath, building up to speak multiple times, then furrowed her brow. "Please know that it was never my intent to have babies and children tortured." She met the piercing intensity of Esther's silver eyes. "But that was terribly naive of me."

Esther said nothing but was slightly persuaded by the glistening in the Speaker's eyes.

"Luther had shared with me what you--*endured*--" She swallowed hard. "But he told me you didn't survive."

Based upon Annette's tone, there seemed to be something she was supposed to infer from this.

"I guess I don't blame him for not trusting me. For letting me believe what everyone else involved in the study believed–"

"Which was what?" Esther prodded.

Demetri's eyes darted to Annette, then back to Esther.

"*Oh*. That you were expelled from the program."

"Why was I expelled?"

"*Because–*"

"Because they were racists," Demetri said bluntly.

Esther frowned. "Luther said there was a fire. He said the fire was the reason they thought I was dead. I thought he meant—and I think he meant me to think that the lab burned down, which didn't make *sense*– and doesn't really make it better, but--" She met Demetri's gaze, then panned over to Annette. "*Oh*, when you said 'expelled,' you *mean*—" she said quietly, taking a deep breath. "*Well*, that's what I get for wandering down that rabbit hole."

Demetri passed behind Esther and sat in the other high-back plaid chair.

Intimidated perhaps by his presence, Annette resituated herself on the couch. "Is it okay if I continue?"

Esther gave a short nod.

"After spending a few years in Congress, I was encouraged to set an example as a strong, single working mother. It was all political theater. Or it was supposed to be. The thought was that it would make me more likable or relatable, which would give me better favorability to reach higher office. It would also help me push different legislative agendas."

Esther narrowed her eyes.

"Not a great reason to have a child." She cleared her throat. "I didn't count on becoming so attached to the baby growing inside me." She subconsciously touched her fingers to her stomach, seemingly lost in a memory. "Things were getting out of hand. I had a political strategist coaching me on every part of my pregnancy and was plotting out what I would do once the baby arrived. It was all too much. I decided *then* I was going to leave politics, do something less demanding, and raise my child. *That* was my plan.

"I went into labor in the halls of Congress, which had been the plan all along. It was all very dramatic. I had unexpected cardiac issues during labor though and lost consciousness. When I woke up in the hospital, they told me that my baby had died, that the umbilical cord was wrapped around the neck and my baby had likely died days earlier." She leaned forward, reaching for a tissue from the box on the coffee table.

"That's heartbreaking," Esther said quietly. "I'm sorry."

"I loved her already, before she had even been born." She paused to wipe her nose, and, in that moment, Esther felt the weight of Demetri's eyes upon her. "I didn't expect that. I'd always advocated for a woman's right to have an abortion without restriction, believing that the baby wasn't a baby until the moment of birth, prioritizing the rights and conveniences of the mother over the life of the baby. But I felt like I knew her. She had such a fiery personality already. I couldn't even wrap my mind around what I had believed before, what I had advocated for." She was becoming quite animated with her hands.

Esther stared at the sleeve of Annette's shirt, mesmerized by the vibrancy of the pattern, saying nothing.

"Just like that, she was gone. I didn't even get to hold her." She exhaled, sweeping the hair from her eyes, finally looking up.

Esther remained silent, focusing on converting oxygen into carbon dioxide, though she was finding even this task difficult.

Annette cleared her throat. "As a part of the strategy to push different pieces of legislation through Congress, when I was to become pregnant, I was enrolled in a program called 'BEST Start,' which focused on prenatal health care--injections of different 'vitamins and nutrients' to support development. They performed weekly prenatal tests 'to make sure the baby was healthy.'" She paused to shake her head. "There was more to it. Several years after my daughter was born, I learned that BEST was connected with a government-funded research program called STRONG."

Esther blinked, her eyes shifting momentarily to Demetri and back.

"I learned that my baby hadn't died in the womb. I had trusted someone I shouldn't have with my plan to leave the District, to leave politics. You see, all their tests had shown that my *daughter* was the most successful child in their program. They weren't going to just give her up. *So*, they manufactured a cardiac episode for me and took her. I guess I should consider myself lucky that they let me live, but they used my loss to their advantage to push for legalization of artificial wombs, funding for 'infant loss prevention' research, etcetera."

Esther appeared to be staring in Annette's general direction, but her eyes no longer focused on anything in the room. Her long, deep breaths pulsated, and her hands were visibly trembling. She stood quickly, moving into the kitchen, appearing lost. She looked around aimlessly, then retrieved her sandwich from the refrigerator, along with a can of Hawaiian passion fruit juice. Upon returning to the living room area, she hesitated to return to the same chair. Her eyes darted around the room before she moved to the opposite side of the coffee table, where she crossed her legs and sat on the floor in one fluid motion.

Annette glanced up at Demetri but found his eyes fixated on Esther, his expression sympathetic.

Esther took two large bites right on top of the other, chewing forcefully, and set the sandwich back on the plate, moving on to pop the tab on the juice drink. She slurped loudly and swallowed hard, her eyes glued to only what was immediately before her. Her face looked determined, but her silver eyes were filled with tears.

She picked up the sandwich again, taking a deep breath, her lip now quivering, her hands shaking. She dropped it back to the plate, giving in to the wave of emotion flowing over her. She squeezed her eyes shut and folded over herself.

The room was quiet besides her rhythmic, but restrained cries. Annette watched helplessly, moving to the edge of her seat. She gave Demetri a questioning look and followed his guidance to scoot to the floor beside Esther. She did this with difficulty, then cautiously placed a hand on her daughter's back. She was rewarded as Esther's sobs seemed to lessen at her touch.

29

seedlings

"Esther," Annette said carefully. "I'm surprised you haven't asked me who your biological father is."

Esther considered this, then shrugged. "If you met my dad, you'd understand."

"*Oh*," she replied, taken back. "Luther said your dad is a *priest*? Those are the ones that can't marry, right?"

"Pastor. He *was* married."

"*Oh*. They divorced?"

"She died."

"*Oh*. I'm sorry."

"It was two months before I came to live with him."

"Was it sudden?"

Esther winced, remembering the look in her dad's eyes when he told her about what happened to his wife. Rachel had been his childhood sweetheart.

"We were so happy," he had said reminiscently. He described their wedding, how a travel agent aunt had managed to get them a deal on a trip to Hawaii for their honeymoon. He talked about their first apartment and how they were saving for a house.

"The first pregnancy took us by surprise," he sighed, his eyes becoming very round. "Our shock and worry had turned to excitement very quickly, but then we found out there was no longer a heartbeat. We hadn't planned on having kids for some time yet, but she really wanted to try. After we lost two more babies early on, we made it to the six-month mark. Things were going well." He swallowed hard, shaking his head. "When we lost him, too, we decided to give ourselves some time. We needed to reconnect as just the two of us, we needed time to heal."

Their situation was becoming increasingly common. Many couples were finding they were not able to conceive, or if they were, very few babies were surviving to full-term. Having it be prevalent did not ease her sorrow. Depression started to close in around her. She went to a counselor, a psychiatrist, and a support group, and they had done a wellness program together. After a few months, she seemed to be doing better.

One day Matteo came home and heard the bath running upstairs. Grateful she was having some relaxation time, he went straight to making dinner. He called up to her when everything was almost ready; he had just started boiling pasta, but there had been no response. He could hear only the sound of the water still running. When he reached the stairs, he found water streaming down the steps.

There would have been no use trying to save her, given how long she had been submerged in the water, as she'd shot herself before he arrived home, but Matteo had still pulled her from the tub, dialed emergency services, and performed CPR for the seventeen excruciating minutes it took for the ambulance to arrive.

The ambulance drove in silence to the hospital.

Esther hadn't thought about it for some time, but it occurred to her as she recounted the story silently that her dad had to return to that apartment. He had to empty that pot of congealed pasta. He had to deal with her clothes, her belongings. He had to deal with cleaning up the water damage, and the warped wooden stairs. He would have had to have settled the lease—she couldn't imagine continuing to live there.

Rachel had left a letter, but when Esther asked him about it, her dad's jaw had tightened and his movements had become very rigid. He'd never not given a response to a question she'd asked, and the uneasiness of the moment was very difficult for her to bear.

"I'm sorry, Daddy. I shouldn't have asked."

He had shaken his head abruptly, turned, and placed his hand on her cheek. "No, mia dolce ragazza. Non hai niente di cui essere dispiaciuto." *No, my sweet girl. You have nothing to be sorry for*. He had taken a long breath. "In ogni tragedia, Dio promette una benedizione." *In every tragedy, God promises a blessing.* "I've taught you that, right?"

She remembered nodding.

"Tu, mio angelo dal cielo, sei mio. *You, my angel from Heaven, are mine.* Sei la più grande benedizione che Dio mi abbia mai dato. *You are the greatest blessing God has ever given me.*"

She hadn't pushed the conversation further but had spent a lot of time afterward wondering what he meant. How was she the blessing that came from his wife's death?

She had finally gotten her answer while staying out at the farm. She was spending some time with Sara, harvesting strawberries, and had shared what her dad had said. "What did he mean?"

Sara had closed her eyes, smiling tightly. "They would have never moved back to Colorado."

"Why? I thought they grew up here?"

"Rachel moved to Texas after her parents died."

"How did they die?"

"Tornado. The biggest one Colorado's ever seen. She suffered from severe depression after that. She had even had a failed suicide attempt when she was sixteen."

"She tried to kill herself then?"

Sara nodded regretfully. "She turned things around though, with Teo's help. Luke says your dad worked two jobs in high school so he could afford to go visit her. It's why he chose the college in San Antonio. So they could be together. She swore she'd never move back to Colorado because she couldn't face the memories. It's why she and I never got to know each other very well."

"*So* it's because she died that my dad is my dad." The thought didn't sit well with her. It made her feel somehow guilty for Rachel's death.

"It was God's hand, bringing you to Teo."

"How does *that* work? If it was in God's plan for my dad to be my dad, then does that mean God *intended* for Rachel to die?"

Sara had dropped her wooden bin. "You know better than that—honestly!"

She remembered fighting back tears.

"God doesn't cause tragedy in the world. *People* do. He doesn't dictate our actions; He gave us free will. He didn't make Rachel kill herself. She chose that path for herself. What He does promise is that He will bring about a blessing from every tragedy. He guided Teo back to Colorado with that opportunity in Wallace. At the time, I thought it was so he could be closer to us, so he'd have support. Then he showed up with you."

"You think God was guiding him to Colorado so he could be my dad?"

She sighed. "I think God was bringing the two of you together, yes. You were exactly what the other needed."

Annette raised her eyebrow curiously and cleared her throat.

"She had pregnancy complications," Esther said shortly, frowning.

"*Oh.* That must have been a very difficult time for your dad."

Esther nodded.

"You're really close with him?"

Esther smiled tightly. "He's the best person I know."

"I hope I get a chance to meet him someday."

Esther couldn't imagine the two of them meeting. It just didn't seem possible for both to exist in the same place. "Does your plan not include coming to the Ark?"

She shook her head. "My plan is to enable what needs to occur for the Arks to eventually not be necessary."

"That's a tall order."

Annette gazed out the window, resolving something in her mind. When she rotated back to Esther, she wore a forced smile. "*So,* do you have a boyfriend? *Girl*friend?" she added quickly.

Demetri released an audible exasperated sigh.

"Actually, I've been sharing accommodations with five young men."

Annette's eyes widened, her black mascara too dark. "*Well*, that's certainly something."

Esther dropped her chin to her chest, chuckling lightly. "Your words sound accepting, but your face tells a different story?"

"That's what the public surveys say. My facial expressions give me away."

"I've been traveling with five young men. Two are acquaintances I don't know too well yet. One I also don't know too well, I spent a little time with him when we were younger, but he's growing on me. He's like the annoying brother I never wanted but love anyway."

"And the other two?"

Esther smiled tightly. "The other two are brothers–" she began, pondering the best way she could describe Josh and Gabe West.

"Gabe is like a protective older brother."

She thought of that very first day meeting them. They were standing in the front drive exchanging awkward greetings. Sara and Luke had been taken off-guard by her presence and had done the usual grownup thing of squatting to her height and asking rhetorical questions. It was all very uncomfortable, all the attention laser-focused on her. She was scanning her surroundings, actively avoiding eye contact, when something caught her attention. Tucked slightly behind the leg of his father was Josh, puffing out his cheeks, pursing his lips, and crossing his eyes at her. She wasn't sure what to make of it; she'd never had this sort of interaction before. He twisted his face once more, tugging at his ears. And then he stepped forward, dropping his chin to try to meet her gaze. He leaned in close to her ear and asked her if she wanted to go on the swing. She hesitated, glancing up at her dad for permission, but Josh was persistent.

He grabbed her hand, pulled ever so slightly, and then he smiled that wide, winning smile of his.

Annette tilted her head to the side. "And the other?"

Esther felt her heart inflate. "Josh taught me how to feel joy." She nodded, satisfied with the brevity of her statement.

30
phoenix

"Canary, respond." Josh's voice had become desperate. He waited long enough to take two forced breaths, and wipe the sweat from his face, his jaw clenched. Every inch of his skin seemed to be caked with dirt, grime, and sweat. He fumbled with the receiver in his hand, waiting another few seconds to clear his throat. His hand smelled of gunpowder, rusty and simmering. "Canary, status."

Miles ran his fingers through his sandy-colored hair, walking away. He shook his head as he anticipated what the lack of response indicated. "I lost focus, I wasn't covering her like I should have," he said to no one in particular. When he whirled around, his dirty face was streaked with tears. In the 14 years he'd known him, Josh had never seen Miles Kent shed a tear.

"*Canary*," Josh's voice cracked. Up until then, he had convinced himself the call sign was indicative of her love of music.

Songbird. Songbird would have been a better call sign, he decided silently. If her call sign was about music at all, he added.

It seemed more likely, and perhaps more fitting given the circumstances, not to mention her occasional dark sense of humor, that her call sign represented her intended role. Miners used canaries to tell them when there was trouble, when the air had gone toxic. When their canary went silent, it meant their world was about to implode.

"Luther said to meet here, right? He said she'd be here," Miles said, pacing.

Josh handed off the radio to Gunner and walked toward the tree line. He spun around in a slow circle, taking in their surroundings--a lush wall of pine trees behind them, the massive, mirrored lake before them backdropped with layers of green mountains. Everything was quiet. He breathed in, he breathed out and turned to the forest. "I need a minute, guys," he said, disappearing into the thick of the trees.

"Josh?" Gunner protested.

"He needs a minute. Give him an effing minute," Miles said roughly, stepping angrily toward the lake shore, chucking the rock he'd been fiddling with across the surface of the water.

And then--a crackle came through the two-way radio speaker, followed by a sweet drawl: *"Say heeeey, good lookin'. Whaaaat'cha got cookin'?"*

Miles whirled around, searching for the source of the voice.

"Is that *you*, Canary?" Gunner asked, turning toward where Josh had disappeared.

There was silence on the radio.

"That was her," Miles insisted, rushing back. He glanced up. "Where the hell did Amnesia go?"

*   *   *

Josh had caught a brief glimpse of her golden-brown hair beyond the thick, century-old tree trunks. He wasn't convinced his mind wasn't playing tricks on him, but he stepped quietly through the pine needles just the same. He'd always had a light tread, which had allowed him to sneak up on her time and time again when they were kids.

He could see another figure in the distance, large and imposing. She appeared aware but unaffected by his presence. She was listening to the voices, the noises on the other side of the trees. She lifted the two-way radio and started to sing. It sounded familiar, a favorite of her dad's perhaps.

"*Is that you, Canary?*"

She was visibly startled when Gunner's voice came through the radio, her face turning uncertain.

"*Canary?*" It was Miles this time.

She raised the radio to her mouth, taking a deep breath.

And then Gabe's voice came through from just ahead of him: "'*How's about cookin' somethin' up with meeeee?*'"

He wouldn't soon forget the expression on Essie's face when she saw Gabe through the thicket. Her unearthly silver eyes were wide. Her bottom lip, slightly parted from the top, quivered. She moved quickly down the incline toward him, gulping the chilly forest air. He'd marveled at the graceful, controlled movements she'd developed doing MMA, but he watched her gait become frantic and inelegant, desperate to close the distance.

With a stride's length to go, she leaped toward Gabe, crashing into his chest. As he closed his arms around her, Josh could see her body trembling.

He remembered, Josh said silently, lips pulling upward.

Miles burst through the trees at that moment and Josh threw out his hand to stop him. "*Ess—she was on—Is she—*"

Josh patted Miles on the chest, nodding lightly toward where Gabe and Essie were embracing. "Why don't you grab the other guys? We'll get going."

Miles widened his hazel eyes. "*Dude*, it doesn't mean she chose him," he whispered, straining to see around the bank of trees. "They're just *hugging*."

Josh pressed his lips together, nodding. "I know. Just give them an effing minute."

When Miles finally went back to the lake, Josh turned on the spot, purposely crunching pine needles under his boot so they'd hear him. To his surprise, Esther was already stepping toward him, her eyes filled with tears, a broad smile on her face. In the same manner she'd embraced Gabe, she came crashing into his chest, wrapped her arms snugly around his neck. She kissed his cheek. "Thank you for not shooting me."

He tightened his hold around her.

31

christmas

"We focus so much attention at Christmas on the newborn Jesus Christ. As we should. But when I sit and think about the story of His conception, His birth, I'm amazed by all the moving parts involved to have things happen as intended: Who was the backup if the angel came to Mary and Mary was like–you *know*, it's not a great time for me right now? What if Joseph wasn't quite so understanding that his virgin bride was pregnant? He *really* did consider divorcing her. What if the angel wasn't able to convince him otherwise? Nowadays being a single mother is accepted, but things were different back then. What if the donkey that carried Mary to Bethlehem rebelled and bucked Mary off? There were so many opportunities for things to go wrong.

"We also don't talk much about Jesus's family tree. We won't go into details here, but it's filled with scandals and some sordid circumstances. These weren't ideal conditions that would easily permit a man to live a perfect life, as He did."

Matteo smiled politely at the young pastor pacing in front of a heavy altar adorned with large poinsettias and candles. The church was built in the 1800s and was made of brick walls and intricate stained glass, and heavy wooden beams. He let his attention drift to the other decorations in the church–the large evergreen wreaths, the towering

Douglas fir trees that glistened with strings of lights. The worship team had selected gold for the accent color so each tree in the sanctuary was filled with shimmery gold ribbon, ornate ball ornaments, and blown glass ornaments filled with golden accents. Initially, he had been uncertain about the selection, but the effect was so stunning it took his breath away.

He couldn't linger over the decorations too long. They just made him think of how Esther would have loved the ambiance. Thinking of Esther not being there for Christmas was difficult but considering the possibility that she wouldn't reach the Ark before lockdown made it difficult to breathe.

Pastor Caleb was still speaking, still pacing in his casual manner, wearing a gray five-piece suit and expensive looking loafers. He must have said something amusing because the congregation was chuckling. To Matteo's surprise, Caleb motioned directly at him and finished his sentence with: "--spoke about how at Christmas, we're not really celebrating that our Savior was born, that this baby was born. The significance comes from what this baby went on to do, that ultimately, He died for us, rose from the dead, and ensured us eternal life in Heaven. Amen?"

Matteo felt the attention in the church shift back to Caleb as they echoed his "Amen," and he released a breath. He wiped roughly at his right cheek, where he could feel a tear, chilled by the crisp air.

The arrangement had been for Matteo to provide the sermon during the first service, Caleb for the second. This had been established back in October. As Caleb was single, he offered to take the second service so Matteo could spend Christmas Eve with Esther. When Esther hadn't arrived by the end of the first service, he had simply not left. He stood in the recessional line, sent everyone off with well-wishes, then helped distribute pamphlets for the second service before making his way to the front pew.

After she left the Ark, Luther had come to the church and shared with Matteo the significance of the work she had been doing, and how the antidotes they had been able to produce were proving to have lasting effects. He estimated she'd already saved thousands of lives. By lockdown, he said that number would be in the hundreds of thousands.

Additionally, he was confident it would change the approach for immunizations, as it seemed far more effective than an entire schedule of booster shots and inoculations without any of the chemicals or ill effects.

Luther had meant it to be a comfort, for him to know that his daughter had made an enormous impact, but Matteo had found himself increasingly agitated.

"You don't think she's going to make it back," Matteo observed.

"It's not that. I just thought you should know--"

Matteo shook his head. "Considering how much time you've spent with Essie, you really don't know her very well," he had said quietly. "You seem resolved in thinking that she's not making it back. And if that's the case, then I strongly recommend that you remember who you're talking about."

He stared blankly toward ornaments on the tree immediately before him, suddenly struck by the lyrics of *Mary, Did You Know?* Though nothing compared to the daunting realization of raising the Son of God, the lyrics struck deep in his heart as he thought of the impact *his* child would have on the world. He was filled with an enormous sense of pride, but also debilitating fear.

The most heartbreaking part of the song for him was Mary knowing that her baby was destined to die at a young age, that she would witness His crucifixion, and care for His body after His death. He wondered if she ever thought of protecting Him from that fate.

Matteo stared at a golden glass ornament, hearing, but not processing Caleb's words. Suddenly, a chilly hand was on his arm, and the music director was crouched before him, her dangly holly earrings bopping against her cheeks as she spoke.

"Pastor Matteo, would you take over guitar? Rebecca's son just vomited all over outside," Claire whispered.

He frowned. "What about Dale?"

"He left after first service."

His mind started to reel through the other potential replacements, but he was starting to feel guilty that he would try to pass this off to others when he was fully capable. He nodded, glancing at the guitar sitting on its stand near the altar. "*Silent Night* is next?"

She nodded enthusiastically, patted his knee as she got to her feet and jogged to the back of the church.

*   *   *

They had finally reached the long, desolate road that led to the picturesque town of Douglas. Once they had made it within the parameters of the Ark, there had been building excitement and lively conversation.

"Hey, Essie," Miles beckoned after some time had passed. "Why don't you sing some carols or something, get us in the Christmas spirit?" He turned from the passenger seat when he received no reply, a smile spreading across his face.

She had leaned against Gabe when they first set off from the meetup location, but there was a heavier slump to her body now. Gabe's eyes were also closed, their heads tilted together. Her breathing came out in slow, heavy snores so loud that Miles could hear her in the front seat. He started to chuckle. "I guess we're in the clear," he said quietly to Josh, who kept his eyes on the road ahead.

Josh waited until they were at the stoplight two blocks from the church to attempt to wake her. It was more difficult to rouse her than he would have anticipated. Finally, she peered through her eyelashes at her surroundings.

"How much further?" She asked through a yawn, starting to sit up. Through the windshield of the truck, her eyes took in the sight of the old brick church, the live nativity set outside in the snowy lot. She smiled with round, innocent eyes.

*   *   *

They intended to slip into the back of the church. Through the windows from the lobby, they could see a young pastor standing by the altar as the congregation sang *What Child Is This?* There wasn't any obvious free space in the rows of pews, so they had resolved to file into the benches along the back wall.

Essie craned her neck, searching for her dad, for the Wests.

"*E*," a voice said in an almost accusatory tone.

She turned on the spot. "Merry Christmas, Thomas," she whispered with a smile.

"You *said* you would be in the Christmas service this year." He was dressed in a sleek black suit and a buffalo plaid tie and looked furious with her.

"Oh. I said I might be. I haven't--"

"*No*," he insisted. "You said 'would be'. I thought you were done breaking promises."

"Thomas," came a scolding voice through the chapel doors. "I could hear you halfway up the aisle." A woman in an oversized evergreen sweater and very heavy-looking holly earrings slipped through an opening in the door and immediately closed it behind herself. "*Where* is your sister? She's up next."

"She was counting on you being here," Thomas said, ignoring the woman and raising an eyebrow at Esther. Her dirty, disheveled appearance did nothing to deter him.

"I should have been here, Thomas," Esther said in as quiet a voice as she could manage, as they'd started to draw glares through the windows from occupants of the back pews. She'd never discussed anything of the sort with Renee, the only mention of the Christmas service being with Thomas several months earlier. "I'm sorry."

"You're here now," came a wispy voice. A very pretty girl with blonde, beach waves was silhouetted in the doorway of the restrooms. As she moved closer, Esther could make out the details of her face.

Renee was nearly unrecognizable. Her face had matured, her cheeks narrowed, her lips plumped, and she was wearing a significant amount of makeup. The detail that gave her away was one prominent dimple on her chin.

Essie smiled at her. "You'll do great, Renee."

"*Oh.* You're coming with me." Renee said, raising her eyebrows, frowning. "Is this your security detail or--?"

Esther turned to see all five young men had created a half circle behind her. "Looks to be," she said with a smirk. "I'm coming with you *where*?"

"We're singing together. I'll sing the first verse, you sing the second, we'll sing together for the third."

"Renee, I can't–look at me." She motioned down to her ripped jeans. She could feel the scab on her knee, tight and throbbing.

"Aren't you the one who says not to worry about appearances? Yeah, you look like you've been mangled by wolves, but who *cares*?"

"'Mangled by wolves'? Really?" Esther whispered covertly to Josh. She gritted her teeth. "Do I look like I've been *mangled by wolves*?"

"You're beautiful no matter what," Miles chimed in.

Esther raised her eyebrow at him.

"But yes."

Renee craned her neck to the side to get a look at him. "Seriously, *who* are these guys?"

"Renee, it's almost time," the woman who scolded Thomas warned.

"Esther, please sing with me."

"*Wait*, you're Esther? Pastor Matteo's daughter?" she considered Essie's appearance.

She nodded, distracted, scanning the pews through the windows in the back of the church for signs of her dad.

"Esther? *Please*?" Renee asked, puffing out her lower lip.

"Fine, I'll do it."

Renee smiled broadly. "Will your security guards be joining us?"

"We'll see you in there," Josh said, kissing the side of Essie's head. He moved toward the doors, Gunner and Corey close behind.

"*No*, come with us," Esther pleaded, scanning between Gabe, who still stood beside her, to Josh. "Both of you."

"*Ouch*," Miles remarked, stepping toward the Sanctuary. "That hurts, Ess."

Gabe squeezed her hand, which she'd nearly forgotten he was holding, and followed the others into the church.

She watched in awe as the five men filed into the back row of the church.

Renee turned to Essie, assessing her appearance. "What if you undo your braid?"

"I can't. My hair will look like a troll doll."

*　　*　　*

"I'm surprised I didn't burst into flames when I walked in here," Miles whispered once they had filed into their seats, earning a glare from the elderly woman on the aisle.

The church was silent aside from some occasional muffled remarks, and some nervous coughing. As Josh raised his eyes to the altar, he saw Matteo adjusting the strap of his Taylor Guitar over his shoulder. He looked uneasy and preoccupied as he began to strum the guitar, making a few minor adjustments to tune it. He repeated the melody a couple of times before raising his eyes to the top of the aisle so he could time Renee's entrance properly. This appeared difficult to do with the spotlights glaring in his eyes. He squinted into the light, nodded, and began to play, lowering his eyes again.

Renee and Esther started a slow procession through the carved doors, each carrying an ivory candle, which illuminated their faces in a soft, golden glow. They were arm in arm, Renee wearing a scarlet red sweater dress and tall fashionable boots, while Esther wore her tattered jeans, a heathered gray t-shirt, Josh's oversized flannel shirt, and a pair of his spare hiking boots. Renee had convinced her to take down her hair after all. Her hair poured over her shoulders and down her back in wild, voluminous waves. As they turned down the aisle, Renee began to sing.

Josh watched Matteo over the shadow of the girls moving up the aisle. He still had his eyes lowered, staring vaguely at the tiled floor.

Until the second verse.

The moment his daughter's rich mezzo-soprano voice echoed in the chambers of the church, his chin jolted upward, and a broad smile overtook his face.

THE DAY *TRILOGY*:

THE RAIN FALLS
THE EARTH SHAKES
THE SUN RISES